GREEN
THE LIGHT WITHIN

S.M. HUGGINS

Green: The Light Within

Copyright © 2014 by S.M. Huggins

All rights reserved. No part of this book may be reproduced or transmitted in any form or by any means without written permission of the author.

© Depositphotos.com/Cokacoka | Branislav Ostojic-Cover

Other Books by S.M. Huggins
Green: The Awakening (Book 1)

ISBN 978-1-63068-441-9

Dedication

This book had been dedicated to Ruth and Robert Plunkett, my grandparents. Grandpa, thank you for reading and loving these books, this touches my heart. Grandma, you are missed and have not been forgotten. I pray that you are the first face grandpa sees when he follows you home. Each of you have left a footprint. I love you both.

"Your greatness
is revealed
not by the lights
that shine upon you,
but by the light
that shines
within you."

-Ray Davis

Contents

Chapter One 1
Chapter Two 6
Chapter Three 25
Chapter Four 36
Chapter Five 61
Chapter Six 75
Chapter Seven 92
Chapter Eight 109
Chapter Nine 129
Chapter Ten 154
Chapter Eleven 169
Chapter Twelve 188
Chapter Thirteen 217
Chapter Fourteen 227
Chapter Fifteen 240
Chapter Sixteen 260

Chapter Seventeen....................................275
Chapter Eighteen 295
Chapter Nineteen 305
Chapter Twenty.....................................321

Glossary...339
About the Author 347
Acknowledgements 349

Chapter One

I vowed to be of service to the greater good—this was my oath. All Light Warriors were bound to honor this pledge. As their leader, I stood before each of them and heard them voice this truth. This solemn promise resulted in my ultimate sacrifice. For love and for the Light, I fell. Gravity drew me downward. My eyes were open. I embraced my decision. Resisting the innate desire to fly was challenging, but this was the path I envisioned. I left that life for them. I died so I could live this destiny...

Kneeling down, my hands find the very spot. In some way, the soil has stored a memory of my final moment. I landed here. This is where they found me. And this is where the Light Warriors learned that I would return to them. Over a thousand years ago I sacrificed myself to save this family. My death was meant to bring hope. But fate will join us in the very same battle from which I had wished to spare them. This war is looming. And we are not prepared.

Using my powers, I appear atop the cliff; the same precipice that I fell from centuries ago. Upon its peak, my robe catches the wind and moves, billowing. It is as restless as I am. I feel misaligned with my path; with my destiny. Closing my eyes, I connect to my breath. I search for my spirit. I seek the driving force that seems to have departed. Then...I sense his presence behind me.

"What do you see, my liege?" Mikiel asks in a soft tone.

"Everything, though I feel detached from all of it. War is coming. We are not prepared."

"We will be," he affirms. "Perhaps we should return to the Light Force domicile? It was once our home and there, we can prepare."

I face my winged protector. His short, blond hair shimmers in the waning sunlight. He runs his fingers through the locks. The tops of his white wings tower a foot taller than him. Wearing an ivory, linen shirt, so thin that I see the outline of his muscles, and fitted leggings that cling to every curve of his strong legs, he waits patiently for me to answer him. With his luminous blue eyes nearly searing me, I answer him.

"Churria is a remarkable vision and Shria is the mother I always dreamt of having. This is my home. I must remain here and protect it."

"But?" he asks, intently gazing into my eyes, the question lingering between us.

Facing the cliff edge again, my head drops downward. My inner doubts continue to climb to the surface. "Mikiel, I worry that I am losing a part of myself; the element that will save all that I know and love. As I am, I fear that I will fail."

"We will not falter," he answers firmly. "You are not alone. You will fulfill your destiny with the Light Warriors by your side." I hear his words, but still, I struggle to believe them. War is coming and I must reconnect with the part of me that is fated to face it.

A gust of wind wafts upward, deeply liberating. I lean into it. Whilst I tilt forward into the vast space before me, Mikiel's hand takes hold of my wrist. Leaning forward a little farther, with his unyielding hold tethering me, I dream of flying. Gently, he pulls me back.

"Do you trust me?" he asks.

"Of course I do. Why?"

"I know what you need."

About to turn and look at him, I felt his arms cinch my waist. The sound of Mikiel's wings as they fan out behind us is so familiar. I long for the ability to fly again. Possessing this memory, but not the capability, is utter torment. He draws me closer to him as I hear a voice from behind us.

"Meelah!" the voice calls.

Unable to see over Mikiel's outstretched wings, I employ another method. In my mind, I see Mikshe as she quickly strides our way. The head elder undoubtedly sent her to fetch me. Twilight is nearly upon us and like birds, all Churrians return to their homes when darkness sets in. But Mikiel has other plans, and so I willingly go for the ride. His chest expands as he inhales deeply. It pushes against me. Then we dive into the open freedom before us.

The exhilarating gusts of warm air touch every part of me. This luxuriating sensation makes me smile. Mikiel's face is next to mine, his cheek is warm and soft. This is what I need; with what I am meant to reconnect. With this thought, I feel his face change shape as he grins.

The wind pushes against us as if it intends to bring us back to the cliff. As Mikiel banks in rhythm with the varying currents of air, I am able to glance over at Mikshe. Our eyes meet as she rushes to where we were just standing.

"I will return prior to nightfall." Acknowledging me, she lowers her head.

For the first time since I returned to Churria I feel free, and it's energizing. Catching an updraft, we move effortlessly in cadence with the shifting wind. Mikiel's heart beats faster and faster. It thumps wildly through his shirt, pounding against my back. Drawing his wings back, he gains speed and again, I feel him smile and so do I. His powerful wings make us soar with such ease.

Below us is the magnificence that is this star. A sea of light-shaded sand is to my right and the shimmering crystal landscape of Ralta is to our left. Gliding forward, we enter Bursa. The air here is sweet and moist. The thick and rich vegetation spans as far as I can see. It's beautiful. It's alive. It lifts some of my emotional burden, which I am happy to let go.

Closing my eyes, I gain a deeper connection to this moment. Every move Mikiel makes, every subtle adjustment is in alignment and harmony with the ever-changing atmosphere. I feel him adjust his wings to maintain not only our balance, but also gain a smoother ride. I had forgotten all of the dimensions of flying, but now the details are flooding back to my mind. This outing has awoken them and something else within me. Extending both of my arms, I place them beneath his wings. I feel as though I am the one making us soar. My hair catches a gust of air and blows across my face, obstructing my sight. Raising my right arm, I lift his wing and redirect us. With this adjustment, the air thrusts my tresses back. I continue to make slight corrections to his inner wings as I feel the need.

Mikiel's arms in passion wrap even tighter around my waist. The lids of his eyes shut. He leans his face in toward my neck—his breath, warm and soft, blankets my skin. I withdraw my arms and rest them at my sides. I had forgotten. The interior of a Light Warrior's wing is quite sensitive and most personal. I should not have touched them. I love Mikiel but I cannot be his. My heart belongs to another.

After I abruptly remove my arms, he is silent. He is dear to me. Moving his face away from mine, he lessens his firm hold. By permitting this closeness, I have injured him. Neither of us speaks. This silence persists. Placing my hand upon his hand, I give it a squeeze. In time, he returns the kindness. His fingers press into my hand briefly, then release. For different reasons, neither of us wishes for this moment to end, though it must. It is time for me to leave. I care deeply for this Light Warrior. I mustn't hurt him by giving the wrong impression. Using my powers, I disappear from his arms. I sense him halt midair, wondering where I've gone.

Standing again on the precipice with the ubiquitous breeze wafting through my hair, I wait for him to locate me. Somehow, Mikiel can always find me. When I see him fly my way, I wait for our eyes to connect. Lowering my head to my dear friend, I send him my sincere gratitude. He knew what I needed and it was divine. I take my leave and teleport home.

Chapter Two

Bursa is quiet and peaceful. The night is nearly upon me. As darkness settles, the flowering flora close, creating a new beauty, and the splendor of this place glimmers in the subtle light from the stars and the two full moons above. This light illuminates my path. But something else draws me home. Shria's pervading energy has permeated everything encircling her humble abode. Flowering vines cover the outside walls of her stone house. The blue blossoms have closed. They also rest when twilight dims the sky. The roof is swathed by a vibrant green moss. This plant has short stems with small, spiralling leaves. Pleasantly, it diffuses a sweet scent into the air. I need not use sight to know I am approaching it.

Rather than teleport, I enjoy the stroll. I sense Mikshe prior to seeing her; before she sees me. My powers are growing. Every day they expand, though my focus hasn't been on refining them. Daily, preparations for becoming an elder have been under my spotlight. This focus must change after I take my orders. I must prepare for what is coming. Not wishing to startle my friend, I clear my throat as I continue her way.

"I waited outside for you," she voices softly, while turning to face me.

"And I thank you."

"What was it like, Meelah?"

"Flying?"

"Yes. Wasn't the chilly air intolerable?"

"The air was not cold, even at that altitude. Perhaps it was the adrenaline that warmed me. But flying is pure freedom," I reply, while closing my eyes, hoping to be immersed in the moment again. But my mind returns to my arms touching the inside of Mikiel's wings and again, I feel the intolerable weight of my decision.

"Light Warrior Mikiel wishes to be with you even though you have chosen Kriyo."

"Mikiel is a dear friend. My heart belongs to Kriyo. Has the head elder heard anything regarding him?"

With a simple shake of her head, heaviness befalls me. Nightfall appears, as if to emulate this dismay. I watch it coat everything around us with gloom. With a whimper, I gaze up at the night sky. Above us, glistening stars speckle the darkening atmosphere and the twin moons are aglow. With every fleeting moment the contrast between the blackening sky and the stars becomes more striking. I am lost in the magnificence of it all and sense Mikshe is as well.

"Meelah, life was uneventful until you returned to Churria."

"Thank you, I think?"

"Perhaps I'm not choosing the right words. What I mean to say is, I'm glad that you're here."

"Then I thank you again," I answer, while studying her profile.

Her alabaster skin radiates in the subtle light from the radiant stars and her long, black hair blends seamlessly into the darkness that surrounds us. She is a true friend to me, the only Churrian since I returned, other than Shria and Trall, that I relate to and thankfully, she lives with me. As the cooling night breeze puffs against us, we enter the house.

"I have made an evening tincture for you both," we hear Shria state.

"I am sorry, Head Elder," Mikshe promptly answers. "I should have been here."

"You were precisely where you were meant to be. As for you, Meelah, how was your flight?"

"I know better than to inquire, but how do you always know... everything?" I wait for Shria to reply though I sense that she won't. Respectfully, I answer her. "The sensation of flying was wonderful. I long for the ability again."

"If you are meant to fly, then I'm sure that you will. Mikiel and you have been spending a great deal of time together," she adds with a raised brow.

"No more than usual." After a moment of silence and a persistent glare from her, I include, "My heart has chosen Kriyo, even though you wish that it hadn't."

"Meelah, you have been chosen for something grand and thus, you must not be distracted, that is all. As for Mikiel, he has deep-rooted feelings for you. Don't give him hope if there is none," she states, gazing intently at me. "I must rest. I have an early meeting and tomorrow we have a great deal of fine-tuning ahead regarding your appointment as an elder."

"I will see you in the morning," I tell her, while bowing.

"Indeed, you will, Meelah. Rest well."

For a moment, my head elder remains before me. The color of her skin is that of a white lily. A smile graces her face. Swept up in a bun, the silver-gray hair frames her ruddy cheeks. The image of health, and buxon in her form, she bows to us. Shria, as she walks toward her chamber, exudes kindness and honesty. I aspire to possess the conviction and wisdom that she applies to her every move. Though I am honored and blessed to be here, I still feel detached from the part of me that I reclaimed before my return to Churria. My inner power and guidance seems misaligned from my higher-self. But, looking at Mikshe as she hands me a cup, I am reminded of why I am here. The present moment is a gift. I will do everything in my power to protect the innocent. This sweet Churrian embodies this purity of intention. I will find my way.

Focused on her kind face, I say, "Thank you."

Swallowing the sweet viscous liquid seems to smooth my jumbled thoughts. Instantly, fatigue moves in and replaces them. Watching Mikshe cover her mouth as she yawns, I do the same. Shria must have put some strong sleep herbs in her little concoction. Observing Mikshe's stance waver, I take the cup from her hand.

"I'll wash these."

Lowering her head to me, she says not one word as she staggers in the direction of her bedchamber. Promptly, I rinse out our cups. Feeling slightly unbalanced, I make my way to my chamber. Struggling to see through the fog that seems to be building around me, I hear the sound of Mikshe snoring as I pass her bedchamber. I finally reach my bed. As my head touches the pillow, my thoughts return to flying, then to Mikiel.

Good night, my dear friend. And Kriyo, return to me. I love you.

Straightaway, I am in a dream. Running, my breath is as rapid as my swift pace. But something catches my foot. My hands, then face, crash into the unrelenting ground. With the wind knocked out of me, I sit up, wondering what I fell over. Then I see it—death! It's everywhere. Churrians and Light Warriors lie motionless as far as I can see. This horrific sight distresses every part of my being. Warm tears stream down the sides of my face, dampening my cheeks and chin. A sense of sheer panic builds as I begin to wonder what has happened to Mikshe and Shria. Fear takes the place of panic as I become unsure if I will see them again. Rising to a stand, I notice that this awful view leads to the river Calla. I see her unusually placid surface in the distance and sense her energy as this body of water shares my despair. Wary not to step on any of the fallen pure, I approach her. With every step, I feel Calla call to me. She beckons me. Making my way to her aggrieved shore, I hear her trying to communicate with me, but can't discern the message. At her waters, I collapse to my knees. Sinking my hands into her cool liquid, I rub them vigorously in an effort to remove the dirt embedded in the palms of my hands. Oddly, this water remains still and unaffected by my movement. Even my tears, as they continue to rain downward, don't alter it in any way. Calla's motionless surface acts as a mirror and I am compelled to study my image within it. I see the white silhouette of wings behind me—my wings. Their magnificence fans out as I honor their need to stretch. Wind generated by their movement swirls around me, lifting my long hair rhythmically. But my senses attune to something else; still looking into the reflective surface, I see a being come into focus behind me. Rising, I see her. It is Drana, the Queen of The Realm of the Mystics. Tears cascade down her cheeks.

Appearing overwrought by the devastating sight, she states, "You had the power to stop this, Meelah. Earth will be next."

The clamorous sound of a male's raised voice breaks into the horrid dream like a hammer striking a pane of glass. But again, I hear Drana intone, "You had the power to stop this, Meelah… earth is next."

As her words fade away, so does the horrendous sight. The ear-splitting male voice persists and it rouses me. Opening my eyes, I wearily come to my feet. The soft light of dawn illuminates my chamber. I feel as though I never slept. Vaguely, I recall the evening tincture that fogged my way into bed, but how is it morning? Nearly conscious, I find myself fumbling around as my senses and body gradually awaken.

A waft of pungent, sweet air pours through my open windows. This distinctive breeze reminds me daily that I am no longer on earth. But again, the raucous voice redirects my attention and this time fully. Twisting my hair up, I leave my chamber and find the culprit of my abrupt rising. The dreadful taste of my nightmare still lingers. The last time I had a dream like this, I was on earth and it came true. But this mustn't. I will make certain of it! But what of my wings, I wonder, while feeling my back with both of my hands. Sadly, there are no wings, just the nearing sound of commotion.

Approaching the unusual shouting, I see Mikshe, the back of her, anyway. She stands at the threshold of the front door dressed in the same blue robe as yesterday. Also affected by Shria's concoction, she appears to have had a difficult time awakening.

Looking past her, I follow the boisterous voice and see him. It's Elder Jael—my birth father. His cheeks are flushed red. Repeatedly, he wipes his sweaty forehead. Piercing and intense, his hazel eyes glare at me. Jael's bald head, also beaded with sweat, shines in the radiance of the new day. This is the only light I have ever seen reflected from this elder. Rotund in stature, his chubby, olive-complexioned figure appears calm, but is belied by hands that repeatedly ball into fists. He insists on coming in. Mikshe is calm and composed. She effectively holds her ground.

"Is there a problem?" I ask.

"Meelah!" Jael exclaims. "I have come to speak with you!"

"I will speak with Elder Jael. Thank you, Mikshe."

"Are you certain, Meelah?" I hear her ask telepathically.

As I nod my head, she stands aside, and Elder Jael begins to barge in. I raise my hand and immediately he halts his step. He appears uncertain of what I may do. His expression and guarded body language is quite curious to me. Why would I harm him? Regardless of his distrustful nature, he is here and I am by birth his daughter. Everything occurs with a higher purpose, even this unexpected visit, I suppose. I end his awkward pause with words.

"Elder Jael, I will speak with you, but this is not my house, therefore I cannot permit you in. You may say what you wish—outside."

I observe him digest my words before turning around. Signaling with his spade-like hand, he asks me to proceed before him. Walking ahead, I lead us to my favorite tree. Its massive canopy covers the back of Shria's cobblestone home. The edible yellow blossoms are as sweet as honey and their heady scent hangs in the air.

As I turn to face this Churrian, I feel the soft, warm breeze as it grazes the skin of my face. I watch it sweep across the landscape, affecting all in its path. The iridescent green leaves of the humbra tree dance and the flora bounce to a melody solely audible to them. Though I fear I have lost my way, I love Churria and I will not allow her nor earth to be destroyed. And perhaps I don't have wings, but maybe I can fly as I did when I was a Light Warrior. My mind begins to process the possibility, but the sight of Elder Jael grounds me and my wingless form. This moment is no longer about my haunting dream, it is concerning Elder Jael. He never introduced himself as my birth father nor has shown any interest in me since I returned to Churria. I wouldn't even know that he's related to me if I wasn't told. So what does he want? I wonder.

Curious, I continue to gaze at him and finally our eyes meet. At first, no words are exchanged. I once had many questions for both of my birth parents, but time seems to have wiped them away. The love that my adopted father bestowed upon me was quite fulfilling. It is Samuel I long for, not either of my birth parents.

In our silence, I sense something. Stirring beneath my feet is an energy that I've never before felt. This presence is both calming and grounding. This unforeseen gift affords me the strength for whatever this moment with Jael may bring. Remaining steadfast and composed, while Elder Jael becomes increasingly uncomfortable, I observe him shift back then forth and sneer with his dry, thin lips. I wait for him to say something. Though neither words nor thoughts have been exchanged, he has already conveyed much. His utter contempt for me is quite evident; I feel it and see it infused in his every move.

Landing beside me is Mikiel. As he swiftly retracts his wings and the fine dust aroused by his landing begins to settle, I lower my head to him and he does the same to me. His armor shimmers as if he just finished polishing it. Pristine and put together, Mikiel fixes his eyes on Jael. He must have felt that I would need his presence, and perhaps I do. With a deep breath, I break the lingering silence.

"Elder Jael, why do you dislike me? What have I done to you?"

After a snicker, the stout elder eagerly answers, "You are not one of us. You never were and you will never be! You are a half-breed; half them and half something else!"

Sensing Mikiel's increasing desire to draw his sword, especially after the "half them" remark, I reach over and place my hand upon his shoulder. This seems to relax him a bit, but I am uncertain as to how long this will last. Elder Jael had the nerve to point at Mikiel as well. Feeling Mikiel's unease mount, undoubtedly because he senses anger rise within me, I telepathically send a message for only his ears.

"I can handle him. Please, let me."

I see Mikiel respect my wishes. His hands relax in front of him, but not his gaze, it remains intent on Jael. I have the power to delve into this elder's mind, but since he's present I'd much rather hear his words.

"Why are you here?" I ask him.

"Yes, Elder Jael, what do you want?" I hear Shria ask from behind me. "Meelah," she says fondly, standing beside me.

An unexpected smile brightens my face. I stand amidst a devoted Light Warrior and the Head Elder of Churria. I am supported and loved. I finally feel a sense of family and home, though the Churrian before me is connected to neither. Elder Jael remains silent, though I believe he has much to say. So again, I try to get him talking.

"What is it that you want, Elder Jael?" This last query opens the floodgates.

"I, along with many others, do not want you to take your orders as the next elder of Bursa. Only a Churrian should receive such an honor. You will bring dishonor to our ways!"

"She is a Churrian, Elder Jael," Shria states. "She was born to you!"

"She was cursed to me!" he shouts with sheer disdain, stamping his feet. "I knew it the moment I laid my eyes on her. She will destroy us, and she is no Churrian. She may resemble us, but she is not one of us! We sent her away, Head Elder! Or don't you remember?"

"Though I agreed in words, my heart never did. That is why I asked Samuel, Pasha and Light Warrior Mikiel to accompany her. I knew that Meelah would rightfully return to take her place with us. I prayed to Natiya and to the mother of the earth. I asked them to keep her safe and here she is. That should be your evidence, Elder Jael. If Natiya, our divine mother, has welcomed her, Meelah is destined to stand precisely where she is. And," she adds, with a powerful pause, "I keep no secrets from Meelah. I keep no secrets for anyone! Are we done?"

"You will regret moving forward with her appointment. I am not alone in this, Head Elder."

"Though here you are—alone!" I affirm. "You are not a father to me. My father died on earth. Your cruel words hold no value in my heart. They only show what is lacking within yours! I don't believe that we have anything further to discuss."

"No, we don't!" Shria exclaims. "And, if you or any elder wish to discuss concerns, please do so at our next meeting. This is my home, not a space for an open forum. Do we understand each other?"

"I understand you completely." Every one of his words are tainted with scorn. "It would be wise to make provisions for your safety, Head Elder."

As we watch him teleport, his rage affects me and I run to where he was standing. Every part of me wishes to follow his teleport and to warn him—to terrify him! He will not threaten Shria; she is the kindest being I know. She is also his Head Elder. What gives him the right to be so disrespectful? Shria and Mikiel, who remain silent, are watching me.

"I am fine. Please don't worry. But the nerve of him! He cannot disrespect you, Shria."

"This is you acting fine?" she asks.

"I am unaffected by his spiteful words, but his sheer disregard for you is what so affects me. You're quiet, Mikiel."

He smirks at me then calmly runs his hand through his flaxen locks. I sense him watching me as I resume my pacing about and so does Shria. I mull over my rather irksome awakening. As I sense Trall, I see him teleport beside Shria. He instantly attunes to my irritated state, but the news that he carries outweighs my unsettled emotions.

"May we speak?" I hear him ask Shria. "Alone."

"When and if you wish to discuss Elder Jael, I am here," Shria says kindly.

"It is always a pleasure to see you, Meelah, but would you please excuse us?" Trall utters. In a weak attempt to conceal the news that burdens him, he pats me on the shoulder.

I observe them as they enter her house. Trall's demeanor is uptight and out of character. Shria is always composed and strong, but she too is affected by Trall's unusual energy. But here I remain, speechless. What a way to begin my day, first that nightmare, then this. What else will ensue?

"You should have allowed me to run my blade through him," Mikiel declares.

"He speaks. I was wondering when you would come."

Taking a few steps closer to me, he asks, "Are you wounded by his words?"

"No. But I worry for Shria's safety. Something amongst the Churrians is changing."

"The other Light Warriors and I sense it as well. This star was once our home, but we no longer feel welcome. I came to speak with you about this yesterday; however, I sensed that you needed some time in the sky."

"I did. Thank you, Mikiel, and again, I apologize if I was inappropriate. Truthfully, I had forgotten about the sensitivity in your inner wings." He answers me with a grin. Wishing to move onward, I change the topic. "With the training of the Churrians nearing its completion, you and the other Light Warriors needn't remain here. Do any of you wish to leave?"

"We do not remain for the Churrians. We are here for you. Your destiny is ours." His radiant blue eyes gaze deep into mine while he closes the gap between us. "The Churrians are not prepared for the task ahead of them. They are no longer warriors. Meelah, we require support. Can you leave with me today? I would like to introduce you to someone who is willing to give us aid."

"We do require support, but I can't leave today. I take my orders as an elder at nightfall."

I feel his desire to come even closer, I also sense his honorable restraint. His beautiful eyes affect me. There is still a powerful connection between us. A part of me will always love him. With that thought I ask, "Will you attend the ceremony tonight?"

"I will be there," he answers softly.

Not wishing to linger, I end the moment by respectfully lowering my head. Turning around, I proceed back into the house.

Mikiel's connection to me reminds me of what I feel for Kriyo. I yearn for Kriyo! It has been a month since he left with the Timeera when we were on earth. I feel the tears as they begin to well in my eyes. Inhaling, I push them back and press onward.

I hear Shria and Trall exchanging words out in the garden. Honoring their need for privacy, I return to my chamber. Opening my door, I proceed in and see the disorder I have left. Ancient tomes are spread all around my room. Every waking moment I have been learning everything Churrian. On top of reading, Shria and Trall have taught me daily. In one month of intensive study, they have prepared me for my duties. As an elder, I will be able to attend the weekly meetings and offer my "unique" perspective. This title is essential. It's a way to mingle and get to know the inner workings of this star and all the beings who live upon it. Shria believes this appointment is critical to my path. But, rather than studying, I feel as though I should be preparing for what's building. Even so, I have faith in my head elder. She loves all that lives and breathes on this star.

Again, I glance around my chamber. The walls are a soothing lavender color. Ahead of me are two window-like openings, both are oval shaped. They appear like massive green eyes against the outside environment, rich with thriving greenery. Blossoming vines climb through these openings. Tenaciously they creep into my room, extending onto and up the walls, dropping blue flower petals everywhere. Soft illumination brightens all before me. With this clarity, I appreciate the disorder encircling me. If my father were here to see the disarray of my bedroom, I know what he would say. Perhaps this space mimics my unorganized and ungrounded spirit. Creating change, I begin to straighten up. After I've collected the wilted petals, I move on to the tomes.

In my hand is a book about Natiya, the mother of this star. Churrians pray to her, though she is not a god. She is the energy that embodies all life on this star. Pure and loving, Natiya is connected to every living thing and every living thing is connected to her. Everything on Churria is threaded to the other. With that acknowledgement, how then is Jael linked not only to Natiya but to saving all life upon her as war threatens us?

A soft knock upon my door distracts me from my contemplation. When I open my door, I see it. My little project has manifested into form. At my feet is a neatly folded pile of clothing. As I quickly glance down the hallway, I see Mikshe walking away. Glancing over her shoulder, she gives me a wink.

"Thank you, Mikshe."

Picking up the stack of garments, I re-enter my room. Eagerly, I slip out of my cumbersome robe, then into the new wear. The ivory linen top is a sleeveless tunic and the ivory linen bottoms are crop-length pants. Though my new shirt is a little form fitted, it will do. I can move freely again—finally! And now I can properly train. I have missed this component. Though my mind has been pushed to its limits, I also need to exercise and train. Now I have the clothing to allow it.

Shria "misplaced" the outfit I wore when I led the Light Warriors tirelessly into battle. I know that she didn't really lose it, she more than likely stored it, wishing for me to immerse myself into the Churrian way and we Churrians wear robes—only robes. Just recently, the use of color has been integrated, refreshing their look. Churrians from all four quadrants are now wearing robes of every color found in nature. This wave of change has not affected the elders. All elders don the white traditional robe. After I take my Orders as an elder, I will join them, but not today.

My thirst for a morning tincture brings me to my door. When I open it, I'm halted by a vision of a star. This bright, blue light overwhelms me. Raising my hand over my eyes, I minimize its blinding illumination. As I move around this three-dimensional image in awe, I notice a smaller star to its left. Impressively manifested within the threshold of my chamber door, their brightness causes me to travel around them to get a better look.

Shria, most definitely drawn to the oddity of me walking in and out of my room while wearing something other than a Churrian robe, joins me. She also becomes mesmerized by the spectacular vision suspended midair.

"Sirius A and Sirius B," I hear her say telepathically.

My amulet lifts from beneath my tunic. Gently, it leads me toward the stars. The chain from which my amulet hangs begins to cut into the nape of my neck.

"You're bleeding. Don't oppose the will of your amulet. Allow it to guide you," I hear her say.

Droplets of my blood float past me then into the image. Minute pools of my life force are pulled to this manifestation like bees are drawn to their hive. They travel slowly and as soon as they pass through this odd materialization, they disappear. I honor whatever it is that my amulet wishes to show me and step forward. The tension of my chain eases, but not for long. Leading me onward again, it causes me to move forward until ultimately, I am within the vision.

The brilliant azure haze of Sirius A is to my left while the white dwarf known as Sirius B is to my right. Standing in the midst of these magnificent stars, I gaze around in absolute wonder. Energy that unifies me with all life everywhere, is suspended within this space. The feeling of adoration and connection to something greater than myself swirls around me. I feel the hairs on my arm lift and stand on end. Each strand seems to act like an antenna tuning into this unique vibration. Then from all around me, I hear it.

"We have been observing you."

I remain silent both in thought and in spoken word, uncertain to whom this voice is linked. My quiet immobility cocoons me. This encasement also becomes infused with the unique energy twirling about me. Vigor emitted from these two stars flows through me, a powerful force. The voice is connected to something inexplicable, yet benign. While breathing in the rejuvenating air, I wait for more.

"It has begun," the strident voice speaks.

With those three words, I know what the being speaks of—war. My vivid dream this morning, then this, there is no coincidence.

"Has the Dark Force taken possession of free will again?"

"*He* has."

I linger in reflective silence. This stillness seems to affect us all; they are also quiet. Then the floodgates open in my mind and I cannot stop processing. The Dark Force has done it again! *He* has unlawfully and immorally taken ownership of innocent beings by saturating them with *his* malevolent Shadows. *He* is building *his* army with the intent of ending my life, then all life that is connected to the Light. Why are *his* actions tolerated? Why hasn't the Creator stopped *his* illicit behavior?

"That is your destiny." the discordant voice states, grounding me.

"You seem to know me and my fate. Who might you be?"

"We need not be named. We are loving beings with the highest of intentions. Our interest in you and your destiny relates to our charges. Planets will be destroyed if the young Dark Force persists. *He* spreads his darkness and like a plague, it ends life. There is a great shift occurring within this universe, specifically upon one of our responsibilities—earth."

"Earth?" I ask, curious. "Did you manifest the dream with Drana?"

"A seed of intention was planted, but it was the Queen of the Mystics who crafted the message."

Instinctively, I assess this unseen being. Its high frequency is connected to the Light and honorably it respects the universal laws; I also assess, this being is many. As I relax and fine-tune our connection, I sense the scope of these benevolent life forms. Perhaps I delve too closely, as these powerful energies begin to pull away. Unsettled energy is quickly replacing their presence. This unease affects me. Then, I begin to understand. The unrest and self-doubt that have overwhelmed me, is me sensing the resounding effects of the Dark Force. As the darkness grows stronger, so must I. I have to find the source of my strength and do so quickly.

"Soon, we will show you the Dark Force's new army," I hear them add in a distant murmur.

As I open my eyes, I'm greeted by Shria and Trall. To my surprise, I am now standing outside in the garden. I wonder how I got here. Both Shria and Trall are still as they wait for me to inform them of what I've learned. But what do I say? As I stand before them, I wish not invoke fear. How do I tell them that I have been contacted by beings who are concerned that the Dark Force will soon be unstoppable? So, I look away and as soon as I do, my gaze is abruptly halted by Shria's soft hand.

Lifting my chin, she waits for me to look into her eyes. Gently, she says, "Though we can no longer hear your thoughts, your actions speak loud and clear. When, Meelah? How much time do we have?"

"I don't know, but the Dark Force is working diligently in *his* pursuit. We are not prepared."

"Not prepared yet," she corrects. "What must we do?"

"I have to leave with Mikiel. We require support. We need many."

An abrupt knock upon Shria's front door disrupts the moment. Without a word, Trall walks off to answer it while Shria moves in closer and takes hold of my hand. The warmth of her fingers as they weave around mine touches my heart. Here we are on the brink of war and she takes a brief yet unspoken moment to remind me that I am not alone.

"We will find a way," she insists.

"I must!" I answer her poignantly.

Rustling movement in the foliage of the garden seizes my attention. As I turn to see what it is, I watch Luther's furry tail spill onto the ground. I observe his furry, brown body roll around oblivious as to what's coming. Since our return to Churria, he has remained in his natural Galidrome form. After a big yawn, he drifts off to sleep.

Trall returns, his long, thin fingers grasping a scroll. This elder's neatly combed, long, snow-white hair is pushed behind his ears. His kind, pale blue eyes appear to avoid me. Fair-skinned and spindly, he reveals his disquiet. Looking at Shria, I see distress upon her face as she makes out what he's carrying. Enough is enough!

"What is going on?" I demand.

"Meelah, you must trust me. I know what I am doing. Go with Mikiel and gather support. I will finish the preparations for your appointment."

Trall gives me a nod of agreement. Then again, I take a gander at Shria. Something is occurring, but I honor their need for space—for now. Bowing to them both, I teleport from their sight, knowing precisely where I must go.

Standing again on the precipice, I wait. I know he'll find me, he always does. In just moments, I sense him. Reaching up, I untie my hair and allow it to cascade freely down my back. The wind carries my dark brown locks in every direction. It feels wonderful, liberating. Glancing over my shoulder, I smile at Mikiel, who is sauntering my way. I know that if my theory is erroneous, he will gladly catch me. Facing forward, I go within my mind and see what the river Calla was trying to tell me. Then, for the first time, I experience Natiya. Actually, I realize that it was she who soothed my nerves earlier with Jael. Again her energy vibrates the surface beneath my feet. Allowing her unique presence to ascend, consuming all of me, I attune to her accordance with my little test and it prepares me. Linking to her innate connection to everything on Churria, I clearly hear fitra. Resembling small birds on earth, they flap their wings in the distance. Through Natiya, I bond with them and our senses converge. I experience their tiny hearts pound in their chests as they drop into the wind. I become one with them and with this gift, I dive into the open freedom…

Chapter Three

As I descend, I feel the air as it harshly thrusts against me. I sense Mikiel as he leaps into the air in an attempt to catch me. Opening my eyes, I see two fitra on either side of me; one is female and the other male. They tell me telepathically that they are a mated pair. Their shimmering golden wings are fiercely drawn back as they follow my rapid descent. Their extended legs look similar to the legs of a frog.

"Are you ready?" I hear the female ask.

"Or do you wish to end this day with your death?" the male inquires.

"Meelah!" I hear Mikiel scream in terror. "You will not fall to your death again!" he adds, as he catches up with me.

"I won't die today. I will fly!" I shout into the wind.

With those words and perhaps with this intention, I do just that. I don't care how, I only revel in the fact that I'm airborne. No longer descending, I have balanced myself and am now soaring. The thrill of flight is just as I recalled it when I was a Light Warrior; but then, I had the weight of massive wings to contend with, and now, I only have me. The fitra, still on either side of me, do their best to keep up with my speed. I see their fatigue as they pant rapidly, so I slow my speed.

"This is your path," the female says while pulling back. I watch as the male does the same before he reunites with his mate.

"Thank you," I say in thought to them.

Silent and at my side, is Mikiel. As he senses me looking at him, he states, "Rather than terrify me, advise me of your intentions. I lost you once from that very cliff. I will not lose you again."

Slowing down, I reply, "Did you really believe that I would give up and end my life?"

Stopping, though suspended midair, I wait for Mikiel's response. Flying next to me, he is pensive. His head is down and he remains silent. I watch his massive white wings flap, keeping him by my side. Little by little, he raises his eyes and in his soft voice, he answers me.

"You do not comprehend how your death affected all of us. Though your intention was to spare us, Meelah, your actions equally injured all of us. You especially wounded me. I wish to never experience that pain again."

"Though we no longer age, we are susceptible to death. I cannot guarantee how long I'll be in this form. But I promise you this; I will not surrender. I am here to achieve my destiny and I will not give up. I am sorry for the pain I've caused you and all of the Light Warriors. I honored our oath. I fell to my death to save all of you. I fell to spare you."

"But what has changed, Meelah?" he asks in obvious frustration. "The Churrians are no longer warriors and we will still die protecting you. Your absence was in vain!"

"Is that truly how you feel? Do all of you feel this way?" I ask, lowering to the ground. I wait for him to join me, gradually he does. Once his feet touch the surface, I continue. "I haven't lost my faith. All things occur as they're meant to, even my death. I was right to fall."

Swiftly he takes hold of my arms, and yells, "No, Meelah! All that has changed is your lack of wings and the Dark Force's increased power. As for the rest of the Light Warriors, no one has uttered a word, but I sense their doubts."

"Mikiel," I say calmly. "As I was, in that form, I would have led all of you to one outcome, defeat. Your death and the deaths of all of my beloved Light Warriors would have been seared into my soul. I knew what I had to do and I stand before you now with that same resolve. My destiny hasn't changed, but I have! The powers that be detained me at length and this, too, was meant to happen. I believe this. In this form, as I am right now, I will lead you and those who wish to fight. War will occur and I will brave it with faith." My eyes locked onto his, I add, "I am sorry that my death destroyed your sense of belief."

"That is not true." Gently, he releases my arms. "I do believe, Meelah. We all do," he adds, gazing into my eyes. "You, standing here, looking as you did when you led us, is evidence that something grand is occurring. Simply...I wish not to lose you all over again. The moment that you regain your memories, war, the very same war that we battled against thousands of years ago, is upon us again. The Churrians are no longer warriors and our forces have greatly diminished. Though I believe in providence, I also know that my heart cannot bear to see you die."

Taking hold of his warm hand, I give it a squeeze. "Have faith. Though the path we tread may appear hopeless, we will defeat the Dark One's army. I will restore balance. I know this. I feel it." Weakly, he is still focused on me. I can see him processing.

"Mikiel."

"Yes," he answers.

"Though I'm wingless, I can still fly."

"Yes, apparently you can," he replies with a smirk.

Still having his attention, I include, "I didn't come back to fail."

"And you won't," he affirms.

I watch him for a few moments. His eyes remain on mine. No words are exchanged between us. As time moves forward I watch his faith return. His wings relax and his tension diminishes. My presence before him allows Mikiel to realize I'm not leaving any of the Light Warriors this time. Even this conversation has been divinely planned. It has confirmed the deep-rooted resolve that lives within me. It has also validated my connection with all the Light Warriors. I am attuned to the unease prevalent within the universe and they are as well. We are linked. I am not only their leader, I am also one of them. Relaxed and grounded, I continue to smile at Mikiel and finally, he smiles in return.

Lifting from the ground, I join the sky above me. Glancing behind me I see him still smirking while continuing to watch me. Diving downward, I fly over his head.

"Allow the breeze to take us on a journey!"

Onward I soar. Quickly he catches up. The two of us glide over the sands of Drista. Looking over at him, I wait for our eyes to meet and when they do, again we smile genuinely at each other. Embracing the moment, we allow our prior heaviness to dissipate.

In harmony with the direction of the wind we allow it to carry us. Consumed by utter bliss, I feel honored to be able to reconnect with this awesome sensation again. Bringing my arms against my side, I gain speed. I hear Mikiel sputter a little laugh. Apparently, he enjoys the competition. I remain half a body length ahead of him. He can go faster than this.

"Come on, Mikiel!"

"You shouldn't push yourself, Meelah."

"That's why you're slow?" I yell. "You don't want me to push myself?"

Without answering me, he gains speed. Swiftly, we move through the air and I do push myself as I am ahead. I feel the presence of other Light Warriors. They join in our frolic and before I know it, I am surrounded by all of them. Hundreds consume the Churrian sky and they position me to take the lead. I am deeply honored by this. To my left is Ruzi and to my right is Mikiel. When I glance at them, they lower their heads. Tears streak across the sides of my face. I am finally home and with my kind again.

Perhaps Elder Jael was correct. I am part Light Warrior and this, I will always be. But, I am precisely where I am meant to be—on Churria again. I take a moment to thank Calla and Natiya for helping me realize my ability to fly. Then I thank the Light Warriors who've remained devotedly by my side. I feel their shared appreciation not only for this moment, but for whatever it may bring. It's time to have a bit of fun.

We change directions with the mere thought of doing so. Our movements seem tethered to one another as we fly in unison over Drista. Below, I see Grawl and Grutiri as they swim through the sand. These two judicious invertebrates resemble enormous earthworms. Nearly twenty feet in length, their cylindrical forms weave in then out of the sand effortlessly. Grawl and Grutiri have been part of this star for as long as I can recall. Both seem to pause as they sense us. Regretfully, I have not yet visited them or Pasha and Faro who live in Drista. We observe them raise their bodies, then lower their heads reverently to all of us. Diving into the sandy surface, their enjoyment is palpable.

Unable to contain my joy, I soar with my family. We move in harmony with the air currents. I feel my hair streaming behind me. The wind wafting around us changes from dry heat to a damp coolness. Scrutinizing what lies ahead, I understand why. Ahead I see a vast body of water encircling Plai. This cool moist air from the water brings a chill to me, but I push forward. In one of the tomes I recently devoured, I learned that Plaians, the Churrians from Plai, built a self-sustaining community on a living foundation known as Zaltan. These Zaltan support the settlement and all upon it. They thrive on the energy that the Plaians emit. Their relationship is truly symbiotic.

As we glide over the still water, beings that live beneath the surface come into view. I read that these large creatures resembling whales are known as Tella. They are the protectors of this quadrant and I watch them follow the water beneath us. I sense their energy and they do the same to us. Appearing satisfied of our benign nature, all but one submerge deep into the murky water.

Now looking ahead, I see Plai. This is the first time I have ever seen this township. This development only dates back 900 years. It didn't exist when I led the Light Warriors. Since my return, I have been quite distracted and never teleported here.

A splash of water grazes my cheek. Looking over my right shoulder I make out the offender. Mikiel's impish smile gives him away. I grin at him in return. As we near the township, my attention shifts from Mikiel to the extraordinary sight before me.

All the description I've read doesn't come close to Plai's magnificence. Structures with high peaks resembling castles are abundant. The stone buildings are exquisite. Decorating the center of this small land mass is a white, stone temple, its gilded peak glimmering. Slowing down to take in the view, I feel all the Light Warriors do the same. Though I'm quite certain that they have seen Plai more times than I choose to count, they seem to enjoy my sense of awe. Below us Plaians dressed in vibrant-colored robes point up, smiling. My eyes connect with an elder donning a white robe. He brings his palms to his chest bestowing on us all honor. This touches me deeply, especially after the unsettling meeting with Elder Jael. It seems that the Bursan elders are the ones who are resistant to change. Below, we are welcomed with joyful smiles.

Mikiel's intent focus as it singes the right of my face distracts me. Our flight seems to have brought again to the surface his feelings for me and my uncertain feelings for him. Though I love Kriyo, I am still very much connected to the Light Warrior on my right and this flight rebirths recollections of our extensive past.

Unexpectedly, there is a shift in the atmosphere—I sense it. It jars me from the magnificence beneath me and I become fully attentive. The air that we are soaring through seems connected to something else. As we slow down, we hear it...

"It is time for you to see," the strident voice from earlier, says from all around us.

As a group, we slip into another world. Arriving in a foreign, dismal land, we land on the very top of a mountain. I hear Ruzi, Mikiel and other Light Warriors as they sniff the air and instinctively draw their swords.

"Wait," I telepathically signal to all of them.

Though my sense of smell may not be as acute as theirs, I realize precisely where we are. "It has begun." I state solemnly. "The Dark Force has found its host and there are many this time."

"My liege," I hear Ruzi say, still sniffing the air. "This is the home of the Epoh and if what you're saying is accurate, we'll need more than support. We'll require a miracle to defeat them."

"What do you know of the Epoh?"

"The Epoh are imposing four-legged creatures who procreate quite quickly. Their thick hide is nearly impenetrable and their single horn atop their head is toxic. Usually they're placid, but under the influence of the Shadows, I fear that they'll be a powerful adversary. They eat vegetation, so thankfully, they do not hunt."

Looking Ruzi's way, I state, "Every enemy has a weakness, even the Epoh. We will discover it."

All kneel as we try to peer through the gloom below us. A layer of substantial haze obscures the base of the mountain. Going within, I use my mind and visualize the air beneath us clearing. I open my eyes. My heart feels as if it falls into the pit of my stomach. Indeed, the view now offers clarity, but what lies there consumes me and the Light Warriors with an overwhelming sense of dread. As far as we can see are Epoh. They have already been devoured by the Dark Force's Shadows, as made evident by the fresh and brutal slaughter of their old, young and newborn. We watch them senselessly continue to stomp on their own kind. We have witnessed this horror before. Only the ones capable of battle are spared.

This seemingly unstoppable sea of malevolence is terrifying. I pull back and force a few deep inhalations. My surmounting emotion continues to steal my need to breathe. This is what will come not only to Churria but everywhere. And this is what I have been reincarnated to defeat. Reaffirming my faith, I take a few deep breaths, but my love for Shria, Trall, and the other members of my newly formed family, create doubt within me. As we are, we will fail.

"They must leave Churria," I say quietly.

"Who must leave?" Mikiel asks me.

"Everyone." I sense something behind us. Rising, I turn around and face it. Protecting my kind, I appear before it and bellow, "Leave! It is no longer safe!"

A beast is charging my way, it's an Epoh. It closes the distance between us swiftly, far quicker than I anticipated such a large creature could move. Its eyes are consumed by darkness; fearlessly, I connect with them. As it is about to pummel me, I use my powers and toss the imposing beast away from the Light Warriors. The ground shakes when the creature crashes to the surface. Its horn has torn into the flesh of my right arm. Glancing over my shoulder, I make certain that the Light Warriors have left. All have obeyed my orders, all but Ruzi and Mikiel. Both are headed my way.

"You have been slashed!" Mikiel exclaims.

Quickly wrapping my arm with a cloth, he tightly cinches the bandage. We hear Ruzi shout, "We must leave, my liege!" Wearily, the Epoh is already to his feet. As he appears ready to charge again, I feel Mikiel take my hand. I know that he wants to make sure that I leave with him. Then we, with a thought, return to Churria.

Gathering myself for a moment, I carefully assemble my words before addressing the Light Warriors. Removing the cloth that Mikiel tightly affixed to my arm, I see that the wound is already healing, but it's red and swollen. Turning, I face them and their unsettled energy.

"Meelah...you must return to earth. We are preparing the remedy," I hear Drana say from all around me.

Almost expecting to see her, I look around. From the corner of my eye I see Mikiel tilt his head as if he's wondering what I'm doing. I realize that no one else has heard Drana. A wave of dizziness affects my balance and I feel my stance waver. My vision also becomes obscure. Through murkiness, I see Mikiel, Ruzi and Nala as they run my way. Now, barely able to stand, I connect eyes with Mikiel and utter, "I must get to Drana."

I hear Ruzi declare, "It's the toxin from the Epoh's horn. There is no antidote."

Feeling disconnected from my body, I fall to the ground. Looking up, I see Mikiel's panicked expression. Sensing Natiya's energy as it rises from beneath me, I become aware of her soothing yet powerful pulsation as it intensifies. Perhaps she is trying to cure me because my self-healing body cannot tolerate the toxins of the Epoh. Maybe she is simply trying to get Mikiel's attention. Fitra and other flying mammals overtake the sky, darkening the atmosphere above. The ground shudders as other mammals surge our way. Natiya is working through them. She knows that I must leave and leave now! Gathering all my remaining strength, I say it again, "Mikiel, get me to earth. Drana will be waiting. She has a remedy."

Without further hesitation, we ascend. I sense the concern of the other Light Warriors as if Mikiel flew through a veil consumed by their emotion. Though I wish to alleviate their disquiet, I too become unsure of my fate. Though my mind is keen, my body lies weighted and unable to move in Mikiel's arms. A flash of brilliance erupts and we travel faster than light. Before I know it, we arrive on earth, then at the outskirts of The Realm of the

Mystics. Still in flight, I feel my body thrust from Mikiel's grasp. Crashing to the ground, I roll to a stop. On my side, facing Mikiel, who is standing, I witness his distress as he remains outside the invisible barrier containing this realm. Running back then forth, I see his sheer panic as he tries to get to me. His movement begins to settle and his gaze remains locked on something behind me. I sense the gentle nature of whatever it is, but unable to move, all I can do is wait.

The dirt on the ground vibrates as the heavy form moves around me. Feeling weaker with every breath, I continue to wait, but not for long. Finally, I see it. A pure white, winged horse with no rider stands before me. I watch the animal as it abruptly lowers to the ground and lies upon its side. With its pristine white back before me, I am gradually nudged forward by something behind me. The gentle prodding moves my immobilized body against the animal's back. As it rises from the ground, whatever is behind me keeps me in place and I rise as well. Now lying upon its back, I see what else has come to my aid; a coal-black, winged horse. The animal sniffs my face, then snorts. Then, it and the creature beneath me lift into the air. The sweet aroma of the equine's fur coupled with its cadenced movement lulls me and effortlessly, everything falls still.

Chapter Four

Raucous sounds surround me as I drift in and out of consciousness. Vaguely, I see what I believe to be Drana's face. In a soft whisper I speak to her, "Mikiel. He's in the woods."

"I am here with you," I hear him answer. His presence is comforting. If I die I want Shria and Kriyo to know and I trust that he would tell them.

"Mikiel, you must warn Shria," I beg him with all of my strength. "All should leave Churria. Promise me."

"I promise," he answers. "You must fight, Meelah! Don't give up."

Too weak to talk, too feeble to think, I lie still. In this peaceful state, I slip into another state of consciousness. In this unusual place all is a muted soft golden hue. A table comes into focus ahead of me. It, being the only thing in sight, draws me to it. Upon its surface is a small clear stone. Without a thought, I hold the stone in my hand, then look around, pondering where I am.

"It is time, Meelah," I hear a voice affirm.

I turn, following the trail of the voice, and see a Timeera ahead of me. Its inimitable golden cloak and boney fingers remind me of the last time I saw Kriyo. They took him away from me. With time, I was able to honor Kriyo's path, even if it was in the opposite direction of mine. I long to see him, especially now. I watch as the Timeera glides across the floor and over to me. I wonder if this being senses my unsettled heart.

"In your hand is the rightful stone for your amulet. You now possess what you'll require," the Timeera states. "Use the full power of the amulet and right the balance."

Every part of me wishes to ask about Kriyo. About to open my mouth and do so, I feel a pain surge through my body, dropping me. This throbbing ache returns me to my failing physical form. Nausea overtakes me. Beings come into sight. Covered from head to toe in serious gear, they help me sit up. Opening my fingers, I see the clear stone on the palm of my hand. Clutching it, I begin spilling out the Epoh's toxins. Red foam spews from my mouth and nose, burning my skin. Forcefully, I eradicate the poison for what feels like hours. When the need to throw up subsides, weakness takes its place.

Placing me on a gurney, they push me out of the chamber. Allowing gravity to roll my head to the side, I see Mikiel; he appears to be waiting for news and the sight of me instantly seems to give him relief. Rushing over to me, he is held back by beings. I hear them try to soothe him.

"We must quickly remove the poison from her skin. You mustn't touch her."

Though their words make him pause, he works hard to remain in my line of sight. Once our eyes meet again, I see the tops of his white wings as he settles down and relaxes. Still clutched in my hand is the clear stone. As we enter a new room, I see a basin being filled with chunks of what appears to be ice. With every passing moment I feel my body begin to heal. The poison was just too powerful for my healing ability. If it affected me so quickly, it must take down an average being within seconds. The Dark Force has selected an inexorable army.

They bring me over to the basin. I clearly view the chunks of ice within the water. Slowly I come to a stand and consider the daunting task ahead of me. One thing I despise is frigid anything! I loathe being cold and now I find myself being disrobed and asked to submerge myself in icy water. My hesitation prompts one of the individuals to try to reason with me. "We must neutralize the poison and rinse it off your skin before it re-enters your pores. If it does, it will kill you."

If I wish to live, I have no choice. Even though I dread the cold, I know what I must do. With the stone still in my grasp, begrudgingly, slowly, I ease myself into the glacial water. No part of my body wishes to remain, let alone find the power to submerge, though rationally I know I must. The rate of my breath increases as my body temperature decreases. This freezing water actually hurts before it numbs the surface of my skin. Now lowering myself to a seated position, I feel a firm and persistent push on both of my shoulders. Nearly breathless, I do it, I submerge. I try to return to the surface, but they hold me beneath the water. I thrash about for a moment, but when breathlessness becomes too much, I use my powers and quickly rise, gasping for air. I see the beings who were holding me down as they attempt to rise to a stand. In my panic, I flung them across the chamber. Grabbing the first thing in sight, I cover myself. I feel an awful remorse that I may have injured them.

The commotion has acquired Mikiel's attention. I see him burst into the chamber. Beings covered from head to toe in gear suited for a toxic waste station surround him as he tries to approach me. Weak and frigid, numb, I struggle to come out of the icy water.

"Meelah," he says calmly. Hoping to ease me, he gives me a weak smile. "You must trust them. This is the only way."

I watch him as he reluctantly turns and leaves. I honor the trust that he has in them. Trying to speak, though the words don't come out, I feel warm tears as they tumble down the sides of my face. Still quite weak, I too must trust them. Again, I allow them to submerge me. I don't resist. I simply do what is asked of me, embracing faith. Gradually, the water above me rests and so do I. The only audible noise is my heartbeat. Moments ago, it fluttered, but now it beats slowly. The last bit of air leaves my nose and mouth. Bubbles of air float to the surface. My hands follow them. The clear stone slips from my grasp. It floats downward, striking the basin's floor, creating a beautiful pinging resonance. Everything falls silent and is now unmoving.

I hear a sound amidst the tranquillity. It's voices. Like tuning an antenna, I home in on them. Gradually comes clarity. It is the oath of the Light Warriors. The words whisper around me. "I vow to be of service to the greater good. I solemnly promise this." Over and over again, I hear it. In a frenzy, this phrase envelops me. The murmurs continue as if hundreds of voices are expressing this pledge. The sound builds. The energy driving these words mounts. It is the Light Warriors; those of the past and the present. They are praying. My faith has brought me to their prayers. They are waiting for me to join them.

I vow to be of service to the greater good. I solemnly promise this. There is silence. They heard me. I answered them, then I declare it again. I speak this truth as my truth, like I did thousands of years ago. *I vow to be of service to the greater good! I solemnly promise this!*

A sensation of heat builds from behind my amulet. This torrid temperature begins to enliven me. Though I no longer have access to air, I don't feel deprived of it. A sense of wholeness blankets me, permeating my every cell. From beneath the water, my body has fully healed. I don't know when the nurses released their hold, but I'm free. With strength, with fortitude, I rise and come to a stand. No longer numb, I feel reborn.

My amulet begins emitting bright, white light. Wearily, one of nurses hands me a robe before standing back. Wrapping myself up, I lift my amulet from beneath the garment. It's still beaming. The sensation of intense heat fills me. It feels wonderful. My amulet is now complete. The clear stone has somehow found its home. The heat from my amulet begins to fade and the light dissipates. Magically, my hair is dry. Running my fingers through it, I lift it over the collar of my robe.

"Who did I injure?" I ask. Two females cautiously step forward. "I am deeply sorry," I say from my heart. "I thank you, all of you."

Bringing my attention to the remaining females, they all continue to stare at me with their mouths agape. Perhaps they have never seen anything like this. Regardless, I am quite grateful for their help. Lowering my head, I honor all of them.

There is someone I must see, Mikiel. I have to find him. As I open the door, I see him down a corridor. His back is to me and he appears quite contemplative. His impressive wings are slightly open, indicative of agitation. He worries for me. I sense his unease. Earlier today he professed his fear of losing me, then this, when he nearly did. Attentively, I watch this Light Warrior. He is always there when I need him. Then...I hear him, "I vow to be of service to the greater good. I solemnly promise this." His voice was one of the many I heard. I overheard their prayers. They trust this oath. My life, my destiny is connected to everything we believe and have worked toward. Appearing to sense my presence, he turns and sees me. For a moment he simply faces me. Then a smile graces his face. Quickly, he strides over to me. Now, nearly running to where I stand, he remains silent as he stands before me. I can't help but smile at his innocence. Though a part of me wishes to linger in this space, my rambling thoughts recall it; I return myself to my appointment. Shria has done so much to make certain that it would occur. I worry that I've already missed it.

"My appointment as an Elder was at nightfall. Does Shria know what has happened?" I ask him.

"You have not missed your appointment," Drana affirms. I see her coming my way. "You needn't worry about Shria. She is well aware of what occurred."

Queen Drana is stunning. Her ash blond curls fall to her waist. A gilded crown bedecked with jewels rests atop her head. The corkscrew curls secure it in place. Her dark brown, almond-shaped eyes are alluring. Though she is slender, her presence is grand and robust. Adorned in a rich red, velvet gown, tapered at the waist, her appearance complements her full, ruby lips as they form a smile.

Bowing to the mistress of this realm, I address her. "You saved my life. I thank you, Drana."

"As you saved mine," she readily answers. "But I am not as selfless as you. My words in your vision are quite accurate. Earth will be destroyed if you don't defeat the Dark One's army."

"I must be leaving. There is a great deal for me to do."

"Yes. You must leave, but not in a bathrobe. An elder of Churria must dress as one," she says, handing me an elder's robe, in my size.

"One would wonder how you possess an elder's robe? It's not as if they sell them anywhere on earth. How could this come to be?"

"Destiny is a curious thing, Meelah. You must leave, to remain on your path with your complete amulet."

"Who removed the correct stone? Was it the Timeera?"

"Valid queries, but the answers are not meant to be spoken by me. Kriyo has the information that you require," she replies, while lowering her head in deference to me. "And Meelah, the Noori that brought you here is now bonded to you."

"Are you referring to the Pegasus? I have also bonded, and am indebted to him."

"To her, they are not Pegasus. To my knowledge, those mythical creatures no longer exist. I am referring to the last of the Noori. And, when I mean bonded, this signifies that she has found her rider. Once a Noori bonds with its rider, they will only accept the one rider in their lifetime. You must take them with you, for wherever your path leads, they are now destined to follow. They are a gift; the female is yours and the male is for Kriyo." Turning toward Mikiel, she adds, "I mean no disrespect to you, but as you already have wings, Mikiel, I figure that the Noori might be of greater benefit to him."

"No disrespect taken," he answers.

Reaching into her pocket, she says, "Mikiel, I have this for you." Handing him a small object, she adds, "After all, it was you who brought Meelah to earth. Without her, a chance of any future honoring free will would be unattainable."

"Thank you, Queen Drana, but a gift will not be necessary."

"Oh, it is, Mikiel," she affirms. Opening his hand, he studies the object. His expression intrigues me. Turning toward me again, Drana concludes with, "The Noori will be waiting here for you, Meelah."

"Thank you, Drana, truly, thank you." I bow, then return to the room with the basin. When I enter the chamber, I see three beings still adorned in full gear, straightening up. As they proceed to the door, I thank them again.

While changing, I hear Drana telepathically transmit a bewildering message. "Meelah, I must thank you. You may not understand the significance yet, but soon you will. Your discernible voice gave me hope. Cila is as you said—she's safe."

Her message is baffling, but I know that I'll understand it when I'm so destined. As hurriedly as I can, I prepare myself to depart. Again running my fingers through my hair, I brush it out. A small medical instrument acts as a spear to hold my twisted bun in place.

"I need shoes," I say quietly to myself.

A knock on the door redirects my attention. When opening it, I see Mikiel holding a pair of sandals. Not really my style, but I appreciate them nonetheless. They too are Churrian. This is all quite curious.

"There was only one antidote for the Epoh's toxins and rightfully, we administered it to you," I hear Drana inform telepathically.

I know that this news is not meant to be frightening, but it terrifies me. I must be careful and far more aware. Mikiel continues to stand before me as I process. He takes my hand into his and I feel not only his passion but also his deep-rooted love. I look into his eyes and recognize that he sees the concerns within me.

"Thank you, Mikiel."

"Don't thank me for doing what comes natural." He steps even closer to me.

"Will you tell me what Drana gave to you?" My question brings space between us, he takes a step back and adjusts his stance.

"In time, perhaps." he answers.

I am left intrigued. Respecting his need for space on this matter, I prepare to leave. Placing the sandals on the floor, I slip my feet into them. Dressed and prepared to depart this realm, I notice Mikiel lost in thought with a light smile brightening his face. Whatever Drana gave him appears to please my dear friend. His happiness brings joy to me, satisfying my curiosity.

The sound of the Nooris' hooves as they strike the rock-faced floor brings my focus to them. Proceeding into the vestibule, following the sound of their stomping hooves, I see them amidst an open space. Four gilded archways lead to extravagantly decorated corridors. Within this massive space, each partition has a prestigious wall hanging that appears to be of the past Kings and Queens of this realm. I even see a portrait of the current leaders; King Kune and Queen Drana. This vestibule is a breathtaking as the Queen who oversees it. The sweet scent of the Noori brings my focus back to them. As I come to the female, she drops her head to me.

Touching her withers, I tell her, "I will name you Blessing, for you were mine. As for you, you big boy, Kriyo will have the honor of naming you, assuming you wish for him to mount you."

The male Noori tosses his head up and down as if he understands me. Mikiel stands before me and takes hold of my hips. He closes in as if to kiss me, but instead he lifts me onto the Noori, seating me on the animal's back sidesaddle. I watch him smirk as he takes the male Noori's reins in hand.

"Mikiel, take my hand. I will return us to Churria. Don't let go."

"I won't," he solemnly affirms.

I close my eyes and squeeze his hand. All four of our hearts connect and beat in unison. I have no idea what I'm about to do, but somehow, I know I can succeed. I see Bursa, the platform of the square, in particular, and as I open my eyes, that is precisely where we stand. Looking downward I see Mikiel, who's still gazing at me.

"How did you do that?"

I don't answer him. Truthfully, I can't explain how I returned us to Churria, but here we are. The astonishment of not only my appearance, but Mikiel's and the Noori's, is shared by many. Both of the Noori become agitated and move about as they attune to the encircling nervousness.

"Here, here, Blessing." Stroking her neck, I add, "You're all right."

"Meelah, you're back."

Even though I recognize Mikshe's voice, I continue to look at Mikiel. I feel that once our hands part, we will not be like this again. I reach down and caress the side of his face. His warm cheek presses against my hand. With no words spoken, he hands me the male Noori's reins. For a moment longer, he focuses on me. Then, veering away, he walks in the other direction. Following the sound of Mikshe's voice, I ask Blessing to go forward. I don't look back though a part of me wishes to. When I see Mikshe, I keep her as my beacon and don't waver. Behind her is a man running toward me, nearly passing her, and I make out his face.

"Kriyo!"

Blessing attunes to my ardor and cantors his way. With the other Noori in tow, I keep my attention on Kriyo as we come closer and closer. Slowing their gait, we finally stop. There he is. He is standing below me. With love reflected in his brown eyes, the orbs abundant with flecks the color of honey, he remains focused on me. His luscious, full lips form a smile that brightens his face. His ash-brown, long hair tethered behind his ears is a frame for his glowing complexion. The top of his tan robe clings to his well-defined chest. This being, who has my heart, is striking, and finally present with me. Reaching up, he extends his strong arms and I slide into them. His sweet, irresistible scent enlivens my senses. Not restraining myself any longer, I reach up and pull his face against mine. Our lips in passion meet. The warmth of his mouth makes me weak at the knees.

"I have missed you, Meelah," he whispers in my ear. The restless Nooris begin stomping their hooves behind us. This peculiar sound seems to intrigue Kriyo "What are these beautiful creatures?"

"They are a gift to us from Drana. This is Blessing and he is yours to name."

I didn't have the heart to tell him about his needing to be its rider. I watch Kriyo as he stands in wonderment looking at them. I hand him the male Noori's reins and allow the man and beast to bond. Luther flutters above us. Appearing winded, his plump, furry body lowers onto the male Noori's back. As his feet touch down, with one buck, he's thrown into the air.

"Calm yourself," I hear Kriyo say to the Noori. Kriyo's composed demeanor eases the animal. Looking at me, he chuckles. "I guess he didn't like poor Luther."

I feel Mikiel's pleasure in the near distance, though I don't see him. He thinks that it was Kriyo who was thrown off. But it won't be so. I keep my mind clear, wanting this revelation to be his.

Kriyo should know the truth, so I tell him. "The Noori will only permit one to be his rider." He appears fascinated by my words. Conversely, Luther continues to kick his little feet in the air. I can't contain my need to laugh. "I'm sorry, Luther! But the Noori isn't a bench." He continues to hiss and squawk, not only at the animal but also to me. "Come here, Luther. You can rest in my arms." With my invitation, Luther makes himself at home in my embrace.

I overhear Kriyo quietly speaking to the Noori. "Do you suppose that I'm your rider?" The two of them remain silent. Curious, I observe them. His question is satisfied with one look. Circling within the dark pools of the creature's eye, he gets a glimpse of something quite spectacular. "It is me…I see me soaring on your back," Kriyo continues, in a soft whisper of wonderment.

Instinctively, he pulls the reins over the Noori's head and leaps onto his back. Kriyo mounts the animal as if he has been doing so all of his life. The Noori bonds with his rider. Jumping about for a moment, their connection is forged. The Noori's eyes turn bright green as the lids of Kriyo's eyes close. Something grand is occurring, but this bond is solely between these two, horse and rider. Their movement settles and the Noori's eyes gradually return to their natural color. Both drop their heads and I sense their silent communication. While watching them, I process my day and all of the events that led me to where I now stand. Breaking my contemplation, Luther licks my cheek. Our eyes connect for a brief moment before he flies away.

"It's time, Meelah," I hear Shria's voice say. "Thank you, Kriyo," she adds, as though I've missed something.

Standing before me, I delve into her thoughts and rewind the day. I see me leaving and feel her concern. Next, she hands the scroll that Trall held to someone. Moving around to learn the identity of the person, I see Drana. Then I hear Shria pray to Natiya for my safe return. Finally Trall enters with Kriyo, and explains the relevance of the stone that rightfully belonged in my amulet and why the Timeera extracted it. He goes into detail about the Timeera needing to see my pure intentions. They wanted me to avow the oath of the Light Warriors as I once did. Honoring my free will, they allowed me to naturally return to this pledge. Though the amulet possessed most of its power, it was muted without the true stone. Raising my eyes, I understand the connectivity of the entire day. *It was a test!*

"Everything is a test," I hear Kriyo reply as he stands before me.

"How can you hear my thoughts?"

"The Timeera gave me several gifts. One is a safe-haven for the Churrians, another was the scroll that saved your life," he says, while taking my hand. "It is time, Meelah. Become the next elder of Bursa."

I break the mesmerizing connection to him and face Shria. With a gentle nod, she validates his words. A male Churria comes toward us and stands alongside her.

Addressing him, Shria says, "Thank you, Hetry. Please bring the Nooris to their new home. And Kriyo, your parents are anxiously awaiting you." After she lowers her head to them, she focuses again on me, repeating, "Meelah, it is time."

"Shria, if I am the one supposed to have all of these powers, how is it that you always seem to be one step ahead of me."

"It is one of my many talents," she answers with a smile. "A talent that maturity and time have bestowed upon me, a gift that I will do my best to teach you. Today was a test, an assessment to show everyone not only who you are, but it also revealed what drives you—purity. You were injured protecting the Light Warriors. You possessed faith when you were asked to remain beneath the icy water and through devotion, you reaffirmed the sacred oath of your kind. I wouldn't have survived even with the antidote, no other mortal being could have. Meelah, you did. You were destined to survive. You are meant to be right here. Natiya and I both recognize this. Never stop listening to her."

Bowing to me, graciously, she then proceeds to the platform. Following her, I see Trall in the nearing distance. His relaxed demeanor is again true to form. When he extends his hand to me, I take it. Looking into his kind eyes, I see tears well up. Tears, born of pride for me, glisten as they slip down the sides of his face. He squeezes my hand gently, then leads me to the platform. Ahead of us I see an ocean of robed Churrians. Pausing, he directs me to the moss-laden stairs leading to Shria and to my fated title of elder. Carefully, I ascend them. All I need is to slip and fall. What faith would they grant me if I still must master walking? With that thought, I grin, and for the first time in a long time, I feel my father, Samuel's, presence. I have missed him terribly. Looking around the platform, I expect to see his energy. I don't see him, but he's here and I'm grateful. He honors me by choosing this moment to be present. Though I wish to see his face, I accept any moment that has him in it. While I appreciate his gift, the light of day gradually comes to rest. Twilight steadily takes its place.

Amid the transition of lightness to darkness, I hear Shria announce, "I am honored to introduce Meelah Neegry, the next elder of Bursa."

Silence follows this introduction and I steadily make my way to my Head Elder. Her kind smile draws me naturally to her. As I approach, Shria places the palms of her hand together, rests them before her chest, then lowers her head. Her reverence resonates within me. Churrians don't clap. Instead, if they are in harmony with the event or the person, they simply bring their palms to their chest and lower their heads.

Drawn to the hushed mass of Churrians standing before me, I find myself observing them. The front rows are for the elders of all four quadrants. Only a handful have chosen not to honor my appointment. Their hoods are raised for all to see. Amongst the opposing group is Elder Jael. I feel his spiteful glare, but choose to ignore it. Behind him I see Raza, my birth mother. She seems to wait for me to see her and when I do, I watch as she lowers her head and places her palms in front of her chest. I am honored by her gesture.

My spoken words break the stillness and all raise their heads. Every eye is fixed on me and I feel utterly grounded and calm. I commence my speech in ancient Churrian, as is tradition.

"Reeditta." This means, Welcome, my friends.

I continue speaking from my true source, the part of me that is again connected not only to my higher-self but to the Light. I feel the heat from my amulet as it rests on my sternum, but I remain steadfast and focused on my words. The ancient Churrian flows from me. I sense some of the older elders who chose not to honor my appointment begin to waver. A few of them even lower their hoods. Change is here and with change we will move forward as we are fated. I feel this. I know this. And my words reflect this truth. In summation, I honor our Head Elder, who selflessly has dedicated her life to Churria, and the sacrifices that she has made. I remind them that with unity, we will prevail. Shria takes center stage and continues.

Kriyo's powerful gaze pulls my eyes over to him. His small, knowing grin sears my insides, birthing heat deep within me. He is the most beautiful man I have ever seen. He beams and his brow rises as my complimentary thought reaches him. I must grow accustomed to him being able to attune to my thoughts. I hear Shria as she ends her speech. Respectfully, I bring my palms to my chest and bow to her. Repeating this gesture, I honor all in attendance, even Elder Jael.

The ceremony comes to an end with divine timing, darkness has settled. Additional luminaries are lit and gently they diffuse radiance. This illumination is beautiful. It reminds me of lightning bugs on earth. I even expect them to twinkle and flash. But, these lights are steady. They are as solid and stable as the head elder before me. Already engaged in conversation with a few of the elders, Shria seems amazing as I observe her.

Sensing someone, I turn around and notice Mikiel in the near distance. Leaving the stage, I mindfully tread down the stairs. On solid ground, our gazes connect. He bows and honors me. I volley with a smile as I continue to close the space between us.

Landing beside him is Ruzi. His short black hair, ebony-colored skin and wings blend seamlessly into the encompassing obscurity, while his white uniform and gilded chest armor reflect the soft lights encircling us. His presence is quite evident. My eyes don't need to see him to sense his powerful and commanding charisma. As more luminaries are lit, his muscular form becomes clearer.

"Only you would survive an Epoh's lashing," he expresses. "It's good that you did, my liege."

"We have seen what lies ahead, my friend. A meeting at first light must be held. Please have the Light Warriors assembled. I wish to speak with them."

"Perhaps unity should begin at first light," I hear Shria say, joining our conversation. One moment she's on the stage, the next she's by my side. She truly cares for me.

"Unity shall begin at first light," I agree.

"Congratulations, Meelah." I hear the sound of Pasha's voice and follow it. Holding Faro's arm, she comes over to the small group. "We are quite proud of you, dear."

"Look at you, you're a Bursan Elder," Faro adds softly. "I know that you'll use this appointment to do great things."

Acknowledging their kind words with a smile, I then listen to the soft repartee already present from the small group. But I am drawn to one voice. Now separate from the group, I connect again to Mikiel. For a few moments, he simply looks at me. His stare bores through me. This is not easy to decipher. A sundry of emotions surface within his eyes, yet I cannot clearly identify any. Without provocation, he ends this moment by turning around then proceeding into the shadows of nightfall. I watch his exit. Gradually, his lightly-shaded wings fade from my sight until they disappear.

Bringing my attention back to Kriyo's parents, I enjoy the compassion that they both exude. I use this moment as a distraction from Mikiel's peculiar egress. Continuing to observe these wonderful beings, I distinguish what drives them: benevolence. Kriyo is a true reflection of this kindness. I will do my best to exemplify this honorable trait.

Before I see him, I sense Kriyo. With great anticipation, I wait for him to emerge. I yearn for this closeness. I have missed his presence. Finally the wait ends. Standing at my side, he takes my hand into his. His warm touch makes me lose a breath.

Addressing the group, he asks, "Will you all excuse Elder Meelah and me?"

"Of course, son," we hear Faro quickly reply, as if Kriyo's question was directed solely to him.

"Scoot, you two. You have some catching up to do. We understand," Pasha adds.

"Use this time wisely, Meelah. Kriyo has attained knowledge that you will soon require," Shria affirms. Her mind is always processing. Truthfully, there is a great deal that I must learn from Kriyo's time with the elusive Timeera. In every respect, Shria is accurate.

As my mind begins to reel, I notice Ruzi step toward me. His dark brown eyes focus on me. He stands before me, choosing not to communicate in any form. In time, I understand this unspoken sentiment. Silence is powerful. His undeclared message reminds me that all we possess are moments. Perhaps it is time for me to enjoy a few. As I project this epiphany only to him, he smiles contentedly and steps back to join the small group. With the din of their chatter in the background, I continue to consider this Light Warrior. He is not only a member of the Light Warrior family, Ruzi is and has always been a true friend to me. He has always had my back and the backs of those I love. I have never needed to ask him for this support, even now, when I require a reminder of the need for balance. Sending him a private message, I thank him for his pure devotion. Again, he answers me with silence, but includes a smile.

Turning toward Kriyo, I sense that he didn't attune to the silent communication between Ruzi and me. Always the gentleman. Validating this, he lowers his head to me. With a thought, he teleports us to the interior of Bursa. Though it is dark, I can sense where we are. He stands very close to me. The distant, joyous noises fall silent.

"You owe me a dance," I say to him.

"I owe you more than a dance," he whispers into my ear. "There is a great deal that I must share with you, Meelah. But," he expresses with a pause, "I missed you."

"As I have missed you."

"I am here now and wish to never leave you again," he states with passion.

Lowering his forehead, he rests it against mine. Cinching his arms around my waist, he holds me, and we remain in this lull for what feels like hours. I rest my head against his chest. We don't exchange words or thoughts. Simply, we honor our time together. All around us is swathed in dimming light. The noise from the square has quieted. The only sound to be heard now is our hearts beating and our breath. We both know what lies ahead of Churria. We choose not to immerse ourselves in this reality right now. At present, we recharge our hearts with each other's presence. Ruzi saw that this is what I needed. This is what had diminished within me. Love births fire and drive. This restored passion will fuel me. I find it telling that Ruzi recognized Kriyo as this source. Again, I feel honored by his loyalty.

The sound of someone clearing their throat ends this perfect moment. Masked by a veil of darkness, I make out this being by my other senses.

"Is Shria all right, Mikshe?"

"Yes, Meelah, she is fine. I was sent to—"

"Get me?"

"Yes."

"It appears that I must be leaving," I say tenderly to Kriyo. "Eyes are everywhere."

"And I have nothing to hide," he replies softly. "At first light?"

"Yes. Shria has summoned all the elders. They are to meet with the Light Warriors. A sense of unity shall commence. This should be an intriguing fusion."

"I will see you at first light, then," he whispers into my ear.

"Until then."

Against our each yearning for the other, I step back. Before I release his warm hand, I give it a squeeze. Then, I leave. Now that I am at home, Mikshe enters the house. Since the assistant of the Head Elder lives with their leader, perhaps if Trall was Shria's assistant they could be together. Change is coming. I hope that this wave affects their relationship as well.

"It is late, Meelah, and tomorrow will arrive before you know it," I hear Shria say from somewhere inside.

"Indeed it will. But why are you still awake?" I reply, following her voice. There she is.

"To tell you I am here for you."

"I know, Shria. You have always been present for me. I do have a question. Was the visit from Elder Jael a part of today's scripted events?"

"No. But he too was a test. Everything and everyone, each day, are tested. The results reveal who we are and what we believe. I am proud of how you handled his…"

"Contempt," I answer.

"Yes. He and a handful of other elders are having difficulties. Change is a fearful concept for them."

"I would like to thank you for addressing me as Meelah Neegry. I am honored that Trall allowed me to keep Samuel's last name. Shria," I add pensively. "I don't know what I would do if Jael harmed you."

"I know who Jael is and you are not a reflection of him. And Meelah, I feel the same way about you. Perhaps his presence here today was for both of us. Is there more that you wish to discuss?"

Though I know that she cannot hear my thoughts, she certainly acts as if she can. I wanted to confide the conflict I feel between Mikiel and Kriyo, but something inside of me halts my words. Instead, I hug her, not a Churrian thing to do, but it feels right in every way. Fatigue sets in and even though not many words were exchanged, enough were shared to find peace with the day. We know what each other's heart is conveying. Honoring our need for rest, we go our separate ways.

I hear Shria's chamber door close as I enter my room. After brushing my teeth and letting down my hair, I find myself lying in bed. Taking hold of my amulet with the palm of my hand, I drift off to sleep, but not for long.

"Meelah," I hear Mikiel telepathically call. "Meet me outside. It's important."

Sitting up, I wonder if I dreamt him speaking to me; but no, I feel his presence and his concern.

"I'll be right there," I say telepathically while slipping into my sandals.

Then it occurs to me. My trusty boots that have been with me for ages, I was wearing when the Epoh cut me. The poison must have destroyed them. My new clothes were destroyed and so were my special boots. Apparently it's time to let them go. Change isn't too terrible, though I am not fond of these flimsy sandals.

Before leaving I find myself standing before Shria's door questioning whether or not I should wake her. I know that she needs her rest and I don't know Mikiel's message. I choose not to disturb her. Continuing to the front door, but not quietly, I sense Mikshe coming behind me.

Turning around, I address her. "Mikiel has a problem and needs me." I see the confusion on her face as I struggle to articulate my words. She mustn't get the wrong idea. So I simply say, "I have been asked to meet with the Light Warriors. Please don't disturb the Head Elder as she has had a great deal to contend with today."

Perhaps I stretched the truth a bit, but Mikiel is a Light Warrior and Shria does require her rest. Closing the front door behind me, I see Mikiel pacing. He is here on business.

"Take my hand," he states bluntly.

Not questioning him, I extend my hand and before I know it we are at Ameira. This powerful teleporting station is amazing. Though the light of a new day hasn't fully arrived, the darkness of night is slowly lifting, revealing the beauty around me. The sleek glass-like surface resembles an enormous ice rink. Its surface is even slippery underfoot.

As I follow Mikiel, I sense Ruzi and Nala ahead of us. Their forms, immersed in the faint diffusing of light, begin to appear gradually in the dark as we approach. Entwined together like vines, I feel their passion and hear their increased heartbeats and rapid breath. I had forgotten how passionate Light Warriors are. Their animalistic fervor makes my cheeks blush red. Being polite, I make a little noise as we approach.

"Our liege," I hear Nala say with a giggle.

"I apologize, my liege," Ruzi adds, adjusting his stance. "Mikiel has asked you to come because of this," he says, pointing to his left. "Tonight Ameira didn't power down and this has never occurred."

"She is powered by the light of day. How is this occurring?" I ask.

"I don't know. But this is a great security risk," Mikiel responds. "Feel her energy. Something is amiss here."

"It's already a danger that the Churrians have no security measures nor restrictions regarding the use of Ameira," Nala includes. "But if she begins to operate at night as well, she will give the Epoh an added advantage."

"We must increase our patrol of Ameira to all day and night, regardless if she powers down," I affirm. "Perhaps both Churrians and Light Warriors should carry this responsibility from now on. This integration is crucial and the training for the Churrians is still necessary."

"Then it will be done, my liege," Ruzi promises. "The morning patrol will be here shortly for the light of day is nearly here. We will remain on guard until they do."

For as long as I can recall, Ruzi and Nala have had a romantic relationship. With what lies ahead for all of us, each moment is precious. I wouldn't have them waste time needlessly. I am here and quite capable of keeping watch.

"I will wait for the next team."

"Are you sure?" Ruzi asks.

"Yes," I answer firmly.

I watch the two take to the sky. This prompts a remembrance from when I was a Light Warrior to burst out of my mouth. "Light Warriors prefer to be together sensually while in flight."

"That is correct," Mikiel answers. I see in his face, his amusement.

"I'm sorry, that was quite inappropriate of me. I'm recalling so much from my past incarnation and that reminiscence surfaced."

As those words spill from my mouth, another memory plays like a film in my mind. This recollection is of Mikiel and me. We were passionately engaged in flight. I see my wings as they encompassed his body while plummeting through the atmosphere. I experience the intense, nearly breathless fervor that stirred between us. As we ascended, he touched me, all of me. Our wings struck harshly against each other, sending deep pulsations, affecting every cell within our forms. This action enlivened our senses, making them more acute. With each strike the moment now consumed with ardor became tumultuous. But before we fully connected, forging an everlasting bond, we were summoned by the Light Force to battle. We were never together. With this epiphany, I note Mikiel incessantly sniffing the air. Instantly, I'm alert. Looking in every direction, I wonder what he senses. Approaching me, he sniffs the air around my shoulder. Oddly, he lingers with his eyes closed.

"What are you doing?" I ask him.

"You are ready."

"Ready for what, Mikiel?"

"For mating," he replies, intensely.

"That is none of your business. I will not discuss that with you." Warmth rises to the surface of my face, flushing my cheeks.

Calmly, he observes me as if my discomfort is his entertainment. "Meelah, there is nothing to discuss," he states, still smirking. "I'm only telling you what I know."

I can't help but sniff the skin of my arm. This only prompts laughter from him. I watch this Light Warrior turn away, acting as though he's patrolling. He's not, he's wondering who I will choose to satisfy the task my body requires.

"So, there is still a choice to be had," he says, hearing my thoughts.

That's it! Fatigue has lowered the shield protecting my thoughts, but not for long. Both he and Kriyo have no business in my mind. My thoughts are private, and if I wish to share them, it will be my choice to do so from now on. I close my eyes while taking hold of my amulet and seal my thoughts. Opening my eyes, I see Mikiel sauntering my way. The light of a new day is nearly here, lifting any and all residual darkness of the night. I wonder why Mikiel wasn't poking around my thoughts when I recollected the intense moment from our past. Perhaps it was all of his sniffing that distracted him. Engaging with Mikiel again, I don't only see him. There is something else here as well and it towers behind him.

Chapter Five

With a wave of my hand, I move Mikiel from harm's way. Though I only wished to relocate him, I regrettably may have hurled him instead. I need to work on my powers. Thankfully, I see that he's safe. Not at all pleased with me, but safe.

The being in question is now in my full sight. Appearing winded or perhaps injured, the imposing life form's stance wavers. Grasping onto something beneath his shirt, he seems in need of aid. Bald-headed, the being has a kind, round face. Wearing a drab loose shirt with a leather belt that threatens to slip off his hips, he heaves his barrel chest with each breath. His leggings are torn and tattered. The large, pale-skinned creature radiates his benign nature, causing me to begin my approach. Appearing like a fairy tale ogre, he towers above me as I now stand before him.

"It's only an Opala!" I hear Mikiel spout in an agitated tone.

I find myself wishing to sneer at him. Could Mikiel be a tad more ungrateful? I didn't know that this being was an Opala or what an Opala even might be, though I find myself standing before one. Daylight is here and beings from throughout our universe begin to use Ameira to further their travels. Even these life forms know that Ameira functions with the dawn. Chaos would ensue if she never shut down. Individuals would use her continuously and the risks are too grave. Oblivious to this change, beings appear, then disappear from sight en masse.

"Kriyo," I hear the large creature say telepathically.

Then he speaks outwardly in a foreign dialect that I somewhat understand. He rambles on, then pauses, appearing as if any moment he may lose consciousness. I work to attain eye contact with him. As soon as our gazes unite, I witness the hell that he has only nearly escaped. Within this being's eyes, I witness the horror of war.

"Get Kriyo," I say to Mikiel. I feel his hesitation. "Now, please," I demand.

As soon as Mikiel leaves, I see movement from beneath the Opala's shirt. Again, I use my instincts and know that it too is benign.

"Help them," the Opala tells me telepathically.

He falls to the ground. Thankfully, this massive being landed on his back or whatever is in his shirt most likely would have been flattened. Tearing his shirt open I see what lies behind it. Distinguishing what he's been protecting, my heart nearly stops. Two very young Opala are nestled together. One appears very badly wounded and the other slightly injured.

"Save them," I hear the Opala mumble. "They are all that's left."

I take the two younglings into my arms at the same time I see Mikiel and Kriyo running my way. Beings from all over the universe begin to surround me and the downed Opala. Kriyo looks at me then at the being I'm kneeling over. Instantly he joins us.

His face appears wrought with concern. He knows this Opala and judging from the grief registered on his face, they are quite close.

"Lador, what happened?" his soft voice asks. "Drink this, it will help you," he adds, pouring a vial of herbs into his mouth.

Gently I handle what I believe to be the Opala's progeny. Placing them on the warm glass-like surface, I sense Kriyo's gaze follow my every move. I feel how deeply affected he is by their injured state. The weaker one is quite limp. His life is tenuous and I fear that I am already too late.

"Mikiel, your sword please."

As he draws his sword, I raise my wrist and slice it against his blade. I drip my blood into the mortally wounded Opala's mouth before I give the balance to the other. Before my body heals, I reach over and rest my wrist on Lador's lips, giving him my final drops. I look again at Kriyo. He returns an intense expression denoting his gratitude. Giving my attention again to the younglings, I immediately note the improvement in the stronger one but not the other.

"Let him go," I hear Mikiel say softly. "His injuries are too grave."

"It has begun. The Darkness has commenced its devastation?" I state telepathically only to him.

"It has, Meelah," Mikiel answers solemnly.

We both know what happened. This is not the first time we've discovered an entire kind almost extinguished in a matter of hours. The Light Warriors have spent their entire existence battling this precise destruction and the force behind it. Thousands upon thousands of years have been dedicated to this plight before a lull came, a time that ushered in a counterfeit peace, because here we are again. Utter annihilation has reared its ugly head and it must end. The two Light Warriors just beginning their patrol worked through the throng and now stand before us. When I witness their faces, I see that they too are affected by the plight that has haunted us.

As the weaker youngling's body fails, I hear him gasp for air. Its suffering pains all of me. I know that I should end its misery, but I can't do it. I know that Mikiel waits, expecting me to find the strength. I once possessed this selfless ability, but now I just can't muster it. The adult Opala, with Kriyo's help, makes his way to me and his offspring. He takes hold of his distressed son and with absolute love, he silences him, ending his pain. I watch the youngling's arms drop, then hang lifeless. I honor this father for possessing what I lack. His son's suffering has come to an end. This noble act moves me, but quickly other feelings replace it.

Distraught and crushed by the variety of emotions, I sit immobilized. I feel the other youngling as it crawls onto my lap, then nestles against my chest. In time I look down. Our eyes meet and I witness the dreadfulness that this young being experienced. With no warning, in the light of day, they were aggressively attacked. Her mother shielded this little one, but the other wasn't fully protected by its mother's corpse and thus, badly injured as a result. Their father hid with them through the night and as dawn arose, teleported them here.

Feeling a presence above me, I look up. "If I give him to Natiya, may my daughter and I remain on Churria?" the Opala asks, holding out his deceased offspring.

The Opala wears his pain as plainly as I am wearing my robe. I see him grapple with it, so that it doesn't overtake him. Kriyo kneels down beside me and engages with the youngster, who appears at home in my lap. He communicates with her as though they've known each other her entire life and obviously they have. I feel Kriyo take my wrist into his hand and inspect it. His warm lips press upon the area that just healed, distracting me for a moment, but I redirect my attention to the Opala's request.

First, I wonder why he's asking me, as I have no authority to make such a decision. Furthermore, judiciously there is a channel one must use to permit any outsider residence on Churria. I just learned this process, but how can I explain this to the innocent being that has just gone through such loss. Put simply, I don't possess the ability to provide him with an answer. With that thought, I'm aware of Natiya's energy welling beneath me. I close my eyes and hear her answer the Opala's request. I ask her what I am to do and she instructs me.

When I open my eyes, I see that the little Opala has vacated my lap and taken residence upon Kriyo's. Ahead of me is the father standing with his back toward me, with his son in hand. I feel his guilt and remorse as if it was mine and perhaps it is.

"I requested Shria," I hear Kriyo say. "She will answer him."

"That was wise of you, but I have his answer," I tell him, rising to a stand.

Taking hold of my wrist, Kriyo tethers us together for a moment. He says, "His name is Lador. We have been very close my entire life—he is like a brother to me."

"Natiya has granted their stay," I say, trying to ease him. "But she must take his son."

"Please allow me to tell him?"

I lower my head in acknowledgment and take the Opalan youngster as he hands her to me. Barefoot and wearing a thick, ivory tunic, her warm hand gently touches the side of my face. Like her father, she is bald and pale-skinned, but her little face is quite feminine. Still within the dark pools of her eyes is the horror that she and her family experienced. What she's seen at such a young age is deplorable. Remembering that her father easily communicated with me telepathically, I ask her, "What are you called?"

"Dalia," she readily answers.

"My name is—"

"Meelah," she answers. "We all know who you are."

I smile at her innocence. Her face reflects a brief moment of glee before returning to the previous somber expression. Within her eyes, I also see the reflection of her father still holding her brother.

"Yidor," I hear her emit telepathically. "He saved us, didn't he?"

I nod yes, while restraining my tears. It is I that should have saved them—all of them! And the cost of her little brother's body shouldn't be the reason that they are permitted to remain here on Churria. Anger from pure frustration begins to rise within me then a gentle hand warming my shoulder eases it and settles me just as swiftly. Without looking, I recognize who it is, Shria.

"Do as Natiya wishes," she states, still standing behind me. As I turn to face her, she adds, "Honor our mother. I will witness the exchange and we will report it to the elders at the meeting this morning."

Without speaking a word or forming a thought, I do as Shria instructs. I hand Dalia to her then head over to Lador. His pain as he hands his son to me further injures my heart. With the deceased in my arms, I allow Dalia to bid her goodbyes then I do the same for Kriyo, then again, Lador. Taking Kriyo's hand while clutching the wee male against my chest, I follow Natiya's instructions.

Attuning to her, she leads us away from the gathered masses and over to the sand. I kneel down and Kriyo does the same. Placing the small body atop the warm sand, we wait. A breeze begins to encompass us. My hair lifts and whirls about in every direction. From the corner of my eye, I see Kriyo bow completely forward, honoring the mother. I ask if I may remain kneeling. I feel her answer within the breeze. Curious, I watch. The wind shifts. Like a cyclone, it centers its funnel directly over the small body. To my utter astonishment, a small essence lifts from the deceased form. It looks at me and I look at it. We each see the other's light. Then I make out Natiya as she manifests before my eyes. Golden rays of light assemble her outline. Her essence, infused with love and purity, consumes the golden contours depicting her svelte figure. Here she is. Her radiance is standing before me holding the life force of little Yidor. Her beauty is divine and her presence quite powerful. As Mother lowers the palm of her hand to the ground, Yidor's physical body sinks into the sand. Slowly, sand overtakes his form until finally, it's gone. I raise my head and look at Natiya. She is already staring at me. When our eyes unite I sense the insurmountable work that we'll do together. Lowering her head to me, she lifts from the ground and continues to ascend, taking Yidor with her. I come to a stand. As if she needs me to understand what she's doing, I follow. Instinctively, I take to flight, and I feel Mikiel do the same. Ascending at a lesser speed than she, I observe her in the distance. She leaves the atmosphere and I do the same, never wondering whether I physically could. Again, I sense Mikiel as he closes the space between us. Surrounded by the absolute darkness of space, her brilliance is ahead of us. Like a beacon, she draws us to her.

I witness her reverently place Yidor's essence down. As she does, a luminous golden web awakens, brightening the area around us. Churria is encased by this amazing net and Yidor willingly joins it. His essence makes it stronger. When the golden mesh senses his benevolent heart, it beams.

"It is this shield that has protected all of us from the Dark Force and now the Epoh," we hear Natiya declare. Descending back to Churria, she adds, "This shield is weakening, and thus I will soon require your help. Darkness has found its way to Churria. Be aware, Meelah, it sees you."

Her words affect me. *What has found its way to Churria? What sees me?* As I watch her luminosity return home, an overwhelming sense of need trumps the intrigue of Natiya's words. I must see what happened to the Opalas' home. I must learn from this travesty and outwardly I say, "Something good must come from their annihilation."

"Why do you wish to go there?"

"You know me, Mikiel. I must go. I will understand when I am there."

"I know where to go, but this is dangerous, Meelah."

"Trust me."

"I do," he answers, taking my hand.

Escorting me through the darkness, moving only forward, I question why he needs to hold my hand. I also wonder why he just doesn't take us there using his powers, but with time, I have my answer. The Opalas' home is relatively close to Churria and to earth, meaning that our fated battle is imminent.

Looking at planet earth, I feel Drana and the love she possesses for her home. She was the first creation of mother-earth, the being to oversee all that earthlings now consider to be mystical.

A blue grid encases earth and I sense Drana's intimate connection to it. This net energetically protects this planet, for now. It's also weakening.

Another epiphany rises to my mind's surface. The Dark Force will attack all the many planets and stars that are home to peaceful beings. If *he* succeeds, the balance will continue to weigh in *his* favor. All protective shields everywhere will fail. *His* pursuit will become effortless, especially with the Epoh as his army. I send this realization to Mikiel and watch him as he digests it. I stop processing and afford all of my attention to what lies below us. We are here; slowly we descend.

"We need not be here. I have a feeling where *he* will attack next."

Though I receive his words, something in the distance catches my attention. As our feet touch ground, we choose our steps carefully. I am mindful to not dishonor the dead underfoot. Then I make out what the movement is.

"Qanti, the scavengers that feed on death," I say softly, crouching behind a rock. "If they are here the Epoh have already left."

"It's still not safe, Meelah."

A tug on the hem of my robe arrests my attention. Below, a female Opala, closer to death than to life, extends her hand to me. I kneel down, and before I say a word, she transmits, "I know who you are. Save our younglings. They're beneath...."

Too weak, her telepathic message ends with a final exhalation. There are survivors. I knew there was a reason to come. Hope fuels me though I have no idea where the younglings have hidden.

"I spent some time with the Opala," Mikiel says quietly after hearing her plea. "They are known to hide a handful of their young when threatened. They conceal them underground. The space will be too small for the predator, but large enough for one adult Opala."

The sound of rustling redirects our focus for a moment. Both Mikiel and I tune into the noise and see four Qanti tear into an Opala's corpse before moving onto the next. With so much meat available, they can afford to be picky, and choose the most palatable parts, which appear to be their stomachs. Qanti resemble huge vultures. They stand as high as I am and scavenge by tearing through the midsection of their prey before extracting the tasty insides with their claws and beaks. More arrive close to where we are. Peering around the enormous rock that shields us from their line of sight, we realize that we are nearly out of time. The Qanti thankfully have a poor sense of smell or they would have already learned of our presence. Their eyesight isn't much better, but their hearing is acute. Unfortunately, even more clunk down and feast.

Closing my eyes, I use my powers to scan beneath the surface. I hear rapid heartbeats, many, and not of the Qanti. Taking hold of Mikiel's hand, I watch his lips lift, forming a smile as he tunes into the sounds of life. But the Qanti's incessant grazing brings them even closer to us. Realizing precisely where they've been hidden, I ask Mikiel to create a diversion. Within his eyes, I see his concern at leaving me alone. If I am to lead us he must trust my judgment as he once did. Squeezing his hand, I remind him of this notion.

He gives me that look of his, then takes to flight. Startling the nearing Qanti, he rises as they scatter, giving me an opening. One of them fires off a distress call then others join the shrieking. An intolerable sound fills the air. Focusing on the life beneath the large rock, I use my powers and fling it to the side. A deep hole appears and only darkness is revealed, but I sense the younglings.

"I am Meelah," I communicate telepathically. "We must hurry before the Qanti return!"

Still nothing from the young Opala. But the sound of Mikiel's sword as he draws it, reminds me of the little time I have. The ground begins to shake and I realize that the Qanti were notifying something, perhaps an Epoh, of our presence. I see Mikiel prepare to battle the beast—I will not lose him! Trying one more time to lure them out, I choose words that will be effective.

"I will not die here, but all of you will if you choose not to leave with us NOW!"

That did it! I see them hurriedly climb to the surface. Extracting them one by one, I urge them to huddle close together. One of the younglings screams as a Qanti runs our way. Creating a shield that bubbles us, I foil the several Qanti that join in and propel their bodies at the invisible barrier then bounce off. Finally, the last Opala surfaces, but I no longer hear Mikiel. Sheer panic begins to rise within me as I look in every direction. Finally, I see the Epoh on its side and Mikiel extracting his sword from the beast. Taking to flight, he soars over to me and the Opala, but he's closely followed by a group of Qanti.

"Leave, Mikiel!" I order. I watch him disappear from sight and now it's our turn. "Hold hands," I telepathically instruct them.

I sense their tiny fingers weave together while the Qanti continue to violently bash into my shield. Closing my eyes, I feel our heartbeats unify as one while visualizing Ameira in my mind. As I open my eyes, I see that we've made it. With no authorization from Natiya, the council or Shria, I return with twenty-two young Opala.

Kriyo is running our way with Lador slow to follow. Dalia squirms in her father's arms, appearing antsy to have her feet on the ground. I look for Mikiel, wondering where he is. Concerned, I call to him. Though I used my mind to do so, Kriyo hears it. His expression becomes difficult to read, but my concern for Mikiel takes precedence. Finally, I see him soaring above with Ruzi.

"You did well, my liege," I hear him state.

I follow his flight with my eyes and though a part wishes to join them, I remain grounded. Next to me is Kriyo, who is already communicating with the younglings. Lador's breathless form has finally reached me as well. Tears fill his eyes as the overjoyed youngsters climb up his legs.

"I am proud of you, Meelah," I hear Kriyo say.

I smile at him, but another gets my attention. "Words are not enough," I hear Lador transmit in thought. Lowering his head, he bows. I return the gesture. I had help. It wasn't only I who saved these younglings.

"If Mikiel didn't give me the time I required, I would have been forced to leave without them."

After hearing my words, Lador promptly walks off. I observe him, wondering where he's going. Following his direction, I see Mikiel, who landed a few moments ago, his wings not yet fully retracted. I watch this Light Warrior comically tilt his head as the large Opala remains focused on him. Now standing before him, Lador takes hold of his arm, then yanks him against his chest. Lifting him from the ground, he gives my dear friend quite the squeeze. I see Mikiel gasp for air and I can't help but smile. As Lador lowers him back to the ground and releases his grasp, Kriyo makes his way to Mikiel as well.

Both stand facing the other reticently for a few a moments. Perhaps they're communicating solely between themselves. Maybe they wish not to talk for fear of what would be communicated. Kriyo places his palms to his chest and reverently bows to Mikiel. This authentic gesture touches my heart. Kriyo's integrity is one of his greatest strengths and his finest quality. He's also very easy on the eyes. I observe him rise and smile at Mikiel before he returns back to me. He seems lost in thought for the first few steps, but then locks his eyes on me. Instantly, he creates a smile on my face.

Now standing quite close to me, he says, "So, you can fly. Is there anything that you can't do?"

"I couldn't save the other Opalas nor was I able to save Lador's son."

"Perhaps you weren't meant to," he answers, while touching the side of my face. "But Meelah, we are late for the meeting with the elders."

"You waited for me?" I ask him.

Taking hold of my hand, he answers, "Of course I did."

He makes me smile, but I cannot get lost in his eyes. We are late. With a sigh, I remember who I forgot to invite to the meeting. "Kriyo, I didn't get a chance to ask the Light Warriors to join me at the gathering."

"Possibly, it's not the time for your Light Warriors to meet with the elders. Today, the elders are fated to meet with the Opala. That might be enough."

"Maybe you are right. We should go, Kriyo. Shria is waiting, I feel it. Gather the Opala, and Mikiel, please join us on the green in Bursa."

Mikiel joins with the sky. I watch him soar as effortlessly as I breathe. I feel Kriyo's stare as he watches me.

"I am indebted to him," I hear him say, still looking at me. He is aware of even my doubts. "Mikiel is a true ally," I tell him.

"Is that all Mikiel is to you, Meelah—an ally?"

"I love you, Kriyo." I say in earnest.

"I know that you do and my heart will always belong to you, Meelah. But, in time, I hope you'll be able to answer my question."

"Time, it is a curious thing, isn't it? It keeps moving forward. We must go. Everyone, please gather."

Without the interlacing of fingers, I group all the Opala, Kriyo and myself as a whole and with my intention, we leave. As I open my eyes, I see that we have arrived on the platform, behind Shria. With the elders' mouths agape, I wait for my Head Elder. I observe her pervasive calm and composed demeanor, even if behind her stands a mass of foreign beings in need of a home.

I hear her ask Kriyo to the podium then see her almost glare at me. Now standing beside me, she quietly and privately asks, "Is this all of the surviving Opala?" I nod yes while maintaining my forward gaze. "They may take residence in Drista, but I am unsure if they will be permitted in the Underground City. We must seek approval from the Timeera."

"What underground city?" I ask.

Chapter Six

Intrigued, I devour every word that exits Kriyo's lips as he shares his knowledge of the Timeera and of the mysterious Underground City. The Timeera have granted the Churrians refuge from the wrath of the Dark Force. Then I hear Kriyo announce, "But." It's not the word, it's the way in which he used it that heightens my interest.

After a pause, he explains, "Only those who truly honor and respect Natiya are allowed passage."

With these spoken words unrest swirls amongst the elders. Emotions of all kinds surface and seem to tangle into a knot. The emotional upheaval is all but tangible. I look at Lador and the young Opala and see their discomfort. After all they have just endured, they don't need this. Circumventing the proper channel, perhaps for the first time, I ask Shria if Mikiel is permitted to bring them to Drista. Abruptly she nods yes, before returning to the podium.

Hesitantly, Mikiel agrees and removes the Opala from the mounting tension. I am aware that he doesn't appreciate me sending him off on errands so often. I know that he wishes to be at my side. Nonetheless, I require his help for at this moment someone else is in need of assistance, Kriyo. Still standing next to Shria, he's in the direct line of fire from the elders. Finally Shria pulls on the reins and begins to resume control. With a forceful tone, she seizes everyone's attention.

"Enough—we will soon be under attack!" she exclaims. "Let us not forget this! It is an honor that we have been offered any support from the Timeera! I will not tolerate this useless and fearful exchange any longer. We will recess then with dignity we will reconvene when the light is mid-sky. At this time, Kriyo and I will do our best to answer all of your questions."

She stands resolute and poised as the elders begin to disburse. Her patient and reassuring demeanor, as she maintains a strong sense of leadership, is like nothing I have ever encountered. Once the final elder teleports from sight, she relaxes and turns toward Kriyo.

"Your intentions were good, but panic is rising to the surface and overtaking all reasoning. Is it possible to have a member of the Timeera present when we reconvene?"

"I will leave and inquire."

"Thank you," she replies.

"Meelah, do you wish to come with me?"

"Very much, but I must speak with Shria."

"Then I will see you when I return," he answers.

"Indeed."

Intrigued by where he's going, I watch him teleport from sight. The idea of an underground city here on Churria is exciting. Sensing Shria's presence, I turn around and note her ruffled spirit. Her ungrounded nature is quite disconcerting. The air is unsettled.

"We are not alone, Meelah. Darkness has come to Churria. I fear we are being watched," she says quietly. "I will wait for you at home." Closing her eyes for a moment, she includes this, "Natiya has been calling you. She said she requires your help and it is important. We will request a meeting with her at home."

Abruptly she teleports from sight. Behind her, I see Elder Jael. Perhaps he is the darkness that she's referencing. I bet Natiya was trying to warn us about him. Oddly, I haven't sensed her since I returned. But here and now, I do sense this elder's wickedness. Jael seems to be lurking in the shadows. I observe him beaming in utter content. Enjoying the upheaval, he even blurts out an obnoxious snicker.

Quite unexpectedly, I feel the presence of Blessing, my Noori. Though I don't see her yet, she's near. Her distinctive scent grounds me. A smile forms on my face when her white, winged equine form comes into my view, particularly because of where she's standing.

"What are you smiling at?" Elder Jael asks.

"I am pleased to see Blessing."

"Pleased with whom?"

No sooner do his words depart from his mouth, than Blessing nudges him hard in his back. Fear overtakes him as he braces himself from falling forward. Jumping away from my winged beauty, he glares at me. Jael's natural contempt alters his facial expression. Pure disdain births a wicked sneer.

"Blessing, come here, my good girl. Leave that old Churrian alone."

"I will have her seized for attacking me!"

I smile at him, then to the young female Bursan who's approaching my Noori and me. Appearing quite enamored, she is fixed on the foreign winged creature. I feel the youngster's excitement and see her eyes continue to brighten.

"She likes you," I say, as she lifts her slender hand to touch Blessing. "Would you like to bring the Noori to the humbra tree? She loves the blossoms. And what is your name?"

"My name is Grya and I want to be just like you when I grow up."

As I sense Elder Jael's annoyance from her statement, I wonder why he has remained here on the green. I know he doesn't want bonding time with me. I won't leave this young lady alone in his presence. Her innocent giggle captures my attention. In her, I see a young Mikshe. Slender, with a swan-like elegant neck, this young brunette wears a bright yellow robe. Cascading down her back, the Churrian's brunette hair is festooned with small, pink flowers. A cheerful crown-like embellishment rests atop her head. Grya's virtue and purity are apparent, especially in the presence of her polar opposite.

"So you wish to become an elder?"

Her brown eyes connect with mine, powerfully. "No, I want to be a warrior. Will you truly save us?"

Her query derails me for a moment. She possesses the same innocence as Dalia and I have discerned what her eyes have witnessed. I wish for Grya to never know that kind of pain. I reply, "Grya, you can become anything you wish." Connecting to Blessing I add, "Take care of Grya for a moment. Keep her safe and I'll meet you at the humbra tree."

I observe Blessing as she receives my request. Slowly and mindfully, with Grya at her side, she honors my words. From the corner of my eye I see Elder Jael's shifty presence. He's up to no good. Addressing him to break his silence, I ask, "Elder Krall is the name of that young Churrian's father? He outranks you, doesn't he?"

"That is irrelevant," he answers, fired up.

"No, Elder Jael, nothing is irrelevant! And I will not tolerate your threats! We are on the brink of war and I am only trying to save this star."

"It is you," he says, taking a step closer. "Perhaps I should have killed you when you were a mere infant. Here you stand, Meelah, and here war threatens. IT IS YOU!"

Shuddering as I feel the emotion that drives his words, I see several elders emerge from the dense greenery. They join his alliance. Their rage and fear all wrapped up into one sledgehammer of emotion thickens the air encircling me. Then I feel it! Something has happened to Blessing. I run to her.

"Leave her be!" I scream. I see four Churrians continue to violently strike Blessing with metal tools as I run her way. Ropes are thrown over her neck.

"Get away from Grya, you beast!" I hear them shout.

I hear Blessing squeal as they harshly pull on the lines, choking her. Overwrought with terror, the Noori rears. Grya is right there! Faster than I knew I could travel, I shield the young Bursan from Blessing. Appearing behind her, I pull her close to me. Tremendous weight upon my back steals my breath as I crash to the ground. Using all my strength, I try not to crush Grya beneath me. I feel a thud beside me. Blessing has fallen. If they have killed her, I'm unsure what I'll do to them!

"Mikiel, I need you," I whimper.

In just moments, I know that he's near, as a hush befalls the crowd. Fearing my back is broken, I remain as motionless as possible. Quietly, I call to Grya. She lies beneath me without a sound.

I hear her muffled heart beating and feel her breath as it stirs around the skin of my chest—thankfully she lives.

"Meelah," I hear Mikiel say. "Do not move. This will hurt, but you must remain still for me to remove it."

"Remove what?"

Then I feel Shria and her sheer panic as she assesses what I cannot see. Rousing beneath me is Grya. Subtly her body moves as she begins to come to. As her eyes connect with mine, she asks, "Did they hurt her?"

"I believe they did, but I will do everything to help her. May I ask you something?" As she nods yes, I say, "Remain still for a moment?"

"Of course," she answers. "Did you save me?"

"Yes," I answer, wincing in pain. Persistent tugging nearly lifts me from the ground.

"Your robe is all red," Grya voices, trembling.

As Mikiel rolls me gently into his arms, my gaze remains connected with the youngster. Promptly she's lifted from the ground by female Bursans. They seem to discard me, as if hoping I'll succumb to my injuries and rot. I'm pained watching Grya's terror as she sees Blessing, and I instantly fear that I may have lost her.

I hear Grya scream, "Why did you do this? She was only protecting me from those elders! Why?"

In Mikiel's arms, I am reminded that he's always where I need him. Grasping his arm, I state, "I will not leave her here!"

"Nala is here now. She is using your blood to heal her. I believe she'll recover."

"I must see her."

As I am carried over to Blessing, I see Bursans gather. Perhaps they're a lynch mob. At this moment I don't have a clue what they're capable of doing. Looking for Shria, I hear Mikiel telepathically update me with, "I told her that I'd get you out of here. Ruzi will protect her."

"Where will they go?"

"I asked the Light Warriors to stand guard at her home. They will protect the Head Elder."

My heart thanks him and I see him receive this message as he closes his eyes briefly. He lowers me to the ground. Blessing is in my line of sight. There is a puncture to her side, gradually it's closing. Nala holds a metal object still swathed in my blood. Gently, she wipes my blood onto Blessing's tongue. The tool that Nala holds is what I saw the Churrians use to strike Blessing. They also must have impaled her with it. I piece things together. One of them must have thrown the long metal tool at us. I'm relieved that Grya remained unscathed, at least physically anyway. I witnessed her emotional horror.

"I think they wished to kill the young girl and you blocked their attempt," I hear Mikiel say, alerting Nala. "That way they could blame you for her death. It is no longer safe for you here," he determines, rising to a stand. Spreading his massive wings, he lifts us from the ground.

"Where are you taking me?"

"Somewhere secure."

"I will not hide nor will I run. I have done nothing wrong. Bring me to Shria's."

"No!" he shouts. "I will not lose you, especially to them!"

"Bring me to Drista. Grawl, Grutiri and the Light Warriors can more easily keep watch. We know the protection of the wall that encompasses the township. We built it."

I watch him grapple with the thought for a moment, but he too knows it's irrefutable. The Light Warriors constructed the barrier that surrounds the small township of Drista. We made Drista our home for two reasons: the dry fountain of knowledge, and the location. Drista is surrounded by a flat sandy landscape. We could see anyone approaching for miles. A small group of about two hundred Churrians took residency regardless of the harsh arid environment. Only those close to Natiya can thrive in this place. Without this connection one can't manifest the water needed to substantiate the herbal nutrients required for survival. Dristans are rumored to produce water from thin air. I can't wait to see this. It's fitting that Kriyo was born here. He is a natural in manifesting.

As Drista comes into view, I am able to move my legs again. My body is healing and my strength returning. I never thought that a Churrian would be capable of such malfeasances, but apparently I am wrong. My welling emotions aside, I see the incredible protectors of Drista. Below, Grawl and Grutiri swim through the sand. They seem to know what has occurred and are escorting us home. Their presence is welcoming and most appreciated. As I observe them, my mind returns to Blessing. If she heals they may seize her. What about Shria and Mikshe? Then there's Kriyo. He soon will return to the Bursa green, the devastating scene that we just left. All who are close to my heart are still in Bursa, where the unrest has reared its foul head. My worry sets in for all of them.

Outside the Dristan wall, I see Pasha and Faro. The news seems to have travelled fast. Then to my left I see Ruzi with the male Noori in tow. He appears to bring weighty news. Both Mikiel and I sense it immediately. Ruzi and the Noori land within the confines of the Dristan wall. I hear the male Noori whinny. He calls for Blessing. I am overcome by his pain as silence is his answer.

Then a faint sound of Blessing's whinny prompts the male Noori to call again. Anxious, I wait, hoping to hear it once more. The sound of her neighing reaches my ears. Some of my distress is lifted with this gift. Bouncing about while I scan the horizon behind us, I feel Mikiel almost lose his grasp of me. Tightly, he draws me closer.

"I see Blessing. She's with Nala."

Blessing's massive wings carry her my way. I am antsy to see her, but feel Mikiel's unwillingness to release me. I look at him. Within my eyes, he sees that I've healed enough to journey on my own. He can't help but smile and as he does, his grasp releases, liberating me. Immediately my heart brings me to Blessing. By her side, I see that she's winded and still in much pain.

"I had to get her out of there," I hear Nala explain. "There was talk of ending her if she recovered. The elders there have deemed her a threat."

"Thank you, Nala. What you have done here...."

I feel Nala's smile before her face creates it. I didn't finish my thought, she already understands my heart. Directing my focus to Blessing, I see blood painting a thin line from her nostril. Flight is too much for her. Asking her to land, we gradually descend.

"I will walk her the remainder of the way. Go to Ruzi, there is news."

Lowering her head, Nala continues onward. Her massive wings, mottled with white, brown and black feathers, carry her. This beautiful Light Warrior is willowy in form. She is fair-skinned and her facial features are delicate and refined. With chestnut-colored hair, braided and secured in a bun, her beauty is natural and simple. Nala is the most genuine of beings, though ferocious and well-skilled in battle. Shimmering, the armor covering her back reflects the sunlight. Part of the outfit she has always worn, her white skirt continues to flap as it catches the wind. Swiftly she soars. I can sense her curiosity regarding Ruzi's news.

Next to me is Blessing. I acknowledge her weakness and I wish nothing more than to heal her. As we approach the wall I see Grawl and Grutiri are conferencing with Mikiel, Ruzi and Nala. I am aware of their concern. Soon I will learn of this news, but first, I must get Blessing to safety.

Pasha runs our way. I have missed her. "I don't know what to say, dear, but I know what we can do. I have a salve prepared for your Noori and a room for you."

"Thank you."

"Meelah, you are safe with us," Faro says as I approach. "Pasha, it looks like she'll require a fresh robe."

Looking down, I see the front of my robe soaked in blood. Great, another robe destroyed. Then Blessing nudges me as if to say that everything will be fine. Stroking her neck, I also believe that with time, all will be well, but now, we have a bit of a problem. Blessing is too large to fit through the entrance. She'll have to fly over the high wall.

"Is she strong enough?" I hear Faro ask.

"She'll have to be," I say, looking at her. "Let's try, girl."

Still breathing heavy, she expands her wings and begins to move. Her hooves lift from the ground before swiftly they return to it. She tries, but simply, she's too weak.

"Here," I say to her. "It's all right."

In my mind, I see what to do. I can hardly believe that I didn't previously have the sense to do this. Standing by her side, I lay both of my hands upon her, and then…we disappear.

"Meelah!" I hear Mikiel cry.

"I'm right here!" I answer from within the confines of Drista.

No sooner does he hear my words than he runs past Pasha and Faro. Immediately, he relaxes when he sees me standing next to Blessing.

"It's a Light Warrior thing," Pasha says.

"It's a mad, passionate, love thing," Faro answers.

"She made her choice. On earth she chose our son."

"Meelah might have, but does that Light Warrior know?" Using his cane, Faro makes his way to Blessing. "I have the salve for this beautiful creature," he assures me. "We will set you back to rights," he sings. "Meelah, do you trust her in my care?"

"Absolutely," I answer him. Handing Faro the reins, I give him my sincere gratitude.

"Come with me, you beautiful Noori," he croons in bliss as he walks alongside her.

As I watch Blessing and Faro walk onward, I'm wondering just who is helping whom to walk; both seem to lean on the other with every step. Lador, with Dalia resting in his arms, comes to me. I see him shake his head as he approaches. The news of what happened in Bursa seems to be everyone's knowledge now. Not that I wish to hide it, I just wish that he had no need to carry more than what he already does.

"You are hurt?" I hear him ask telepathically, as he looks at my soiled robe.

"Not anymore, but thank you for your concern."

"Where is Kriyo?"

"He…" I pause. Truthfully, I don't know where he is. "Kriyo was asked to meet with an ally of ours."

"The Timeera?" he inquires.

That surprises me. I wonder how he knows of the Timeera. I simply answer, "Yes." No sooner do I provide him a response than he lowers his head and turns around. "Lador," I shout, halting his step. "Kriyo was asked to return with a Timeera and meet the elders in Bursa."

As he turns to face me, he responds, "I will go to him. He will be safe with me."

I see in the dark pools of his eyes that he is willing to die trying. Their bond is illustrated by his selfless desire to lend his aid. How did I not know that this massive yet modest being is Kriyo's closest friend? Perhaps there is a great deal about Kriyo I still must learn and I look forward to it. Bringing my attention back to Lador, I ask, "How did you fit through the entry of the Dristan wall?"

"One of the Light Warriors flew me over."

"That was kind of them, but may I suggest another way?"

Indicating yes by the bobbing of his head, he waits. I reply, "Give me a little time to change. I'll meet you at Pasha's house."

I can't imagine that a being of his size would want to be handled by anyone, let alone lifted from the ground. Which Light Warrior was strong enough to carry him? I wonder. It doesn't matter. The wheels in my head are spinning. I begin to create a plan.

"Meelah, how will we get to Bursa?"

"I will take us."

"But I cannot teleport like you," he replies, brooding. Lost in thought for a spell, he then adds, "You'll bring me the same way that the Light Warrior brought us to Drista, like teleporting, but faster? You're not a Light Warrior."

"Give me a few moments and I'll remind you. I brought you and all the Opala to Bursa the same way." Realizing that I have no idea where Pasha's home is located, I turn back to Lador and see him gazing sweetly at Dalia. Amorously they simply each stare at the other. Perhaps this is their way of communicating. Regardless of what it is, I am mesmerized for a moment. Dalia is lucky to have him as her father.

"Thank you," Lador says in ancient Churrian to me. "Words cannot express my gratitude for what you've done for us, all of us."

Dalia sits up in his arms. When she sees me, she grins from ear to ear. But she notices my soiled robe. "Meelah, you are hurt!"

"I am fine now. Lador, would you direct me to Pasha and Faro's home?"

With a nod of his head, he begins his slow troll forward. Journeying away from the Dristan wall, we enter an oasis. Outside the wall is an environment, abundant in nothing more than a sandy flat terrain, but in here it's quite different. Ahead of me are two pathways leading to lines of clay homes. In the midst of the paths is lush greenery that surrounds the dry fountain. This incredible tool is in the very same place that I remember it. It was a gift from our Creator and we used it see where the Light would send us next. I am unsure what the Dristans use it for now or even if they understand its true function.

Walking onward, I'm astonished by the beauty of everything I see. Trailing behind Lador, I study the abodes as we pass them. Made of red clay and moderate in size, each one is distinctively adorned. Some are festooned with thriving ivy and flowering greenery, while others are bedecked with colored ornaments and vibrantly painted pieces of art. Each dwelling is colorful and exudes an aura of bliss. The dry air is consumed by the sweet scents from the abundant blossoms. Dristans, dressed in vibrantly colored robes, greet us as we pass. This quadrant is both welcoming and beautiful. Ahead I see Pasha waving to me. Her bright-blue robe moves about as she continues to gesture with her arm. Picking up our pace, finally, we are here. I need to change, then meet with Ruzi and Mikiel before I leave.

"Come on, dear," she says. "A clean robe awaits you. I know that you and Lador must depart."

While wondering how she knows this, I turn and thank Lador for the escort. Inside, the charm of this small home embodies the essence of who they are. I feel welcomed and loved, and this represents Pasha; the abundant eclectic artwork symbolizes Faro, and then there's Kriyo. I sense him in the very air and I readily inhale. Reminiscent of him, it seems infused not only with his sweet scent, but also with integrity, which personifies his nature. An open room with a vaulted ceiling greets me. Small pieces of vibrant-colored clay art are everywhere. Each wall has shelves with little clay creatures on them. They are incredibly detailed. I almost expect to see them move as I walk past.

"Your home is stunning, Pasha."

"I appreciate the compliment, dear," she returns. As our eyes meet, she adds, "Faro has spent his entire life making our home what it is."

"I can see that," I say, looking in joy at the room.

"Meelah, you will have time to become acquainted with our home, but now you must be going," she says, prodding me along.

"Pasha, how did you know that Lador and I were headed back to Bursa?"

"Faro has seen it. Come, let me show you." Swiftly, she proceeds into another room. "Come on, dear! I can't bring Faro's chamber to you."

Following her voice, I enter a large chamber, again with a high ceiling. Drawings on each wall consume every inch of space. Standing beside Pasha, I am drawn to her finger as it points to a specific creation. I see an illustration of Blessing as she's attacked, then of me, shielding the young Bursan. Continuing, I see Light Warriors, Ruzi and Nala specifically, with the Nooris as they arrive in Drista. The last picture is of Lador and me. This drawing has captured my desire to return to Bursa. But there is more, the Light Warriors fill the sky. This is unsettling. It makes me itch to leave, eager to learn what prompted my kind to take to the sky.

"What's happening in Bursa, currently?"

"My prophetic partner is tending to Blessing. Perhaps I should find him."

"Perchance I shouldn't know, but I must prepare to go."

"Bring our Kriyo home."

"I will, but where is home?"

"What's that human expression, oh yes, home is where the heart is. Once you know where your heart feels alive, you'll always be home. Until then, you're welcome here for as long as you like."

"Thank you, Pasha. Where can I clean up?"

"Follow me. I have a chamber set up for you. There are many positives to Faro's gift. I always know when we'll be having a house guest," she continues, proceeding down a corridor.

Stepping into the chamber, I realize that I'm somewhere new again. Like my time on earth, I continue to be nomadic. I sense that my time living in Bursa has come to an end. Perhaps this feeling is simply brought about by being in Drista. This quadrant was my home, though at that time, it didn't look as it does now. We didn't have physical homes like humans and Churrians do.

Nevertheless, here I am, no longer a full Light Warrior, and yet quite different from all Churrians.

As quickly as I can, I wash off the dried blood and slip into the clean robe Pasha left for me. It's burgundy in color and a little short. The hem of most robes sits on the ground. I can see the toes of my feet. It will have to do. My clothes seemed to be ruined by each day's end. I wonder what this robe will look like after a few hours? Keenly, I sense Mikiel. He's waiting for me with bated breath. The news from Ruzi seems to be pressing. When I open my door, I am startled by Faro, who is standing at the opening.

Taking my hand, he says, "You must see this."

Back in Faro's drawing chamber, is Pasha. Her focus is intent on the wall. Upon my approach, I too become engrossed by what Faro has just created. The drawings are of the green in Bursa. I see a gathering. Darkness is present. Behind several Churrians is a malevolent mass. Shria stands on the platform beaming, the only light. Witnessing her radiance, I sense Kriyo but don't see him in the drawing. Death hangs in the air.

"Who?" I demand, while searching Pasha's and Faro's eyes. "What is the timeline here? Has this already occurred?"

"I fear we are too late," he says, spilling tears.

"Don't allow fear to steal your hope. I must leave."

Appearing outside, Lador is waiting for me as I exit the home. But first, I must speak with Mikiel, sensing his unsettled nerves. "My liege," he greets me, intensity in his voice. With a thought, he sends me a picture of symbols and my soul instantly recognizes their meaning.

"These symbols manifest a curse. Darkness wishes to gain a stronghold over the Churrians. This could deplete the shield protecting them. We must go." With a nod of his head, he prepares to leave. Closing my eyes, I summon the rest of our kind. I don't know what lies in Bursa but I know I can trust them. Light Warriors are unaffected by such curses, they don't possess the necessary iniquity within. Like attracts like and in this case, darkness needs its likeness in order to affect the host.

Taking hold of Lador's hand, I already see my kind soaring above. They blanket the sky, mirroring my worried heart as I fear for those I love. Uncertain of what we'll find when we arrive, I close my eyes and bring us there.

Chapter Seven

* * *

Following Jael's visit to Shria's, demanding that Meelah refuse her appointment as an elder of Bursa, he was visited by an odd little creature. Waiting on his doorstep, it stared at him while it cocked its tiny head. "What do we have here?" Jael asked the peculiar black bird. "Shoo, be gone with you!" Ignoring the flailing of Jael's arms, the unusual animal stood perfectly still. "I have never seen a creature such as you," Jael whispered. "What are you? You are not indigenous to Churria, of this I am quite certain."

"I am not from here. I heard your pleas and am here to help you, Jael." Intrigued, the elder lowered to one knee for a closer look. The creature began to fly, circling around him a few times before it perched upon his shoulder. Their eyes met and something entered Jael. A connection to the Darkness was forged. After some time, Jael lifted his head, rose to his feet, and stood as something else.

Later that day, the first of two secret meetings was called to order. All of the elders except Elder Trall were asked to gather. All in attendance knew not why they'd been called, nor the heinous events that would ensue. The birth of a malevolent plan was upon them all.

The sudden scuffle of feet intruded into the silence, capturing the attention of all the elders. Elder Jael lifted the hem of his robe as he proceeded up the few moss- and vine-laden steps leading to an aged stone platform. Amid the dense greenery of Bursa, this location hadn't been utilized formally in over a thousand years. All eyes remained fixed upon Elder Jael as he settled himself. After a moment, he searched every face in attendance, and in a dynamic tone, he began.

"I have asked all of my brother and sister elders from all quadrants of Churria to join me here. Your loyalty to our traditions, our very ways of governing, will heal the fracture in our current leadership."

A sage amongst them interrupted Jael by coming to the front of the gathering. He began by stating, "I am Elder Fithro of Plai. I would like permission to speak." The mass hushed as the eldest of all the Churrians proceeded over to Elder Jael. His withered form mindfully navigated the decrepit steps that time and Natiya had reclaimed. Pale and long, the fingers of his wrinkled left hand grasped a wooden staff. Slowly he ambled, pressing on the rod for support, each stride seeming more arduous than the last. Adorned in a brilliant white, loose-fitted robe that billowed behind him, the elder possessed thinning, gray hair, tousled in the wind. All could see his exemplary and profound connection to Natiya. Even in the wind, she communicated with him. Once upon the stone platform, his eyes closed and stillness overtook him. All knew whose counsel he sought, and Elder Jael became increasingly antsy as a result. Ascertaining a clear answer from Natiya, he addressed Jael. "What is it that you want, Elder Jael? For the path you navigate leads to treason."

"Treason, treachery, betrayal, all of these words define our current leader, not me."

"You wish to take her title then?" Fithro asked.

"We wish for proper leadership!"

Facing the unsettled elders, Fithro indicated only this, "I have time and wisdom on my side. I have appointed our Head Elder and I believe that her intentions are pure. I've sought the counsel of Natiya and I pray that all of you will do the same. My place is not in alliance with this elder. He will walk his path—but not with me beside him."

Elder Fithro teleported from sight and the elders of Plai, Drista, eleven elders from Ralta and seven from Bursa joined him and left. The remaining forty-three elders faced Elder Jael. The eldest of them came forth.

"I am Elder Krall of Bursa, and though I am not pleased with some of the recent choices that our Head Elder has made, what do you propose we do?"

No sooner had the words departed the elder's mouth than the black bird perched on Jael's shoulder. A peculiar exchange was transmitted between them. Intrigue amongst the elders had them wonder what the creature was. They watched Jael as he nodded his head a few times; oddly, he seemed engaged in a dialogue with the peculiar winged animal. Both bird and Jael turned back to the crowd. After a brief moment to collect himself, he said, "We will permit Meelah to take her appointment as elder then destroy all connected to her. After that, I will kill the Warrior herself."

"You wish to kill your own daughter?" Krall asked, astounded.

"I am willing to sacrifice whoever stands in the way of justice."

"Justice, you say? What injustices have occurred? And Meelah is the chosen one, she possesses great power."

Jael grinned, and answered, "War is nearly at our door. What has our current leadership done to prevent this? Oh, she returned Meelah to Churria. She has returned the being that the Dark Force seeks," he added mockingly. "As for powers, Meelah is not the only one who possesses similar abilities."

The remaining elders initially found absurdity in Jael's claim to power. Hilarity rose to the surface and erupted in laughter. Jael joined in their amusement for a moment or two, then, like a predator waiting for the precise moment to seize its prey, he extended his arm and made a fist. He raised his outstretched arm, lifting Elder Krall from the ground. Silence followed. Elder Krall struggled to breathe as Jael clutched his fist. Kicking his feet in the air and flailing his arms, the elder neared sheer panic as his life flashed before his eyes. Crashing back to the ground, he eventually caught his breath and Elder Jael effectively possessed the attention and fear of them all.

"Your daughter is Grya, is this correct, Elder Krall?" Jael asked, with the black bird still perched on his shoulder. Both cocked their heads in unison while awaiting the elder's response.

"Yes, that's correct. Why do you ask?" he questioned submissively.

"All things in time," Jael answered. "Do I have your support?"

As Elder Krall teleported from sight, Jael expresses amusement with a cackle "It has begun, elders! My plan is under way. Now who wishes to join me?"

The remaining elders still knew not of his true intentions, but joined his alliance. The fear that Elder Krall exuded hung in the air. With that fear affecting each of them, these elders attentively focused on their new leader. With the black bird still on his shoulder, the next details spilled out.

Elder Krall burst through his front door, startling his partner, Shala. "Where is Grya?" he asked.

"She's tending to the garden. What has happened?"

He hurried over to the hall to see their daughter. She was the only progeny they would have in their lifetime. Churrians only procreate one offspring. This was the will of Natiya. It was written that all females only have one viable egg in their lifespan. Grya was their heart.

"I must leave. Keep Grya within the confines of our home."

"What is happening? I can feel your fear and it's affecting me."

"Just promise me that she will not leave," he stated adamantly. Before Shala was able to respond, Krall departed.

He found himself at his Head Elder's front door. His betrayal of her, even if it was for a moment, had the best of him. As he gently pulled on his wiry, ginger whiskers, guilt and fear worked against the other, in a futile battle that took him nowhere. While immobilized, he recalled Elder Fithro's words, "I've sought the counsel of Natiya and I pray that all of you will do the same." The brawny elder closed his eyes, grounded his emotions and cleared his mind. What was shown to him by his Mother invoked dread. As he opened his eyes, his Head Elder stood before him. "We've been expecting you," she said placidly. "Please come in and join the others in the garden." First, the feeble Elder Fithro came into his view, then all of the elders that chose not to join Jael. He was met with a feeling of hope. Amid these honorable and unwavering elders, his guilt rose again, but this time it was met by a kind hand on his shoulder. "You are here now. You made your choice," Elder

Trall said to him. Grateful for Trall's words, he relaxed enough to join the group. All present settled in Shria's garden, waiting for their Head Elder.

Standing before them, Shria remarked, "Free will, it is a powerful gift indeed. Let us not judge the other elders, for something larger than judgment is occurring here. A balance between the light and the dark is being restored universally; naturally, this restoration would affect Churria. Our Mother has shared a few of Jael's malfeasances with me, but what is of concern most is what he truly wishes to gain."

"Head Elder," Elder Krall said, while drawing his palms to his chest. "It is not only his plan that you should fear, it is his powers."

"Of what powers do you speak?"

"Like those of his daughter's." Exposing his neck so all could see the marks that streaked its surface, he added, "He lifted me from the ground by raising his arm, but there is more. His eyes were bathed in darkness."

"Thank you, Natiya," Shria answered. "If she didn't keep you there, we would not possess this knowledge. Tonight Meelah will become an elder of Bursa." She paused reflectively then continued. "The chosen one, at this precise time, is being tested by the Timeera before she is given the key to her amulet. They must be certain that Meelah's will is strong and resolute. They know the unsettled nature of Churria and they have offered a safe haven, but with conditions. I will share those conditions with all of you at tomorrow's meeting. Change is occurring as fast as light can travel. I ask all of you to maintain your close connection with Natiya and have faith that I'm doing the same. Go now. Appearances are important. We need not invoke panic, but prepare your family for the move."

All faithfully bowed, then exited her abode, all but Elder Trall and Elder Krall. "My daughter," Elder Krall spoke softly, but his piercing blue eyes registered concern. "Elder Jael knows my weakness, my vulnerable soft spot, and I fear that he will—"

"NO!" she stated. "Do not speak of it. No Churrian has left in such an unnatural manner."

"My son Samuel did," Trall replied. "Darkness brings death," he added mournfully.

"Then we'll need an abundance of light. The Light Warriors are here and I know that Meelah will return, having passed the Timeera's test. She is the light. Go, join with your family, Elder Krall, and keep Grya close to you."

After he bowed, hope seeped back into his being, restoring his faith. As he left, Mikshe entered with a guest. For a brief moment Shria stood facing her garden. Perhaps she was merely collecting herself, or perhaps she was consulting with Natiya; regardless, when she greeted her company, she did so with a renewed sense of well-being.

"Reeditta, Drana. Thank you for coming."

"Reeditta, Head Elder."

"Take care of this scroll, Drana, for this is the only one in its existence. Once opened—"

"The paper will quickly deteriorate," Kriyo finished the thought, while entering the room. Bowing to both ladies, he explained, "Drana, you must do exactly what it says. Meelah has to live."

"And she will," Drana promptly answered. In obvious admiration for the mature Churrian before her, she added, "It is good to see you again, Kriyo. Time has nurtured your essence." Closing her eyes, she whispered, "Ah yes. Meelah is now being taken to my castle. It seems that she's passed the Timeera's first assessment. She still must reinstate her oath to the Light." After another pause, she included, "Mikiel is asking to be allowed entry to my realm. What are your thoughts, Kriyo?"

Without hesitation, he instructed, "Permit him to enter."

"It is done," she replied. "You intrigue me. Why have you allowed a being with such strong feelings for Meelah to be by her side?"

"If Meelah's heart has truly chosen me, then I have nothing to fear."

"Possibly."

"Your highness, I recognize that they share an extensive past and love surely bonds them, but there are endless variations of love. What I feel for Meelah and what I have felt from her is what builds an everlasting relationship. I know the kind of love that binds us."

"You still intrigue me. What I will say is this: You're in a category all of your own." Closing her eyes, again she paused. "I must leave. They require the scroll." Turning to Shria and Trall, she concluded by saying, "Jael is communicating with the Darkness through the raven. Be safe, my friends. We'll be watching."

"The raven must surely be the odd black bird that is currently watching us," Shria affirmed, pointing to her garden.

"Be gone with you!" Trall blurted, while he chased it away.

"No part of my day is uneventful," Shria stated to Kriyo. "Now we have a mysterious raven with a direct line to the Dark One."

Grinning from Shria's refreshing sarcasm, Kriyo walked into the garden and stood beside Trall. Dropping down, he knelt and prayed to Natiya. He pleaded for Meelah's safe return. He prayed for a peaceful resolution. Kriyo's actions became contagious for, from her chamber, Shria did the same.

As twilight ushered in the night sky, Meelah was made an elder. It was this night that Jael called the second meeting to order. Within the confines of his abode, the elders gathered. The fear that bonded them with Jael was also a bridge to darkness. Slowly, iniquity seeped into each of them. At first, this connection severed their bond to Natiya; but after that, it replaced their light, hope and consciousness with darkness.

Standing before their leader, they heard, "Tomorrow morning will commence with a meeting." Jael stated this with a sparkle in his eyes. "Let us make it memorable."

"What about Elder Krall? Do you think he spoke with the Head Elder?" one of them asked.

"Of course he did."

At length a plan was laid out. Details were formulated by the now evil elder, and panic grew in Raza as she digested his scheme. She learned not only of the treasonous act that would ensue, but also of the lives that they intended on ending, including Meelah's. She quickly sent Natiya this knowledge. A strange wave of energy overtook her. It was a gift. Natiya appreciated Raza's unwavering light amid the surrounding darkness. "Fear is an illusion," Natiya told her. "Alert your Head Elder for I cannot interfere more than I have." Opening her eyes, Raza saw that the gloom of night had almost completely lifted. Dawn would soon come. Proceeding to leave, she was abruptly halted.

"Where are you going?" Jael asked, standing before her.

Thinking quickly, she replied, "I'm headed out to the garden to harvest herbs for our morning tincture."

"Be sure to cut enough for all the elders. Perhaps you'll need my help?"

"That won't be necessary, Jael."

"You look tired, Raza. Allow me to help you," he said, escorting her by her arm out into the garden.

"You are hurting my arm! Let me go!"

"Feisty, aren't we. Where's your knife? Show it to me."

"I don't have it."

"Where was Raza off to then? Obviously you have no intention of cutting herbs without a knife."

"Leave me be, Jael."

"NO! Where were you headed?"

"How can you think of killing our daughter? Taking her away from me once deeply wounded me—you will not do it again!"

"Or what will you do?"

Concealed under her sleeve was the knife. Grasping it, she pointed it at his neck. "Let me go!"

Releasing his hold, he stepped back and smiled. "I didn't think you had this within you. Do you want to kill me?"

"Do I have a choice?" she asked, as the elders joined them. As if they were summoned, one by one they encircled Raza and Jael. She witnessed the darkness within them, it consumed their eyes.

"There is always a choice, Raza."

"Then stop this! All of it!"

"I intend to," he whispered.

With all of her might, she threw the sharp knife directly at Jael's chest. The raven, perched on his shoulder, swooped down. The weapon struck its side with a thud. At their feet, the bird lay dead. Raza looked at Jael. Terror overtook her. Darkness clearly commanded him. His eyes were black, his breath had turned rancid. It was pure evil. Raza began to shudder at this sight. The raven stood up, the knife having fallen from its side, then flew onto Jael's shoulder again. Smiling at Raza for a moment, Jael lunged at her neck. As she raised her hands to shield herself, silence arose. Opening her eyes, an invisible barrier encased her. Taken aback, Jael fell still for a moment, but she was wiser and left.

At Raza's banging upon Shria's door while gazing over her shoulder in fear, the door finally opened. "Mikshe, where is the Head Elder? It's urgent!"

"She is not here. The Head Elder is meeting with a group of elders in Bursa."

"Please, permit me in!" Raza said, nearing panic. "I must leave her a note."

Sensing her alarm, Mikshe allowed her in. Hurriedly, Raza scribbled Jael's plan on a piece of paper. After she folded the note, with a shaking hand, she gave it to Mikshe. "Make sure she gets this," she said softly. "Or all will be lost."

Pounding on the door jarred them both. "Raza, go to Plai and ask for Elder Fithro. You will be safe there. Teleport from the garden."

"Thank you, Mikshe, and whatever you do, don't answer the door! The Dark Force has found a way to Churria. Hide!" she ordered sternly. Again, Raza attuned to Natiya and the lids of her eyes closed. Bestowing another gift, she vanished from Mikshe's sight.

"Do as she said, Mikshe," Natiya calmly stated. "The Head Elder must read this note. Conceal it here." In Mikshe's mind, Natiya showed her what to do.

Abruptly her stillness was disrupted by persistent banging. Jarred awake, she followed the instructions. The sound of the door flung open, chilled her. Already in the Head Elder's bedchamber, she quietly slipped the note into Shria's favorite book before ducking into her closet. She settled against the rear wall. Numerous robes hung before her. Breathless from fear, Mikshe knelt down in the far corner. Emptying her mind and clearing all thoughts in hopes of hampering potential telepathy, she closed her eyes.

When Shria returned, she felt beckoned to her chamber. As if guided, she pulled her beloved book from its shelf. While she held it in hand, something caught her eye, so she placed the tome upon her bed and opened her closet door. Only robes were present there.

"Head Elder!" Ruzi called.

"I'm in here," Shria answered, coming in to the great room.

"There was a distress call from my liege. Mikiel is with her. I promised that I would protect you. Let me take you to her."

"I just left her. How bad is it?"

Ruzi simply took hold of Shria's arm and with a thought, they arrived. Both grasped the import of the message when they saw Meelah, on her stomach with a metal object embedded in her back. Mikiel was knelt down assessing her injury. Then the sight of Blessing—her white coat, painted in blood, and lines still tightly affixed around her neck. She lay lifeless on her side as Nala tended to her.

"Ruzi, it is not safe here for the Head Elder," Mikiel stated. "Please return her home, then request that she remain guarded by only our kind."

"I will not leave Meelah," Shria answered tearfully.

"You must leave," Ruzi answered. "It is what my liege would want. I am deeply sorry for bringing you here."

"Sincerely and painfully, I am sorry," she murmured, taking his hand. "Mikiel, keep her safe."

She teleported back to her abode with a shattered heart. She saw Trall waiting outside and fell into his arms.

"What has happened?" he asked. "We all feel a shift. What has Jael done?"

"The unthinkable," she answered. "Why are you outside, Trall?" she asked, wiping her face.

"No one answered the door," he replied. "Allow me to help you in then tell me what has happened."

"That is a fine way to begin," she answered.

"Head Elder," Ruzi interjected. "I've stationed four Light Warriors to keep watch over you. May I have your permission to check on the other Noori?"

"Of course," she was quick to reply. "And thank you, Ruzi. Where would we be without the support of your noble kind?"

He lowered his head and hurried off. On his way to the barn, he felt that something was gravely amiss, and he now feared for not only the other Noori but others close to his liege. The scent of fresh blood inundated his keen sense of smell. Quietly, he drew his sword. Then the muffled sound of labored breathing drew him to her. Slowly entering the barn, he saw a most dreadful sight. Against the stable wall was Mikshe, naked and near death. Quickly, he ran toward her while returning his sword to its sheath. Mikshe's hands were tightly bound together and raised above her head. Upon closer inspection, Ruzi saw nails pressed through her skin, then into the wall holding her in place. The nails ran down the length of her body. Her ankles were also tied and the scents of several Churrian males lingered upon her skin. Still conscious, but nearly, she wept. First, he sent a message to the Light Warriors standing watch, asking two to come, then one message to Shria.

"Please don't look at me," she whispered. "What they've done," she added, before succumbing to tears again.

"I must get you down," he affirmed, turning his winged-back toward her.

Her crying fell silent, prompting him to face her again. Sensing she was nearing lifelessness, he knew that he must work promptly. Shria and Trall entered the stable, terrorized by the scene before them. Ruzi quickly assessed how to get her down and with the other Light Warriors' help, that is precisely what they did. Trall grabbed a blanket hanging from a hook in the barn and covered Mikshe. Blood oozed from the corner of her mouth.

"My liege would want to help. I will go to her," Ruzi stated.

"No," Mikshe said telepathically, for all to hear. "Let me go. I choose not to live with these memories haunting me. Let me go…."

Shria's tears cascaded down the sides of her face. Kneeling beside Mikshe, she gently took hold of her hand and sang a lullaby that her mother used to sing to soothe her. Gathering herself, she controlled her unsettled emotions and gave Mikshe all of her attention. With love, she remained present. She honored this young Churrian's request, and she wasn't the only one to do so. From beneath them, golden threads of light rose from the ground. Gradually they enveloped Mikshe, affording her soul peace. Readily, she received this gift. As her head dropped to the left, Shria lovingly moved her hair from her face. Continuing to sing, she noticed that Mikshe had fallen completely still. Natiya's golden light encased her form fully. From within this luminous stillness, Mikshe left them, taking her physical body with her. Still gazing at the blanket, though now it covered nothing more than dirt, Shria began to release her tears again. In moments, another emotion began to consume her—rage! Trall knelt down and took Shria into his arms, but the strength that anger provided her, raised her to her feet.

"Enough! My heart has had enough!"

Abruptly, she headed back to her home. Trall rose to his feet. He remained there for a few moments to give thanks to Natiya. Ruzi, who had seen thousands of years of heinous acts, pulled himself together as he checked on the male Noori. Seeing him seemingly unscathed, he slipped the bridle on the Noori then opened his stall door.

"Mikiel and my liege are headed to Drista. I will bring the Noori there as well. But I will return. Elder Trall, the Head Elder is not to leave!"

"Yes, yes," Trall answered. "I should go to her." Gathering himself for a moment, he saw something above them, written on the ceiling. "What's that? Are those symbols, and in what language are they?"

"They've been written in blood," Ruzi answered, after following his line of sight. "This cannot be." Fully comprehending the message, he handed the Noori's reins to Trall, then sought counsel with the other Light Warriors. Trall watched as one by one the winged-warriors sniffed the air. Appearing to have caught a scent, they left the barn. Curious, Trall followed with the Noori.

There lay Hetry, the Noori's keeper—dead. His chest, completely open, exposed his inner organs. Trall wrestled his immediate reaction to throw up. With his hand tightly pressed against his mouth, he struggled to pull himself together.

"They knew to write this with his liver," he heard Ruzi mumble. "This hasn't been practiced in thousands of years." Addressing the other Light Warriors, he spoke quietly before he turned to Trall and said, "Make sure the Head Elder doesn't leave and don't move anything here. I wish for Mikiel to see this just as it is. And it might be best if you don't share this with the Head Elder. Wait for my return." After taking hold of the Noori's reins, both Light Warrior and equine took to the sky. Trall ambled back to the house, in shock.

"We must be leaving!" Shria said as Trall entered the room. "You are pale, Trall, sit for a moment."

Eagerly he took a seat and tried to clear his mind so Shria wouldn't see what lay beside the barn.

"Drink this," she said, while handing him a tincture. "Poor Mikshe, if I was only here, if Meelah was here. Trall, why can't I hear or sense her? Do you think Meelah was unable to recover?"

Trall stared at her blankly, unable to answer. Bringing the small cup to his mouth, he swallowed the herbal elixir. Shria recalled that she hadn't shared what happened to Meelah and the Noori. Then, she heard something. The odd sound redirected her focus and curious, she followed it. In her bedchamber, she sensed Natiya's presence, calming and grounding. Hoping for guidance from her Mother, she remained still. Silence surrounded her and she knew that Natiya had chosen this form of communication rather than words. This moment was a gentle reminder that she was supported and loved; words weren't needed. The book she drew from her shelf was lying on her bed. As she picked it up, she heard the sound of Trall crying. With book in hand, she went to him. Hunched over, he was releasing his emotion.

"What did you give me?" he cried.

"You know the tincture, Trall, you gave me the ingredients. It will help ground you, just as it helped me."

"Sit with me and tell me what occurred earlier."

"I can't, Trall. I must return to the meeting."

"NO!" he shouted, attempting to stand. "It's not safe, Shria!"

"Perhaps it's not, but what about Kriyo? It was I who asked him to return with a Timeera. I could not bear the thought of telling Pasha and Faro what befell him. Then there are the Bursans, and the others from all the quadrants. No further calamity can come to us."

She saw something in Trall's eyes. Like a film, the sight of Hetry's desecrated body reeled in his thoughts and readily Shria received it. Dropping her favorite book from her hand, again, she covered her face as if to block the visions.

"He still lies there?"

"Yes. Ruzi asked me not to move anything so Mikiel could review what was done. I wanted to tell you, but he wished for me to wait until his return."

"And when will he return?"

"I am here now," Ruzi answered, as he entered with Nala. "You dropped something," Nala said, pointing to the neatly folded note on the floor, next to the book.

Picking up the note, Shria unfolded it and began to read. Terror filled her face, its affect resonating in all of them. Handing the note to the Light Warriors, she walked into the hall, gathered herself, then asked, "Ruzi, where's Meelah?"

"According to this note, precisely where Jael expects her, she's headed to the green."

Chapter Eight

"You understand what we've told you?" a Timeera asks Kriyo.

"Yes."

"Then it is time. Take this knife and do precisely as we have instructed. And Kriyo, Meelah must leave when the Light Force calls for her. She must leave," they repeat, for emphasis.

"I will do as you have requested. You have my allegiance," Kriyo avows, lowering his head.

Taking the knife the being hands to him, he watches the Timeera fade from his sight. The dagger radiates a golden hue, its blade sharper than anything he had ever held. Engraved in its handle are symbols. As his finger grazes over them, he hears their meaning—*To balance all light.*

Gathering his thoughts, he closes his eyes. In his mind, he sees Meelah. He relives the painful acts that the elders, under the influence of darkness, had inflicted on her. Subdued by the Timeera's powers, he was forced to watch Jael and his followers as they thrashed Blessing and attempted to kill Grya. He released his welling frustration and screamed when Meelah was mortally wounded and discarded by his own kind. He heard Meelah call to Mikiel then watched as this Light Warrior tended to her—again! Pacing back then forth, he could not intervene due to their command. It was Meelah's free will that brought her there. They reminded him that both he and Meelah were a part of something grander. They spoke of the balance that must be restored, then of his and Meelah's destined roles. "She must leave," he hears them repeat. Those three words haunt him, though he understands that Meelah must train. She must live in her powers, not in her emotions and fears. With this adjustment, her amulet would show her how to defeat the Epoh. He must make sure that Meelah leaves or she and everything that lives in the light will fall.

Sensing the darkness controlling Jael, Kriyo acknowledges that it is time. Opening his eyes, he teleports to the green with dagger in hand. Churrians are everywhere. They are fearful, even angry. The news of Meelah and the Noori has spread through the star, affecting everyone. This information has been convoluted. Unsettled emotions are directed at the one destined to save them. This is the effects of the curse, like a plague it spread darkness, resulting in unbridled anger and fear. This wll give strength to the Dark Force, depleting the shield protecting all of them. Soon they will learn the truth. Even Jael's murderous malfeasances will be revealed, open to their knowledge. Change has arrived. But this wave of transformation is moving slowly. He sees Meelah. Stones are thrown at her. Encased by her shield, she looks for him.

"Meelah!" he calls.

Following the sound of Kriyo's voice amongst the building chaos, quickly, I appear at his side and shield him. "I feared the worst."

"I am fine," he states with passion, touching the side of my face.

Hours ago, she was impaled and close to death. His love for her is palpable, but time is growing short. He is near. "Please forgive my actions. They are not meant to injure you."

Delving into his thoughts, I can see the knife, then what he's been asked to do. If he cannot kill the raven then he must end Jael's life. I see the Timeera, but surprisingly, nothing more. Blocked, his innermost recollections remain private. Curious as to why I have been prevented from their exchange, I gaze into his eyes.

"In time, Meelah," he answers. "But now, the connection to the Darkness must be severed. Only this dagger can do that and only I have permission to wield it."

"I will help you. Together we will do what must be done. The curse must end. It will otherwise destroy our shield. So many are already influenced."

Closing my eyes, I send a directive to the Light Warriors above us. I request that the Viox prepare, then remind the others to remain in the sky. This group of Light Warriors is well versed in this kind of operation. They are equipped with bisers, small hollow tubes that project a dart saturated with sedating oils. With this weapon they are able to subdue most beings under the influence of a Shadow, or in this case, a portion of the Darkness himself. Flying low, always keeping an eye on me, is Mikiel. Thankfully, he honors my request and remains in flight.

"Meelah," I hear Kriyo intone. "You must trust me. This battle is not yours."

Still gazing into his eyes, I am baffled. The Light Warriors are preparing to fight the influence of the Darkness. How is this battle not mine? Then I see them. Within each of his eyes stands a Timeera. They are present. They are guiding him. I trust Kriyo and honor his wishes. Lowering my head, I agree.

The dark presence of the elders lures me away from Kriyo's gaze. I sense them. The Viox do as well and begin to land. The elders emerge from the surrounding dense foliage. I watch my kind as they strategically disburse. Under the influence of the Dark One, these elders challenge them. A few Churrians join their alliance, striking the Light Warriors with stones and sticks. This infuriates me! The existence of darkness has disaffected so much. We stand witness to this change as we see their fear and aggression. Kriyo's hand lovingly takes hold of mine, grounding me. I promised not to intervene and it's difficult to honor my pledge, but I do.

At last, the upheaval comes to an impasse and I release my shield. The bisers have taken down the influenced elders, even a few Bursans. The sight before us must pain Kriyo's heart. These are his people. Intently watching something to his left, he remains still. It is Jael. Though I don't see him, I begin to sense his presence.

Attuned to the looming darkness, Light Warriors Ruzi and Nala, with Shria and Trall by their sides, arrive out of sight. In the distance, Ruzi turns to his liege and Kriyo, stationed precisely where Jael wants them, on the platform for all to see. Shria's panic causes him to grab hold of her arm, preventing her from teleporting. "No!" he says sternly. "Today is not your day to die." Appearing before Meelah and Kriyo, Ruzi takes them into his arms and spreads his massive black wings, shielding them. The

Light Warrior falls. Crashing down, his body thrashes about. An arrow has hit him, the head of it is protruding from his chest. Churrians flee in fear, chaos ensues.

Kneeling, I do my best to keep Ruzi still. He flails uncontrollably back and forth. The arrow snaps; the sound, chilling. Witnessing this reaction, I surmise it must be poisoned. With this epiphany, I watch as it overcomes him.

"Ruzi, don't give up!" I order. "Don't let *him* win!"

A line of black fluid streams from the curve of his mouth. By my side is Kriyo. Strangely, he's calm and composed. His reaction confuses and irritates me. Does he know something that I do not or is he willing to have this Light Warrior die for the greater good? From the corner of my eye, I notice Kriyo retrieve a vial from the pocket of his robe. He leans over and pours golden fluid into Ruzi's mouth.

"How bad is it?" I hear Mikiel call out as he lands besides us.

"We must remove his armor. The arrow has run through his chest, we have to take it out," I express to him.

Taking hold of my hand, distracting me, Kriyo assures me, "Meelah, he will be fine."

"What aren't you telling me? What was the liquid you gave him?"

"Nala and Mikiel will remove the arrow." Standing up, he adds, "I asked you to trust me and I am telling you he will fully recover. We must go and finish this."

Nala kneels by Ruzi's side. The expression on her face registers her pain, but somehow she restrains it, to work on the one she loves. With Mikiel's help, they tend to our wounded friend. Members of the Viox land around us. Swiftly, they kneel down to help. Looking up, I see Kriyo's outstretched hand. I do trust him.

Grabbing it, I rise to a stand. Though my heart wishes to remain with Ruzi, I acknowledge that this must end. Kriyo believes Ruzi will live and I have faith in his conviction.

"Protect them," I transmit to the Light Warriors soaring above.

We proceed off the platform. Glancing over my shoulder, I watch them land. Encircling their fallen brother, they stand guard. I can no longer see Ruzi, only the light that surrounds him. Closing my eyes, I attune to my friend. His heart still beats. He's getting stronger. Now, I must focus on the task at hand. The dark connection to Churria must be severed. This will end.

With this objective, Kriyo and I move through the chaos. The Dark One is near, both of us subject to his malevolent presence. In the distance, our eyes finally lock on Jael, a bow is in his hand. He tried to kill me. He nearly killed a member of my family. His eyes, bathed in pure blackness, become my focal point. With the raven still perched on his shoulder, he pulls someone out from behind him—Shria. Fear of losing her slows my steps.

"Trust me," Kriyo reaffirms.

Every part of me trusts him, but no part of me trusts the Dark Force. This is no longer Jael. He has been thrust aside. "What do you want me to do? I will help you, Kriyo."

"So will I, my daughter," I hear a female voice declare.

Standing beside me is Raza, with a restored sense of self. She smiles at me. For the first time I am aware of love in her heart. Wisps of her graying hair float across her face and her pale-green eyes reflect her affection for me, the true love that a mother bestows to a daughter.

"Too long I've lived in fear, Meelah," she says in earnest.

"A family reunion!" Jael howls.

"All of your followers have been captured!" Kriyo shouts. "You stand alone. Release the Head Elder."

"I am not alone!"

"Who was it, Jael? " Kriyo bellows. "Who raped Mikshe and left her hanging by nails to die? Was it you who tore Hetry's body apart? Two died, Jael! Two!"

The remaining Churrians can hear his words and the horror within them, especially me. Within Kriyo's mind, I witness the terror that both Mikshe and Hetry experienced. While I digest this, the remaining elders arrive by teleport. Channels of light brighten the green as they appear en masse.

"Meelah, he means to kill the Head Elder. Whatever happens to me, know that I'll always love you," Raza whispers. No sooner does she speak than she disappears. No one but Light Warriors can travel in this manner. I realize that my mother has powers and if Raza does, Jael might as well.

"I believe that they have powers," I express to Kriyo.

"Who has powers?"

"Both of my birth parents," I answer him.

Appearing behind Jael, Raza separates Shria by pushing her abruptly to the side. I raise my left hand and create a shield, protecting her. Unharmed, Shria comes to a stand.

"Bring the Head Elder to safety," I ask the Light Warriors.

Two Light Warriors whisk her away. Returning my attention to Jael, I see Raza standing amidst a translucent bubble, shielding herself. With pure rage, he reaches into her casing, rips through it vehemently. Grabbing Raza by the neck, he lifts her from the ground. Letting go of Kriyo's hand, I appear by Jael and snatch the raven from his shoulder. The bird, held tightly by its feet, violently flaps its wings and screeches.

"Let my mother go!" I demand.

Walking onto the platform, Kriyo raises his hands, freezing everyone but me. The instant hush silences me. Following the sound of footsteps, I turn and watch Kriyo coming toward me. First his gaze is downward but gradually he raises his head and connects with me. I hand him the raven to end this. He takes the bird while stroking my hand with his.

"How are you doing this?" I ask him.

Instead of answering me, he continues to look into my eyes, and within this reflection, I see Jael and Raza and again am immersed in the present moment. Walking over to them, I look at my mother's seemingly lifeless body held midair.

"Has he claimed Raza's life?"

"No," Kriyo answers softly.

"Look at him, Kriyo. He killed my friend. Poor Mikshe, I should have been there."

"Yes. You should have been there," he answers coldly.

"Are you blaming me? I would have saved her had I known. It enrages me that *he* killed her!"

"You are the one destined to end this suffering, Meelah. Natiya was warning you of Mikshe and Hetry's fate. Why didn't you hear her?"

His words bring pain to my soul. In truth, I should have been in tune not only with Natiya, but also to the horrors that afflicted Mikshe. We were close and had a connection, so how was it that I didn't hear her cries or sense her fear? I have lost my way.

"Anything that is lost, with effort, can be found." Gently he lifts my chin so our eyes meet. "Hope has not been lost. The Timeera and Natiya believe in you. And," he says, "I have always believed in you. Meelah." He concludes, "It's time, my beautiful. I must end Jael's connection with the Darkness."

With a flick of his wrist, out comes the dagger from the sleeve of his robe. With his turning away from me, time resumes. Chaos and noise fill the space around us. He severs the raven's head, disengaging the tie between Jael and the Dark Force. Raza's feet touch the ground. Wearing an expression of shock, Jael continues to lower her down.

"What have I done?" All can hear Jael mumble. "Did I kill her?" he asks. His body trembles.

Going over to her, I kneel to examine her. Thankfully, I feel a pulse in her neck. Healthy color returns to her face as her breath deepens. "You called me mother," I hear Raza whisper. In her eyes, I see a glint of white light. This brilliance grows. It is the Light Force. I feel His love. He assisted her. His presence saved her. I witness His radiance. It then steadily diminishes as it leaves her. In its wake are her green-colored irises and they focus on me. "It has left me," she voices. "The powers that made me a little like you, they're gone. Perhaps I'm not worthy of possessing them."

"Maybe you no longer need them," I answer her. "As for being worthy, I see the light in you. The Light Force does as well or He wouldn't have come to you. Thank you for assisting me. You are more powerful than you realize."

Helping Raza to her feet, I look over at Jael. Kriyo is talking to him. Pure panic consumes this elder as he appears to piece together the gaps in his memory. When he sees the blood smeared on the front of his robe, he becomes overwrought by fear.

"Whose blood is this?" he cries.

Going over to him, in Jael I see nothing more than fog. "What is the last thing you remember?"

"I saw you, Meelah. I was at Shria's and that Light Warrior was there," he says, pointing to his left. Following his finger I see Mikiel coming my way. Jael stops talking, but I continue to process. The outburst at Shria's was all his doing. But I can only hope that the Dark Force had something to do with that as well. Kriyo's loving presence as it moves closer to me reminds me of the polarity in all things. This Churrian is my light.

Mikiel is on my other side. He still doesn't trust Jael. His hand rests atop the handle of his sword while he sniffs the air around Jael's robe. "My liege, it was this elder. His scent was all over the blanket that covered Mikshe's body." Addressing Jael directly, Mikiel adds this, "The Dark Force seeks those like himself. *He* saw your natural obscurity and used it to *his* advantage! You did this, all of it."

Jael cringes. Standing before his peers, he digests the Light Warrior's words. He doesn't speak. He doesn't move. Fear and a deep sense of remorse appear to have immobilized him. This elder is no longer a threat to anyone.

Placing my hand on Mikiel's shoulder, I gain his attention. When our eyes meet, I ask the question that my heart needs answered. "How is Ruzi?"

"Whatever Kriyo gave him, has saved his life. He's weak but he'll recover. Nala brought him to Drista."

Hearing Mikiel's words in the lingering din brings me solace. "Thank you," I say, lowering my head to him.

I feel a warm hand as it takes hold of mine. It's Shria. Her grounding presence embraces me. As I face her, we both smile. "She has been calling you," she tells me. Furrowing my brow, I have lost my connection. "Natiya has been summoning you."

"Why can't I hear or sense her anymore?"

"Go to Drista, Meelah. She waits for you there." Addressing Kriyo, I hear her repeat, "It's time."

With Mikiel still close by my side, Kriyo takes my hand and faces me toward him. Shria lowers her head, then turns to Raza. I sense her sadness and like a contagious virus, it affects me. I bring my attention to Kriyo as he gently squeezes my hand. In this space, we teleport to Drista. Mikiel follows. As we arrive, I am astonished by the sight before me. A line of large mammals stands facing us, roughly fifty of these creatures.

Kriyo quietly announces, "They are Grana."

"What are they doing here?"

But before he answers, I observe him lower to one knee, then reverently bow his head. I sense Natiya but not as I did before. My connection to her is muted, dull and feels blocked. The golden outline of her form materializes before me. I face her, but before I lower my head, she taps on my chest. Taking my hand, she guides me away from Kriyo. She waves her hands in the air, revealing Mikiel, who is watching. With another wave of her hand, she relocates him next to Kriyo. Then again, she taps my heart center.

"You have grown weak from distraction," she exclaims. "But now, you must ground yourself for the task at hand."

"What do you wish me to do?"

"These Grana are a gift from Reetra. They will strengthen our shield, but only temporarily. The Dark Force slipped a tiny Shadow through a weak portion of our defense. This silhouette embodied his rage. Then you…" she utters intensely. "You lost your way. You no longer heard me or the cries of those you have come back to protect. You have lost your way," she repeats emphatically. "Two Churrians were forced to ascend as a result! It was not their natural time; they still had knowledge to attain."

I do my best to restrain my tears. I honor my disconnection. Natiya continues to circle around me. I own my mistakes and experience the pain of losing my friend anew. In Natiya's mind, I see the timing of Hetry's death. It occurred after I left for the Opala's planet. I despise choosing who lives or dies. It wasn't wrong to save the Opala but it came at such a cost! Mikshe perished after Blessing and I were attacked. When did I disconnect from those close to my heart? What else have I missed?

"These are relevant questions. You will find the answers when you depart. But, before you and many of the other Light Warriors leave Churria, I need your help to strengthen our protective shield. The curse depleted it greatly."

"Where am I going?"

"You must return to the Light Force realm. There, you will remember who you are and why you've been chosen to live this destiny."

For a brief moment, I'm lost in thought. Closing my eyes, I feel the truth in her words. I also feel the longing gaze from Kriyo for I will be leaving him as well. I sense Natiya's powerful presence as she stands patiently before me. As I open my eyes, she hands me a long dagger and says, "The Grana are here willingly. This gift will protect the countless lives on Churria until your return."

"You wish for me to kill them?"

"Yes," she simply answers. "Then, I will take their essence as it leaves their physical form. If you listen, truly listen, and do as I instruct, the Grana will be honored, and most importantly, they will experience no pain. They have come freely."

"And what does Reetra want from me in exchange for the Grana?"

"Ask him yourself. He's right behind you."

I turn and face the unusual being standing near Kriyo and Mikiel. Holding a long staff, the thin reptilian creature standing on two scaled legs hobbles toward me. His gait is off balance and seems labored. His hands appear like claws. One of these claws holds his staff while the other dangles in the air. His scent is oddly sweet as it travels in the soft arid breeze. Our eyes lock. It is here that I sense his integrity, honor and the love he feels for these mammals. I can't help but wonder why he's allowing them to die.

Then I hear a series of clicks and clacks that seem to be coming from his mouth. He telepathically communicates, "Though I care deeply for all life upon my planet, I respect their decision. All life that is born into existence is temporary. Eventually, the body will die. The Grana also must face their natural mortality, but here they will leave with great respect." Reetra takes my hand and draws me closer to him. "I need a vial of your blood in exchange," he includes, slipping a tube into my hand.

"You may use the knife I gave you," Natiya instructs.

I look at the tube rolling back and forth in the palm of my hand. I feel both Kriyo and Mikiel's attention on me. I look up and see Mikiel, who appears as though he wishes to whisk me away from all of this and is just waiting for me to signal to him. Kriyo attunes to my distress, but somehow he gives me strength for the tasks ahead. Kriyo nods his head in agreement and walks over to me. Looking again at the tube in hand, I firmly grasp the razor-sharp dagger and cut into my wrist. Kriyo takes the vial from me, opens it and fills it with my blood. As the tube is nearly filled, my body begins to self heal, staunching the flow. The last drop tops off the tube. He presses the cap onto the vial and brings it to Reetra. Returning to me, he tenderly wipes the area that was bleeding with the sleeve of his robe. Once the blood is gone, he promises, "I will faithfully wait for you, Meelah. Though I understand that you must leave, I will miss you."

I caress the side of his face. For a moment, we simply look into each other's eyes. "It is time, Meelah," I hear Natiya repeat. Wearing a brave face, Kriyo smiles. After that, I am led away from him.

Both Natiya and Reetra bring me to the first Grana. Gently, the creature lies down upon its side. Its heavy scent engulfs me. I watch its enormous rib cage rise and fall with every breath. Every part of me wishes not to be here. I wish not to harm these innocent creatures. My heart begins to race.

"Meelah, you don't have to do this. This is not the responsibility of a Light Warrior," Mikiel asserts as he approaches. He seems to have received every one of my insecure thoughts.

I feel Natiya's power as she turns and glares at him, but this is inadequate. He persists and continues to come toward me. "Enough, Light Warrior!" Natiya announces firmly. With the wave of her hand, she freezes his step. Coming to a stand before me, I hear her affirm, "I have never had an issue with your kind so don't be the first to cross me."

"It's all right, Mikiel." I get up and walk over to him. Struggling to free himself from her hold, when I lay a hand on his, he relaxes and Natiya releases her restraint.

"I will do what Natiya wishes," he asserts. "You are my liege. I will do this for you." While hearing Mikiel's sincere words, I sense Kriyo's increasing pain regarding the connection we have. Kriyo seems to naturally understand what Natiya is asking of me. He doesn't question it. He has faith and so must I. This action is for the greater good, my heart has no place in it.

I direct my attention to Mikiel. "I appreciate your desire to help me, but I have been asked to do this, not you. This is done of my free will. I trust Natiya, and if she believes that this will protect all on Churria, then this is what I must do, even if it may pang my heart. Mikiel, this action will spare thousands of innocent lives. That is the role of the Light Warriors. This is our oath. As your leader, it is fitting that I honor these creatures."

He remains before me for a moment, then he respectfully steps back. I rejoin Natiya. She kneels beside the animal and I do the same. I'm drawn to the Grana's eyes. They appear innocent and placid. The peaceful demeanor and energy of this mammal makes the task ahead of me that much harder. One by one, all of the large four-legged, wooly creatures, similar to the earth buffalo, lay upon their sides. Willingly, they embrace their self-sacrifice. Emotion begins to rise within me. Like an active, volatile volcano, it mounts with such velocity that I feel the eruption and cry. Natiya chants words over and over again. I join her. A profound connection binds us.

"Raltgada… Gitulia… Falas…"

Though I have never spoken these words, I feel their meaning as Natiya's powerful voice dynamically repeats them. *Eternal... Honor... Light... Raltgada… Gitulia… Falas...*

As if guided, both of my hands take hold of the dagger. Standing over the Grana, I abruptly drop to one knee and press the knife precisely through the space between the ribs, piercing its heart. Immediately, the Grana's life has ended. I feel its heart fall still, my knife embedded in its heart. Its breath comes to a rest. Then the words flow from me and with reverence, I express, "You will be eternally honored for the gift of your light."

I stand before the next animal, but now I'm alone. No longer guided by an invisible force, I drop to one knee and with trembling hand, I end its life and repeat, "You will be eternally honored for the gift of your light." I continue the wretched task while Natiya,

Reetra, Kriyo and Mikiel watch. Am I being punished? I wonder. Ending innocent life injures my soul. Blood covers my hands and the handle of the dagger as I near the end. Weak and pained through and through, I am finally at the last Grana, but this one is different than the others. It's young, not even fully grown. It raises its head and looks into my tear-filled eyes. This Grana is different from the rest. I sense its desire to live. This creature has not surrendered itself like the others did. I drop the knife to the ground. No more. I will not. I cannot!

I sense Reetra as he stands beside me. I exclaim, "I will not kill this youngling! I honor its free will. It wishes to live!"

Silently, he remains at my side. I sense from him that he's pleased with my constraint. Reaching down, he extends his claw-like hand to me and politely, I take hold of it and rise to a stand.

"Meelah, you have honored them," he conveys to me in thought. "All but one of these mammals was closer to death than to life. You liberated them from their failing bodies." He bows to me; his reverence, touching.

Gazing at the youngling, I honor the one to whom he was referring. Again, I have been tested. I listened to my heart, my inner knowing. Because of this voice, I didn't end this creature's life. I also understand why Reetra didn't mention the deteriorating health of the other Grana. I needed to possess faith and honor Natiya. This was her will. Truly, I hope that this exchange will sustain our field in my absence.

A soft tap on my shoulder grounds me and my mind. In my line of sight is this unusual being. I hear Reetra ask, "What do you think now, Meelah?"

Unsure of what he means, I follow his oddly shaped, scaly arm as it points to something behind me. Turning around, my eyes behold an impressive sight. The sandy surface has effectively drawn the bodies of the Grana beneath it, leaving something unforeseen in their wake. Brilliant white luminescence stands before me. One by one, this radiance bounds into the air. Following Natiya, the herd of light ascends into the sky. It is beautiful and deeply moving. I feel privileged to witness this. Once in the upper atmosphere, its burst of luminosity spreads as far as I can see. Gradually, it dissipates, leaving the sky a soft, yellow hue.

"It is quite amazing," I hear Shria say from beside me.

There are words I must say. Using this time, I speak from my heart. "I'm sorry for not being there to save Mikshe and Hetry. I have adversely affected many, and I have hurt you."

Taking my hand, she answers me. "Meelah, my heart has been injured by the passing of two Churrians but I have faith that time will heal it. Both Mikshe and Hetry are home now. No one can change this and no one is blaming you. Jael and his followers are responsible for those deaths, not you."

I feel the truth of her words. Like the soft breeze touches all in its path, her words commence my healing. At that moment, something indiscernible lures my gaze to the upper atmosphere. Inexplicably drawn to the sky above me, I see another light. It brightens this space. The white light gradually builds. It speaks to me and to my amulet. Extraordinary heat nearly sears the skin of my chest. Pulling my amulet from beneath my robe, I watch Trall as he positions himself by Shria. Lovingly, he takes her other hand. Then again, my attention is pulled to the radiance that streams from above.

"It is happening," Ruzi declares to Nala. All the way from the Dristan wall, they feel it as well. "He is calling the Light Warriors home. We must go."

"But we are no longer permitted there," she replies.

"We are among the many that will feel the call. They too will not be permitted. We are the eldest of them. We owe them our support." he explains.

"Do you have any regrets, Ruzi?"

"Not a one!" he swiftly answers. They both fly up.

As each Light Warrior connects to the call, the group take to flight. One by one they arrive and stand in appreciation of the luminosity above them. The Light Warriors who have obeyed the rules of their creator are the only ones summoned home. This is affirmed by a light radiating from their heart centers. White radiance from my chest beams as it connects with the brightness.

From within the gleaming, a private conversation commences. "Mikiel's light is not illuminated," Leva says. "He has obeyed every law. Why are you not summoning him home?"

"I am not certain Mikiel is ready," the Light Force replies. "What if he doesn't choose you? His feelings for Meelah may blind him." After a brief moment of contemplative silence, the Light adds, "Free will is to determine the outcome."

"Meelah and Kriyo are destined to be together. Making her forget her connection to Mikiel will only please your Father," Leva reasons with cunning.

"Free will, Leva! Allow the outcome to evolve on its own," the Light Force insists. With this statement, Mikiel's light illuminates.

I feel someone take hold of my other hand. Unable to disengage my gaze from the female Light Warrior standing within the radiance, I sense that it's Kriyo. "She's beautiful," I utter softly. Her long blonde hair shimmers as it undulates in the ensuing breeze. Her massive white wings appear grander than all others as they fan out. I observe Light Warriors heed the call and join the conduit leading home. Mikiel walks by me. He pauses, resisting the incredible draw, and turns toward me.

"Let me take you home," he says.

I feel Shria release my hand, but for a moment Kriyo cannot. As the Timeera's words sound around him, he lets go. Standing before me is Mikiel and his eyes are intense as they seem to see right through me. The blonde female Light Warrior comes forward and stands alongside him. Once Mikiel faces her, he drops reverently to one knee, as do all the remaining Light Warriors. In the background, Ruzi and Nala also honor her, dropping down to kneel before her.

While the Light Warriors faithfully waited for me to reincarnate into form, a story was whispered through space. Each of them heard it. It was said that when another Light Warrior was gifted to the Light Force, a destined one would be born from her. This female is she. All in attendance realize this.

Introducing herself, I hear, "I am Leva."

Lowering my head, I greet her. The front of my robe and both of my hands are covered in the Grana's blood. I am not ashamed to wear their selfless deed. With the wave of her hand, she appears to direct Mikiel. I notice him proceed into the light. To my right stands Leva, deeply connected in thought with Kriyo. In this space, I see something in this Light Warrior, it's obscurity. I don't trust her even though we just met. I have never felt this way about one of my kind before. Unsure how I feel about her close proximity to the one I love, I clear my throat, loudly.

She addresses me. "It is time to leave, Meelah." I turn to the Churrian who has my heart, fully. "Kriyo will be fine. All life on this star will be protected until you return. But, if you choose not to leave, all will be lost. The choice is yours."

There is no choice in that scenario. "I will honor the Light Force's call," I answer her.

As I step forward, I look back at my family. Shria and Trall are unaffected by Leva. They both smile at me wholeheartedly. Knowing them as I do, I see their grins thinly mask their sorrow. I bow to them both. Kriyo remains spellbound. I walk over to him and press my lips to his. Gently, I stroke the side of his face.

I whisper into his ear, "I will return to you, my love."

In the background, I see Reetra with the young Grana in tow. "My warriors will be prepared," he transmits telepathically.

Acknowledging him, I lower my head. Then, I am drawn to the white void. In the distance stands Leva. She raises her hand, signaling for me to join her. Honoring my path and the many lives that have already been lost, I begin my journey. I step into the glorious light. It engulfs me completely. This light nourishes me. It begins to restore what has been lost within my essence. This is my path. This is home.

Chapter Nine

"It has been done," Shria confirms. "I let her go."

"Yes, you did," Trall answers, giving her hand a little squeeze.

"Not yet," Shria utters, as if to herself. "Please, I have never been self-seeking but here and now, I ask this of you."

Trall is witness to Shria's peculiar exchange with no one he can see. Not using his literal eyes, he delves deeper to make out whom she's communicating with. He cannot hear anyone speaking to her, but he senses Natiya. A feeling of nausea sweeps over him. He understands the conversation, but usually there is never a discussion when it comes to ascending. Ashen, he watches Shria.

"Oh, stop fretting," she tells him.

"I can't lose you."

"Trall, all life is merely borrowed. One day it must be returned. Even I am held accountable to this law."

"Natiya wants to take you, doesn't she?"

"I have achieved my growth. Letting Meelah go was my last test and it's time for me to leave, but…" she says with a long pause. "I have asked for her to give me time."

"And what did Natiya say?"

"I must appoint the next Head Elder at the meeting with the elders tomorrow."

"You already have. You appointed Meelah," he states, confused.

"Yes, but Natiya has asked me to consider another in exchange for time."

"And?" he asks with bated breath.

"Why do I love you so?"

"I know you love me. And since you're still here and I'm not left sobbing over your robe, who will you appoint?"

"I must appoint a Churrian who is NOT an elder. This is all that I can tell you."

"What do you mean, they're not an elder? We can't afford another lynching."

Smiling at Trall for a few moments, she scans the area, as if searching for something. She's drawn to Ruzi and Nala. They, along with about sixty other Light Warriors, remain on Churria. Her cheerfulness dissipates as she senses their pain and sadness. She also sees Kriyo to her far right, still lost in thought.

"Are you well, Kriyo?"

Surprised by her query, he answers, "Yes, I suppose."

"Good. Would you ask Ruzi to join me, please?"

He honors his head elder's request and proceeds over to the gaggle of Light Warriors. Immediately, he tunes into their solemn energy. Though Ruzi is communicating to the group in a manner that is only heard by the Light Warriors, Kriyo's new abilities allow him to hear his kindhearted words.

Joining the group, Kriyo adds, "Separation hurts, but we cannot fall victim to its powerlessness. We are all stronger and wiser than this illusion."

Astonished that a mere Churrian has articulated their opinion, a few of the Light Warriors snicker and ignore his sentiment. But this doesn't affect Kriyo. In fact, it seems to have the opposite reaction. Continuing, he states, "In reality, you are home and free to live in your truth. You are all paired and in love. Live from this divine space. Being with your soul mate is far better than leaving to train, if you ask me. Besides, you can always train here."

Kriyo's candid and succinct message affects the Light Warriors positively. Ruzi asks, "How did you know that mating was the reason why we are no longer permitted in his domicile?"

"I heard you say it, and besides, home is where your heart is. Earthlings like this phrase. I can see that your hearts have found their counterparts; therefore, wherever they are, the two of you are home. And Ruzi, the Head Elder, has asked to speak with you."

"Where is she?"

"Right over there," Kriyo says, then, perplexed, "that's strange, she did ask to speak with you."

"She knows precisely what she's doing," Ruzi chuckles. "You're something else, Kriyo. You are different from the other Churrians. I can see why our liege has feelings for you."

"And for Mikiel," Kriyo's words slip out.

"Yes, she does possess sentiments for Mikiel, but he is not her soul mate."

Ruzi's words give Kriyo hope, especially since Mikiel and Meelah are together and completely out of reach. He must have faith.

"You needn't worry, my friend. And thank you for planting that seed. Tomorrow we'll commence training!" he yells to his comrades, effectively rousing them. "But for tonight," he says quietly to Nala. "Let's go for a long flight."

"Indeed, let's," she answers.

Lowering his head to all before him, Kriyo begins his journey. Nothing but sand encompasses him. As a child, he enjoyed the long walk between Drista and Ameira. To his recollection, it took under a half a day's time by foot. Though most Churrians travel by teleporting, a good stroll nurtures the essence, at least this is what his mother would always tell him. Moreover, he is not needed at the moment and Meelah, his Meelah, has left. It is time for him to leave as well.

"Your Meelah," a familiar deep voice says with a chortle. Rising to the surface, he adds, "I did not think that you would ever take ownership of another."

"Grawl, it has been far too long, my friend."

"Indeed it has. How long has it been since you've been home?"

"Longer than I care to voice. I should have made time to see you. Where is Grutiri?"

"She's warming herself by the Dristan wall. Do you want a ride? I remember that a ride on my back always elevated your mood."

"Thank you, Grawl." The large invertebrate begins to burrow into the sand, making it easier for Kriyo to sit atop him. "I'm still young and quite able to climb up on you."

"I forgot! You now ride the male Noori. If you can mount that beast, you should have no problem with me," he retorts, fully rising to the surface.

"You haven't lost your sense of humor, Grawl."

Kriyo strolls around his massive form. When completely out of the sand, Grawl's cylindrical shape stands twice as high as he.

Kriyo ponders how to mount his friend. Humble to his core, he states, "I need your help. I'm not Meelah. I simply cannot fly."

"No, you're not Meelah," he jests. "She is much prettier and she smells better too."

"Thanks! Meelah is quite beautiful though," Kriyo says, for the moment lost in his words. "She left, you know."

"Yes, but her absence is temporary. I watched the whole thing."

"She was standing next to me and then she was gone. Not even a goodbye."

"You Churrians! Do you lack a sense of smell? Her scent is," he says nearing Kriyo. "It's all over your face. Meelah did bid you a farewell, but Leva's presence did something so you don't remember."

"Leva, who or what is Leva?"

"That female has great power if you don't even recall seeing her," he answers, burrowing into the sand. "Get on and I'll explain."

He admires the enormous invertebrate. Encased by a dense hide, Grawl's tan, leathery exterior appears weathered and rough. Within this creature's brown, rounded eyes is a softness that personifies his nature. The lids of his eyes are thick, pitted and wrinkled, repeatedly they close. As he moves his body back and forth, lowering into the sand, he draws in air from his single nostril. Now that half of his body is well beneath the surface, he stops and waits for Kriyo.

"Thank you, my friend." Patting Grawl's side, Kriyo mounts him then settles atop his back. Patiently, he waits for him to continue with the Leva conversation. But as time passes, they both enjoy the calm. In the nearing distance they see Grutiri as she makes her way toward them. Slightly smaller than Grawl, she swims through the sand with ease, closing the gap between them.

"Well!" she exclaims. "You just left me to cook in the sand, didn't you, you old thing! Kriyo, it is always nice to see you," she adds.

"I did no such thing. I mentioned to you that I was going but you must have been sleeping," Grawl answers. "And, I wasn't going to wake you! You told me that I should never do that again," he smirks.

"I told you," she answers with sass, "never to roll me down the embankment when I'm not awake, you cantankerous rebrase!"

"You called me a rebrase! How dare you. Those pathetic creatures are nothing like me!"

"They are old like you." she mutters.

"The last rebrase died over one hundred years ago. And, as I have always said, I thought that you were awake when I bumped into you by accident. By the way, it was only a little hill."

"Things have not changed between you two," Kriyo inserts.

"I missed everything, you old crust! You should have awakened me. I am grateful that Natiya updated me. I missed a great deal: the Grana's ascension strengthening our field, the Light Warriors being called home, Meelah leaving, and Leva. If she was bestowed to The Light Force, a birth is imminent," she whispers.

"I know," Grawl answers, just as quietly.

"Perhaps it's just as well that I slept through it all. My sense of imagination is running wild."

"You would have just talked through it anyway," Grawl mutters.

"Did you say something, Grawl?"

"I said we should get Kriyo to Drista. It will soon be dark."

Kriyo chuckles at their exchange. The two fall silent, though he wonders for how long. Some things never change, and these incredible allies are a sound example of this. Though they fret and fight constantly, they cannot live apart. When the light in the sky rests and coolness infuses the night air, Kriyo remembers as a child gazing out of his chamber. He would see them in the distance, nestled closely together. In truth, he believes that they enjoy their clashes. It has entertained them for millenniums. Their lives may appear as unending, but they are quite mortal. These judicious beings have seen all the happenings upon this small star. But, soon there will be full-fledged war and this will be a first, even for them.

Ahead, Kriyo sees a familiar being trudging through the hot sand. Steadily moving, Lador continues his journey to Drista. His stare is fixed downward. Each step he takes appears more labored than the last.

"Lador!" Kriyo shouts into the soft, dry breeze.

The gentle wind carries Kriyo's voice and Lador raises his head. Smiling, he patiently waits for them. Moving steadily through the sand takes them minimal time to finally reach the parched Opala.

"Meelah brought me to Bursa so I could help you," Lador says simply. "But I'm unsure what happened. One moment you were there, the next you weren't. I wanted to be of service to you, Kriyo."

"Thank you, Lador," he tells him. Having a difficult time surmising what transpired during the last few hours, Kriyo finds himself at a loss for words. As stillness overtakes him, Lador interjects his thoughts.

"Meelah. It is she who overwhelms you. You have also lost your way, my friend. Your mind is consumed by her, leaving little room for what you must do."

"I love her," Kriyo states, sliding down Grawl's side.

"Yes, you do love her," Grutiri adds. "But there is great wisdom in your friend's message. You mustn't allow love to cloud your vision. It should embellish, not control you. You are governed by your sentiments."

"Is this how you all feel?" Kriyo asks them. "That I have lost my better judgment?"

"No need to be defensive," Grawl states. "You certainly aren't the first nor will you be the last to fear losing the one you love. Even I had to balance this fear."

"Thank you, Grawl," Grutiri says softly.

"I do fear losing Meelah to death and—"

"To that Light Warrior, Mikiel," Lador interrupts.

"We should make our way to Drista. Soon the night will come," Kriyo states.

"Would you like for us to bring you the remainder of the way?" Grutiri asks.

"No, but I thank you. A walk will be therapeutic," Kriyo answers. Facing both Grawl and Grutiri, he bows. Then he and Lador continue their journey. In the distance he sees the Dristan wall and vaguely he makes out Light Warriors patrolling the very top of it. But his mind rebounds to Meelah. Perhaps they are correct. He accused Meelah of being solely emotionally based. He nearly treads the same reality. She does distract him, but the idea of not knowing her as he does almost immobilizes him. A life without love is a life not worth living. He recalls his father always saying this. But where is the healthy balance in this premise?

Being deep in thought makes for a rapid trip for now they stand at the entryway of the Dristan wall. Kriyo looks upward as if an invisible string lifts his chin. His eyes lock on a wondrous new friend. The black Noori hovers above him and then, transfixing him, the animal floats down. With each flutter of its massive wings, the tiniest grains of sand dance whimsically into the air.

Lador's open mouth seems to collect an excessive amount of the debris. When he spews it out, Kriyo can't help but chuckle at his friend. Lador continues to wipe his tongue with the sleeve of his shirt.

"You are quite funny, my friend. It's only sand. It will not harm you," he explains, while patting the Noori. "You are a beautiful creature," Kriyo says softly to the animal. "I shall give you the name Seli."

"Hope," Lador mutters, still spitting out sand.

"Yes, hope, in ancient Churrian. How is Blessing?" Kriyo asks, as if the Noori can answer him. With the consistent nodding of his head, he does. "Then she is well. I am relieved. Do you wish for me to ride you?" Again Seli bobs his head repeatedly. "Let's take to the sky, twilight is quickly approaching." Mounting the creature, Kriyo advises Lador, "I will return soon. Please excuse us."

Still removing miniscule elements from his mouth, Lador raises his hand in acknowledgment. Kriyo cannot help but smile at the Opala. He is a true friend. To think that he went to Bursa, wishing to be of aid to him, touches his heart. For as long as he can remember this Opala has been a faithful part of his life. Lador lived on a nearby planet and frequented Ameira. Even though it was forbidden for Kriyo to travel with him, he did. Many adventures were had in their youth and now they are rejoined by war and the devastation it causes. Kriyo's heart sickens, recalling Lador holding his deceased son. In reality, this is merely the beginning. If Meelah doesn't awaken and connect with her true power, and if he cannot ground his fear of losing her, all will be lost.

After a brief moment of reflection, the epiphany that all must change to allow room for growth, settles in. Pressing his heels gently into the Seli's side, he rides the Noori cantering on the soft sand. Kriyo connects energetically with him and moves his body in cadence with the spectacular equine. Once their movements synch, so do their minds. With the simple thought of flying, they lift from the ground and join the sky.

"Astounding!" Kriyo shouts.

The muted sky before them makes the journey all the more special. The small airborne mammals have settled in for the night, freeing this space for them. Though the air temperature in the upper atmosphere is quite refreshing, it's also chilly. With the skin of his face and hands too cold, he asks Seli to descend.

"You'll require new attire," a voice states.

Following the sound, Kriyo sees Ruzi flanking them in the sky. "What's wrong with my robe?"

"You should answer that yourself," Ruzi laughs.

Looking downward, Kriyo sees that the repeated lifting and lowering of Seli's wings has caused the back of his robe to catch the air, exposing things. "I suppose that I was too cold to know that I was giving you a show.

"It was not a show for me," Ruzi remarks with a chortle. "Land down there. You and the Noori must work up your endurance."

Kriyo sees the plateau ahead and asks Seli in thought to stop there. Slowly they descend and all four hooves rejoin the land. "Both you and he should walk. If you don't, your muscles will cramp," Ruzi states.

"How do you know so much about the Noori?"

"I hear him."

"I have named him Seli."

"Indeed, and he appreciates it."

"If I am the one who has bonded with this magnificent creature, why can't I understand him?"

"As your bond deepens, you will. But Light Warriors have no language barriers. When we communicate, our thoughts translate into the language that the other being speaks. But having worked with mammals spanning the universes, I have learned to use this same translator with them."

"Please tell Seli that our ride was amazing!"

"He knows. And Kriyo, I would like to thank you."

"For what?"

"You saved my life after I shielded you and my liege. How did you know to have that remedy on hand and where did you get it? Nala was told that you simply went into your pocket to retrieve it."

"The Timeera prepared me, but I envisioned Mikiel requiring it. He's always protecting Meelah."

"Would you have given it to Mikiel?"

"Of course! He is a part of Meelah's life."

"You are so different," Ruzi expresses, with a pause. "Truly, you are noble."

"I'm not as altruistic as you may think," Kriyo quickly answers.

"You question this quality because of my liege. You are not prepared if she chooses death to fulfill her destiny?"

"No, I'm not. Where's Nala?" Kriyo asks, changing the subject. "I thought that you two were going to take a long flight together."

"She stepped in to help another Light Warrior patrol Ameira, but we had our flight," he answers with a wink.

"In flight? You choose to be together in the air? It's freezing up there."

"When what you're doing creates heat, you acclimate to the cooler temperature."

"It must be a Light Warrior thing."

"It is," he replies, closing his eyes for a brief moment.

"Why is Ameira patrolled at night?"

"No one told you? A portion of it is not powering down and we cannot risk any silent entry."

"The battle on Lador's home began right before dawn and his teleporting station was also powered by the light, perhaps it too never powered down," Kriyo says.

"We will take no chances. If there are visitors after dusk they will be terminated."

"Ruzi, may I ask you a question?"

"Of course."

"Did Meelah ever…in flight with Mikiel?"

"No, not with Mikiel, not even with any Light Warrior. When she defied our creator it was with a being that looked like you, as a matter of fact." After a moment, he adds, "Why haven't I seen this before? May I touch your arm?"

"Yes," Kriyo answers. Ruzi takes hold of Kriyo's shoulder and the lids of his eyes close.

After a brief pause, he drops his hand and begins muttering, "The timing, the timing of it all. It was right in front of me."

"Are you going to share your findings?"

"It's you, Kriyo! You were the being that she fell in love with when she was our leader. It must be with you somewhere. I saw it, so you can as well. You two were fiercely connected and it almost destroyed Mikiel. That's how I recognize you. I was with Mikiel when he followed Meelah. When we saw the two of you, it was something else!"

"What happened? If we were in love as you say, why did she end her life?"

"Your planet was destroyed along with all life upon it," he states sorrowfully. "My liege was shattered, but her broken heart wasn't the only reason she left us. Our forces were greatly diminished. She had a plan, she always does. Not long thereafter, she made an agreement with the Creator of all life and fell to her death. My liege was an irreplaceable leader with a pure heart. We loved her and we waited for her to reincarnate, but possibly, too much time elapsed, for she is only a mere fraction of who she once was."

"Perhaps her time with the Light Force will rebirth her innate spirit. There is a reason why she had to leave. The Timeera insisted that I let her go."

"Yes, Kriyo, there is a higher connectivity to all of this and that being said, I would like to include you in our training. I will help you strengthen Seli as well. I am assuming you will ride him into battle."

"Thank you, Ruzi. I'd be honored to join you tomorrow."

"Again, it is I who must thank you. Now that it's dark, allow me to lead you and Seli back to Drista. He'll follow me."

Kriyo pats Seli on his withers then mounts him again. Truthfully, he knows that his robe is cumbersome and not proper gear for this task, but this is what he has and for now it will have to do. This time he makes certain that his robe is tucked in. Asking Seli to follow this kind Light Warrior, they leap off the plateau and take to the dark sky. The air is even cooler than before, bringing with it an effective chill. While in flight, Kriyo drowns out his temporary state of feeling uncomfortably cold by thinking about the intimate, yet unrealized connection he had to Meelah when she was not just a Light Warrior but the leader of these judicious warriors. He has always felt an intense closeness to her, even when they'd just met. This past connection is quite plausible. It sits as comfortably and as naturally as he sits on Seli. Not able to see a foot in front of him, he closes his eyes and faithfully allows Ruzi to navigate them home.

As the air temperature begins to warm the exposed portions of his skin, he feels them descending. Upon opening his eyes, he sees that they are again on the surface. In the near distance he sees his parents standing outside the Dristan wall with luminaries in hand. Their perfectly timed greeting further warms him.

Dismounting, he proceeds over to his parents with Ruzi at his side. His parents' steady smiles illustrate the depth of their adoration for him. His father wavers a bit. He shifts his weight from his cane to his healthy leg.

"Are you well, Father?"

"Better that you're here," he answers. "The Noori must fly over the wall. He stands too high to fit in the entryway."

"Your friend, Lador, also has the same issue. I flew him over before I joined you," Ruzi explains. "Allow me to bring Seli to his stable. Blessing is waiting for him."

"Thank you, Ruzi. I'd appreciate that." Kriyo and his parents observe both the Noori and Light Warrior blend seamlessly into the night sky.

"Seli," Pasha utters. "I like it. No one speaks our ancient language anymore."

"It's old!" Faro exclaims.

"You never liked it, Father," Kriyo avers. "Whenever Trall gave me a tome to master, you would hide it from me."

"I only wished to spend the little time that we had together—together! Is it so hard to believe that I missed you?"

"I missed you too," Kriyo replies, resting his forehead briefly against his father's.

"This is nice," Pasha comments. "Come to think of it, this is the very first time since I've returned from earth that all three of us will sleep under the same roof."

"That's right!" Faro shouts. "And, I made your favorite tincture, son."

"He did. He has been stealing herbs from everyone's garden all day to make it," Pasha remarks with humor.

"Stealing? No, I asked them."

"Asked who?" Kriyo inquires.

"I asked each plant for their permission. That seemed sufficient to me," Faro answers while ambling toward the entry. "You don't have to drink it, even though I spent all day preparing it for you."

Standing before Kriyo is his mother. Her smile stretches from ear to ear. Her ivory skin glows in the subtle light emitted from the twin moons. A vibrant red robe casts a rosy gleam over her cheeks, while her silver-white long, wavy hair gently moves in the arid breeze. Though he briefly saw both of his parents in Bursa when Meelah was appointed, it feels like so much time has passed, and he realizes how much he's missed them.

"And we have missed our son," she replies. "I also miss Meelah. Since our return to Churria I have only seen her twice. The burden that has been bestowed on the both of you hardly seems fair."

"I have no regrets, Mother."

"I know you don't," she agrees.

Hooking her arm around his, they walk through the entryway. All is quiet and tranquil as they proceed. The darkness of night has a nesting influence on this township. Inhaling deeply, Kriyo enjoys taking in the scents that hang in the air here. This is home to him and he instantly feels affected by his reminiscences. His youth was spent running down the very pathway that he and his mother now tread. Ahead is the dry fountain. Daily, he used it as target practice. He recalls Elder Hiro. He would chase him whenever he heard the pings created by the stones he threw. At

Meelah's appointment, he saw how time seemed to have altered this elder, rendering him unable for such a pursuit. For fun, Kriyo halts his step and feels around the ground for a small stone.

"Son, what are you doing?"

Not answering his mother, for he knows that she would somehow talk him out of such an immature deed, he impulsively throws the stone and waits to hear the sound of the little chink. But instead he hears, "Why did someone just throw this at me? Show yourself!"

As a perturbed Light Warrior makes his way out of the gloom and over to Kriyo, his mother says, "You threw it, so deal with the consequences. I will be at home with your father… drinking the tincture that he spent all day preparing. We'll see you when we do."

Kriyo watches his mother stride off, leaving him to deal with the agitated Light Warrior. "I'm terribly sorry," Kriyo explains. "Honestly, I didn't see anyone. Why were you over there?"

"I was using the fountain!" the Light Warrior states as if Kriyo is an imbecile. "And why would you throw a stone at it?"

"It's what I used to do when I was young," Kriyo replies, realizing how ridiculous it sounds. As intrigue slowly builds in him, he asks, "What do you mean, using the fountain? It doesn't work."

After hearing the Churrian's query the male Light Warrior pays it, and Kriyo, no mind. Turning around, he proceeds back from whence he came. Kriyo observes his pale wings as they slowly melt into the darkness. Intrigued by the possible use of the relic, he quietly follows. As his eyes acclimate, he observes the Light Warrior kneeling down before the fountain. He doesn't know what he's looking for or even why he's drawn to linger. Curiosity tethers his feet to the ground. As time passes, the Light Warrior remains as still as the fountain itself.

Startling him from his lull, he hears a soft whisper. "He's seeing his next step." As he follows the voice, he makes outs Nala. "The fountain guides us. It keeps all of the Light Warriors on their path. These are for you," she adds, handing him a small bundle. "Ruzi asked me to get them for you. These are his spares."

"What is it?" Kriyo asks, inspecting the small cloth-covered package.

"They are apparel," she answers quietly.

Kriyo smiles as his mind swiftly returns to his lifted robe exposing him. "Thank you, Nala. Please tell Ruzi that I will don this with honor." She lowers her head, then studies the Light Warrior, who is deeply connected to the flowing knowledge of the fountain. "Can someone other than a Light Warrior use the fountain?"

"I am uncertain," she answers him. "It is an intriguing inquiry. Do you feel the call? The fountain beckons when our essence is ready to obtain information, or understanding."

"A draw," Kriyo answers softly. "I feel a peculiar pull to it."

"Then honor it. We will never know if you are attuned to its prophetic power if you do not try," she says, while signaling to him where to sit.

Kriyo finds the spot and kneels down. The rock-strewn ground is not comfortable by any means. It's also cold. As he tries to settle himself, he becomes mindful of the noise he's making. He already agitated the Light Warrior beside him, he doesn't want to disrupt his trance as well.

"I will leave you now," Nala speaks again in a soft whisper.

Nodding his head, he watches Nala as she silently departs. Not a noise from her to be heard. Beginning to have a deeper sense of how incredible these beings are, he considers the other Light Warrior. He's alone. These stealthy beings continue to astound him. Though their wings make them appear massive, they can silently maneuver even in tight places. Also not making a sound, is the fountain. Using the Light Warrior's meditative state as his guide, Kriyo closes his eyes.

Initially, his mind centers on how uncomfortable the obtrusive rocks beneath him feel. They poke and dig into his legs relentlessly. Rocking from side to side, attempting to relieve the persistent irritation, he is aware of a presence. With this distraction, he finally settles. Gradually, even the most irritating jabs soften. A sense of peace overcomes him. Even his breath is influenced by this change. Shallow and yielding, each inhalation carries him to an unusual space. Profound tranquility moves all around him, relaxing every muscle in his body.

Content and completely at ease, he hears, "It is nice to see you again, Kriyo." This female voice speaks from all around him.

Opening his eyes, he realizes that he's no longer kneeling before the fountain. In fact, he's no longer anywhere that he recognizes. Standing in a white, muted reality, he sees a form walking toward him; a female Light Warrior with massive, intricately feathered white wings. The tips of her wings stand well above her head. Barefoot and light on her feet, she appears as if she's walking on air. Adorned in a pearly gossamer gown that flutters as if caught in a breeze, she mesmerizes Kriyo as she approaches. Her flaxen, shimmering tresses, falling to her waist, also move about in the stillness that surrounds him. Silent and nearly awestruck by her presence, he sees something within her dark blue eyes, he sees Meelah. About to speak, she quickly raises her pointer finger and presses it firmly against his lips. Hushed, he remains silent before her. Hoping to see Meelah again, he searches her face for answers.

"Meelah certainly has an effect on males," she says, while walking around him. Stopping, she stands directly before him and lowers her head. "I am Leva. And, we have a similar goal."

"Goal? What objective do we have in common?"

"You wish to be with Meelah and I wish to be with Mikiel."

"I love Meelah but I want her to choose me." As she resumes her strolling, he asks, "What could I possibly do for you?"

"Are you certain that Meelah has chosen you?" she poses her question while looking at him. "Oh, you have doubts. I see many of them. You worry that her attachment to Mikiel will cause her to waver. As to what I want from you? Soon you will find out. But for now, do you wish to see Meelah?"

"Yes, but I respect the need for our separation. I want her to embrace who she is and if this means that we must be apart, then I honor it."

"You are her mate," she asserts. "Though you're judicious and honorable, these qualities will not alter her course."

"What do you mean?"

"Shhh," Leva says softly, closing her eyes. "*He* will soon arrive and I am being summoned," she whispers. "Watch, there are players in this game that even I have never seen...," the Light Warrior expresses, while fading into the opaque background.

Pacing about, Kriyo waits in this surreal space. Anxiety grows within him. With each breath he wonders what Leva meant. Frustrated, all he can do is wait, but not for long. Ahead of him he sees a large round object. Slowly, it rolls his way. Wondering where it came from, he looks in every direction as the object taps into his leg. He leans down to inspect it. As he runs his hands along its smooth surface, he spots movement from within it. Feeling his heart beat faster as intrigue continues to build, he moves closer. With every passing moment, the images within the orb come into focus.

He observes Leva. Her long ornate gown trails behind her as she approaches a being seated in a gilded chair, raised on a platform. A brilliant silhouette announces this life form. Kriyo knows who this individual is—the Light Force. Appearing similar in form to a human being, the Light Force has short, chocolate-brown hair. Wearing a thick ceremonial, white robe with a heavily embroidered red stole over it, His back is straight and His presence is commanding. Unlike any being that Kriyo has met, He emits virtue and radiates utter power. Leva, now standing in front of Him, lowers her head, then steps onto the platform. Confidently, she stands beside her leader.

Following their line of sight, Kriyo sees her. Meelah makes her way toward the throne. Dropping to one knee, she lowers her head as if she's been doing so her entire life.

"Please rise, Meelah," the Light commands.

She rises to a stand. Meelah's presence has already grown from merely being in His realm. Her stance is strong and her essence is again pure. She is one of a kind to Kriyo. Even though Meelah just arrived, she has begun her restoration. Wisps of darkness appear behind her. Quickly they build.

In front of me, I see the Light Force rise abruptly to a stand. Closing my eyes, I attune to the looming malice welling behind me. I turn around and face it. As something materializes, dressed in a black attire, a being appears from the murkiness. With medium-length, coal black, greasy hair, slicked behind *his* ears, here *he* is. Thin and noticeably devious, the Dark Force has managed *his* way to *his* brother's domicile. Shifting back and forth, wearing a cunning grin, *he* extends *his* gnarled fingers, revealing sharp, talon-like nails.

"What are you doing here, brother?" I hear the Light bellow.

"What? I can't visit?" the Darkness asks. "I have been invited, after all. I heard that Father has given you another gift. Oh, look," *he* says addressing me. "The other gift from our father. You're not looking well, Meelah! Are you tired? The bloody ensemble is encouraging." Moving closer to my face, *his* beady black eyes glower at me. "Did you have fun slaughtering whatever you killed?"

With energy from the palms of my hands, I thrash the malevolent monster, pushing *him* back and away from my face. "You killed my father and you've amassed an army again. It has killed thousands of innocents! You will be stopped!" Again, I send an energetic pulse *his* way, and this time *he* nearly falls over.

"That felt good. I suppose I had it coming!" *he* quickly retorts. Casually, *he* dusts off *his* robe and proceeds to the throne. "Brother, make this thing…" *he* offhandedly states, "stop! I'd hate to further upset our father by stomping her into oblivion! Today my battle is not with her. But soon, Meelah," *he* hisses with a slithering tongue.

"Meelah," the Light Force assures me, "this is not your war." And with these words, I respectfully lower my head to the Light.

"No, indeed, it's not. Though I'll win that war and thoroughly enjoy spreading my gloom," the Darkness states, continuing to *his* brother's throne. "I guess Dad had some doubts about Meelah. I love it when He fails!"

"No, brother, no one has failed, and you are no longer welcome here. I formally rescind any invitation that you may have received," the Light Force declares. He directs his glare at Leva. Between them is a private exchange.

"You didn't know that she invited me," the Darkness utters sarcastically, winking at Leva. "This is interesting. Well, thanks for the invitation, you beautiful thing. It seems that you and I both like to get under my brother's skin. And wow! I can smell your alluring scent from here. That must drive you crazy, brother! What I would do to her if she was mine," *he* mutters, licking *his* lips.

"Undoubtedly you would destroy her like everything else you touch," the Light answers flatly.

Sneering, *his* wickedness clenches *his* fist, squeezing my midsection as a result. Gasping for air, I struggle to breathe. The pain is unbearable. It feels like all of my ribs are about to break!

"My brother has no power here, Meelah," the Light assures me. "You give *him his* power. It resides in your doubts."

Baffled that *his* brother chooses not to intervene, the Darkness tilts *his* head. Everything occurs with a higher sense of purpose. I use *his* moment of confusion to my advantage. Unaware that I now stand at *his* side, I launch *him* across the room. Before the Light, I lower my head to Him. He was right. In a heap, the Darkness gradually rises. Shifting forms, the malevolence grows in a wave of pure evil. I stand strong. Here, *he* is no threat.

"You have no power here, brother. Leave!" the Radiance demands.

Laughter is all that comes; pure, wicked, iniquitous amusement. Then silence. Transforming into energy, both brothers, one a brilliant light, and the other a dark shadow, ascend into the space above them. Still observing the incredulous sight, Kriyo watches. I sense him, the man I love is near, and I lift my head to find him. Our eyes meet. Before a word is exchanged between us, I also change into energy; one half brilliance and the other portion dim. I ascend.

"Meelah," Kriyo says softly, resting his hand on the orb.

"She cannot hear you," Leva communicates. Standing on the other side of the clear object, she seems indifferent. Composed, she remains silent.

"Where did she go?"

"She has gone to a place where even I am not permitted." Flicking her wrist, she moves the rounded object. "Will you help me, Kriyo?"

"With what? What do you wish for me to do?"

"Will you help me!" she shouts.

"If what you wish will right the balance between the Light and the Dark, then yes. I will assist you."

"You are quite unique. Many would give their souls for personal gain, but you…you are truly righteous. If I need you, I'll be in touch. It has been enlightening meeting you," she adds, brooding.

As she turns to leave, all fades to darkness. Kriyo opens his eyes. It is dark. He struggles to rise to a stand. His legs have fallen asleep. Heavy and weighted, he moves them about in an attempt to rouse them. The power of this fountain leaves him astounded and speechless. Finally able to bear weight on his legs, he senses a presence behind him. Turning, he notices the Light Warrior from earlier. He's wearing a grin. Lowering his head to him, Kriyo acknowledges his ignorance.

"I linked to your vision," the Light Warrior says in a low voice. "My name is Duzri, and in all of my years, I have never experienced a vision such as yours."

"It was not a vision of what is to come. This, I know," Kriyo answers. "If you saw everything, where did Meelah go?"

"Somewhere that only a few are permitted. I believe my liege was summoned by the Creator. This energy is the only one who can beckon the Light and Dark Forces."

"But why was she called there?"

"I am unsure why my liege was summoned. I am equally uncertain about Leva. Why did she invite the Darkness into our realm?"

Both remain quiet and reflective for a few moments. Then Kriyo replies, "With all due respect, Leva is not like Meelah. Both are a gift from the Creator, but Leva's motives are questionable. And Duzri, do all Light Warriors link into another's vision?"

"No, and I apologize for doing so," he answers, lowering his head in shame. "But I was curious as to what you were doing. I have never seen any other beings use this fountain. Perhaps we are even then? You did throw a stone at me."

"Again, I'm sorry about that. Admittedly, I was unaware of the useful power of the fountain. Churrians are not educated about it."

"Perhaps they are naïve, but Kriyo, they are not meant to use it. The fountain was sent here by the Light Force. It connects us to Him. I have never seen it communicate with any other being. I have witnessed many attempts. What are you?" he asks, sniffing the air around Kriyo.

"I am Churrian."

"You are more than that," Duzri answers, with his eyes closed. "But perhaps you aren't ready for the truth. These are Ruzi's," he adds, touching the bundle.

"Yes, he lent them to me. He asked me to train tomorrow."

"Even Ruzi knows that you are more than a mere Churrian, so does Leva. She would not have been able to communicate with you through the fountain otherwise. I will inform the remaining Light Warriors of her actions. I am grateful that I was able to see them for myself. It was unwise of her to betray our maker," Duzri replies in earnest.

"You speak of the Churrians as if you dislike us."

"Light Warriors only detest the Dark One. We remain on Churria for our liege. She also sees who you truly are."

"Perhaps our meeting was fated. Though again, I am sorry that it began with me throwing a stone at you," Kriyo tells him with contrition. "Tomorrow we train and I, a simple Churrian, need to rest. I hope to see you then."

"You will," the Light Warrior answers.

Kriyo steps into the darkness and makes his way home. As he opens the door to his parents' house, the familiar fragrances of his home waft all around him. Too tired to do anything other than go to sleep, he continues to his bedchamber. Entering his room, he smells Meelah's soft scent. Having nothing more than faith to hold onto, he lies down while staring at the ceiling.

"Be safe, Meelah," he murmurs.

Chapter Ten

Feeling disoriented and quite nauseous, I struggle to get my bearings in this new place. Traveling the dimensional levels makes me feel off, but not like this. Waves of dizziness make my stance waver. Holding onto the wall beside me, I feel like a miniature figure. Before me are two extremely high doors. What walks through them? I wonder. Despite the odd panoramic view, I hope to find some clues that will tell me where I am. I also wish to promptly acclimate so these dreadful bouts of nausea come to an end. A few deep breaths seem to ease my queasy stomach.

Similar to the oddity of a dream, or perhaps a nightmare, the oversized objects encircling me, make me feel as though I am a Barbie doll. At that moment, the massive doors spanning higher than my eyes can perceive begin to open. Unsure of what or who lies ahead, I stand to the side and, filled with intrigue, wait. With a resounding boom, the doors crack into the walls. I feel myself shudder. The sight before me continues to be peculiar. I seem to have arrived in the land of giants and I wonder when I'll see these hopefully peaceful enormities. As the nausea dissipates, another discomfort takes its place, a searing headache from behind my eyes.

"Perhaps this will be easier for you," I hear a soft female's voice say from all around me.

No sooner do I hear the soft-spoken words than I find myself standing in Central Park in New York City. Observing two women stroll by as if they don't see me, I hear their laughter and sense their happiness. The familiar scene of the city is nostalgic. Then everything changes and I'm now standing on a cliff in what I believe to be Ireland. Overlooking the ocean, I hear the waves thrash against the rocks below with force. Fine mist rises upward, filling the air. The cool, moist air blankets the skin of my face. Subsequently, I'm on Churria. Looking around, I see Shria's home. The sweet scent of the humbra tree greets me, relaxing me. Before succumbing to this peaceful moment, again, I am standing before two massive open doors. Like an invisible string is tethered to my waist, I am pulled through the opening. Walking down a long corridor, painted in subdued pastel hues, I see a sylphlike female, with a graceful long neck and ink-black, straight hair. Her facial features are elegant and delicate, though Her presence is powerful. Adorned in a lavish ivory robe, heavily decorated with intricate symbols, She appears to be waiting for me. As I approach, the energy encircling Her is like nothing I've ever felt and again my head aches.

"Touch my hand," She tells me.

Nearly defeated by the pain in my head, I take hold of the female's outstretched hand. Consequently, I feel restored. There is no pain, no nausea, I instantly feel righted and balanced. With my hand still in Hers, the two of us now stand in my old apartment in

New York, in my bedroom, to be precise. Walking over to touch my special books, I realize where I'm standing and the painful memory of my father's death consumes me.

"How are we here?" I ask, restraining my tears. "All of this was packed up and moved."

"I can bring you anywhere you wish," She plainly answers.

"Who are you?"

"You already know, Meelah."

"If I knew, I wouldn't have asked."

The female smiles at me. Then the scene before me changes again. At the present, I'm standing behind the Light Force and the Dark Force. Ahead of them, I see two enormous beings seated on thrones. The female is the very same from seconds ago and the other being is an unassailable male. Both appear to be in a private, silent exchange with the Light and Dark Forces.

"Thanks for the family gathering," I hear the Dark Force spout obnoxiously. "It's been amusing, but I'm on quite the schedule."

"You understand what has been told to you?" the commanding male seated on the throne asks both Light and Dark sternly. With a nod of the Dark Force's head, He adds, "Be gone then, my sons."

As the forces disappear into thin air, I realize who these magnanimous beings are, the Creators of all. Standing before me, in my size, are the two of them. Dressed in elaborate, ivory robes ornamented with complex golden symbols, both look at me as if they can see through me. I am not intimidated, I hold myself with pride.

"We simply are. There is no need to define us," the impressive female affirms, Her almond-shaped brown eyes fixed on me. "We can appear as anything and for you we chose to separate our polarity and appear to you as male and female. We felt that this would be the most pleasing for you."

"What are your names?"

"We have an abundance of names to speak, but your essence knows us as a sound." The two of them release a soft resonance.

Hearing the two harmonic pitches, recollections of me standing in this precise location wash over me. After I fell to my death as a Light Warrior, they summoned me here. Glimpses of all varieties of memories find their way into my mind, but only bits and pieces of them. Like the shards of a broken mirror, each holds my reflected image. I hope I'll be able to put them together and see what is created. This minute awakening has revealed one relevant fact.

Addressing the two powerful energies before me, I declare, "You created me."

"Yes," they answer. "You used to call me Feena," the female explains.

"And you would address me as Ta," the male adds, before continuing. "Do you know why you are here?"

"I have lost my way," I answer, owning my actions.

"Nothing has been lost. It's time for you to understand," Ta replies. This commanding bearded male has gentle, light brown eyes, and I connect with them. His ash-brown mane is wiry and long. Possessing innate vitality, yet exuding deep-seated wisdom beyond all limits, He continues. "Meelah, we contacted you once before. When you were the leader of the Light Warriors, you were not ready to comprehend that you always possessed the power to save the Light Warriors from total annihilation. But now, you are ready. It is time that you understand."

With my curiosity piqued, my mind races, creating an abundance of questions. How did I possess the ability to save the Light Warriors and why didn't they just reveal this then? Continuing to process, I realize that all my queries will be satisfied in due course. Reining in my wonder, I allow them to continue.

With a gracious nod, Feena begins. "You, as the leader of the Light Warriors, were created in my image. We gave you to our son. He used this inspiration to create others like you. You, and the first creation of our son's, were made differently. Both you and he could procreate, whereas no other Light Warrior can."

"You're speaking of Mikiel?"

"Yes, this is why you and he have always shared a deep connection. You were meant to be together and raise another army."

"But we were forbidden to mate! The Light Force still shuns the Light Warriors that have."

"Our son never knew that you and Mikiel were able to procreate. It was Ta's idea not to enlighten Him. He wished to see what would occur without this intervention. When we heard your plea to save the remaining Light Warriors rather than inform you of the solution, we accepted your request to reincarnate into another form, Churrian form, where you will live out your birthright."

"Wouldn't it have been easier to just tell me that I could have created a new army?"

"Meelah, at that time you were carrying heavy emotion. You lost the being that you now call Kriyo. We saw your path and we felt that respecting your wishes would be best."

Closing my eyes, I am lost in memories that bring me back to that fated day. Standing alone, I out of desperation and irrefutable heartache called out, pleaded for help. I forged a plan and I was unyielding and stubborn. They knew what I was able to handle. When I open my eyes, Ta continues.

"Honoring the law of free will, we observed your journey. Our allowing all to navigate freely is their right. Look at you! This is your destiny. It is quite satisfying that free will has returned you home."

"But the Dark Force, *he* has taken the free will of thousands upon thousands of innocents. *He* kills and destroys at will. Why don't you stop *him*?"

"This is what we created you for," Feena says gently. "Return our son back to *his* domicile. *His* darkness balances *his* brother's light. They are needed for all perceptions of reality, everywhere. Worlds among worlds on all dimensional levels require their polarity and honoring the laws that we created, we choose to have faith in you, Meelah."

"Does Mikiel know that we were destined to be together?"

"No, we honored free will and allowed the two of you freedom in this decision," she answers.

"We created Leva and gave her to the son who has been unfailingly faithful to the universal laws. Leva possesses a stronger connection to the darkness. But, she and Mikiel will be able to breed for the benefit of the Light Warriors."

Pain in my heart builds. I feel wounded deeper than I knew I could. Mikiel is fated to be with another. Though I love Kriyo, I feel pained by this news. A part of me can't let Mikiel go. I gather myself and as I do, I hear them.

"Again, we honor free will," Feena explains. "It will be Mikiel's choice to mate with Leva. If he does, Leva will bear a son. This Light Warrior will have the power to maintain the balance that you are destined to restore."

"We are the creators of all; every soul and every emotion. But what each soul chooses to do with these emotions is what creates all that we see."

Setting aside my wounded feelings regarding Mikiel, I ask the question that my soul needs to know. "Did you create Leva because you believe that I will fail?" Dreading their response, though ironically, needing to hear it, I wait.

"No, Meelah," Ta replies. "That would mean that we would have lost our impartiality. Leva is merely a gift to the son who has faithfully abided by the universal laws."

"Do you believe you will achieve the task of righting the balance by returning the Dark Force to his domicile?" Feena inquires.

"Yes," I answer firmly. "I know that I have changed from who I once was, but standing here, before you now, I feel power deep within me. I will live my destiny."

"You have changed," Ta confirms, walking around me. "Being immersed into the humans, and raised by the Churrian you called Samuel, has softened you."

"But change is good!" Feena states adamantly. "Meelah was taught emotion by experiencing it and this will make her a stronger leader."

"We will soon find out," Ta states.

"What about Mikshe? Is she well? I should have been there to protect her."

"Her essence has ascended," Ta explains, closing his eyes.

Before me, I see her come into form and as soon as she does, I pull her into my arms. Still wearing a simple robe, she is radiant.

"Meelah," I hear her say, squeezing me back.

"I should have been there to save you," I affirm, unable to let her go.

"Everything occurs as it's meant to," she answers, stepping back to look at me. Joyful now, emitting a soft glow, she continues.

"Meelah, you are the strongest being that I've ever known. I believe in you!"

"They did such terrible things to you, Mikshe," I say, with tears pooling in my eyes.

"Shh," she answers, raising her pointer finger, then pressing it against my lips. "Everything is fine now. I have faith in you, Meelah. Thank you."

"For what? Why are you thanking me?" I ask, wiping my eyes.

"For what you will do. Soon, you will save all that I know and love," she answers, while fading into the background.

I remain fixed upon her sweet face, and manage to say, "Goodbye, my friend." Again, I gather myself emotionally then face Ta. "Thank you," I say from my heart. I observe him slowly lower his head. Within the stillness that encompasses me, I know what I must do—obtain answers. Now is not the time to succumb to emotion.

"May I ask the two of you another question?" After a nod of acknowledgment, I query, "Who are the Sirians?"

"There are many dimensions housing evolved beings and the Sirians are amongst them. They are connected to earth and their interest in you is in your destiny. These beings, like many higher dimensional life forms, understand the larger picture, as do we. They wish for your success. Standing outside the perception of time and space affords us an interesting view," Ta explains.

"What am I?"

"You may appear as a Churrian though no Churrian created you in their traditional manner. The one you know as Raza birthed you though you are not biologically connected to her. We created you from the same DNA, or genetic information, used when we created you as the leader of the Light Warriors, but now, you have no visible wings. You are ageless, but also mortal, and your added powers are a gift."

"And my amulet?" I ask, pulling it from beneath my robe.

"You stored your memories in the stones of your amulet and those recollections birth strength from that incarnation. Protect your amulet. If it falls into the hands of our son, *he* will learn the way to defeat you. But," Feena states with a long pause, "what about Kriyo? You have feelings for him."

"Who will the chosen one select?" Ta asks, appearing as Mikiel.

"Intriguing, isn't it? To be in love with two," Feena says, appearing as Kriyo. "But Meelah, every decision comes with a consequence, and I will age while you will remain youthful," I hear Kriyo's sensuous voice speak softly.

"Meelah," Mikiel's sultry tone says. "We have always yearned for each other, but if you let me go, I will bear a son who is destined to maintain the balance."

Torn by my emotions for the both of them makes me want to scream out of frustration. I love them both, but...

"But?" Feena asks, in her physical form. "Regardless of whom you choose, your first born will be given to our Dark son as payment."

"What! What payment?"

"Perhaps *he* must remind you," Ta states, waving His hand.

Out of thin air, the Dark Force stands before me. With a sigh, *he* scans the drab robe that *his* parents have adorned *him* in.

"Really! Why am I back again? What have I done now?" After a short period of silence, *he* realizes that I know. "No, No, No! That was underhanded of you! Is NOTHING SACRED?"

"Tell her, son," Feena demands.

"Killjoy, killjoy! Meelah...I will be taking your first born in exchange for the key that freed Queen Drana from her quaint prison. That's a load off my chest! This has been entertaining, but I must go and pillage some little town."

"NO! I never agreed to this!"

"Yes, you did," the Darkness answers, rifling through *his* pockets. "Here it is...the contract! You Meelah, whatever, whatever, will be given the key to liberate Drana from her prison and I, the inimitable Dark Force, will get—"

"It's blank!" I shout.

"But not for long," *he* snickers joyfully as the words, *Meelah's first born*, appear in blood. "Darling, you have the looks, let me tell you, but not the brains. You signed the contract and that's that," *he* affirms, rolling it up.

"And if I choose not to bear children?"

"Like that's an option!" *He* laughs. "Your hormones are on overdrive! Your denial of that desire is just as entertaining," *he* says, licking his lips. "Anyway, I'll only take your firstborn, you have enough eggs to build an army...oops, that's what you were supposed to do your last lifetime! But really, you will have other offspring. What's the big deal?"

"What can I do to reverse this?"

"Yes! The question I was hoping for," *he* exclaims, thoroughly elated.

"What do you want from me?"

"It's simple, Meelah...LOSE!" Blackness consumes *his* eyes.

"Not a possibility."

"Well then," *he* says, looking at *his* creators. "What relation is Meelah to me, a sister or something? Don't answer, simply listen. It will bring me extreme pleasure when I tear her apart! Naturally,

I will wait until she slips and gives birth, then I'll revel in the moment, making it full of agony!" *he* states with a sinister grin.

I glare at *him*. Choosing my words wisely, I respond. "When I destroy your army and return you to your domicile, I will equally take pleasure! One day I will die and you…you will be trapped there for all eternity." I watch *him* shudder.

"Well," the Dark Force states. "This has been enlightening, but," *he* says, glancing at the skin of *his* wrist, "I'm late!"

"And I smell your fear," I reply calmly.

"You have so much to learn!" Exploding into a murky shadow, *he* swirls about. I feel the part of me that is connected to *him*. I need this rage. This fury will help me annihilate *his* army. Sensing that I take pleasure in *his* malevolence, *he* withdraws, disappearing completely from sight.

"*He's* theatrical," Ta remarks.

"*He's* your creation," Feena quips. Then, to me, She explains, "Meelah, free will is yours, but tread out your future wisely." She says, joining Ta.

"Together we are one." They say in unison.

As the Creators fuse together, their light grows and intensifies. No longer able to bear the brilliance, I close my eyes. The vigor created from their fusion twirls about. Love, hate and a sundry other emotions tickle my insides. Extreme heat, then a cool chill fills the air, coiling around me. My hair dances in every direction while my robe twists and turns. Finally, peace brings stillness. Opening my eyes, I witness the radiance as it dissipates.

Leva approaches me. I've returned to the domicile of the Light Force. Regardless of Leva striding my way, my mind recalls seeing Kriyo's face right above me. But how is that even possible? Thinking of Kriyo, I become attuned to Leva's impatience as she stands before me. Cleary, she cannot delve into my thoughts. I'm quite certain she would have an opinion about my thinking that I've seen Kriyo. I bet she's the one who contacted him. She probably believes she can persuade him to help her regarding Mikiel. Raising my line of sight, I allow our eyes to connect. I feel her contempt for me, her annoyance that I am here, even her anger that I was the one called by the Creator. Intrigued by her reaction, I recall what Ta told me. Leva possesses more darkness than I do. Perhaps it is this obscurity that brings her to me now. I smile at her.

"You will tell Mikiel that he's to be mine," she orders in an authoritative tone.

I continue to smile. Baffled by my actions, she furrows her perfectly shaped blonde brows. I observe not only her beauty, but her welling irritation. The truth is, she is not my enemy. Sensing Mikiel before my eyes even see him, I look around.

"Meelah!" He runs to me. "The Light Force told me that you were also summoned." Closing the gap between us, he gently rests his forehead against mine before wrapping his arms around me. "I know, Meelah. I know what we were destined to create," he speaks, in a manner only to be heard by me.

Leva reluctantly departs. With our eyes closed, we remain together. No words or thoughts are exchanged. Silence and peace blanket us. As his warm breath caresses my lips, I use all of my restraint to remain still. I honor him and our lineage. He's the correct Light Warrior to bear a child. Mikiel is devoted, honest, and I love him. Breaking the spell…I tell him.

"I will always love you, Mikiel," I say, looking at him. "But—" Before I can utter another word, he presses his lips against mine.

His lips, soft and warm, seem to melt into mine. All the love that we feel and have ever felt, erupts into a sweltering exchange.

Our breath instantly becomes heavy. Sweeping me into his arms, I hear his wings spread. Quickly, we ascend into the vast space above us.

"Why can't it be us?" I hear him whisper.

Within his words is the truth that both of us have chosen to veer away from. Gently, I disengage our intimate connection, ending our passionate kiss. As tears well in my eyes, we descend. Our eyes remain fixed upon each other's. This ephemeral moment of fervor continues to dissipate. His soft blue eyes sear my soul as they fill with sorrow. He holds me tightly as his feet touch the ground.

"A part of me will always love you," I tell him again.

"All of me will forever be yours," he replies.

"Not all of you," I answer. With these truthful words, his arms relax, lowering my feet to the ground. Again, we're silent. Until I say it, the words that must be spoken, the truth could not be realized, though neither of us wish to hear it.

"Mikiel, you must be with Leva. You and she will have a Light Warrior that is destined to maintain peace. Perhaps it is this Light Warrior's fate to ensure that the Darkness remains in his domicile."

"We were meant to do this!" he shouts. "Why did you act so rashly?"

"Mikiel, I am no longer that Light Warrior. This cannot be altered. I am walking in this form, but my destiny has not changed. Create the child as you are meant to and I'll balance the Forces as I'm destined."

"And our love, are we supposed to—deny it?"

"We are more than our sentiments. We are destined to walk a path that will send the Darkness back to his home and your child will only benefit this pursuit. We vowed to be of service to the greater good. Your son, his path, is our solemn promise."

"And you will choose Kriyo?"

"You will choose Leva. This is the right path. It will benefit all that we know and love. I meant what I said; a part of me will always love you. I have summoned Leva."

As I turn away, he grabs my hand, halting my step. His warm grasp further injures my heart. I feel his love and passion, yet I know it's right to deny it. I simultaneously refute the love I feel for him. I don't look at him for I wish not to get lost in his eyes. Our destinies now move in opposing directions. This way we can accomplish the same goal. Finally, I see Leva as she saunters our way and I briefly glance at Mikiel. His eyes are consumed with the same emotion that unsettles me and with no words exchanged, I watch as he releases my hand, lowers his head and subsequently places his palms together at his chest. Acknowledging me as a Churrian and no longer as his liege, is boorish. I lower my head reverently to him, but then, I turn and greet Leva by saying, "We have the same objective. Bear the child that will ensure our success."

Leva seems to scramble for words. I feel Mikiel's focus on me as it burns my back, but his anger softens as frustration replaces it. I wish not to hurt him. I love him, but walking away is right. I also love Kriyo and he is the intended being for me.

"Perhaps I have misjudged you," I hear Leva say, silencing my inner musings.

"But I have not misjudged you, Leva. I see you just as you are. That said, you will never contact Kriyo for your own personal gain again. Are we clear?"

"Meelah, Meelah, Meelah," she says wickedly. Like the flick of a switch, she's filled with contempt again. "You will not threaten me. I am your leader! The leader of all Light Warriors!"

"No!" the Light Force commands, materializing into form. Striding our way, He continues. "You, Leva, were a gift. You will bear an heir. Meelah is, and will forever be, the rightful leader of the Light Warriors," He affirms. Addressing me, He adds. "Meelah, it is time. There is work to be done."

Leva bows in shame, then stands aside. I feel sorrow for Mikiel, for whom he is destined to be joined with. He deserves so much more. His Radiance extends His hand to me and I am moved by His powerful and generous statement. Again, I lower my head to dear Mikiel before joining hands with the Light Force. My destiny has begun.

About to leave, the Brilliance says, "Mikiel and you have a choice. Destroy the army and return my brother to *his* lair. When you achieve this, an heir may not be needed. You and Mikiel could be together." Gazing over my shoulder, I see Mikiel's face. He too has heard His eminence's spoken words. Hope is restored in him while disdain builds within Leva.

"I will defeat the Dark Force's army," I announce. "To do this, I must find myself. What occurs after the war is still to be written, but now I must prepare."

Departing His realm, I hear the Light say, "The future isn't written in stone. I will show you what you'll need in order to defeat my brother's army."

Chapter Eleven

Before the dawn of a new day, Kriyo awakens. As his head settles to the right, he considers the chamber that housed him as a youth. Though now he's an adult, these walls still afford him the same comfort they did growing up. He watches the dark of night as it begins to lift. With this clarity, he sees the bundle from Ruzi and chuckles. The thought of donning something other than what he has always worn, especially a Light Warrior's uniform, is as strange as learning to fight like one, but that's exactly what he's going to do. Sitting up, Meelah's face appears in his mind. Her perfect, delicate and beautiful countenance engrosses him. Rather than getting lost in it, he replaces those thoughts with the objective of making his parents a morning tincture.

Slipping into a clean robe and sandals, he ponders which ingredients to use. As he passes the clothing from Ruzi, he can't help but shake his head. Though he's honored to be loaned them, he has never worn anything so revealing. For now, he uses the security of his robe to ground him.

In his parents' yall, he combs through his mother's herbs. A specific recipe calls to him, but it requires thame; a small purple grass that happens to grow in abundance beside his neighbor's front door. Journeying outside, he stands before the herb. Since it is too early to wake the elder that lives here, he rationalizes the thought of asking the herbs for their assent in his plucking them. In the same spirit as his father's, that it's not stealing if the herbs give you permission, he bends down to ask the plant. *What a way to begin my day; I'm speaking to grass.* Unable to contain the grin on his face, he smiles, laughs and proceeds to stand up. The elder's door opens.

"Kriyo!" Elder Hiro exclaims. "Just the Churrian I was thinking about."

"Reeditta, Elder Hiro. May I have some of your thame?"

"No doubt you were at my door ready to ask, unlike your father," he responds. "Many Dristans have been talking. He's been taking their herbs too without asking."

"Perhaps my father asks the herbs instead."

"You have not lost your sense of humor, boy. But look at you, you are no longer a youth, what do you intend on doing? Perhaps you wish to become an elder?"

"All prospects are open. May I have some of your thame?"

"Of course, help yourself. Oh! I have a message from the Head Elder. It's for you. Where have I put it?" he says, flustered, feeling around the pockets of his robe. Scampering back into his house, he cries out, "I know where it is. Ah, yes! Here we are."

Handing over the envelope, he watches Kriyo examining the elaborate seal upon it. Kriyo asks, "When did you receive this?"

"It came late last night. The messenger said that you were over at the fountain. He gave it to me and asked that I deliver it in the morning."

"Thank you, Elder Hiro. It was a pleasure to see you again. And, thank you for the herbs."

"Perhaps you would like to open the letter here?" the curious Elder Hiro asks.

"I will read it at home."

Quiet, so as to not wake his parents, Kriyo returns to the yall and places the freshly cut thame in water. Looking again at the intricate seal binding the envelope, he mindfully opens and reads it.

Kriyo Fallis of Drista,

Your presence has been requested by Head Elder Shria at nightfall on the Bursa green.

The Honorable Head Elder,
Shria Retalias

Walking into the yall, Pasha observes her son with the letter in hand. "Is there news?"

"News?" Faro adds, ambling into the yall as well. "What's the news?"

"It's just a letter from the Head Elder," Kriyo explains.

"Just a letter from the Head Elder? I have never received a letter from her personally," Faro states. "May we see it?"

Handing the letter to his inquisitive parents, Kriyo takes the herbs from the water and begins to grind them. A sugary scent from the thame disperses into the air. Curious himself as to why the Head Elder has requested his presence, he harshly presses the herbs into oblivion.

"Keep churning the herbs and even I, who will try just about anything, will not drink them," Faro says with a smile.

Realizing that he's destroyed the thame, he sighs. "I didn't mean to do that, I'm just wondering why the Head Elder wishes to see me on the Bursa green? Father, what do you feel?"

"See, Pasha, he leaves the juicy predicaments to me."

"Perhaps you had a vision?"

"No, son, I haven't, but it doesn't mean I won't. Let me try your creation. It's thame grass, right? I could smell it when you first started grinding it."

Turning to his father, who simply waits for a response, Kriyo sees this Churrian's innocence. Purity is evident in his smile. He simply exudes it. Uncomplicated and genuine, is the authentic Churrian before him. Kriyo can't help but smile back at his father. As their silence ensues, reminiscent of one the games they would play, Pasha grows impatient with it all.

"Of course it is thame, Faro. And Kriyo, you will see what the Head Elder wants when it's time. The two of you can complicate things," Pasha mumbles, walking off. "And," she yells to them, "don't ingest the thame now that Kriyo has turned it into a soup. Your stomachs will ache for a week. I'll pick more."

The sound of the front door closing reaches them and they resume their little game. This diversion rejuvenates Kriyo. Staring into his father's eyes, he notices how time has altered his appearance. The skin of his face is wrinkled and worn. His father's hair is more gray than not. He appears so weary. Even his eyes have changed into a lighter and softer shade of brown. Frail and in obvious discomfort, Faro remains steadfast. Though physically, time has changed his form from his glory days, his personality remains the same. Dropping his eyes, Kriyo concedes this victory to his father.

"I knew I still had it in me," Faro spouts. "Thanks for giving me that. You have matured into greatness. I am very proud of you, son."

"If I am anything worth noting, it's because of you."

As tears well up in his father's eyes, Pasha returns with fresh herbs. Glancing over at Faro who's overcome with emotion, she rolls her eyes and sighs. "Kriyo, you know how he gets. He'll be teary all day now."

"Do you see how she treats me? Ever since she returned from earth, she acts as though she has a handful of thame jammed up where the light doesn't shine."

"Father!"

"What is the matter with you, Faro? I regret returning from earth with books. Listen to how he speaks now!"

"Well, it's true," Faro adds. "I apologize if I offended you, though. My Pasha, the day you returned home was special indeed."

Kriyo observes his mother as she beams over her shoulder at Faro. Their love is what Kriyo wishes for with Meelah. As her face begins to consume his mind again, he commences the task of making a morning tincture. "Mother, allow me," he says gently. "This was my idea, after all."

"Not too rough this time. Elder Hiro looked like he was counting the thame after I cut some."

"But you did ask before cutting them?" Kriyo asks, with a wink.

"Of course I did!"

"I inquire because of the rumor I heard this morning."

"Do tell, son," Faro states, anxious to hear the news.

"A wild Dristan who resembles my father, has been stealing herbs from everyone in this township."

"It's not stealing if the herbs give their consent. That's my story and I'm sticking to it!" Faro declares as he folds his arms. "And to think, I thought you had some enthralling hearsay, like Tilly forgetting where he placed his robe again. Why does that Dristan only have one robe? If I had one robe, I'd be wearing it or drying it—not losing it," he states, shaking his head.

The musical sound of laughter fills their small yall. Kriyo's mixture is ready for tasting. Carefully, he pours the viscous liquid into the small cups and hands one to each of his parents. "To our health," Kriyo toasts, raising his cup.

"To our future," Pasha adds.

"To a life with a little less pain," Faro says feebly.

All are affected by Faro's words. Gradually, one by one, they down the concoction. The herbal mixture, syrupy yet clean, nourishes them. The startling sound of a cup striking the stone floor instantly redirects Kriyo. Following the sound, he sees his father convulsing. Darting behind him, he allows Faro to fall backward into his arms. Trying to stabilize him, Kriyo holds onto his father tightly.

"It's the visions," Pasha cries. "They are stealing his life away."

Kriyo closes his eyes and with his arms wrapped firmly around his father, he asks for help and prays to Natiya. Warmth, infused with a deep sense of calm, emanates from the cool surface beneath him. Kriyo watches the effects of this soothing wave as it washes over his father. Every tensed muscle within Faro's rigid form gradually eases. His limp body surrenders peacefully into his embrace.

Waiting for his father's eyes to open, he hears his mother ask, "What did you do to him?"

Unsure of what happened, he chooses silence instead. A faint noise comes from Faro. As the resonance builds, they hear the distinctive sound of snoring. "He's asleep!" Kriyo exclaims.

"He was asleep."

Coming to, Faro mutters, "Bring me to my drawing chamber."

"No, my dear, you have had an episode, far worse than ever before. If our son wasn't here, you would have collapsed onto the floor."

"That is why he's here!" Faro announces. "Thank you for calling Natiya, son, now please help me to my drawing chamber, this you must see."

Progressively, Kriyo and Pasha get Faro to his creative workshop. With a groan, Faro sits down. Once seated, he immediately begins to prepare the vast array of paints. An unforeseen wave of vigor appears to have rejuvenated him.

"Kriyo!"

"Yes, Father?"

"Nice tincture! It was sweeter than I thought it would be. Isn't that wonderful?"

"Isn't what wonderful?"

"Isn't it divine when things turn out better than you expected, son?"

"Yes, Father," Kriyo answers, unable to contain his grin.

"Go. Ruzi, the strapping Light Warrior, is waiting for you at the stable." Painting with unbridled passion, Faro adds, "That Light Warrior sees in you what we see in you."

"And how do you know this, Father?"

"It was in my vision. Go, I'll be at this all day."

"Mother," Kriyo says, unable to make sense of what happened moments ago.

"I'll be fine!" Faro states in a shrill voice.

"Son, I'll take care of him. I love this old, incorrigible curmudgeon."

"You wouldn't know it by that flattering comment," Faro spouts. "Go, son!"

With a grin, Kriyo bows in respect before bolting back to his chamber. "Now the daunting task," he says coolly, gazing at the bundle of clothing. Opening the package from Ruzi, he inspects the garments. With a nervous sigh, he slips out of his robe and into the new attire. To his surprise the uniform fits quite well. Though Ruzi appears so much larger than he, everything is well-fitted, with the slight exception of the white sleeveless shirt. He feels the air against his skin from the two openings for Ruzi's wings. The bottoms have two parts; a skirt-like bottom reaching mid-thigh, and a form-fitted inside. Raising his brows for a moment, he wonders if all of this has just been cleaned. Sniffing his top, he hears a burst of amusement.

Laughing louder than Kriyo has ever heard him, is Lador. Kriyo's mother, standing behind Lador, has had her attention drawn by the uncontrollable mirth. At the threshold of her son's door, she bites her tongue, though she can't control her grin at the sight of him.

"They are a gift from Ruzi and I am late," Kriyo says defensively.

"They're quite interesting, my son," Pasha says, struggling to restrain her laughter.

"You'll need this, too," Lador says, picking up the chest armor. But again Lador releases a chuckle. "Are you wearing this for Meelah?" he asks, wiping the tears from his eyes.

"Are you done?" Kriyo shouts, trying to regain his dignity.

"No…but I'll stop."

"I should be leaving."

"Yes, you should be leaving," Lador affirms, regaining control. "Ruzi asked me to collect you."

"Kriyo!" they hear Faro shout. "Let me see you before you leave. I've just drawn you in attire I could never image you wearing. Allow me to test my visionary talents."

Dropping his head, Kriyo walks into his father's creative space. When he is not even a step into the chamber, Faro says, "I've still got it! Too bad Meelah isn't here. You have nice legs."

Again, laughter erupts at Kriyo's expense, but humble, he manages a smile. Holding his head high, he proceeds out the door when he hears his father yell, "That's my son!"

Striding about in this unusual attire catches everyone's attention as they pass by. His legs feel the air and heat upon them as never before. Picking at the holes in the back of Kriyo's top, Lador says, "Are these openings for your wings?"

"No," he answers. "But watch me fly." Rounding the corner to the stables, he calls to Seli telepathically. "Lador, please tell Ruzi that I know where to go. I'll be there shortly. Thank you, my friend."

In a canter, the Noori approaches them. Kriyo leaps onto his back. Linking with the animal, he feels Seli's wings expand and thrust downward, lifting them from the ground. Off into the sky they go, and this time there's no worry about his robe lifting. They soar over the Dristan wall. Relaxed, the two move together, each in synch with the other. With every fleeting moment, their connection deepens. Move left, Kriyo thinks. Seli does just that. With the horse attuned to his every thought, the harmony produced makes them travel swiftly, as one. Kriyo sees their shadow ahead of them, and they chase it. Soaring like this is pure freedom. The wind, as it moves all around them, is invigorating. Kriyo and this incredible Noori were fated to melt into this state of oneness.

Becoming winded, the horse slows down, allowing their shadow to triumph for now. In the lull of their flight, Kriyo wonders how Seli's body will be protected during battle. Making a quick detour, he decides to fly to Ralta. He knows just the Raltan for the task. This welder is a master of metals and Kriyo knows he'll do Seli justice with a grand creation that will protect him.

On their way they approach Ameira. The magnificent teleporting station is already in use. He observes life forms of all shapes and sizes appear, then disappear from sight, all but one. This being grabs his attention. Curious, Kriyo watches. Frantically, the being gazes in every direction. The individual's hood catches the wind, revealing that she's a young female. Appearing like a Churrian or even an earthling, her long black locks bounce around as she anxiously shoots glances around her. Kriyo slows down on his approach. The female sees him riding the Noori. Once this connection is made, her eyes remain fixed on his. He realizes that she's searching for him.

"Kriyo," she intones, telepathically.

The female collapses to the ground. Swiftly, he instructs Seli to land. Joined by the two Light Warriors who are patrolling Ameira, he makes his way over to the female. In a heap, the female lies on Ameira's smooth surface. While kneeling down to get a closer look at her, he overhears the two Light Warriors snicker at him. Despite their continuing to scoff, undoubtedly because of the attire he's wearing, he chooses not to dignify them with a response.

Kriyo realizes that this female is with child. As she lies flat on her back, her pregnant belly is prominent. He wonders why she would be travelling at the end of her term? It's dangerous to travel between dimensional levels as an adult. A developing child could suffer permanently. But here she is.

Curious, Kriyo asks, "Where are you travelling to and how do you know me?"

Reaching for his hand, she answers, "I came to Churria to find you. I am from The Realm of the Mystics."

"Find me?" he inquires, shocked. "Did Drana send you?"

"No, I am fleeing from Drana," she replies, squeezing his hand. "This child must be born here and you—ahh!" She shrieks. "My baby is coming!" Drawing her knees into her chest, she bears down and begins to push. Wishing that she was able to tell him why she was searching for him, he hears her wail of pain. Uncertain of what to do, he looks up at the Light Warriors who offer nothing more than protection. From behind the female he sees—wings, beautiful pointed wings the hue of purple. Her cape must have concealed them.

Blood soaks the hem of the female's gown. Though pale and weak, the female prepares to bear down again. The bottom of her clothing is saturated. He requires help. Her cry, this time softer and weaker, reminds him of what he must do. Rather than panic, he does what feels right, he calls Natiya for the second time today. Amid his prayer, he quickly senses her presence. As he opens his eyes, she materializes into form before them.

"This child must be born. She is the one!" Natiya declares.

"And the mother, how do I help her?" Kriyo asks.

"She will die. I cannot save her. The infant will also fail if she's not removed and," she says with a pause, "I must enter your form. Do I have your permission?"

"Yes," he answers, though he is uncertain of what she means.

In less than a breath's time, he finds out. Natiya's essence enters Kriyo and pushes him out of his body. Watching his form as it lies the female down, is quite surreal. Hurriedly, Natiya works using Kriyo's vessel. Lifting the female's dress, revealing the extensive blood loss, she lances the girl's abdomen. A blood-curdling wail rings out.

Ruzi lands by the chaos. Beads of sweat glisten on the surface of his brown skin as they catch the sunlight. Hastily he assesses the scene before him. Since Kriyo appears to be ravaging this innocent, he flings him away from the female. Swiftly rising to a stand, Kriyo's form walks intently back to the female, but before Natiya resumes her work, she pauses and focuses on Ruzi. When this Light Warrior sees Natiya's presence, he immediately stands down. Realizing that something larger than he could know is occurring here, he converses with the two Light Warriors. While listening to his comrades, Kriyo sees Ruzi look around. He finds Kriyo in his energy form and looks directly at him. Reverently, Ruzi bows. Though he's surprised that this Light Warrior is able to see him, he is also honored and returns the gesture.

The cries of a newborn infant fill the air and Kriyo is pulled back into his body. In his arms is the infant. Clutching her close to his chest, he hears the mother as she tries to speak. Weakly, she attempts to raise her head to see her daughter. To ease her, he lowers the baby. Gently he rests their cheeks together. He witnesses the unspoken, loving exchange that will bind them. Kissing her new child, she whispers, "Tell my daughter what I did for her. Let her know that I died so she could be free." Her words puzzle Kriyo and silence befalls the mother. Facing her progeny, with her eyes still open, the life within her lifts—she's gone.

"This being gave her consent. The child may remain on Churria," Natiya affirms. "Please bring her to the sand."

Still in shock, Kriyo stands. Looking at the lifeless female that mere seconds ago kissed her baby, wounds his heart. With no time to wrap his head around what just happened and no time to mourn the female, he consults with Natiya. He knows what must be done. After all, if Natiya didn't intervene, the child within his arms would have also died. Ruzi steps in and reverently, moves the female's body over to the sand.

Following this noble Light Warrior, Kriyo kneels down and closes the mother's eyes. Gently removing her hair from the front of her face, he sees how peaceful and youthful this girl appears. "So young," he whispers. Placing her hands together on her chest, he rises, then stands back.

Her corpse sinks into the sand. Tiny granules envelop her body as she's quickly drawn beneath the surface. He simply cannot believe what has just happened. Squirming in his arms, the infant releases a howl. Shedding tears, the newborn cries as if she's mourning her mother. As if she's aware of the loss. Drawing the baby close to his chest, he sways back and forth. This motion soothes her. Calming, she gazes up at Kriyo. As his eyes meet hers, a connection between them is forged. Lost in this precious moment, he notes something within her, a glint of light or perhaps a glimmer of hope. It's not the inexplicable gleam that moves him, it's how this light makes him feel that affects him most.

"I see peace in your eyes," Kriyo speaks to her.

"Kriyo, we should go," Ruzi states. "The Head Elder has been in contact with Drana. Bring the child to Drista. Your mother will be waiting."

"How does the Head Elder know about this?"

"I sent one of the other Light Warrior to notify her. We must leave. You still need to train."

"You wish for me to still train? All I want are answers."

"It's not safe for the newborn here. We must go," he persists sternly.

Kriyo becomes aware of the crowd that has gathered. Beings from other universes and dimensional realities all face them. From behind the masses, he spots Rhana, the siren from The Realm of the Mystics. He clearly recognizes her cloaked in a green hooded cape.

"Seli, fly home," Kriyo tells him.

Lowering his head to Ruzi, he allows the Light Warrior to use his power and bring them to Drista. Unwilling to risk the infant not being able to teleport, he trusts Ruzi to get them home. Just as foretold, his mother is waiting for them.

"There, there," she comforts, touching the newborn's face. "She's cold. Give her to me, son. A nurse-maid from The Realm of the Mystics is on her way."

"What is going on?" he asks, handing the infant to his mother.

"Life is never dull," she answers, swathing the child in a blanket. "Ruzi, please wait for the nurse. She should be arriving anytime now. I trust that you'll see her true intentions. Only return with her if she's pure at heart. And thank you. I don't mean to order you around," she murmurs. "I trust you and your infallible instinct."

"Thank you," Ruzi answers. "I will return shortly."

As Ruzi disappears from sight, all of the events thus far begin to mount in Kriyo's mind. Hoping that his own mother will tell him what she knows, he waits impatiently. Pasha, lost in the infant's innocence, is no help. "Mother!" he exclaims. "If you will not explain what has occurred, I'm off to the Head Elder!"

"You needn't go far, my son. She and Trall are with your father. Let's go to them."

"Did Father see this in his vision?" he asks, escorting his mother.

"I'm uncertain," she readily answers. "You left with Lador and I went to the yall to straighten up. I knew that all was well with your father since I heard him whistling. Then there was a knock on the door. I knew it was Shria, I could just sense it. Walking past your father's vision room, I saw him. He also knew it was Shria. Actually, he was quite rude, to my recollection. He told me to stop walking backwards and to open the door already. Sometimes I just don't know about him. Anyway," she says, regaining her composure, "Shria told me to meet you at the Dristan wall and that you were returning with an infant from earth. Apparently, she conversed with Natiya. Our Mother was quite impressed with how you handled things."

Already home, Kriyo didn't gain any useful information from her other than that he was not the only one cognizant of these events. Opening the door, he hears the lively exchange from his father's drawing room. No sooner did he and his mother enter their home, than Ruzi returns with the nurse-maid and Drana. Most certainly having sensed Drana's presence, Shria meets them as they step into the main room. There, Trall is trying to help Kriyo's father into the room, so Kriyo quickly moves to assist.

"I am here, Father," Kriyo says, relieving Trall.

Sitting his father down in his favorite chair, he attentively tunes into the exchange. But, the absence of his mother and the infant diverts his focus. Wondering where they are, Kriyo looks in the yall. There he sees his mother wiping the remnants of birth from her sweet little face. Oddly, the newborn appears to have already grown.

"Is she larger?" Kriyo asks.

"I thought I was losing my mind, son, but yes, I believe she is. Drana will be able to explain all of this. I thought that the little darling should be cleaned up."

"Clean or soiled, please allow me to see my niece," Drana asks, standing behind them.

Pasha walks over to hand the baby to Drana, but her eminence takes a step back. "I cannot touch her. What has she done?" Drana intones. "Please, hold her so I can see her."

"Mother, allow me," Kriyo offers.

With the child in hand, he extends his arms so Drana can see her. Emotion wells in the Queen's eyes, resulting in tears. "Why, Cila? Why did you do this?" she asks in a heartbreaking tone.

"The mother was named Cila?" Kriyo asks.

"Yes. Cila was my half-sister and this child was the sole heir to my throne. She is very special. This child was fated to bring new leadership to my realm."

"Then take her home, she appears quite healthy," Pasha utters.

"She can't," Kriyo responds. "This child can never go to The Realm of the Mystics."

"That's correct, Kriyo. Only those born in that realm can remain there. Because we are ageless beings, we are capable of procreation only when one of our kind perishes. It's been thousands of years since one of my bloodline was born. And this child is part...it doesn't matter, and perhaps it's better that you don't know. The facts remain the same. My sister is gone and this very special child can never step foot in my home."

"What is this child, part mystic and part what?" Kriyo asks, intrigued. Silence is his answer. "Churria is now this child's home. If we are in any danger as a result of this, we must know."

Pleased by his assertiveness, she respects him by answering. "All you need to know is that there are no more of this kind. Someone went to great length to make sure that all of this kind would cease to exist as we know them. This child possesses half of these beings. I cannot speak their name. I gave this promise to my sister. She loved one, with her heart. This was her first and only love in an otherwise lengthy life. He was also destroyed. A Shadow found him in our realm. We still do not understand how a single Shadow breached our field. I suppose that traitors come in all shapes and sizes," she states, sadly, gazing at the newborn. "She has Cila's eyes; they're blue and as bright as the sky."

"I am sorry for your loss, Drana," Pasha responds. "Can you and Kune produce an heir?"

"No," she answers. Pain is threaded through the single word. Gathering herself, she tells her, "Cila is with our father and her mother. Soon this child will join them all."

"Why? Your sister told me that she died to free her child."

"Freedom from reigning our kingdom, then liberation through death. This is the freedom of which my sister was speaking. She never wanted to succeed me. The thought of her daughter having the same birthright was sheer torment. Soon, Kune and I, along with many other leaders throughout the dimensional planes, will step down, and I have no heir," she proclaims.

Looking down at the child, Kriyo can plainly see that she's growing noticeably larger with every passing moment. Her blanket is now a tad too short, revealing the toes of her feet. She releases a soft cooing noise. Looking at her face, he realizes that even the hair on her head has grown.

"How much time will the child have?" Kriyo asks, disrupting the conversation.

"I am uncertain of the precise time," Drana answers, approaching her niece. "But I fear she will live no longer than a Churrian month or a month and a half. Her cellular matter is not attuned to the vibration here. Her physical body will age quite rapidly. In The

Realm of the Mystics she would have stopped aging at twenty-five, similar to Meelah. Her physical form will also cease aging at this age, but she, still possessing the DNA of a Light Warrior, is unaffected by changes in dimensional levels. When you, Pasha and the Northeast team spent time in my realm, all but you, Kriyo, were affected. You are more than you know, but I am very much like my niece. The assistant that I brought with me is a Curlaze and these beings age at a slower rate than any other from my realm. She has been instructed to care for the child, though the baby will not need to drink breast milk or even eat. Her body will grow, mature then die on its own. The Curlaze will last no longer than two months here on Churria." Tears well up in Drana's eyes. The reality of her niece's fate hits her with great force, to which both Kriyo and Pasha bear witness. Trying to compose herself, she takes a deep breath before continuing. "This should be more than enough time."

"There is no need for anyone from your realm to needlessly age. I will tend to the child," Pasha declares.

Wrinkles form on Drana's face and before their eyes, an entire lock of her hair turns white. Acknowledging that she is willing to age before them, they see the love that Drana possesses for the child. "I wished to hold you," she whispers. "And it gives me pain to no end that I cannot." Again, her eyes fill with tears. Between the two is a silent yet succinct exchange. Though no one present can hear Drana's words, they feel her overwhelming emotion as she says goodbye to her niece, and to the hope of the throne remaining in her immediate bloodline. Drawing back her tears, Drana regains her composure. Addressing Kriyo, she says, "You gave something to my sister that no other could—relief. Though I don't support what she has done, I am grateful that you appeased her soul. Thank you." Turning toward the remaining group, she lowers her head, then asks Ruzi if he would return them to Ameira. The child still in Kriyo's arms continues to make delightful cooing sounds.

"Kriyo," Shria states. "We are quite proud of your ability to honor your flawless sense of judgment."

"Indeed," Trall adds.

"I will see you at dusk on the Bursa green. Today you must train with the Light Warriors. I say this, for I know that you will require this knowledge. Both your father and I have had visions foretelling your need for such teachings. And," she continues, "it seems that you and Meelah have both outgrown the use of your robes. Perhaps it is time to create proper attire for all Churrians who choose to train. But Kriyo, you will don a robe tonight!"

"Yes, Head Elder," he answers with a grin.

Kriyo overhears Shria and Trall converse with his father. It gives him comfort to hear his father's voice. It always seems to ground him. Sensing his mother, he turns and sees her. She continues to observe her son as he holds the new baby. Though she's snuggled in his arms, he hands the youngling to his mother. He feels tethered to the infant somehow and moving away from her is difficult. But in time, he does. Passing the drawing chamber, he is stunned by the magnificence created by his father. He intently follows the detailed account of Ameira and of Cila's demise. He sees a drawing of himself standing precisely where he is. Then his father drew Meelah. He illustrated her flying. Anxious and hopeful to see her, he walks past his father and toward the door.

"Not even a goodbye?" his father asks. "Son," he calls, halting Kriyo's step. "Meelah will return before the day's end. Now go and train!"

Chapter Twelve

"Look, Meelah," the Light Force says, closing His eyes. As contradictory as His words may sound, I know precisely what they mean. Closing my eyes, I see through another source. His sight becomes mine as our minds converge. He shows me vast planets and stars, home to beings connected to His light. Everything encircling us is beautiful and colorful. Each color of the rainbow exists in space; though here, there is no ending or beginning. Blending together, these hues twist and turn, creating unique fusions all their own. Even the stars glimmer in every shade. These masses are homes to life forms seen and unseen, realized and unrealized. His brilliance exists ubiquitously. It extends through all space, through every universe. All life can feel His presence, if they so choose. His radiance births hope and peace.

Amidst the contrasts of light, we stop before a dead star. It no longer possesses luminosity of any kind. I sense that it once teemed with life. Then I recall the beings that lived here, the munads. These beings integrated their very essence into the star, creating an amazing reality. This star appeared like a gaseous mass that generated energy by thermonuclear reactions, but this was merely an illusion. This star was fully functional and able to support the munads. During my life as a Light Warrior, I remember seeing the intense light that beamed from this star's altruistic totality. In wholeness, these beings remained as one consciousness. As the darkness began to overtake the scale, the munads turned their light inward, creating an external reflective surface, camouflaging them. Though they became invisible to the naked eye, recently, the Dark Force has located them. Their energy as it intensified with purity must have been what ultimately revealed them. Keenly, I sense the utter delight of the Dark Force as *he* shattered them to pieces. I wonder why *he* personally made sure that they were eradicated? A righteous anger builds within me.

Like catching an alluring scent that tantalizes my senses, I sniff the air. With my eyes still closed, I trail a specific smell and with my mind I chase it. Sensing that I've arrived, I open my eyes. I'm standing in a familiar spot, The Realm of the Mystics. The Light and I remain connected though He chooses silence. There is something here I must learn. Honoring my free will, He wishes that I use it as a guide from this point. This knowledge must be earned.

I stand waiting, though not for long. I hear voices headed my way. Ducking into the brush, I wait. Rhana along with three other beautiful sirens stroll by. Immersed in their dialogue, Rhana gazes upward as if she senses something. Then I see it, a sparkle of light streams down from above. Through the atmosphere, this glimmer descends and, due to its high and unique vibration, it readily enters their realm. All four sirens shield their faces as this peculiar light crashes onto earth. Once the airborne debris settles, Rhana is the first to inspect it. As black and gray smoke rises, obscuring her view, Rhana bends down to take a closer look.

"What do you see, sister?" one of the sirens shouts to her.

"Perhaps it's a male?" the other laughs. "The perfect mate," she adds.

But Rhana has no response and this intrigues me. She is never silent. In fact, she's always open with candor tainted with insolence. As she intently studies something, the other sirens grow curious. With caution, they approach the smoking object embedded in the soil.

"It's nothing," Rhana states, rising to a stand. "It's just matter that space didn't desire."

"I want to see it! I have never seen anything that is not from this planet."

"No!" Rhana shouts. "You will only injure yourself and soil your new gowns. Look at yourselves! Do you really wish to smell like char and ruin your dresses?" she asks, approaching the two of them. "Remember who you wish to charm this twilight, sisters. Stay on task, it's nearly dark and we should be going," she adds cleverly.

All four sirens leave. Everyone but Rhana giggles. I watch as she glances repeatedly over her shoulder at the steamy mound. After they depart, I approach the smoldering arrival. It's a charred mess, but there is something within it. Drawn to it, I reach down, but before my hand touches the object, I sense Rhana again. She rushes over and walks right through me. I watch as she pauses, looking around. Perhaps she senses me though she obviously cannot see me. Swiftly, the siren extracts the mass and places it in a cloth bag. Trailing Rhana, I arrive behind her at the water's edge. Again she scans the area in all directions, making certain she's alone. Focusing, she places the bag down, gently.

"I know what you are," I hear her whisper. "You're a male from a distant land. I can feel your unique energy. Reveal yourself, you are safe with me." With those words, light from inside the object grows in intensity. Rhana equally beams with anticipation. Her golden locks shimmer in the luminosity as gradually a form appears. A male similar to a human, without a speck of clothing, stands before her. The weak male crouches down as he appears to catch his breath. As if breathing for the first time, he exaggerates his inhalations and exhalations for a few moments. The brilliance fades, obscuring my sight. Then a glimmer of soft light emits from what I believe to be the male's hand. Rhana quickly removes her cape, draping it over him as she silences his light. Though it's becoming dark, I can see him shaking. The male appears in shock and to my surprise, Rhana seems to care. She kneels beside the stranger and rubs his back with her hand. Softly she sings to him. I witness a side of Rhana I never thought existed.

The noise of a branch cracking in the nearby woods alerts all of us. Following the sound, I expect someone to present himself, but instead the female Noori comes to the water's edge for a drink. As I return my gaze to where Rhana and what I believe to be the last munad stood, I find they are no longer there.

For a brief moment I watch Blessing as she intakes her fill of water. Free and relaxed, she spreads her white wings as if to give them a little stretch. Raising her head, she turns and proceeds back to the woods from whence she came. I see her abruptly stop. Lifting her head as if she's attentive to something I do not hear nor see, I too become uneasy. I watch as her ears move in every direction as if they're tuning in a signal only audible to her. Blessing turns and joyfully trots my way. She appears to be able to see me, though how could she? Her eyes even connect with mine and I am shocked! Standing directly before me is the Noori that in my future, will bond with me. I will become her only rider.

"How can this be?" I whisper to her. "How do you know me when we, at this time, have not yet met?"

Though I know better than to ask for answers that are seemingly unexplainable, I remain contemplative. Lowering her head, Blessing nuzzles her nose against my chest as if she's been doing so for all time, and she pushes me. This creature can touch me as well as see me. I cannot explain why Rhana didn't notice me, but perhaps it wasn't her destiny.

"Thank you, Blessing." I say softly to her. "You have reminded me of something quite relevant. What is destined and fated to be—will be. Now, my friend, I must see what Rhana is conjuring."

Blessing nods her large head as if she understands my every word. She positions her long white back in front of me. Without a thought, I hop onto it. Adjusting myself, I'm hit with another epiphany. In the woods with Mikiel, she found me, but I had bonded with her long before that moment. I am precisely where I am meant to be.

With this profound understanding I send Blessing a message meant only for her. "We are destined to be together. Show me what I must learn." She ascends into the sky. Though the night is too dark for me to see anything clearly, I close my eyes and feel our bodies move as one. Effortlessly, we soar. The air, clean yet crisp, flows all around us. I know to open my eyes as if guided by my intuitive sense and as soon as I do, I spy a dim light below. Circling above the dense canopy, she finds a clearing and we descend. Hoof by hoof, we are on the ground. Dismounting, I pat the Noori on her withers. Her fur, soft and warm from our ride, emits the most wonderful scent. Inhaling this sweet aroma, I hear her digging her right front hoof into the supple ground beneath us, her head repeatedly bobbing. She directs me away from the light that I viewed from midair. My taking a few steps in this direction, pacifies Blessing. No more digging and tossing of debris. I continue traversing through the deep thicket. It's still dark. I can barely see in front of me. The sounds of crickets fill the air. To thank my friend, I turn, but she is no longer there. I inhale deeply, hoping to catch her sweet, heady scent, but it too has disappeared. She has given me the knowledge that I required. I am precisely where I'm supposed to be. Everything that is fated will occur, but the process is what's unwritten. With this premise, I journey onward into the obscurity of night. Navigating through the dense coppice, I travel onward, but my movements are silent, concealing my presence. Amid the cooing of all the nocturnal life, I hear Rhana's voice. Pausing a moment to gauge where she is, I hear her distinctive tone again. Closing in, I hear her and someone else communicating in soft whispers.

"You will no longer owe me any debt," I hear Rhana say. "But no one is to enter Cila—no one!"

"You love this being?"

"How do my feelings affect your decisions?"

"Answer truthfully and you will see," a gentle voice tells her.

"Yes. I cannot explain how this is, but I've seen him in my dreams and here he is," Rhana explains pensively. "What is your answer, Cila? Nightfall will soon lift and all will see him."

"Kune and my sister must know of his arrival. I'm quite certain that our Queen already senses him."

"No. Please, Cila. Only you have the power to conceal him until I devise a plan! And I know you wish not to see nor speak with your sister Drana. Just give me time."

"Our debt will be nullified, and in trade, I will hide him for one month. No more than that, Rhana! Spring will be early this year."

"Thank you," Rhana says, surprisingly humble. As Rhana whistles, I see the munad emerge from the shadows and walk over to them. "This is Hanu," Rhana voices.

"He is a munad! What is he doing here in The Realm of the Mystics? He even looks like a human. But, I can smell what he truly is. Kune and Drana must know this!"

"You gave your word, Cila!" Rhana states, insistent.

I continue to observe the exchange between the two females, though silence has fallen over them both. Rhana glares at Cila and within her eyes appears the callous being I know. Darkness overtakes the irises of her eyes. They turn as black as the night. A chilling ruthlessness emits from them and I see Cila shudder. Backing down, I hear her say, "One month, Rhana, then I will go to Drana. Though this munad is welcome in my home, you are not!" With those words, both Hanu and Cila disappear from sight.

Rhana stands alone. Her golden locks blanket her back. Slender and tall, she fills out her green, velvet gown, as it rests heavily on the ground. I watch her shoulders drop as emotional pain seems to overtake her. While the sun begins to lift the gloom, she remains immobilized. Physically she is quite beautiful, her face is delicate and the features are perfectly shaped, but her personality destroys the illusions of this beauty. Deadly and manipulative, her devious ways have proven to be grotesque. Tears cascade down her cheeks. Repeatedly, she wipes them, leaving a glittery residue behind. I wonder if her pain is a reflection of what her anger has done. The darkness that rose to the surface of her being has separated this siren from the one that she wishes to be near, the one that she wishes to keep all to herself. Days go by and her feet remain planted like they've rooted into the soil. By the fourth day she no longer sheds tears. On this day, I see the corner of her lips rise, birthing an evil grin. Wiping her face and straightening her shoulders, she turns and leaves. I wait and see if she looks back, but she does not.

Curious, I use my senses to locate Cila and Hanu. I discern their energy beneath the ground I stand upon. With the thought of seeing them, I arrive at a warm and quaint little home below the surface. Herbs and colorful festoons of flowers decorate the walls, every wall but one. This space is a quiet nook with what looks like a bed. Sitting on the edge this bed are Cila and Hanu.

Cila is quite stunning. Her long hair is as dark as mine and her eyes sparkle. Her wings are a violet hue. When they flutter about, golden specks appear within them. She is happy and Hanu is beaming. Though it has been only days, a profound connection between them has been forged. Hanu looks at her with love in his eyes. His hair is also dark and his skin fair. His chest, muscular and bare, ripples as he shares her laughter. He gently touches her face. I watch Cila press her cheek into his hand. Silence ensues. Realizing what may occur next, I look around, wondering how to leave. I think of the surface, but here I stand. Amid the heavy breathing as they kiss, I will myself to depart but to no avail. I turn around, affording them the privacy that I would wish. Again, I bring my full intention to leave, but here I remain.

"It's time to leave, it's time to leave," I repeat like a mantra in my mind to cover the intimate sounds behind me.

But again, I remain tethered to where I stand. Time has passed and silence hasn't come. Curious, I glance over my shoulder and see what their love has created. Bashful, I look away, but curiosity overtakes my blushed cheeks and again, I bring my gaze over my shoulder. Free and unencumbered by restrictions, they gratify their desire for each other over and over again. Their exchange is beautiful, raw and full of love. Since I cannot leave, I turn around and fully face the moment. I watch Hanu gently hold and caress every part of Cila's physical form. She melts into the moment in utter ecstasy. Her wings flutter about though her feet remain in place. Her form becomes deeply rooted in his. Their synergy ignites into two brilliant golden hues of yellow. This energy fuses into one. Their brilliance intensifies in rhythm with the sounds emitted by each of them. Louder than I knew sound could be and brighter than I knew light to be, their union, their passion engulfs me. I can't help but cover my ears and close my eyes as their radiance all but blinds me. Amid the deafening exchange, I hear a familiar voice.

"You have witnessed the event," the Light Force states. "You can leave at any time."

Honoring their love and the exchange, I leave. "Show me what I must see next."

Upon opening my eyes, I observe Drana and Rhana on the surface of Cila's home. Drana summons her sister. Moments later, both Hanu and Cila appear before them, holding hands. Rhana's expression is one of disgust. She approaches Cila and sniffs her hair.

"You just couldn't resist!" Rhana bellows with contempt.

"Allow my sister and this munad a chance to explain, Rhana."

"I didn't expect this. It happened naturally and I'm sorry if I have hurt you," Cila cries.

"You asked me if I loved him. Why? Did you wish to tear my heart out?"

"No, Rhana! We did not plan this."

"I never belonged to you," Hanu affirms. "My heart has chosen Cila and she will bear our child."

"Is this true, Cila?" Drana asks.

"Yes, sister, but this child will never be trapped as you and our father were. My daughter will be free!"

Shaking her head vehemently, Rhana spouts, "Cila, you will regret your actions."

"Sister, take my hand. Our father's home was once your home. Come with me, the both of you." Sensing the siren's fury, Drana faces her. "Stand down, Rhana! You will not harm my sister or the child she is carrying."

"Indeed, Rhana," Kune states as he approaches. "Think wisely or your actions might be your last."

"I will do as you wish, my leaders! Not one hair on Cila's pretty little head will be harmed by my hands, and as for the child… whatever it is, it means nothing to me," Rhana communicates, spitefully. Bowing to the leaders before her, she leaves.

I sense that Rhana is still quite near. Her unbridled anger is all but tangible. She's listening while planning her next move. I do not trust her. Thankfully, Drana doesn't either.

"Cila, it's not safe for you. Come home where we can protect you."

"Her words are wise," Hanu says, taking her hand. "Go and protect our daughter."

"Are you certain the child will be female?" Kune asks.

"I know that she's female," Cila answers. Then, to her sister, she adds, "She's special, Drana, I already feel this."

"Then you must do everything you can to protect her," Drana affirms.

"I will go to our father's abode but this child will not reign!"

"At this moment, I only wish for your safety. Come with me, sister."

Drana's words affect Cila and all four commence their journey back to the castle. I sense Rhana then see her emerge. The expression she wears illustrates the level of her scorn. I see her wrath as it rises, altering the expression on her face. This darkness overtakes her. Driving her reeling thoughts, hatred distorts all remaining rational thinking. The heinous reflections of her mind erupt, inviting an iniquitous Shadow to this realm. She beckons it and like a moth to a flame, the wisps of the Dark One approach. I intervene. Using all of my power, I attempt to stop it as it flashes by, but it passes through me. I warn Hanu of what's coming, but I am invisible to him as well. Desperate, I send him, in thought, a warning and I see him pause. Hopeful that he heard me, I fire another warning to Drana and I see her step also halt. Abruptly turning around, she sees the black Shadow heading their way. Hanu rushes over to Cila and holds her. Cila vanishes from sight. He remains. The Shadow is too close for anyone to form an adequate defense, though I see Kune try. We witness the Shadow as it overtakes Hanu. The horrific sounds of his death are haunting. Kune restrains Drana. She mustn't have seen Cila disappear as I have. Drana's pleas are threaded with torment. Each word is contorted with deep-seated anguish as she thinks that her sister has also been caught up in the malicious brawl.

Why didn't Drana call to me? In a breath I would have stood by her side and perhaps I would have been able to spare Hanu. How did a Shadow slip onto earth, then into their realm? Earth, like Churria, has a shield, and similar to Churria, this protection is failing.

As the Shadow disburses and darkness lifts, I am again reminded of what malevolence can affect. Only bits and pieces of Hanu remain. I see Drana as she falls into Kune's arms and I remember that she didn't see Hanu conjure the power to send Cila to safety. Closing my eyes, I use my power and find her.

"Cila is alive," I explain to Drana. "Hanu sent her to your castle."

Drana's anguish repels my message so I try again, then again, and persist in this. After my tenth attempt, I see her head rise. Unable to see me, though she tries, she says, "Meelah! Is it true?"

"Yes, Drana. She is safe, though her heart will bear a scar."

"Thank you, my friend. Thank you," she repeats, while rising to a stand. Both Kune and Drana quickly resume their journey home. Rhana emerges from the coppice. Running to the remains of the being she professed to love, she drops to her knees. Crying, she kneels in what her wrath has created.

"You told me he would be spared!" I hear her plea. Tears streak her face as she rocks back then forth upon the unsettled ground. "He was to be mine. He was to be mine," she murmurs over and over again.

Her pain seems to have saturated the molecules suspended within the air, for I feel her sorrow as if it were mine. I experience pain in my heart and a sickening sensation within my stomach. Shaking it off, I place a barrier between us. This is to be her experience alone.

Overwrought by heartache, I see the truth in her essence like never before, humility perhaps. All I hope for is accountability. It was she who contacted the Darkness or one of *his* Shadows and made a deal with a being who consistently changes the rules. And no amount of pleading or ranting will change the fact that Hanu is gone. Every action has a consequence. This outcome has reunited the last munad with his kind. Rhana must own her actions, for this is free will.

Through her cries as she is wallowing in despair, I hear a small voice. It asks me to raise my gaze. As I do, I witness a new star emerge in the sky. It's Hanu. He's taking his rightful place. This munad can forever keep watch over Cila and their daughter no matter where life or death brings them. Perhaps all the new stars are the munads shifting into their destined form. Compassion guides me and I approach Rhana. Though she cannot see me, I wish for her to sense my hand on her shoulder. We have never been close, but I hope more than anything else that this experience births good within her. If the earth is to remain safe, everyone upon it can do their part by increasing the higher vibration around them. I hope that this simple act of kindness assists Rhana in doing her part.

As my hand creates warmth on her shoulder, her essence seems to calm. "Look up, Rhana. Hanu has found his rightful place in the sky. Though daylight is upon us, we can still see his spirit twinkle as a new star."

She lifts her eyes and finds his light as it flickers and glistens in the upper atmosphere. "Why are you showing me compassion, Meelah? I recognize your voice and sense you. I am not worthy of any good thing. Please, tell me that you've come to liberate me from this wicked form?"

"Your form is not who you are, your actions are. If you were able to love, then you equally possess the light. You have time to right your wrongs. Use your time wisely." Removing my hand, I prepare to leave.

Before I depart, I hear the heartfelt whisper, "Thank you."

Returning to the Light Force's domicile, I see His Brilliance appear before me. Bowing down, I hear Him ask, "Do you understand the gift?"

Confounded, I ponder all the events he has showed me. The only gift I can reflect is the knowledge I've gained.

"I have given you the solution. Dream about it, think about it, and I'm sure you will soon understand. Free will, Meelah. Free will...."

After those two soft-spoken words I am again alone, but not for long. Through the awakenings of muted light, I see a Light Warrior headed directly my way on foot. Holding a bundle, this male is muscular and built strong. He looks like a combatant who is rested and ready for battle. The golden armor protecting his chest shimmers with every step. This Light Warrior is new to me. He is among the batch that the Light Force concealed, even from me. I have faith that these actions will soon prove fruitful.

The serious warrior now stands before me. Politely, I lower my head to him. He takes a step back and bows to me. When the Light Warrior rises, he presents me with what he's carrying. After handing me the elaborate white bundle, he takes a few steps back. Looking down at my hands, I see the package has vanished, but I am now wearing new attire. On my hip is my sword and I readily draw it and see my reflection within its polished surface. Returning it to its sheath, I admire my new garments. Golden armor coats my chest and back. Form-fitted to my body, it moves as naturally as my skin. A sleek shimmering white skirt rests above my knee. On my feet are golden-armored boots. Something rests atop my head. Using my hands, I remove a golden tiara and stare at it, dumbfounded.

"Queens and princesses wear such things, not warriors," I state.

"Leaders carry symbols, so all who see them, recognize them for who they are," the Light Warrior answers me. Politely, he takes the tiara from my hand and returns it to sit atop my head.

"What is your name?"

"I am Teese."

Following his introduction, he bows, again. I am humbled by this reverence, especially since I have never led him. Nonetheless, he views me as his leader. Abruptly, this young warrior turns around as if he's been called by the Light Force. Following him with my eyes, I see who he's joining. In the distance, there they are. The sight of these winged-warriors lights up my heart. All the soldiers of this realm have gathered and now stand before me. But my heart is pained, since many are still missing. They remain on Churria and this must be corrected. Unity is our only hope. This oneness begins now. I summon them home; swiftly, they answer my call. As always, Mikiel has positioned himself to stand in the front. Our eyes meet for a brief moment. He lowers his head, then vanishes from sight. He heard me call for our alienated family members, they all have. I use my powers and follow his trail. He has opened the realm and welcomes them home. Instantly, I attune to their presence as they join us. I am joyous.

Now, standing before me is every Light Warrior in existence; those I've taught to battle and those I'm just meeting. Together we will honor the Light. With this unity we possess the hope of a future. I see Mikiel as he resumes his post, but this time, with Ruzi and Nala by his side. All three lower their heads to me.

I stand silent. This massive group remains in wait. This pause connects me to something wondrous. All life that lives, breathes and consciously exists, with love and peace driving it, bonds with me. My amulet warms quickly and begins to burn the surface of my skin. This is what I hid in the stones of this talisman—the source of my power. It's derived from all the life forms who honor the Light Force. It comes from their faith. It fuels me.

That area of my heart beams, its white light validating this truth. I watch this radiance affect every warrior in attendance, illuminating their heart centers as well. The Light Force, to my knowledge, was the only one who could activate this power source, until now. My luminosity continues to connect to each and every warrior before me. With this unification I attune to their heartbeats; I hear, even experience the thumping as if it was my own. I harmonize every beat, blending them seamlessly together. With time, with patience, our hearts become one unified pulse.

Brilliant white light, our cohesive tie, overtakes our vision. I close my eyes and they do the same, deepening our bond. The source of my powers and the connection to these warriors is concealed in the stones of my amulet. It is separate from me, creating a security risk. Within this space, I know what I must do to protect this knowledge. Our unification begins now. As this truth leaves my mind, I command the amulet to enter my body. The connection to these Light Warriors and this knowledge will die when I do.

Giving me excruciating agony, the talisman pushes through my skin, tearing it. The sensation nearly floors me, but the light from my warriors affords me strength. Ultimately, it passes through my sternum, cracking it. I breathe through the throbbing ache as my body restores itself. Opening my eyes, I see that my pain has affected all before me, dimming our unified radiance. They too have experienced it.

Amalgamating with my heart, the amulet is home and now protected. Luminosity brighter than the sun erupts from my form, connecting again with the Light Warriors, restoring us. Reeling through our minds is the truth of who I was, each secret, every inspiration and all of my faith. I share with them the knowledge from my past, what I have come back to achieve and what we are destined to accomplish. We remain in this way for a spell. As a singular conscious being…we are as one.

In my mind, I ask our connective light to wane, then watch the Light Warriors as it dissipates. The luminosity from our hearts fades, leaving silence in its wake. No longer connected to all before me, I stand on my own, as something new. Mikiel drops down to one knee. One by one, all follow his lead, honoring me. This undulating wave of reverence is overwhelming. This is my place. I am again their leader. With this unity, we will succeed. Moved by their respect, I lower my head to all of them.

"Please rise." I wait for all to come to a stand. "There is a war to be won and a force that must be returned to his rightful home. Some of you have battled beside me at length, while others of you have not. We will not allow this to separate us from unity. You are all Light Warriors! And we will battle for our creator! We wage war in his pursuit of righting the balance! Soon sweat will run across our brows. Soon the war will be won!" The Light Warriors and their mission are the passion driving my words. This connection will strengthen us as a whole. But as individuals, they still must train and prepare for what we will soon face.

Devoted and able, they await my orders. They needn't linger a moment longer. "Resume your training!" I shout, rousing them.

My words are rewarded with unbridled enthusiasm. Departing to the training grounds, they honor my orders. But a few choose to remain and their presence pleases me. Ruzi and Nala are among them. Heading over to me, I see their spirits have brightened by simply being here. Their love, each for the other, is exemplary. Though it's forbidden, it's also quite right, and herein is the contradiction.

"My liege, you returned to us," Ruzi affirms. "And thank you. We heard your call."

"When Mikiel opened the portal…," Nala adds with a pause. "We simply never thought that this day would ever come. We are home. Thank you."

"This is where you belong. Look at your faces, they're glowing. It was thoughtful for Mikiel to open the realm for you, but had he not, I would have. This is indeed your home."

"But who will protect the Churrians in our absence?" Ruzi asks.

"The shield will protect them for now. Train with your brothers and sisters. To prevail, we must have unity."

I see the unease on Ruzi's face. His heart has bonded with the Churrians, especially with the Head Elder. The two of them were cut from the same cloth. Both are patient and wise. But another captures my attention, the Light Force. He summons me. Following His call, I see Him come my way. Everyone is gone, everyone but Him. He seems to have removed me from the gathering. He's displeased.

"Free will is intriguing," He intones. "Utilizing it, you chose to defy one of my rules. However," He adds with a pause, "you have gathered all but a few of the puzzle pieces. Unity, one of the missing pieces, has been realized not only by you but also by me. You will require all the Light Warriors to succeed. But Meelah, do not become accustomed to disrespecting me!"

"I followed my heart. My intentions were not meant to disrespect you. I wish to honor you by being victorious. I wish to finally right the balance."

"You will. But there is a truth you must understand. Once my brother is weakened, you and only you, Meelah, can return *him* to *his* domicile." Taking a step closer, with intense eyes, He stresses, "You possess a touch of *his* darkness. You will require this component to enter *his* realm. You must depart immediately or leaving will be near to impossible! Do you understand?"

"Yes," I answer, disquieted by His tone. "I will not linger and will return home."

"And where is home; earth, Churria, here?"

"My heart will know," I answer Him.

"You are always welcome here, " He replies with a smile. Walking around me, He continues. "Your light, Meelah. You have finally connected with it. Free will has returned you to me with an understanding you didn't possess in your last lifetime. As you are, you are able to connect your light to all of my creations; to your warriors. You have found a part of your solution. The Light Warriors respect you."

"But many of them will perish." After I utter these dark yet truthful words, I detect something else shadowy, Leva.

Though I have not seen her yet, I sense she's near. Glancing around, I hear the Light Force state, "I have summoned Leva. I would like her to explain why she did not attend the gathering in your honor. Unity, as you have rightfully confirmed, is essential."

Strolling past me, Leva bows to her ruler. She places her winged back to me. I afford her immature actions no attention. Instead, I process my next step. Like an intricate game of chess, I must be several moves ahead of the Darkness. Amid my plotting I sense another, Mikiel. Before he passes me, he turns, faces me and bows. I resist my impulse to smile as our eyes connect. Instead, I honor him and lower my head in return. His eyes, consumed by the heaviness of disappointment, drop before he turns around and heads over to the Light Force. Perhaps Mikiel was also summoned. Regardless, I feel like a third wheel who is placed outside their personal conversation. Taking a few steps back, I observe the exchange between them. Our ruler speaks passionately to them. Though much of the exchange is directed toward Leva, I watch Mikiel nod his head repeatedly. Then it occurs to me, though I summoned the remaining Light Warriors, it was Mikiel who allowed them entry. He also defied the rules and he too will be appropriately disciplined. The call was my choice.

I send a message for only our leader to hear. "Do not blame Mikiel. I will fully shoulder his punishment."

"Is that truly what you wish, Meelah?"

"Yes."

"No," Mikiel answers. "I will accept the consequences."

"And you will," the Light Force tells him. "Leva has a difficult time accepting Meelah as her leader, so I propose this: a battle between them. The first to submit accepts the other as their commander."

"I accept this challenge," Leva promptly answers.

"This is not necessary. Our battle is not here, Leva."

"You continue to insult me!" she roars. "Do you think that I am not worthy of this challenge?"

"I am not saying that."

"Then bow to me, Meelah, and accept defeat."

"No!" Mikiel returns vociferously. "Meelah is our liege. If you attended the gathering you would know this! You shouldn't challenge her, Leva."

"Though the exchange between you has been quite enlightening, the decision is mine to make," the Light Force declares.

"Leva, you mustn't," Mikiel pleads.

"Mikiel, stand down. This practice has been utilized to resolve differences since the beginning of time. Allow their actions to speak for themselves. No death will occur, though humility may come. As is tradition, an audience of your peers will be in attendance." The Brilliance closes His eyes and summons all the Light Warriors. "And finally, one last detail, an arena."

Now standing at the very center of an open stadium, I watch as Light Warriors fill the stands encircling me. Amongst the raucous cries of the crowds, I hear familiar voices, cheering me on; Nala and Ruzi are the loudest. Who knew a fight would also unite us. Then I see Leva land across the opening, and she saunters my way. This feels wrong. We should be gathering our strength for the battle against the Epoh, not each other.

"Meelah," I hear Mikiel say from behind me. "Don't do this."

"I agree, Mikiel. This is not the way it should be." Addressing Leva as she nears us, I say, "We are not enemies." Though I believe she heard me, she only looks at Mikiel. I feel her rage build. "Leva, Mikiel wishes for me not to fight you, nothing more." And again, she chooses silence, though her body language screams at me. Her hands, tightly clamped together, are as crimson as her cheeks. Her disdain is palpable; I seem to effortlessly bring this out in her. Mikiel tries to reason with her as well. This effort appears to increase her fury.

Appearing between us, the Light Force hushes the anxious audience. "No death will come from this battle, but a victor will be revealed. All of you will name the conqueror. Whoever loses will submit to the other. Let the game begin!"

"But this is unnecessary," I say to Him. "I don't care if Leva is my leader. It's not about who leads. Prevailing against the Darkness takes precedence."

"Honor my wishes, Meelah. Everything occurs as it's meant to, even this," the Light Force communicates for my ears only.

I lower my head to Him and honor His wishes, though I don't understand them. Closing my eyes, I go within. I feel the Light Force depart, taking Mikiel with Him. With a space between us now, they re-materialize and watch. The overwhelming sound of the Light Warriors is deafening. I tune it out. The encompassing din begins to lessen and I hear my heart beating. I also hear Leva's heart. It's pounding. She's approaching me. I try to connect to her heart, hoping to illuminate this center and end this, but I can't. Something blocks me from forging this bond. My eyes remain closed and my hands are relaxed by my sides. I sense her take to flight. My hair lifts as she roars by. I do my best to pacify her need to fight, but this seems to bring with it increased rage. I hear her sword as she draws it. The ground beneath my boots vibrates. She has landed. This Light Warrior nears me with intent to kill. Though she has been explicitly told the rules, the hatred she possesses for me seems to have cast a shadow over her judgment. I open my eyes and face her wickedness. The hush from the crowd makes the stakes build with their anticipation. As she is about to thrust her sword into my abdomen, I disappear from her sight.

Reappearing behind her, I whisper, "We are not enemies."

"Yes, we are!" she bellows.

Turning around, she gives me a devilish little smile and vanishes. Again, I close my eyes and use my acute senses. I sense Leva and open my eyes. I want to see her face as she begins this battle. In her eyes, I only see shadows of darkness and draw my sword. Our blades clash, the sounds of the fight rouse our peers. With ease, I defend myself, then I recall the fun times of practice with Tali when I was on earth. I fell into the same pattern. I almost sense her watching now. I know what she'd tell me. Defend when you must. A good offense is when you see your opponent's weakness and use it to your advantage. I take note of Leva's limitations and I know I could quickly defeat her. Instead, I vanish from her sight. Appearing with distance between us, I wait until her eyes find me. When they do, I return my sword to its sleeve.

"Are you tired?" she shouts, breathless.

I choose not to answer her. Tali was more competition. I haven't even broken a sweat. She dematerializes. I know she's the kind of coward that stabs someone in the back. I sense her behind me. Twisting around, I grab her sword. In a flash I am behind her, pressing the blade against her neck.

"Do you give?" I ask, relieving the pressure.

"Kill me. Defy our ruler."

"I will not end your life," I answer, pushing her to her knees.

"Meelah, no!" I hear Mikiel shout. Looking up to find him, I see him struggle to come to Leva's aid. The Light prevents him from intervening. I release my grasp and drop her sword at her feet.

Heat and pain overwhelm my abdomen and I gasp. Looking down, I see Leva on her knees, pressing a knife into me. "How does it feel to have Mikiel want to come to my aid?" I hear her ask.

"How does it feel to be kneeling before me, Leva!" I backhand her face, something I learned while on earth. Collapsing onto her back, she flails about, attempting to catch her breath. Pressing her shoulder into the ground with my foot, I stand over her. "Leva, I possess an ability that you do not. My body will heal." Pulling the blade out of my midsection, I kneel beside her. "You, however, will surely die if I press this knife into your abdomen."

"No, Meelah! Leva is with child!" I hear Mikiel yell.

Though I've been stabbed, his words are what injure me. I look at Leva and see the truth of Mikiel's utterance. Dropping the knife, I rise. As I do, I see Mikiel run our way. I turn and walk away. I hear Mikiel as he checks on Leva before proceeding toward me. I sense Leva's heartbreak and I pivot. Vehemently, I fly his way. I push him hard, so he lands by her. I restrain my tears. All actions have a consequence. Landing before them, I extend a hand to Leva. She avoids the sight of me.

"Congratulations," I say to the two of them. "You," I add, looking intently at Mikiel, "have chosen wisely. Creating this child is prudent."

"Meelah," I hear him say softly.

"All of you have chosen a victor…Meelah!" the Light boasts from all around us. Cheers fill the air. I feel nothing close to a winner. Mikiel rises and helps Leva to her feet. She stands before me. She loathes me. This senseless battle has not changed a thing.

"Leva, I never wished to challenge nor fight you."

"My liege," she utters, swollen with pride. I continue to gaze directly at her, though she still looks away.

I don't speak another word. Talk seems futile and useless when directed at her. I simply lower my head to be polite. Swiftly, she turns and marches away, leaving Mikiel in her wake. I feel a tap to my right arm. Thankfully, I see Nala's kind expression. Her gentle authenticity brings a smile to my face. Glancing back to where Mikiel was standing, I see that he, too, has left.

"Did Mikiel mate with that thing?" Nala bluntly asks.

"He did what was necessary. We all must make sacrifices. He and Leva will bear a son. This Light Warrior also has a destiny."

"Whatever she creates will not be like us. She's so dark. She'll birth a demon spawn."

"Mikiel's purity will balance her obscurity."

"Perhaps. But when you flung Leva across the stadium, I was overjoyed! Those white wings of hers became as dark as her soul." Nala quips, "Look, a genuine smile! I haven't seen one on your face in…I don't remember when."

Drifting away for a moment, I enjoy the smirk that has found its way to me. The crowd has begun to disburse, though a small group of Light Warriors is coming to join me. They continue to bring life to my soul. They are the light.

"My liege," I hear Nala say. "May I remain here to assist with training? Ruzi is dead set on leaving with you when you return to Churria."

"You are a skilled warrior. Help them train and revel in the abundance of light."

"Thank you," she says, also with a smirk. "And my liege, perhaps you should change your clothing before departing. You're quite the mess," she chuckles.

Looking down, I see that a change of clothing is quite necessary. Apparel and I have issues. As soon as I don fresh clothing, blood, usually mine, seems to destroy it.

"I suppose you're right. Also, please address me as Meelah."

"Thank you, I will," she says. "Meelah, I thought you should know that Ruzi and Kriyo have formed quite the bond. He even lent Kriyo his spares."

"Kriyo wore them?"

"And he looked fine in them, if you ask me. He filled out his uniform in all the right places. The holes for Ruzi's wings may have looked odd, but nothing else did."

"How is Kriyo?"

"He's missing you. Or more accurately, he was missing you, until sweat poured from his brow."

"What happened?"

"Kriyo trained with us. He was amazingly agile in the air. We worked him to exhaustion!"

"Kriyo was flying?"

"Yes, he was. He and his Noori possess a deep-rooted bond. It is a gift to behold."

"It is," Ruzi agrees, joining our conversation. "My liege, I have more to do on Churria. I believe my rightful place is there. May I leave with you?"

"Of course you may. I have a team already prepared to leave, join them."

"My liege, can you return us so no time has been lost? There is an event that I wish to attend."

"You will return a second after you received my call home. No time will be lost. What event?"

"You will see, my liege, you will see."

"The portal is opening as we speak. You and the others may depart. I'll be right behind you."

Bowing, he then rises. As he does, his focus is committed to the one he loves. Taking Nala's hand, he and she both vanish from sight. This is the first time in a long while that the two will be apart. The wave of change is affecting us all. Lowering my head to the group encircling me, I take my leave. Alone, I prepare to return to Churria, but before I depart there are words I must say to all who remain in this domicile.

Projecting a message to every Light Warrior, I announce, "The fight is not with anyone in this dominion. Our war is very real and quite imminent. Continue to train. Nala and the others who just returned are skilled warriors, so learn from them. They have battled for thousands of years. These Light Warriors can teach you from this experience. Soon I will call for all of you; be prepared."

"Are you injured?" I hear Mikiel ask.

Like always, he's found me. "You needn't worry about me. I must return to Churria."

I leave. But I don't get far. The Light Force redirects me and now I wait for Him. Though I don't see Him, I know He's all around me.

"None of that was necessary. Leva wasn't humbled by her defeat. In fact, now she's angrier than your brother!"

"The humility was both of yours to bear," He answers as he comes into form. "Your unwillingness to battle her was insolent and her overall demeanor is riddled with arrogance."

"I didn't want to fight her because it wasn't necessary. She is not my enemy!"

"She is your adversary. It's unwise of you to ignore this. You must always trust your instincts. Leva will betray all in this realm."

"Then why is she here? If you know who Leva truly is and what she'll do, why allow her to remain in your domicile?"

He grins at me as if I'm utterly daft. He knows a great deal more than He chooses to share. Perhaps He's forbidden, maybe it's His free will. Regardless of the sundry possibilities, He continues to look at me as if He can see my every notion, even the thoughts that haven't yet been formed. I have nothing to hide, so I open my mind and my heart and permit his search. He readily delves into my mind. Nearing a migraine, I honor His need for as long as I can. Then it lifts. His search has ended and again, with a soft smile, He remains before me. Whatever He was searching for was not within me. Is this a good thing? In any case, it simply is what it is.

"Free will," He utters. "Though I gave you hope of a possibility of you and Mikiel, he made his choice."

"It was the right choice, although Leva concerns me. If she knew she was with child, why would she fight me? There is darkness within her. A child born from her could be a mistake."

"She will birth a son and that Light Warrior will have the power to…ah, perhaps time should reveal this. As for Leva, I know who she is. Don't forget all that I've shared with you. The amplifier is already on Churria. All of the puzzle pieces have now been collected. It's you who must assemble them. Clarity will be yours. And Meelah, remember to leave quickly when you return my brother to his realm, leave immediately."

Again, I'm alone. I wonder what He wanted to find. Pondering all of His words, I arrive at a conclusion, to win I must be modest. Simplicity—

"Meelah," I hear Mikiel say.

Again he has found me. Apparently, he has words to express, so with modesty, I state, "Speak your peace."

"I didn't mean to injure you. I have fought alongside you and we have buried and burned thousands of our kind. I must do what I can to assist our Creator. After this war, who knows how many of us will be left," he states, catching his breath. "Do you remember when Drana gave me a gift and I wasn't ready to show it to you?"

"I do."

"She gave me a gilded coin with an image engraved on its surface. The image was of me holding a winged-baby. Beneath this picture were the words: *The child of destiny*. Meelah, it should have been you who bears this child. IT SHOULD HAVE BEEN YOU!" he shouts, pushing me against the barrier behind us. "I wanted it to be you. I have always loved you. I waited for you," he says in a whisper. Resting his forehead against mine, dreadfully, he shows me the moment that he and Leva shared. Both took to flight and quickly they entangled themselves together. But specifically, he shows me that his eyelids were pressed tightly closed. I hear the couple's heavy breath and it sickens me.

"No!" I shout. "If you don't release me, I'll injure you!"

"I thought only of you," he mutters. "I pretended she was you."

"And what do you wish from me, Mikiel? What's done is done! You chose your path and must walk it. You and she have created a son. Take care of your child. Protect him. He has a destiny of his own to achieve. Remain here with Leva. Neither of you should step foot on the battlefield." Taking a deep breath to regain my composure, I include, "You will be a great father. You made the right decision." Using my powers, I move through the wall behind me. I take leave of this realm and as I do, he leans his head against the barrier as if defeated. The pain in my heart is not because our paths were never meant to be joined, it is his fate and who he is paired with. I wish for more for him. He deserves better than Leva.

Leva emerges from the shadows behind Mikiel. Though she cannot see me, I distinguish her essence as it reveals that she heard every word spoken word from Mikiel's mouth. In my mind, I hear one of the many messages from my leader, Leva will betray us all. Fearing that her treachery may involve Mikiel, I send a message to the Light Force. When I know He's heard it, I begin my journey to Churria.

Encasing myself in a protective shield, I fall down and through the dimensional levels. On my crossing, I notice that my attire has again been renewed. I have no idea when or even how this change occurred, but I am grateful for it. Pressing onward, I build speed and am travelling faster than light, nearly home.

Chapter Thirteen

"Here he is, here he is," Kriyo hears his mother sing. At his feet is Drana's niece. Now a toddler, she stands on her own and reaches up to him. Bending down, he picks her up. Readily, she nestles against his chest.

"Look how she has grown," Kriyo says in amazement.

"It is quite remarkable. Your father has named her Cila."

"That was your mother's name," Kriyo tells her.

"She likes you."

"The feeling is mutual."

"Remember, my son, her days are numbered. You will soon have to let her go."

"But that day is not today," he sing-songs in a silly voice. "She gives me strength and hope. How can one love another so deeply, when they've just met?"

"You asked me the same question after you met Meelah. And, I seem to recall feeling that way when I laid my eyes upon you for the first time."

Memories wash over him as he recalls talking to his mother regarding his natural feelings of love for Meelah. That day seems like ages ago, though his love for her has not diminished. Then again, his thoughts are drawn back to Cila and he smiles. She wants nothing from him. Their exchange is honest, simple and uncomplicated. Why can't all relationships come with this ease, he wonders.

"Clean," he hears Cila say.

"What? She spoke!" Kriyo exclaims.

"She did, I heard it. It sounded like clean. I've been doing cleaning all day, perhaps she learned it from me. Or perchance, " Pasha suggests, walking over to her son, "Cila is trying to tell you that you need to get washed. You're quite ripe."

"I was forced to train with the Light Warriors and I'm worn out. No," he says, with a reflective pause. "I was exhausted moments ago, but Cila has taken away my fatigue somehow."

"She has many gifts. I too have been affected by her unique energy."

"Mother," Kriyo voices in a somber tone. "I fear that all of the Light Warriors have left Churria."

"Are you certain?" she answers with a grin. "Ruzi is standing right behind you."

Whirling around, Kriyo sees his friend in shimmering new armor. His glistening breastplate conforms to his muscular chest and, similar to his new attire, he also appears renewed and refreshed. Though his broad retracted wings prevent him from entering their yall, he seems just as pleased to see Kriyo as Kriyo is to see him.

"You left, all of you, and I feared you wouldn't be coming back," Kriyo says in earnest.

"My liege summoned us home," he explains, beaming. "There is still a war to be won. We would never abandon you."

"Is Meelah well?"

"Her essence has been fully restored."

Kriyo notes how Meelah's return has affected this Light Warrior. Ruzi stands a little taller. He even emits a light Kriyo hadn't witnessed before. Meelah's disconnect dimmed her warriors, but now, they and their leader have reconnected with their destiny. Referring to Cila, Ruzi asks, "Who do we have here? This is not the infant that I last saw. Look how she's grown! This being's essence is reminiscent of a species that was recently extinguished by the Dark One. I don't see how it could be possible," he mutters of this youngling's unique energy. Adjusting his stance, Ruzi breaks from Cila's alluring charm. "Time has a way of revealing what we need to know. As for you, Kriyo, several Light Warriors and I have returned and here we'll remain. I stopped by the Head Elder's home and she asked me to advise you that she and Elder Fithro will be present at your house momentarily. Perhaps you should wash up. Your scent is quite fragrant."

"Why would she and Elder Fithro be coming here? I am supposed to go to Bursa. And Elder Fithro—isn't he the eldest of all of the elders? Why does he wish to see me? I'm not an elder."

"Son, all valid questions, but perhaps you should wash up so you can ask them yourself. And please wake your father. He's fallen asleep in his drawing chamber." Gently, she takes Cila from him.

Addressing Ruzi, Kriyo has a few words he needs to express. "It's great to see you, my friend. Before all of you departed, one moment we were flying and the next I saw you react to something I didn't hear or see. In unison, all of you—"

"Went home," Ruzi answers, finishing Kriyo's thought.

"Ruzi, I see that your brief return home was quite beneficial, but I'm glad that you've returned."

"I wished to do so. Now off with you."

Kriyo strolls down the corridor. Stepping into the drawing room, he sees his father fast asleep. Faro's head is supported on his folded arms. With tools still in his hands, he remains in a deep slumber. This sight awakens dormant memories from Kriyo's childhood. The soft lull of his father's steady breath is soothing, as he stands observing him. His father's nose begins to scrunch up.

"What is that stench?" Faro mutters, his eyes still closed.

"I don't smell that bad!"

"Son, either you've lost your sense of smell or you've acclimated to the unpleasantness that's emitting from your entire body." Sitting upright, he stretches his arms. "Are they here yet, the Head Elder and Elder Fithro?"

"No."

"Good! Clean yourself. I'm up now."

Kriyo shakes his head and walks to his bedchamber. Entering his room, he sees his mother sprinkling fresh herbs onto the steamy water in the washbasin. Cila giggles and tosses the remaining herbs everywhere. Her delight brings him joy.

"Good girl," Pasha says to her. "Kriyo's entire chamber will smell fresh."

"Kreeeyo," Cila voices, looking at him.

"I have never seen anything like her," Pasha states fondly.

"Nor have I."

"Let's go, Cila. Kriyo has some deodorizing to do."

Pasha takes the diminutive female's hand and begins to escort her out. Cila looks over her shoulder and remains connected with Kriyo. Her brown hair now has soft waves and nearly touches her shoulders. Reluctantly, she, in her small white robe and bare feet, departs. He feels an odd ache as she and he are separated by the door. If a brief parting wounds him, he wonders how her final departure will affect him?

Putting his concerns aside, he focuses on the task before him. Undressing, he takes a whiff of his soiled clothing.

"They're not that bad," he says out loud.

"Yes, they are," his mother answers from the other side of the door. "Hand them to me so our home doesn't succumb to their horrific scent."

Rolling his eyes, Kriyo stands behind the door, opens it and hands the small pile to her. "Thank you, Mother."

Vapors infused with the clean scent of hinna emit from the heated water. They call to him. Walking over to the steamy water, he crunches the dried herbs under his feet. Using a cloth, he commences the cleansing. Clean, hot water feels wonderful to his aching muscles. He recalls how he stood erect and acted unaffected by the rigorous training with the Light Warriors while in front of Ruzi, but here and now, his weariness sets in. A soft bump against his chamber door brings his attention to the muffled sound of Kreee-yo from Cila, and makes him chuckle. Every time the little miracle utters his name, he feels his body become stronger and his fatigue lift. There is something miraculous about her. With a renewed sense of vim and vigor, he scrubs every inch of his body. He breaks up the hinna by rubbing it into his skin to ensure that he's refreshed. Next comes his hair, and with a relatively small basin such as this, cleansing it poses a problem, but he makes do. Wringing the excess water from his long hair, he finishes by combing it. With the final addition of a fresh robe and sandals, he's restored.

Opening his chamber door, he sees Cila waiting for him. She reaches up and he bends down to pick her up. Voices, many of them, come from the sitting chamber. He and Cila go to greet them.

"Cila waited all day at the door for you, Kriyo. I lured her into the yall moments before your return. Now she has you and I can relax for a moment," Pasha enthuses.

"Kriyo," Head Elder Shria remarks. "I would like to introduce you to Elder Fithro."

Bowing, Kriyo honors the oldest of all of the breathing Churrians. The elder is bowing to him. Weak from nearly 900 years of living, the elder slowly makes erect his form.

"Do you know why we've come?" Elder Fithro asks him.

"Though it is an honor to have you in my family's home, truthfully, I have no idea why you've made such a trip."

"I have had visions. Our Head Elder has had the very same revelations. These images consumed our dreams when we slept and our thoughts when we awoke. They were about the future of Churria. Do you know who sent us these reflections of our future?"

Without a pause, Kriyo answers, "Natiya."

"Indeed, Natiya. Our Mother has spoken to us and to you. It is a rarity for a Churrian to personally be guided by her, let alone be able to receive her essence. Meelah also has a unique connection to our Mother but she is no ordinary Churrian."

Meelah certainly isn't, Kriyo considers. To respect the elder before him, he pushes Meelah from his thoughts. Cila's squirming in his arms effectively removes any further musings about her. While bending down to place Cila on the floor, Kriyo's eyes fall on the cutting shears in the elder's hands and he fuses everything together.

"Meelah has been chosen to succeed Shria as the next Head Elder," Kriyo states.

"Yes, she was," Shria answers. "But a new path has been carved out. It is you who must don my robe."

"I'm not even an elder. I'm a simple Dristan."

"You are more than you realize," Elder Fithro declares. "Natiya has appointed you and even I do not question her decisions."

"When, Shria? When will you ascend? Meelah will be heartbroken."

"Truthfully, I don't know. Natiya has granted me time."

"When will this happen?" Kriyo asks again, trying to digest the information.

"You will take your rightful place amongst our people tonight. But first," Elder Fithro says, snapping the cutting shears.

"You must cut all of my hair."

"Yes. Every Head Elder when appointed, whether they're male or female, must commence their leadership with the same innocence they possessed when they were born. The cutting of their hair signifies this rebirth of virtue."

Kriyo processes what he's being told. Standing by his legs, Cila's intent face turns up at him. Her giggling brings some levity. Emanating from beneath the floor is Natiya's unique golden light. Her luminance appears to tickle the little one.

"Noteeya," Cila shouts. "Noteeya, Noteeya, Noteeya," she repeats, creating a contagious sense of oneness in the small chamber.

"This is your course, son," Faro says softly in his ear. "I have seen it!"

"And I, as your teacher, couldn't be prouder of you," Trall exclaims.

"It's time, my son. Follow your path," Pasha adds.

But another voice, audible only to Kriyo, that of the Timeera, chimes in and reminds him that soon their doors will open and a safe haven for all Churrians will be ensured, provided he takes this appointment.

He considers Shria. Taking her hand, he unites it with Trall's and whispers, "The two of you have waited too long. Be together and with honor, I accept." Then, addressing Elder Fithro, he repeats, "With honor, I accept. But may I ask a question?" The elder nods his head. "What about the other elders, traditionally this appointment is voted on by them?"

"It was put to a vote," Shria proclaims. "Your appointment was unanimous. Natiya made certain that all of them knew this was her wish."

"Kneel before me," Fithro tells him.

Kneeling down with his back facing the elder, Kriyo's hair is gathered together and with one snip, the length of it is sheared off. Shria takes the clippers in hand and removes more. Trall, Pasha, Faro, and even Cila cut off the remaining length of his hair.

Running his hands over his head, he feels less than an inch of hair left. After hearing footsteps, he glances over his shoulder. No one is in sight. But something else is—a golden robe, the robe of the Head Elder. He rises to a stand and with a deep sense of honor, dons it. This extraordinary robe is thicker and heavier than anything else he has worn. He never thought that his journey would bring him to this appointment. Opening the door, Kriyo steps out of his parents' humble home as a streak of light, similar to a falling star, paints its way across the night's sky.

Closing his eyes, he knows who it is. "Meelah."

"Meelah," Cila repeats, waking him from his reverie. Her single word is clearly spoken. Kriyo notices that her robe now ends at her knees. Cila is growing quickly. Taking his hand, she continues to patiently gaze at him.

"You were left all by yourself?"

"Pasha waited for you to open the door," she tells him.

"Cila," he says softly. "You cannot teleport. We must bring you to Bursa another way."

"Seli is over there," she says, pointing into the darkness.

"Very well spoken," he answers, taken aback by her accelerated development. Whistling to Seli, he feels the ground move as the Noori trots over to them. "Is there no one in Drista?" he asks, since, despite all the unlit luminaries, he hears nothing more than Seli's breath.

"They are waiting for you," Ruzi says, landing beside him. "Do you like it?" he asks. Realizing that Kriyo has no idea what he's referring to, he lights a luminary and adds, "The armor for Seli, I made it from the lightweight material that we use for our new armor. It suits him, doesn't it?"

"It does, indeed," Kriyo says, running his hand over it. "It's wonderful! Thank you, my friend."

"You are welcome, Head Elder."

"Not yet," Kriyo affirms, lifting his robe as he mounts the Noori. This new robe fits perfectly as he sits on Seli. "Will you hand Cila to me?"

"No, I'll bring her," Ruzi answers, taking her hand.

"If you're going to bring her with you then I will teleport."

"Ride Seli," Ruzi says in earnest. "You may need him later this evening."

Trusting Ruzi, he nods his head. "I'll see the two of you at the Bursan green."

"Yes, you will."

Ruzi and Cila are off into the obscurity of nightfall. Having a little fun, Kriyo signals Seli to run. Into the cover of night they go. With the thought of flight, Seli's wings expand and push them up and into the air. This is exactly what Kriyo needs. He doesn't have to process. He doesn't think. He simply feels a connection to everything past, present and even the unwritten. He simply is. And, for the very first time in his life, this is where he chooses to remain. Soaring, he moves closer to his providence.

Chapter Fourteen

Finally, I'm home. I sense Kriyo as if I can smell him in the air. Landing on the precipice overlooking Ameira, I realize how much I have changed. I am no longer who I was when I stood at this very spot as a Light Warrior. I am no longer who I was when I leapt from this very edge, realizing that I could fly. At present, I am something or someone else. The one element that hasn't changed are my feelings for Kriyo. Connected with the ground, I feel my attachment to him; to our love. Closing my eyes, I focus on my destiny and as soon as I do, I connect to the Light Warriors patrolling Ameira below me. Telepathically I send them a warning.

"The shield protecting Churria is very weak. Keep a sharp eye on it."

After they acknowledge me, I'm drawn to face Bursa in the far distance, where I see lights. Curious as to what is occurring there, I am pleasantly greeted by a special friend. Emerging from the shadows is Blessing.

"You always know when to show up," I say to her as she nuzzles me. "You want to take me somewhere, don't you? Is it over there, at the Bursa green perhaps?"

After a persistent nudging, I mount my white beauty and enjoy the exhilaration of leaping off the edge. Her massive wings propel us forward. A sense of peace envelops the two of us. I am precisely where I am meant to be. This incredible beast has a knack of reminding me of this notion.

In my state of harmony, into and through the upper atmosphere, I notice Hanu's star. Surrounded by the dark space, his light is quite magnificent. He guides us to what looks like an amazing gathering. Though it is night, it appears that every Churrian has assembled. I know this is atypical. The last time a gathering was held, I was named the next elder of Bursa, but even then there wasn't a crowd such as this.

As we land, I sense Kriyo. I even smell his sweet scent as it dances in the air and whisks by me. I tune into his voice while sliding off Blessing. Immediately, she trots into the darkness. Perhaps she senses something or maybe she did exactly what she was meant to do. I follow the sound of Kriyo's voice. I see him, but in the far distance. Approaching him, I stand behind a sea of Churrians from all four quadrants. Using my powers, I locate Ruzi then appear beside him.

"My liege," he says softly, lowering his head. "I'm glad you made it."

Following Ruzi's eyes, I see Kriyo standing on the platform, donning the robe of the Head Elder, and my heart feels as though it fails.

"I am right here," I hear Shria whisper into my ear as if she felt my concern. "And you, Meelah, you are truly here as well. The crown atop your head suits you."

I am greeted with her warm embrace and I'm overjoyed that she is alive and well, but why is Kriyo wearing her robe? Pulling back, I see that Shria is wearing the white robe of an elder, quite content. Missing a few pieces to the puzzle before me, I'm confused by all of this.

Attuned to my energy, Shria explains. "Meelah, you are now prepared to lead all into battle and Kriyo is equally ready to lead all on Churria. His appointment was made by Natiya and agreed upon by all the elders. And I," she adds with a soft smile, "have been granted time to honor my heart."

From deep within me, I acknowledge her will. Finally, she and Trall can be united and the burden of solely overseeing Churria has been lifted. Beside her, I see the large outline of Lador and next to him is Dalia. Both of them watch with steady eyes as Kriyo speaks. Everyone is here, even sweet Luther. I see his plump, furry body snuggled in Trall's arms. I see Kriyo and I hear his voice, truly, I hear him. He has changed. Now mature and collected, he speaks to all as if he's been doing so his entire life. I honor him for the being he's become. His face is perfect and I love his short hair. I study the audience, his peers, and the elders. They too are enamored. I have learned the rules, the "Churrian" way, and this is not that way, he isn't even an elder, yet this is right. All who share this moment believe this truth, I feel it from them. Kriyo is honorable, honest and judicious, and he will dutifully serve Churria. And now, we are fated to be apart. He mustn't unite with anyone. This, too, is the role of the Head Elder. I push down the pain that tries to rise within my heart. This moment is not about me. Proud and strong, I hold my head high. I give allegiance to my Head Elder.

Time moves forward and I, like everyone in attendance, hang on Kriyo's every spoken word as if he has bewitched us somehow, but one, a small one, has escaped his charm. Persistently this diminutive being taps on the armor covering my midsection. Looking down, I see a child. Similar to a human child and wearing a bright, yellow robe which appears a tad too small, she connects with me and I connect with her. Kneeling down, I sense Ruzi's joy as the child and I bond. Her small hands weave through my hair and I hear her quietly speak my name. Raising her hand, she points to the night sky.

I hear her voice, "My father lives there and he has a message for you, Meelah."

"What does he wish to tell me?" I whisper.

In my ear, she expresses, "Don't deny your heart. Though my father's life was short, he lived. He says that you were there when I was conceived. He wants you to know my name. I am Cila. I have been named after my mother."

In shock, I pull back and gaze at the phenomenon before me. I wonder how she came to be on Churria. She hugs me and I return the loving gesture. Closing my eyes, I savor the moment. I catch my breath. She releases me before I wish to release her, though in time, I do.

She says, "*He* cannot take what isn't *his*." Laying her hands upon my belly, then she adds, "You will have daughters."

"I hope that they'll be as special as you are."

Smiling, she nestles into my arms, and both of us listen to Kriyo's closing speech. Time moves onward and Cila and I become lost in the special space that encases us. As silence reminds me of where I am, I sense Kriyo behind us.

Cila looks up and says, "You two are destined to unite."

I see him. Rising, I stand before him and he sees me. Amidst the abundance of movement and continuous din, here we are.

Whether we are fated to walk this lifetime together or not, it doesn't matter. We have an appreciation of who we have both become. We are no longer two halves of a whole. We now stand before the other complete.

"You are always so beautiful," he murmurs. Bowing, he adds, "Your highness."

"You only see my physical form and this crown, my Head Elder?"

"No. I see all of you, Meelah, your past, the present and the unwritten. All of it is beautiful," he replies, with passion.

His words melt away any rigidity I retain regarding my expectations of the future. I will fulfill my destiny, this I know. I also will not deny my heart. I look into the sky and see Hanu's star twinkle as my epiphany settles as truth. Leaning forward, my lips dissolve into his. Tried and true, our love is witnessed by all in attendance. He is donning the robe of the Head Elder and I am geared for battle, but we embrace.

As our lips separate, he whispers in my ear, "My first decree is to nullify the rule that prohibits unity while wearing this robe."

"Sounds wonderful to me," I readily answer with a grin.

"Will you be mine, Meelah?" he asks in a whisper. "Will you faithfully walk with me to the end of our days?"

I must tell him about Mikiel and what almost happened between us. The words do not form, they remain trapped by my remorse. I feel my hesitation harms him so I meet his eyes and somehow he knows what I cannot speak. He doesn't waver, he continues to look at me, not with anger but with love. His courage brings life to me and as I open my mouth, he rests his finger against it.

"We are no longer who we were. We have both changed. At present, I am asking you, the leader, the warrior and the being who is still blossoming, to faithfully make this commitment to me."

I honor my truth and reply, "Yes, Kriyo, yes! But I affirm that my innocence is true. I have shared it with no other. Faithfully I wish to be your partner."

"You have always been my partner," he answers, embracing me. "I will advise the council at tomorrow's meeting."

"Rhana is dying," we both hear Cila say from below us.

Kneeling down, Kriyo asks, "Where is Rhana?" Cila raises her hand and points into the darkness. Kriyo states, "Meelah, I saw Rhana at Ameira. She was there after the child was born. I fear she is a threat."

"She is no threat," Cila explains. "Rhana brought my mother here. She told us to find you, Kriyo."

"I will locate her," I tell him. "Remain with Cila." I also emit another statement, but only for Ruzi's ears. "Protect the Head Elder. Rhana, the siren from The Realm of the Mystics, is here."

Walking away from the gathering, away from the celebratory noise, I immediately sense her. She is no threat. Rhana is weak and near death. She is slumped in a heap against a humbra tree. She also senses me. I see her attempt to rise. As I near her and my eyes fully acclimate to the darkness, I see her diminished form. Severely aged and weak, she extends her hand to me. Shaking and frail, her wrinkled hand drops. I catch it and sit beside her.

"I did something right," she murmurs.

"Why did you bring Cila here to have her child?"

"Cila told me that this was Hanu's wish. She could hear him. Even though he died, they remained in contact. He must have had nothing to say to me," she mutters, nearing breathlessness.

"Then, what you did was right."

She asks, "Does it hurt, Meelah?"

"Does what hurt?"

"Does death hurt?"

"I feel that your death will hurt less than the pain you have already endured."

"I could have left Churria but I had nothing to which I could return. Drana will never forgive me." Then after a short pause, she squeezes my hand and asks, "Will you stay with me? I have done nothing to earn this, but I wish not to be alone."

"I will remain right here."

As we sit together the sweet scent from the blossoming flowers that surround us, hangs in the air. My enjoyment of them is interrupted by a small warm hand on my shoulder. I instantly know it is Cila. I sense Kriyo's panic and telepathically I provide him with a brief update.

"You have the shape of your mother's eyes," I hear Rhana whisper to her.

This young being's powerful essence brings profound peace to the siren. Serenity washes over her frail form, affecting her breath. Softer and shallower it becomes, until finally…all breath ceases. Stillness befalls her as she dies before us. With her eyes still open, fixed on Cila, Rhana is gone. The aged form begins to rapidly decay before our eyes. Rising to a stand, I take hold of Cila's hand and move her back. Rhana's physical form seems to have caught up with her actual age, for now, she is reduced to nothing more than ashes.

"She is free," Cila declares softly.

"Yes, she is free and you," I say connecting to her eyes. "You shouldn't scare Kriyo by running away from him. He worries about you."

"You mean he loves me?" she asks innocently.

"Yes, he loves you. And we should head back to him."

Silently, I bid a final farewell to Rhana. She brought this incredible child to Churria. In the end, she listened to a higher source. She was, for perhaps the first time in her life, selfless. Leaving Rhana's ashes, I feel her relief, her freedom and liberation from the heaviness and the burden of regret. What Cila did, if anything, I need not understand. This death doesn't come with sadness, it was a release. In the near distance, we see Kriyo. I sense his relief as the two of us emerge.

Once close enough, I gently bring his forehead to mine and show him Rhana's passing. I tell him her final good deed. Cila pushes her way between us and we smile, but not for long…she's is trying to warn me! Before she can utter one word, I feel it! Gasping, I pull back from Kriyo. Instantly I find Ruzi here and shout, "Protect the Head Elder!"

"What has happened?" Kriyo exclaims.

"An Epoh has slipped through our failing shield and a Light Warrior has already fallen! Kriyo," I say, gesturing at the sea of Churrians, "they mustn't return to their homes until the Epoh has been defeated. I will update Ruzi."

"I understand. Go!"

He embraces my path wherever it may lead. Vanishing from sight, I return to the precipice. Below I see several Light Warriors battling the one Epoh. I realize that all of these Light Warriors have never seen battle, nor do any of them understand that this beast's horn is toxic. Quickly, I appear before them. The Epoh uses the break in warfare to dart into the darkness. It runs toward Drista and I realize what it seeks, it wishes to destroy the child. The Dark Force is threatened by Cila. Four of the Light Warriors drop to the ground. I see tears in their skin from the Epoh's horn. Death will surely ensue.

"The horn is toxic. One small jab and the rest of you will also succumb. Now follow me," I inform the remaining warriors.

Taking to the dark sky, we soar. Traveling through the air faster than the creature can run, we quickly catch up with it. We are met by another battle. Grawl and Grutiri encircle the beast. Seemingly unaffected by its venomous horn, the two of them use their massive tails to bash the Epoh repeatedly onto its side.

"This is enthralling!" Grawl shouts, sensing our approach.

Unconscious but not dead, I see the Epoh as it finally lies still. Punctures and deep wounds riddle both Grawl and Grutiri's sides. Slicing my hand with my knife, I give them both my restorative life force. I sense Teese's presence, the kind Light Warrior that bestowed upon me my new attire. Intently, he watches as I repeatedly cut into my own hand.

"Your wounds will heal," I assure them. "But, how are you not affected by the poison?"

"Sometimes, I wonder if we'll ever die," Grawl jests.

"Eventually, all things die, my friend. This creature's search will die with him."

Walking with my sword drawn, I sense Teese land in the near distance, watching. The remaining warriors remain by Grawl and Grutiri. I feel their unsettled nerves. At present, they are of no help to me. They are wet behind the ears, new to battle and loss. They must toughen their skin if they are to survive. But Teese, he is different. Curious how his leader will handle this, he is studying my every move. This intrigue will birth a great warrior.

Focusing on the task at hand, I see the creature as it comes to a stand. Rather than charge me, it runs directly at Teese and again toward Drista. Closing my eyes, I appear by his side. I feel his rapid heartbeat as I stand beside him. His sword is drawn where mine is resting in its sleeve. Confounded, he looks at me. Honoring me as his leader, he returns his sword to its sheath as well. Under our feet is the thunderous pounding of the heavy-footed creature as it heads our way. The beast wavers and I realize it can't see well surrounded by utter darkness. I believe it uses its sense of smell to locate us. This ability draws him to Drista. Cila's scent must remain there, though thankfully, she does not.

"With unity, we will prevail," I say to Teese. "Follow my lead and remember, one touch of its horn is fatal."

About to draw our swords, Ruzi sends me a desperate message, "Cila has left. I sense she has returned to Drista."

With anger I bellow, "NO!" This passionate word ignites the light from my chest. This illumination slows the beast. Although weakened, its unrelenting desire to smite Cila keeps its hooves and body pressing forward. "Take hold of my hand, Teese." I feel him grab my hand and I synch our heartbeats. Activating his center, we collectively emit a blinding light, so powerful that the beast stops. The Shadow consuming the creature lifts from its host.

Quickly, I separate our hands. Our beam dissipates, but the Shadow remains. Teese draws his sword and prepares to end the Epoh. "No," I order. "These beings were once peaceful. Look at it. It is no longer a threat to anyone. Grawl!" I shout into the gloom. "Advise this being of what has happened to his kind. Tell him that I am sorry." Even though it's dark, I see the Shadow hovering above as if in shock. It lingers and I use this opening to my advantage. "This I must do alone. This murky darkness will meet with my light," I say to Teese, before I take to the sky.

Surrounding the malevolent energy with my shield, I encase it. Forming it into a ball, I hold it between my hands and ascend into the upper atmosphere. Above me, I make out the failing shield protecting Churria. I also distinguish the breech. Maneuvering the encasement through the opening, I am surrounded by space. But in this moment, nothing will be freed, as this Shadow, a mere fraction of the Darkness's essence, will be destroyed.

"I am stronger than you'll ever know!"

Emitting purity directly into the encasement, I feel the Shadow's distress and I persist. My light dissolves the gloom. Now, another is before me…the Dark Force.

"And how do you feel, Meelah?" *he* asks artfully. "A slaying always makes me feel wonderful." *He* continues, "Consider your weakening shield. Actually, all the shields in this universe are FAILING! In no time, I'll have my victory. Death, death and more death. The cockles of my heart will soon be warm."

"You have no heart!"

"Actually, my dear, you would be surprised. I," *he* proclaims with a pause, "have a deal for you. Only someone or something with a heart would care to modify a contract. You will no longer owe me your firstborn."

I afford *him* no attention. I know *his* deals and I want no part of them.

"Wait for it, wait for it," *he* adds, playing his own game. "I want the munad."

"You destroyed all of the munads. I personally witnessed your Shadow destroy the last of this race."

Appearing nostalgic, *he* says, "Yes, I also watched. I especially appreciated that cute little vixen of a siren inviting me in. She's sultry and quite—"

"Dead," I state.

"Well, most things come to an end, even you, my beauty. But I like how my brother shined and polished you. Tell me, do you find him to be dull? Being a goody goody all the time is—boring! Now about that child, give her to me and your contract," *he* says, holding it in hand, "will disappear."

Moving progressively back toward the shield, I say, "You're quite the magician." Then slipping through the hole, I pull out my knife.

Barking out a laugh, *he* asks, "What do you think that little thing could do to me? I am immortal!"

"This is not for you," I say, slicing my wrist. "It's for our shield."

Severing one of the veins in my wrist, I ensure that I will steadily bleed. I pray this will be enough. I watch as my vital life force repairs the opening and finally, it closes. From the corner of my eye, I see the Dark Force's open mouth catch a few drops of my blood as they float by *him*. *He* is disgusting!

"You are delicious! But Meelah, you're getting weaker. I see your blood pump slower and slower from that severed vein of yours. Though the suspense here is quite entertaining, give me that child and I'll sweeten the deal by giving you an ageless life."

"She already possesses one!" I hear from behind me.

Weak and nearing unconsciousness, I turn my head and see Natiya with the four essences of the fallen Light Warriors. Three of the honorable energies join the shield and fortify it. The last one...its golden light engulfs me. That light is replaced by darkness. All around me fades to black.

Upon Churria, Ruzi has brought Kriyo to Drista to locate Cila. Teese updates Ruzi. He can sense that something has happened to his liege. Teese, following his wise comrade's lead, feels it as well. About to spread his wings and take to the sky, Ruzi takes Teese's arm and orders him to wait.

"It is time," Ruzi says to Kriyo. "Save her! Save her now!"

Then Kriyo feels Ruzi's words and realizes that Meelah is free-falling all the way down from the uppermost atmosphere. No one, not even Meelah, could survive such an impact. Already at his side is Seli. Leaping onto his back, Kriyo lifts into the brightening sky. He doesn't see Meelah but he senses her. In the distance he finally makes out her lifeless form dropping from the sky.

On his way, with great distance between them, he hears Natiya say, "I could not return Meelah safely to the ground; Bastaine of the Timeera has forbidden me to intervene. However, you must. Go quickly!"

Chapter Fifteen

I see a gilded ceiling engraved with intricate symbols above me. This shimmering golden hue is beautiful and the drawings are amazing, like nothing I have ever seen. Where am I? The last thing I remember is slicing into my wrist to restore the breech. After that, everything faded to black. Slowly, I sit up in bed and as I do, my back greets me with deep, throbbing pain. My back aches, I struggle to remain upright.

Although I'm in pain, something else continues to worry me. I have no idea where I am! I sense that I'm somewhere on Churria, but I have never seen a chamber such as this. The room is golden—all of it. The walls, the floor, the bed frame, all before me is covered in a glistening gold. Sitting on the edge of the bed, I'm wearing a plain robe. I'm alive! Churrians leave their robe behind when they pass on and if this robe follows me to my afterlife, I'll laugh. Again, I wonder where I am. I sense that I'm not in Bursa…Drista…Ralta…or Plai, so where on Churria am I? Tuning into the abundant energy that surrounds me, as odd as it sounds, I recognize it though I can't identify it. A fog obscures my clarity. Pressing my hands into the bed, I rise and fully stand and wow, that's a mistake! My back is riddled with so much pain that it guides me to sit on the edge of the bed again.

"Ruzi," I call with my mind. But only silence ensues. "Teese," I call. But again stillness. "Kriyo," I speak softly and once more I am reminded that I'm alone. Sitting upright feels wrong. The mounting pain in my back is screaming! At least something is communicating with me, even if it's my body. I listen to it and lay back down on the bed. It conforms to my back and in this position I feel some relief. Though my body wishes for me to remain still, my mind takes off like a horse at the races. I recall that Grawl and Grutiri were somehow immune to the Epoh's toxicity. There is something within their blood that, if it can be isolated, could effect a cure or antidote. As the situation stands now, too many will fall. In less than a minute, one Epoh killed four Light Warriors. Even if we prepare an antidote, there are still too many Epoh. We require support. Though my body isn't moving, I'm utterly exhausted. But I have no time to lose, not even for healing. I need my body to fall in line so I can get to work! Stubborn to my core, I again try to sit up again and once more, my body has other plans, as the pain immobilizes me. I surrender. I submit, not to the Dark Force, but to myself. I need to heal.

"Faith," I say softly. "I have faith," I repeat, before honoring my need to return to sleep.

Again, my eyes open, but this time, I see Shria. She's sitting on the edge of my bed, then Kriyo comes into my view. "She's awake," I hear Shria announce.

"I was awake earlier, though no one was around to see it," I tell her.

"You've been healing for nearly a week," she informs me.

"Meelah," Kriyo says, taking hold of my hand.

With a smile and a squeeze of my hand, Shria in her sweet voice says, "I will leave so the two of you can talk."

Kriyo takes her place and sits beside me. At first he continues to look at my hand as he holds it. Gently he strokes it. Gradually his eyes meet mine and we both smile. Leaning forward, he presses his warm lips against my forehead.

"I'd much rather feel your lips against mine," I say.

"Your sense of humor is still intact," he replies as he pulls back.

"What happened? How have I lost a week?"

"You repaired the hole in the shield by cutting your wrist. You should have healed and the bleeding would cease."

"But I severed my vein," I say, giving him clarity. "The hole was too large and it required more than a few drops. I wasn't even sure that it would work, but it did."

"Yes, it did, Meelah," he manages. Then, he rebukes me, saying, "But you nearly gave all of your blood. Natiya saved you."

"And the essence of one of the fallen Light Warriors," I say, recalling wisps of my memory.

"Yes. Natiya pleaded with the Light Force for consent to use the Light Warriors' essences to give strength to our field. Though the Light Warriors offered themselves willingly to the cause, the Light Force had to also give his approval. He was reluctant, but once he saw your near sacrifice, he gave his blessing, as long as one of the fallen four would fortify you."

"I remember his beautiful light as it overcame me."

"It saved you. It healed your vein so your heart could replenish your blood loss."

"But I am not healed."

"There is more," he adds, with hesitation. "Once the Light Warrior entered you, you still succumbed to your blood loss. While unconscious, you fell from the upper atmosphere. Natiya was prohibited from intervening and saving you."

"Then who did?"

"Kriyo saved you," I hear a female's voice answer.

"Cila," I hear Kriyo say. "It is polite to always knock."

"I apologize," I hear her answer.

Pushing myself up and this time with far more ease, I see a woman, not a child. "Cila," I say, confounded by her change. "You have—"

"Aged," she answers with a smirk. "It's quite all right. I am not sensitive about my rapid aging and realize you expected to see the child that you last visited with, but enough about me. How are you, Meelah?"

"How much time do you have, Cila?" I ask.

"I will have enough time to help the two of you right the balance. But again, how are you feeling?"

"I am much better than when I first woke up. But I still do not understand. You saved me, Kriyo?"

"And all of the bones in your back snapped into pieces!" he answers, coming to an abrupt stand. "I did this to you!"

"My bones healed. You saved my life! Kriyo, look at me!" I shout. He now paces. "You saved my life and I thank you."

"Meelah, I have been telling him the very same thing for five days, but he doesn't seem to hear me. I'll leave the two of you alone. I just wanted to bring you a tincture. Shria told me that you were awake. She also made mention that tagers herb is your favorite," she says, handing me a cup.

"Thank you, Cila."

With the tincture in hand, I return my focus to Kriyo. He's as stubborn as I am. The door closes and again we're alone. He, staring at the admittedly unique and beautiful golden floor, seems to be carrying a great burden. Gently, I ask him to come over to me and, in time, he does. Once he is sitting again by my side, I touch his face and bring his attention to my words.

"Thank you for saving my life."

"But…"

"There is no but! Accept my gratitude."

"Meelah, when I heard your back break as you landed on Seli, for a moment, my heart stopped."

"But it started again. Had you not caught me, easing my fall, I wouldn't be here."

"If a Light Warrior had saved you, you wouldn't have lost a week."

"Perhaps this is where I was meant to be. But," I ask, "where am I? And please, enlighten me about Cila. The last time I saw her, she was a young child. How in five days can she be older than me?"

"You, twenty of your Light Warriors, Lador, all of the young Opala and the Churrians, are in the Underground City of the Timeera."

"You've done all of that in a week? You moved thousands to their safe haven while I slumbered? Do you think you can win the war as well? I'm still feeling a little tired," I quip.

My jesting seems to evade his sense of humor. With a serious tone, he explains, "As for Cila, her physical form is incompatible with the vibration here on Churria and since she was born here, she cannot return to The Realm of the Mystics. Here she will remain and here she will rapidly age and die. Gauging by the rate of this process, I fear she'll leave us in about fourteen days."

"I am so sorry, Kriyo. I sense your deep connection with her. She is special."

"All of life dies," he says, squeezing my hand. "You will always look like as you do, whereas I will also age and die."

"Just because I will no longer age, doesn't mean that I can't die. Perhaps both of us will cease breathing together."

There is more to the tale. I afford him a moment. Instead of talking, he chooses another route. He rests his forehead against mine. Closing my eyes, I see a Timeera amid the greenery in Bursa. Then I see Kriyo and the elders. The Timeera shows Kriyo and only Kriyo how to open and close the door to the Underground City, though he reveals it to me now. I see the symbols in his mind, then watch as he traces them against a rock face. After the fifth symbol the rock shifts, revealing an opening. Once he steps into the cavity, another door must open by the use of the same symbols.

"You need to see this, Meelah. The Timeera want you to know these hieroglyphics," he whispers.

Next, I see Churrians from all four of the quadrants as they proceed through the door, but I feel something in my gut and then hear Natiya send Kriyo a warning.

"The shield is weakening! There is nothing more that I can do. Save as many as you can. They are coming your way!"

I see the sky and I feel them—all of them. Panic fills the air. The attending Light Warriors draw their swords. Lador takes Kriyo's arm. He forces Kriyo to join the Churrians. The line of desperate Churrians has nearly made it in. All but a few are left. Jael is one of the last. His fear is apparent. It overcomes his countenance.

"Father!" I hear a young voice shout. "Father!" I hear again.

Jael hears it as well. I follow his line of sight to Dalia in the thicket. The clatter of swords begins, announcing a battle. The Epoh seem to know exactly where to go. Jael runs to Dalia and grabs her. An Epoh thrusts him into the air. The door is closing. Kriyo and Ruzi force Lador inside, leaving Dalia. Then I see Teese. He catches her. Just before the doors close, he passes Dalia to her father. Though Kriyo pulls his head back, my eyes remain closed. I search for a connection to the Light Warriors left on the outside, but something prevents the contact. I can only hope that they survived.

"You cannot reach them. Ruzi has tried over and over again," Kriyo says, aware of my need.

"What about Grawl and Grutiri? Were they warned?"

"I do not know. It happened so fast. Down here, even my connection to Natiya has been severed."

"Then we must go up."

"Meelah, that's suicide."

"Kriyo, find Ruzi for me, all of us must talk. I have rested enough!"

"Your father Jael, I closed the doors to him."

"You did what you had to for the greater good. I am proud of him. In the end, he did what was right. Dalia fled from the destruction of the Epoh and again, she was saved. Jael gave her the gift of life, so did Teese."

"Teese was the name of the Light Warrior who intervened and saved Dalia?"

"Yes, and he is a courageous warrior."

"Is? Do you hear him? Do you know if he and the others survived?"

"I don't know, but I hope so. Find Ruzi while I get dressed. And Kriyo, you did right by closing the doors. Only one Churrian perished and thousands were spared."

"No. Several of the older Churrians wished not to leave their homes. The Light Warriors did their best, but in the end there simply wasn't enough time."

"I have learned one hard lesson from thousands of battles over thousands of years—don't have doubts! Learn from when you falter, learn from when you hesitate, learn from when you waver, but don't harbor regrets. They will haunt you! You saved so many and now we must make our plans. If you feel you could have done something different, then learn from your actions. Don't hold on to what you cannot change."

"Thank you. You calm me," he says, squeezing my hand.

"We are partners, right?"

"Yes, we are. I spoke to the elders. Though the vote wasn't unanimous, I won the majority. We can marry, as they say on earth."

"But we are not on earth. We will unite, and we will prevail. And to think…I slept through everything."

"As you said, perhaps you were meant to do so. It could have been you left on the outside."

"And closing the door would still have been the right thing to do. I would be just as proud of you. Doing what is right can be the more difficult path. Losing a few good warriors is far less painful than losing everyone on this star. Here I am, exactly where I'm meant to be. I am rested, restored and ready," I say, downing the sweet elixir. "And," I repeat with certainty, "we will prevail."

"I believe you."

"Then go. Gather the elders, the Light Warriors and everyone who wishes to contribute. All I require is my clothing."

"My love, a robe doesn't suit you anymore?"

Coming to a stand, I pull the robe over my head and toss it to the side. Here I am, before the being I love, completely exposed and vulnerable.

I answer him by saying, "It's either me as I stand before you or my own attire."

With blushing cheeks, he also rises. The passion he has for me is evident as it builds. His alluring, brown eyes fix upon mine. I feel his eyes consume me—all of me. Stepping forward, he closes the gap between us.

Touching my cheek with the back of his warm hand, he utters, "I'll be right back." In a sultry whisper, he includes, "I promise."

He closes his eyes, perhaps so he is able to step away from me. Proceeding to the door, he leaves. I never thought that my naked form would prompt him to go away, but here I am, alone. Deciding to use the time wisely, I peruse the chamber. The room is devoid of windows, yet glowing. I walk around a corner and spy the most wonderful sight—a bathtub. I turn the knobs, and find it has running water, and even better, the water is searing hot! Stepping into the steamy water as it fills the gilded tub, I shed the old and prepare for all the wondrous new. Above me a war is mounting. I use this moment to prepare myself, beginning with a cleansing bath. Immersing myself fully beneath the water, I am surrounded by heat and peace. As I rise, I see Kriyo coming toward me with my attire and armor in hand.

Placing my gear down, he moves near to me. "I wish for only my eyes see your beauty. Here are your belongings."

"You left to get them?"

"Of course I did," he answers, kneeling beside the tub. Then adds, "I also scheduled a meeting for today."

"When is the meeting?"

"Later," he answers, leaning forward to kiss me. His soft lips press against mine. I hear the sleeve of his robe slosh about in the water and I pull back.

"Your robe, it mustn't get wet."

"No, it shouldn't," he answers. "Will you stand with me?"

"Yes," I affirm.

Rising to a stand, I step out of my warm piece of heaven. He envelops me with a soft blanket. Picking me up, he takes me into his arms and carries me over to the bed. Laying me down on my back, he sits beside me. I roll onto my side with a smile.

He says, "I'm traditional. I wish to unite before we are together intimately. I have the authority," he offers. "Will you be mine, Meelah? My heart has always belonged to you. I wish to share my most sacred element with you, all of me."

"I am yours, Kriyo. I am faithfully yours," I tell him, sincere in my promise. "I wish to share the most sacred part of me with you."

"I, as the Head Elder of Churria, declare our unity."

"Is it that simple?"

"Ordinarily the Head Elder officiates the rite for a couple. Then there's a celebration with friends and family, but I wish to be with you, only you. I have chosen this method. Being the first Head Elder to unite with another, I wished for a private ceremony. Is that all right?"

"When is that meeting?"

"We have time," he whispers, slowly removing the blanket swathing me. He waits for me to answer him.

"I wish to celebrate our union privately with you."

"You are beautiful." He rises to a stand.

Unfastening the top of his robe, he removes the rest of his attire, revealing his handsome form. Every part of my essence loves the perfection that stands before me. I feel his intense desire. I also feel him control it. He slips into bed beside me. His breath deepens and his heart rate increases. I hear it. I feel it. Without touching, we intensify the moment. Our desire increases. It builds as we connect on a nonphysical level. Something intense is occurring. Something amazing is mounting. Passion from deep within me ignites my heart, the very place where my amulet has settled. Radiance pours from my chest and it engulfs the two of us. Kriyo for the first time witnesses my light and readily, he joins it. His warm lips press against mine and our bodies melt into a state of oneness. He lifts my hands above my head, and squeezes them. Our breath deepens as our unbridled passion is shared. Fervently, we remain in this heated exchange. Breathless, we are one. Love has created this sacred union. Love binds us.

Though we both wish to remain as one, this ephemeral moment comes to an end. Returning to the pleasant bath, together, we continue to gaze at each other. No words are spoken and no words are needed. No expression could describe what just occurred. Silence ensues. Washing each the other, again our lips meet, but both of us know that we must go. Our lips separate for now. Drying ourselves, we prepare both as individuals and as partners.

I pull my hair to the side and Kriyo fastens the back of my chest armor. Our euphoric connection further dissipates as our minds ground us for the tasks at hand. Then finally, we are prepared to leave, though parts of us wish to linger. Facing one another, we each see a leader. No matter what happens, we will always have this memory, this intense recollection.

"It is time, my love," Kriyo murmurs.

I choose no words as I still find not one that illustrates how I feel. Kriyo understands my silence. He gets me, and I appreciate this. His fingers threaded through mine, we proceed toward the door and exit. Before me for the first time, shimmers the glory that is the Underground City.

Hand and hand, we follow down a long shimmering corridor. Symbols are engraved everywhere. I stop and ask Kriyo to explain them, and he runs his hand over a few as he tells me their meaning.

"You can read them?"

"I hear them," he answers. "May I try something?"

"Of course."

Placing his hand atop mine, he tenderly guides it over the symbols. I also hear their meaning. They speak of war and of destruction. I turn to him and he intuits that I comprehend them.

"It's so sad," I say.

"War always is."

"Kriyo, you're connected to this place. Where are the Timeera?"

"They are everywhere but choose to remain out of sight."

"Everywhere?" I ask him with a smirk.

"Yes, everywhere," he answers frankly. "Even in a bedchamber, if they need to be."

"I like the saying, the more the merrier, but I wish not share our intimate exchanges."

"We won't. But," he reveals, "the consummation of our vows was documented and glyphics have recorded it."

"What! You knew that they were watching and you neglected to tell me?"

"Come here." Gently taking my hand, he leads me back to our chamber. "Place your hand here, Meelah. Trust me. Listen to these symbols."

I position my hand on the markings of our door. Kriyo's warm hand is atop mine. I smile as I hear their meaning. The graphics speak of us and our love, even our unity. Their meaning is beautiful and precisely how I felt, though I was unable to articulate it. Here, my feelings are magically infused into symbols.

Turning around with little space between us, I whisper, "But did they have to watch it all?"

Pressing my back against the door, he answers, "Next time it will just be us. But this time, it had to documented. They told me that you also were asked to view a similar event."

"They are right. That union resulted in Cila. I needed to witness the seeding of the last of her kind. We didn't create life, did we?"

"I am not saying that," he answers serenely.

"Nor are you denying this. Do you know a truth that you are choosing not to tell me?"

"I only know what I have already shared with you. I am not withholding a thing."

Kissing, first softly, then with fervor, our desire mounts. In the distance we hear, "Meelah. Kriyo." Turning our heads, we see Cila. "They are waiting for you."

The sweet being at the end of the corridor beckons us. We step forward, my mind racing. Truthfully, I would love to be a mother one day but not now. Today, I wear the uniform of a warrior. Soon, I will put it to good use. The darkness threatens us.

I must convey this point. "Kriyo, when you know things, share them with me. Especially when unseen eyes are watching us."

"I thought you knew. You always know."

"This place and the Timeera are connected to you, not me."

"Not yet," he counters. "I feel that will soon change."

Standing before Cila, I note her new silver strands of hair. They decorate her long black tresses. Her presence is still quite powerful. I wonder why the Dark Force wants to destroy her, since time will have the same effect. Escorting us down another corridor filled with symbols, I hear voices, many of them. Entering a large chamber, I see the Light Warriors. It brings me joy to see them, especially Ruzi. Kriyo instantly becomes immersed in a conversation with a group of elders. Our hands separate. Cila gently takes hold of my hand. I feel her need to express critical information. Amongst the encompassing clamor, she asks me to close my eyes and I do. In my mind, I see the puzzle pieces coming together. They create a picture to instruct me on what must be done. I single out the sacrifice that will allow us to prevail.

Opening my eyes, I hear her say, "Kriyo mustn't know. He is not ready."

"I understand," is my response.

This feels wrong. Kriyo's heart will soon be wounded. Especially since Cila will be the one sacrificed. I don't want secrets between us, but for now, I honor her request.

"Congratulations," I hear her impart.

"Thank you, Cila." Then I repeat, "Truly, I thank you."

Cila lowers her head to me reverently. Releasing her hand from mine, she proceeds over to Kriyo. His shoulders drop. Though he may be grounded and strong when by her, soon, too soon, that will change. At my side is Ruzi. He is quite pensive.

"Ruzi, I'm glad that you were unscathed."

"I'm grateful that the fatalities were minimal, but losing Light Warriors always leaves scars."

"I'm not certain that we've lost them, not all of them anyway. Teese is alive; I hear his heart beating."

"There is hope. My liege, what is the plan? I'm certain that you have one."

"First, we need order," I affirm, gesturing to the chaos around us.

I draw my blade. As I do this, I feel each Light Warrior look my way. Holding the blade, I strike the handle against my chest armor. One by one, all of the Light Warriors do the same. The rhythmic clanging gets everyone's attention. Slipping my blade back into its sleeve brings silence. I lower my head to Kriyo and he sends a smile my way. He asks everyone to take a seat. Order has commenced.

I remain standing with my Light Warriors as Kriyo addresses the large group. "Meelah," I hear a female say. Turning to my right, I see Raza. She tries to speak, though the words don't seem to manifest from her.

"Jael has perished. What he did was honorable. I am sorry for your loss," I say in earnest.

"I wanted to be certain that you knew. I should leave."

"If you wish to go, by all means depart, but if you wish to remain, please do. We are all equal here."

"Thank you, Meelah. I wish to stay."

"There's a seat next to Shria."

Bowing to me, she rises with love in her expression. When she finds her rightful place, Shria greets her amiably. Consistently, my former head elder is exemplary in all her actions. Within this space of acceptance, Raza's face lights up. For the first time since I've known her, she appears at peace. Intruding on the sweet moment, Kriyo asks for me to join him.

"My liege, the Head Elder is waiting."

"Thank you, Ruzi. I would like all of you to join me. Here, there is no exclusion. We are one."

Joined by my kind, I make my way to the Head Elder, though he's far more than that to me. As I stand by his side, the Light Warriors line the wall behind us. This Head Elder also honors my kind. Lowering his head, he welcomes them all. Once everyone settles, he makes an announcement.

"I performed a ceremony uniting Meelah and I. Though there is still some lingering resistance to this new reform, here we are—proud and true."

Our positive news is quickly overshadowed by the reality of what is looming overhead. Above us, I connect to the malevolent force as it prepares. We must also prepare. Using this time wisely, I assess our capabilities and the task before us, as Kriyo fulfills his new responsibilities with me by his side. I know that he can sense what I'm plotting and planning. I wish not to be rude, but war is upon on us. The Light Warriors and I soon will face this head on. Truthfully, I want to convene a meeting that will discuss a clear-cut plan, but here, we must follow protocol for the elders and the Churrians who wish to partake in the meeting. Questions regarding the Timeera are answered with still no discussion of what's occurring above them. Are they all in denial? Is it truly pressing to know what the Timeera look like? The truth is, their homes and livelihoods have mostly been destroyed! What about the Light Warriors who were left outside? What of the Churrians that chose to face the Epoh? We cannot remain down here forever.

While I honor Kriyo's duties, I work on mine. I allow my mind to drift off, away from the futile droning queries. In my mind, I see the puzzle pieces that Cila and the Light Force spoke of, and I place them all down before me, hoping for more clarity. I apply Cila's vision and I come up with the same dilemma: we need support. I see the support that we require. I must get to the surface so I can leave and call in the favor. Then I see another piece, but again I must get to the surface to connect with these beings and once I'm out there, the Dark Force will locate me. So again, I must modify my plan. As my mind reels I hear a male's voice. I hear a Timeera.

"Meelah, you may use the decahedron chamber."

An inquisitive Kriyo looks at me. He has also heard them. He reluctantly continues to answer questions to appease the group while I again connect with the Timeera.

"What does this chamber do?"

"You can use it to travel from the Underground City without stepping foot on the surface."

Kriyo is displeased. Perhaps he only hears the Timeera's responses and not my questions. Maybe he simply wishes to not multitask. I remain still and as I do, I hear him adjourn the meeting. Quickly, I ask the Timeera my final question.

"When can I leave?"

"You may leave from the decahedron chamber at any time."

I see in Kriyo's eyes that he's not angry, he's worried. He knows me and has already figured that I'm about to leave. We don't exchange a word while the Churrians and elders proceed by. Finally, it's just me, Kriyo and a group that will address matters.

"Kriyo, may I speak?" I ask politely.

"You asked for this meeting, Meelah. You could have spoken at any time," he answers defensively.

"That is not accurate. Those who attended required answers from you. They are not warriors. They have never seen war. You appeased them. Now we can come up with a strategy." Then, I ask Shria and Ruzi, "Are the Retza capable warriors?"

"Yes, they are," they both answer.

"I will ask Reetra to send his army."

"My liege, the Epoh will take you down before that door fully opens."

"There is another way. The Timeera have offered the use of a special chamber. I can use it to leave."

"But the Dark Force, *he* will find you!" Ruzi exclaims.

"What if she was hidden in plain sight? What if she was camouflaged?" Cila asks. "My father's people were quite keen in this way. I believe I can help conceal her."

"The munad can also use the chamber," the Timeera explain.

"What is your plan, Meelah? Enlighten us," Kriyo asks.

"Cila and I will leave. We'll meet Reetra. He offered his army and I will take him up on this offer. The Retza and the Light Warriors together should be effective. I have figured out a way to separate the Shadow from the Epoh. With help," I say, looking at Cila, "I will do just that."

"I don't understand," Kriyo says. "How do you intend to separate the Shadows from the Epoh? And what will do you once they're separated?"

"I will use the light within me. All Light Warriors will invoke this power and together, we will destroy them. I have already ended a Shadow with my light. When the Shadows have been destroyed, the Dark One will be vulnerable and quite weak. I will use this opening to return *him* to his domicile."

"That will work," Ruzi concurs.

"No!" Kriyo exclaims. "There is only death up there."

"Kriyo," Cila declares, "there is hope, but you must believe in it."

Lador ambles over to his friend. Placing his large, warm hand on Kriyo's shoulder, he speaks his truth. "The battle between the

Light Warriors and the Darkness must play out. Meelah is their leader, not just your partner. She is destined to end this. You must allow her to complete her path."

"I believe in Meelah's abilities. I just wish not to lose her," Kriyo imparts from his heart. "When the battle occurs, I will join all of you."

"Do think that is wise?" Shria interjects. "You are also our leader. The Churrians require your guidance."

"Our kind needs a future. If this plan fails, this star will be destroyed, and all life connected to hope will perish. This war calls me."

"Yes, it does, Kriyo," I acquiesce. Pushing aside my doubts about the Head Elder joining the battle, I include, "Tomorrow Cila and I will leave to meet with Reetra. Then we will join the Light Force and prepare the remaining Light Warriors. I will return to the decahedron chamber with Cila and update all of you."

"Then we have a plan," Trall adds, appearing exhausted.

"What can I do to help?" Raza asks us.

"We are absent two elders," Kriyo explains. "Will you take the appointment and start teaching a few students?"

With bright eyes, she replies, "I would be honored."

"Then here and now, before three elders, I appoint you, Raza, as an elder of Bursa. Shria has already begun teaching by age groups."

"Indeed I have. We are desperately in need of help."

Filled with purpose, Raza treads a new path with Trall and Shria. Ruzi's relief is registered on his face. His being resonates with my plan. The Light Warriors again have hope. Lador stands by Kriyo, at his brother's side. And Cila sees the light at the end of her tunnel. A tug on my armor brings my gaze down and I see Dalia's beautiful dark eyes. In her hands is sweet Luther. Bending down, I pick the two of them up. Luther nuzzles his furry little head against my cheeks.

"You have found a friend," I say to Dalia. She gives me a weak smile. Something is weighing on her little heart. "What is it that troubles you?" I ask her quietly.

"Pasha wants to see you and Kriyo. She said it's important."

Figuring that Kriyo knows where his parents are in this massive city, I promptly relay the message to him. Instantly, his face turns ashen. While handing Dalia and Luther over to Lador, I hear him advise the group that we must leave. Ruzi and Cila join us as we swiftly navigate the seemingly endless shimmering corridors. Each hallway appears as the last to me, but not to Kriyo. I feel his welling frustration as he wishes to teleport, to already be there. But here we are forced to travel by foot. I know what he fears, I know what he prays that he will not see. At last, we arrive.

Without hesitation, Kriyo knocks, then opens his parents' chamber door. Lying in bed with Kriyo's mother at his side, Faro appears to have been waiting for him. Beaming at his son, his father's face exudes the pride he feels for his progeny. The love that has tethered them together as father and son is palpable. As we step into the room, golden rays consume Faro's form. Kriyo, realizing what's happening, rushes over to him. Reaching for his father's hand, he takes hold of it for a mere second before Faro ascends. Blinding luminescent light is all I can see. For a moment, this magnificence embodying Faro's physical and spirit body, lingers. All of us feel his relief at being freed from the constant agony he's endured. His light, infused with compassion, swirls around each one of us. Then he departs.

Chapter Sixteen

Pasha sits beside Faro's robe. This is a vision that brings profound sadness to our hearts. A simple robe, still warm from the life that filled it, is now the most precious item in Pasha's possession. This piece of clothing lies flat upon the bed while Pasha's focus remains fixed on it. Kriyo touches his mother's back and she jolts at being startled. With ease she slips back into deep contemplation and resumes her vigil. Kneeling by his mother, Kriyo also looks at his father's robe. I know his expressions, and this is one I wish not to witness. In shock, he sheds no tears, though I see the effects of his welling emotions. They rise to the surface. First his fists curl into tight balls and he stiffens, as if the sight before him is too overwhelming. Kneeling alongside him, I take one of his hands into mine, relaxing it, and rest my head against his shoulder.

Churrians are taught to celebrate this phase of living. It is perceived as a graduation of sorts. One who has lived a life rich with knowledge must take this next step so they may proceed. All of these notions are fine, but the reality of this separation also comes with suffering.

I hear the chamber door close, then see Cila sit behind Pasha. Pasha leans against her for support. All here have borne a loss close to their hearts. Now this bond ties us together. Our tears are released as each one of us frees our unsettled emotions.

"He's gone," I hear Kriyo utter. His sorrow is woven deeply through each word.

"Yes," Pasha answers. "He wanted you to know how proud he was of you, son. Those, over there, are for you." She points to several rolls of paper across the room. "He made me promise that you would have them," she adds. "He was suffering daily. Though I already miss him, the relief that has come his way makes it easier somehow."

"What will I do without him?" Kriyo asks.

"You no longer need him. Your father, as tenacious as he was, wouldn't have left otherwise."

"He has not left you, Kriyo," I tell him. "When Samuel died, he continued to impart his guidance. It helped me heal. He merely shifted dimensions. Faro has not left any of you."

"Meelah is right," Cila confirms. "I converse with my mother and my father every single day."

"We will honor my father tonight. I want you to be here," Kriyo says to me.

"Is this acceptable to you, Pasha?" I ask her.

"Yes, dear," she answers, still lost.

"Then this is what we'll do. Do you wish for me to advise the elders so you can remain with your mother?" I ask Kriyo.

"This is something that I must do, not as the Head Elder, but as Faro's son, but please…."

Not finishing his thought, he watches his mother struggle emotionally. I answer him, "I will go with you."

I sense his relief. "Mother, are you certain of your decision? Tonight will be here faster than you can imagine. I need to know that this is all right with you."

"Yes. I would state otherwise if I felt differently. I will prepare a few words," she replies, holding Cila's hand.

Kriyo rises and extends a hand to me. Standing, I see him bend down again. He embraces his mother and Cila, who still sits behind her. After they separate, he walks over to the rolls of paper, picks up one and proceeds to unroll it. Watching him muster a smile, I join him. I see the beautiful drawing. It is about us. It is of Kriyo and me as we professed our vows of union to each other. Thankfully, Faro drew me as having donned a robe because to my recollection, I wasn't wearing one. The drawing is amazing. Faro captured our love with the use of color. The detailed account of our expressions as we gaze at one another is moving. In the corner of the picture I see this:

The two of you have always had my blessing. I love you both.
Your Father.

"He knew," Kriyo says softly. "Father always knew."

"He did, son," Pasha inserts. "What you are holding was the very last of his creations. He finished them earlier today. Congratulations, you two. He made sure that I knew as well. I believe that he prophetically saw his ascension. I only wish he would have shared it with me. He did what he felt was right. He worked diligently on everything there. They took two days of continuous dedication; take time to view all of them."

"I will, Mother, and thank you for your support. I must prepare. Meelah and Cila will leave tomorrow morning, and the time grows short."

"Leave?" Pasha asks feebly. "Have I missed something?"

"Yes," I hear Cila reply. "I will tell you all about it after Kriyo and Meelah go to join the elders."

With the rolls of paper in hand, Kriyo embraces his mother again. With my heart, I do the same. Close to Cila, I notice how she has aged, even from this morning. Kriyo's estimation of fourteen days I feel is off, but at this time, we need not discuss this. Opening the door, we meet Ruzi's black wings as they partially block the opening. Turning to us, Ruzi drops to one knee and offers his condolences to the two of us, but mainly, to Kriyo. This admirable Light Warrior and Kriyo share a bond, and their connection is quite apparent. Another ready to offer his support is Lador. With no words exchanged, he honors his friend's loss as he lowers his large forehead and rests it against Kriyo's. I watch as Kriyo's eyes close for a moment. As Lador stands upright, he takes his two strong hands and grips both of Kriyo's arms.

"Thank you, my friend!" Kriyo spouts "But I need my arms."

With a chuckle, Lador releases his intense embrace and we proceed down the endless corridors. As we march along, I take in all of the unique symbols. They are truly amazing. Turning left, then two rights, Kriyo navigates us as if he's been walking these halls since he was a boy. With this degree of familiarity, I wonder if this is where Kriyo was when the Timeera took him. Perhaps that was when he learned the meaning of their writing. But this enigma is not mine. This is his path and he journeys it with courage and truth.

His golden robe swirls with each of his steps. He appears at peace with Faro's ascension. It took me such a long time to settle after Samuel died, but this was Faro's time and not a malicious act like that causing Samuel's death. Regardless of the derivation of his peace, here it is. Taking hold of my hand, he halts his step—we have arrived.

Spinning around to fully appreciate the magical panoramic view, I'm blown away. This is the most breathtaking area I've ever seen. The ceiling is at least forty feet high. A gleaming, intricately decorated, ivory stairway leads to a platform above us. The walls, ceiling, columns are all exquisitely engraved. These decorations are not only symbols, they are images that appear to be moving.

"This is the vestibule." Kriyo elucidates. "When everyone from the surface arrived, this was the first chamber they saw. This room took my father's breath away. He felt the stories connected to every demarcation and they touched his heart. His celebration will be held here."

"These etchings are in motion. How are they doing this and what do they mean?"

"Each one represents a moment in time that was so profound that it altered the very consciousness of the beings of that planet, star or realm. They are moving to symbolize that change is continuous. The outcome of this war will soon become a permanent part of this room."

After hearing his words, I close my eyes for a moment. I have faith. In my mind, I see a grand creation depicting the balance and its restoration. This will be. As I open my eyes, Kriyo is already focused on me. He smiles while touching the side of my face as if he saw my vision, my dream, my hope. Bringing my center back to the present moment, I remark. "This place embodies who your father was. It is perfect."

"It is." Kriyo seems lost in the miraculous creations before us. This place personifies the magic that was his father.

Gazing all around, I also fall spellbound to its charm. Drawn to a specific action symbol, I head over to it.

"It's planet earth." Kriyo explains, standing at my side.

"Yes, I understand it somehow. This represents the beings who lived there at that time, the Atlantians." Closing my eyes, I don't only sense what occurred, I experience it. Breathing deeply, I open my eyes again. "When their civilization fell, so did the barriers of consciousness that supported life on this planet. Earth plummeted down many of the dimensional levels." I hold my finger over the pictogram as it drops downward, representing earth's change, its devolution. I sense Kriyo's joy in my understanding the Timeera's symbols. He doesn't use words. He's as silent as the creations encircling us.

"You are more than you realize. I believe in you and in your vision, Meelah. You will restore the balance." Kriyo says softly, kissing my lips. As our lips part, he appears to be preparing for his father's celebration as he continues to look around at this sacred place. "All will honor my father's journey here. It is perfect."

Later that evening, Faro's ceremony was just like the vestibule, remarkable. The massive foyer was adorned with several of Faro's artworks. Cila's contribution was to choose the creations that spoke to everyone. She chose wisely. Each elaborate drawing is filled with energy and life, similar to the Underground City and identical to Faro. Scores of smiling faces are present. In fact, the overflow of those in attendance consumes the corridors branching outward from the vestibule. Everyone has come to honor Faro. Everybody is here because this is their tradition, but there is another reason. Each Churrian has attended to support their beloved new Head Elder. They are safe because of his leadership, and this truth and their appreciation gives all a common bond. During the celebration, no tears of sadness are shed, though tears from hilarity fall in abundance. Anecdotes from the centuries of Faro's life are recounted. He was such a character. Through his creative passion, he brought happiness and joy to those who knew him and to those who did not. During this commemoration, I meditate on how one life truly affects many. I also observe the two dedicated beings who faithfully remain beside Kriyo. Though I haven't left his side, Ruzi and Lador also stand close to him. This brings peace to me. In the days ahead I am assured that Kriyo will have support. He will have powerful beings that will fight beside him and protect him. Then Cila approaches. Her demeanor is always soft and kind. She lowers her head to Kriyo then to me. Her hair is now more gray than black. Wrinkles crease her face.

"Cila, thank you," Kriyo says to her. "In the short time that you have been in our lives, you truly saw my father for who he was. These pieces of his art are perfect. I am grateful."

"You are welcome, Kriyo. Meelah," she continues, addressing me, "I must rest. I will see you at first light."

As I nod, she weaves back through the crowd. First light? I wonder how she'll know when dawn has arrived. Here, beneath the surface, all is continuously illuminated by glowing light. How does one tell when a new day has arrived?

"You'll know," Kriyo answers.

"How are you privy to what I'm thinking?"

"I know you, Meelah," he answers. "We should leave."

"Are you certain you want to depart? The celebration is still ongoing."

"I wish to spend some time with you," he whispers in my ear. "If my father taught me anything, it is that all we possess are moments. I want to create another moment with you."

Nothing could restrain my smile. Navigating through the crowd, we make our way over to Pasha. As if she already knows that we wish to leave, she lowers her head to the both of us. Returning the kind gesture, we do the same. Then we begin our journey through the mass of robed Churrians. Behind them, we see a gaggle of the young Opala. Blissful and very much at home in this incomparable place, they are giggling while communicating in our language. As we pass them, all bow to the two of us. We return the honor, and lower our heads to them. They have been given a second chance at life, all who have sought refuge. Continuing on, I try to place what happened to the Opala. But it becomes difficult. The very same devastation that brought them here to Churria, is now on the surface above us. Focusing on my breath and on Kriyo's warm hand on my back, I immerse myself in the present moment. On our walk, I take in the beauty and the uniqueness of what we now call home. This offers a wonderful distraction. The symbols, each different, never grow old. Kriyo pauses and with his finger he points above us. On the ceiling I see the carvings. Two of them are being etched into form before our eyes. To me, these lines depicting some event are magically manifested, but I see in Kriyo's face that he knows the creator of this magnificence. His eyes are bright and in their reflection is the outline of a being that I assume is a Timeera. All of Kriyo's senses seem fully attuned to the vibration down here and this connection fortifies him. He's alive with vitality. The Timeera and he are deeply bonded.

Without words, we continue. The silence between us deepens our union and amidst this quiet peace, we arrive at our chamber. Sweeping me off my feet and into his arms, he opens the door and brings me in.

As the door closes behind us, he says, "I cannot know what tomorrow will bring, but here and now we have each other."

"But are we alone this time?" I ask, raising a brow.

"Only our heartbeats and our eyes bear witness, I promise you."

Gently, he lowers me onto our bed. As our lips softly meet, the lids of our eyes close. Our exchange is deeper than the mere physical. Our clothing is shed, then our bodies connect and we become one. With fire and heat propelling us, our exchange intensifies and our passion blazes. With heavy breathing and sweaty forms, we share our love, over and over again. If moments are all we have, then this is one we will both cherish. None of us can control the unwritten future, but here, immersed in the present, we create something special.

In repose, we nestle together. As I rest my head upon his chest, I hear his heartbeat. Steadily, it relaxes. This soft rhythmic beating brings with it our need to rest. In our sacred place, we end the day, though swiftly, too quickly my body wakes as if it hears the ring of my old alarm clock. My movements rouse Kriyo.

"It's morning and you are here with me," he says happily while stretching.

"How do you know it's morning? For all we know, it's still last night."

His alluring brown eyes connect with mine, intensely. He wants our lips to touch, I feel this, I also yearn for this closeness. He restrains himself, though I hardly can. The skin of my lips aches to touch him, but we remain unmoving, mesmerized. This space, is my home, my favorite place, amongst all that exists. He yields. Kissing me softly, then with passion, he whispers, "I want every night to be like last night, but the dawn of a new day is upon us. Can you sense it?"

"Perhaps," I answer, closing my eyes. "But perhaps I don't want to greet the day." After I hear a soft knock at our chamber door, I add, "Though apparently I must."

"Apparently, we must," Kriyo says as he dresses. "Cover up. I'll see who it is."

Just like that, fate has moved us forward. I know who's waiting on the other side of the door. I also know that this incredible time with Kriyo must end—all things do. While Kriyo is engaged in deep dialogue, I wrap the blanket around me and search for my apparel. It seems to have landed everywhere. Padding with bare feet, I proceed to the tub and prepare myself. While I'm lacing up my boots, Kriyo returns with two small cups in hand.

"Cila wants you to drink this. Don't ask what it is because she told me three times and three times I forgot it."

"The smell is horrible!"

"Yes, it is. That's probably the reason why I didn't retain its name. It burns my nose," he says as he grimaces, and hands it to me.

"It's making my eyes shed tears!"

"Drink it, Meelah. Cila only wants to protect us."

"Us?" I ask. "How will my drinking this protect you?"

"If this, whatever it is, shields you from danger, then it protects my heart."

How could I resist that? Quickly, I down the liquid that smells worse than a sewage plant. In truth, it's not bad, but what it brings up is foul. I belch, not just a little burp, but the sound that emits from my mouth has come all the way from my stomach. The air it brings up stinks as well. Astounded, I look at Kriyo and see that he finds humor in my newfound ability.

"Watch out, if I need to burp again, the mere scent of it may drop you. What is the other tincture? I require something to wash the vile residue away."

"No, no, no," he answers, lifting his cup above his head. "Cila insisted you mustn't have anything else for the herbs to be effective."

"Great! If my morning begins with this, how will it end?"

"I'm sorry. I should have helped out with a better beginning," he opines soulfully. Downing his herbal elixir, Kriyo leans in and gives me kiss, but he doesn't linger. After a quick peck, he says, "I love you."

"I get it! Next time kiss me goodbye before you hand me sewage. But seriously, I must go. I sense that it's time."

"Give me a moment to change my robe and prepare. I wish to be there when the two of you leave," he says, beginning to dress. "Meelah, I rinsed my mouth out three times. I still taste that concoction."

"You still taste it? I'm the one who drank it! It's still in the back of my throat, and I'm also breathing it!"

"Perhaps it will keep the Darkness away from you."

"It keeps you away from me and you are not the Dark," I readily reply.

"Nothing will keep me away from you, Meelah—nothing!"

"Then kiss me."

Sauntering over to me, he gently guides my step backward to the wall behind me. Taking both of my hands in his, he raises them above my head. First, he kisses my neck, both sides, then my forehead.

"Be safe and return home," he whispers.

"I will return to you, but seriously, you can't kiss my lips?"

With a laugh, he asks, "Must I do this?" Silence is my answer. Leaning in, he brings his lips to mine. He kisses me while squeezing my hands. As he gradually detaches, he gazes into my eyes.

"And I love you," I avow in a soft voice. "Kriyo, it is time. I must go."

Releasing my wrists, he briefly rests his forehead against mine. Pulling his warm face away, he hands me my belt and sword. I have hope that I'll not need it, though we both know it will soon be put to use. I see in his eyes that he doesn't want me to go. With an inhalation, he rolls his shoulders back and adjusts his stance. Poised and ready is my Head Elder. He opens our chamber door and does what he must—he lets me go. Passing over its threshold, I am surprised at finding Cila there. Wearing a smile, she takes hold of my hand and halts my step. In my mind, she shows me the illusion that she intends on using once we leave. This disguise has protected her kind for thousands upon thousands of years. Why didn't they utilize this? It could have saved them all from destruction.

"No," Cila answers. "They are precisely where they are meant to be. They chose their reality as I have chosen mine."

"We have all chosen our destinies," Kriyo states. "The Timeera are waiting. Follow me."

"Meelah, Cila, son, please wait," we hear Pasha shout. "Please wait," she entreats, nearing breathlessness, as she joins us. "Hurry, we're going to miss them."

Pasha has brought an entourage. Swiftly moving our way, they are my family. Shria, Trall, Raza, Lador and Ruzi make up the motley crew. Once they are standing before us, no one utters a word and none is needed. Kriyo takes my hand and we proceed down a different corridor. This hallway has an end. Massive double doors await us.

I am ready. Kriyo signals for me to step forward. I must open the doors to the decahedron chamber. He doesn't voice this truth, though somehow, I know it. Standing before the magnificent doors, I tell the Timeera that I'm ready to live my destiny and right the balance. With that intention, both doors hinge open.

Nearby, Ruzi moves his fist over his heart. "I have faith in you, my liege. I will see you when you return."

As I nod my head in acknowledgement, I also hear, "Be safe, my daughter."

Someone takes my hand. I see that it's Shria. Gently smiling at me, she expresses, "Meelah, I know what and who you are. I'm proud of you. Give my regards to Reetra. I love you."

"I love you, too, Shria. I will extend your regards."

"Meelah, return home to us," Trall adds in his sweet voice.

"I will. Take care of Shria in my absence."

"Of course."

Pasha looks intently at me. I feel the pain she's carrying from Faro's ascension. Lowering my head to her, I send her strength. It means a great deal that she has chosen to see me off. Lador, already by Kriyo's side, lowers his head when our eyes meet. The group sends Cila off as well. As I overhear their thoughtful words, I use this time to be with Kriyo. Taking my hand, he leads me into the odd-shaped chamber. This space is actually in the shape of a decahedron. Ten high walls, in this precise geometric shape, surround us. Each chamber is more impressive than the last. Even these walls are filled with hieroglyphics. As I run my fingers over them, tracing the outline of a few of the symbols, I feel Kriyo looking at me. I see uncertainty in his eyes.

"Kriyo, I will return. I have seen the war that I will fight."

"I must have faith," he answers as he takes a step back. "It is here and now that I honor your destiny, Meelah."

Cila moves toward me. Still fixed on Kriyo, I watch him reluctantly turn and leave. Cila takes my hand and I am reminded of the task before us. Together we step forward. Now standing in the very center of the chamber, we hear the doors close behind us.

"Your breath still smells of the gudra root. That's good," Cila tells me.

"It almost made Kriyo vomit. What is its purpose?"

"Soon you will see. Take my hand, Meelah, and never let it go—no matter what!"

As her stern words settle in the room, the walls begin to circle around us. The floor on which we stand, thankfully remains stationary. I focus on it. Spinning, faster than my mind and eyes can perceive, the walls begin to emit a humming sound. This resonance increases in pitch until it nearly pierces my eardrums. I glance at Cila, her eyes are closed. She stands at peace next to me. How is it that she's completely unaffected by the whipping walls? The effects of centrifugal force shift my feet. My hair flies in every which direction, but strangely, Cila's does not. The disarray persists and I'm drawn to consider her. Though she is silent, I begin to understand the lesson. Moving my flinging hair from my line of sight, I allow this realization to fully come into form. The chaos is a mere reflection of my lack of direction. Amid the pandemonium, I close my eyes and ground my inner self. With this simple action, everything stops. I hear no sound, I sense no movement. Nothing exists in this space. Still hand and hand with Cila, I have a sense of understanding wash over me and I know precisely where we are. We are in the space between space. I must focus on my destination for it to become our reality. But Cila releases her hand from mine. Before processing that, I feel her take hold of my hand again. Peace is registered on her face. With our hands again reunited, I allow my mind to bring us home.

Chapter Seventeen

Before I open my eyes, I hear. "Why have you removed the munad from the protection of the Timeera?" the Light Force asks sternly.

"It was necessary," Cila answers.

"I will answer Him," I say to Cila. "This is what must be done! To be victorious, we require more warriors."

"No, Meelah!" He yells, completely out of character. "All that you require was already in your possession!"

"I know what I'm doing! Cila has shown me a way. Have you lost faith in me?"

"This is not about you! Light is losing its power. I am losing my power. If my brother prevails, then not only will this universe be lost—all will be. Our only hope lies in the being that stands beside you."

For the second time, Cila lets go of my hand and walks over to the Light. Without words she gazes intently into his eyes. Keenly, I watch as their silent exchange intensifies. Slowly she extends both of her arms and takes hold of the Light Force's hands. Both close their eyes. Listening to a soft voice circling around me, I also close mine.

Opening my eyes, I am somewhere else! I am in the very middle of a desert. There is a being heading toward me. Shading my face from the blinding light streaming from above, astonishment makes my mouth fall open. Closing my mouth, I see him continue my way. It is—Jael. With a calm demeanor, he appears as if he has been waiting for me. I am quite surprised by his appearance. To my knowledge, he died saving Dalia. Perhaps this is a mirage; maybe I'm dreaming. Soon, I will know.

Now, he is standing before me, oddly with a genuine smile. He did die. I can see through his energy body. He bows to me. Returning the gesture, I keep my guard up. His form holds no threat to me, but old habits die hard. Waiting for him to speak, I notice that he has changed. Softer and with a kind countenance, he seems to have embraced truth, whereas in life he only seemed to embrace anger. He is no longer who he was. I wait. I wish to know why he's here. I watch as he prepares his words, and I see he's ready. Connecting his eyes to mine and righting his stance, he begins.

"I asked to meet with you. Though you probably would have expected someone else, Samuel or Faro perhaps, I have chosen to convey this message to you."

"What message?"

"My message is a warning."

"What warning?" I ask cautiously.

"All things are not as they appear."

"And you? You have chosen to deliver this warning to me. Why should I believe you? You have only hated and resented me!

Though it is apparent that there is finally truth to you, why would I trust anything that you have to say? Perhaps this too is a lie!"

"Because he has come here in full contrition," I hear Samuel state from behind me.

Turning around, my eyes behold the most wonderful sight—my true father. My heart brings him to me and without a thought, I wrap my arms around him and he embraces me. Pulling back from our encirclement, I sense that he too has manifested before me with a purpose. In his soft brown eyes, I see another within their reflection: Faro. Standing on two healthy legs, exuberant, and bright-eyed, he lowers his head to me. Then he explains his concerns.

"You have not taken the time to see my drawings. They too will validate Jael's warning."

"Meelah," Samuel says. "Nothing is what it seems. Nothing! You are not safe here!"

"Take this," Jael exclaims, pressing a vial into the palm of my hand.

"What is this?"

"It is his essence," Samuel answers.

"Use it wisely," Faro adds.

"But this doesn't belong to you, Jael. Your soul belongs to the Creator."

"The Creator has honored my free will. This is now mine to give you. This is my penitence," he answers.

"You owe me nothing. You gave your life to save Dalia. That was your atonement."

"That reconciliation was between me and my maker. The vial in your hand is the resolve between us. This is my wish, please honor it," he adds with great humility.

"And what will happen to you?"

"Truthfully, I do not know."

"Meelah!" Faro exclaims. "You will soon have need of what you hold. Consider my drawings! Here, nothing is what it seems!"

As their words settle, I study all three of their faces and can see their truth, honor and their virtue. It's healing to witness Jael's choice played out. I never thought he would give me his essence. This is the ultimate of gifts. As I face them, I speak from my heart. "I love you all." As I direct my words to each one of them, I especially stress their import to Jael. Yet, in this special space, I can sense that I have already lingered too long.

"You must wake up, Meelah! It has begun!" Samuel bellows.

As I feel the truth in that final warning, all three Churrians begin to fade from my sight. Bowing to each of them, I pause before Jael, though it hardly seems adequate for what he has gifted to me. Slipping his final honor into my boot, I wake myself and I see it. The Dark Force is in *his* brother's domicile. *He* holds Cila. A knife is pressed against her throat. *He* waited for me to return from my trance. *He* wanted me to witness *his* heinous act.

Light Warriors, more than I can count, lie dead. More, perhaps the remains of my army, go after the Darkness with vengeance. Effortlessly, *he* tears them to shreds with *his* one spare hand. I scan all around me and finally I see the Light Force. He lies unconscious and I race to Him. Shaking Him, I entreat Him to awaken, but to no gain.

"He's not dead!" I hear the Darkness shout. "I cannot kill Him, though I wish to. But, I will kill this munad."

I sense Mikiel and Nala somewhere behind me. Experienced in combat, they know better than to run toward death like the young Light Warriors have. With my mind, I tell all to pull back.

Many of the Light Warriors do, but those who do not, act as my distraction. With a surge of power arising from deep within me, I thrust the Dark Force back. Cila drops to the ground and I ask Mikiel and Nala to protect her. The Darkness is weak and I use this to my advantage. I fly at *him* with my sword drawn. Disappearing from my sight, the knife in *his* hand drops. As if it's falling in slow motion, I see blood run off its blade. Cila has been wounded. As the dagger clatters on the ground, I see that *he* left something else behind—two Epoh. The fear that Cila lies dead is replaced by the two toxic horns that are coming my way! Grounding myself, I close my eyes and feel my connection to the abundant light that encircles me. I sense Jael; I feel Samuel and Faro, too. They watch with fear. But I am not afraid. Connecting to everything I can draw from, my chest expands with a burst of pure white light emitted from it. Quickly, I open my eyes and see the Shadows rise from their hosts. I take to the air and blast them with luminosity. Their shrieks give me pleasure and I persist until silence ensues. Once I am certain that they have been destroyed, I fly down to Cila. Nala has her hands over the gash to her neck. Blood overflows from the small spaces between her fingers. Still alive, Cila allows me to peer into her eyes and within them, I see another behind me, Leva. She draws her sword.

"I am not the enemy, Leva!"

"Mikiel," she shouts. "Watch as I slay her!"

Mikiel materializes behind her. Lifting his sword above his head, he thrusts it downward and cuts off one of her wings. Appearing by my side, he prepares to protect me. Disfigured, Leva has no words. Perhaps the sheer pain has stolen them. Possibly it's the wickedness as it rises within her. Finally, we see it consume her eyes. Darker than twilight, her eyes reflect the pure evil that controls her. Screaming with sheer rage, she disappears from sight and again I focus on Cila. As I take the vial from my boot, she places her cold hand upon mine and points to my left. Leva again appears and this time behind Mikiel. Before I can warn him, before he senses her presence, she runs her blade through his back. I see it coming through him. Removing her blade, again, she is gone, but Mikiel, my Mikiel, falls to his knees.

The two are dying. Both of them possess destinies, but one and only one will leave with me. Cila expresses to my mind that she wishes to spare Mikiel. She knows that days only remain on her path. I hear her plea, I hear her beg, I see her tears, but I pour Jael's essence into her mouth, then I slice my wrist and drip my blood into her wound. This was Jael's ultimate gift and I wish, selfishly, I had another.

"Nala, go to Mikiel," I say, trying to remain focused.

As soon as I see the color return to her skin, I rush over to Mikiel as well. Already in Nala's arms, he's dying. Closer to death than to life, he can barely breathe. He protected me to his death. Tears fall unstoppable from my eyes, though I remain silent and still. Taking Nala's place, I touch his face and with the little strength he has, I see him lean into my hand.

"Save him," he mutters.

"Save who?" I ask.

"My son. Take him with you. Raise him…please."

"Where is he?"

"Nala knows."

My heart feels as though it's breaking in two. The life within him begins to leave. Still looking at me…then, he's gone. He's gone! HE'S GONE! Not wishing to let him go, I hold him close to me as I scream. Overwrought by sorrow, I rock back and forth while still holding him.

The Light Force comes to and rises to a stand. He takes in all the death around Him. I sense Him look at me as I hold Mikiel.

"Is this my fault?" I cry. "I shouldn't have returned here. Look at this. Look at him," I plead. But as anger rises again, I shout, "Answer me! Is this my fault?"

"Not exactly," the Light replies. His odd response causes me to question the meaning. He helps Cila to her feet. Her injuries have healed and her form appears strong. Her youth has also returned. Her hair is again all black and the skin of her face is bright and youthful. I watch as she yanks her hand away from the Light Force's grasp. She seems to discern something that I do not.

Then I hear, "You are more resourceful than I thought. They deeded you a soul." He mutters, wiping dust and debris from His pants. "Go!" He orders Nala, also dismissing the remaining Light Warriors.

With the wave of his hand, all of the death vanishes, all but Mikiel's. I feel that he too will disappear from my sight and from my grasp, so I hold on to him for as long as I can, but he too is taken away. His sword remains. I slide it next to me and in my mind, I rewind the last few moments in an attempt to understand what has occurred. Then I hear Jael's words as if he's whispering them into my ears. "Things are not as they appear." Then I hear my father's voice repeat, "Things are not as they appear."

"He lives!" I shout, opening my eyes.

My words baffle *him*. *His* walk comes to an abrupt halt. I see a dagger partially concealed in *his* sleeve. Rising to a stand, I fly at *him* and seize the knife. I know exactly who *he* is.

I shout, "None of this is real! " With the illusion torn, darkness churns around us. Cila again takes my hand. This time our connection is powerful.

"No!" I hear the distinct voice of Darkness bellow.

"Eat this quickly!" Cila demands, while pressing something into my mouth. I begin to chew and immediately, I recognize the revolting taste. "Never let my hand go!" I hear her shout as we continue to fall into the chaotic darkness.

"You let go of my hand!" I state, swallowing the sickening chewy mass. "Why did you do that?"

"You needed to be tested and I required Jael's soul. Now, the purpose of the gudra roots," she adds, changing the subject. "*He* will not see, sense or even smell you. You, Meelah, you have vanished from the mind of the Dark Force."

Strange light encases the two of us. I hear her speaking in a language I have never heard. Usually, I am able to decipher a foreign dialect, but these words are unique. In truth, they are as distinctive as the being beside me.

Still falling, but no longer connected to *him*, I know where my heart wishes to go. I turn again to Cila. Nodding her head in agreement, she arrives, with me. Still holding hands, I order Leva to reveal herself.

In the domicile of the Light Force, the actual one, not another illusion, I call to her again. The Light Force materializes and both Cila and I take His hand and reveal the trickery of His brother. I watch the suffering in His face as He learns what we just experienced.

"Leva cannot be trusted!" I exclaim.

"I know," is His response. "She has been banished."

"But Leva will try to kill him!" I shout.

"She cannot return!" He proclaims. His words bring Him pain, reflected in His countenance. "This is no longer her home. And my brother, *he* has no powers here. At present, even *he* must have permission to enter my realm."

While listening to the Light Force, I sense Mikiel before my eyes spot him. "All is as it should be," I hear the Light state. And I understand His statement. Cila required Jael's offering and I have chosen Kriyo.

Mikiel, with a newborn baby cradled in his arms, comes into view. My heart fills with relief, but also curiosity. How did Leva bear a child that quickly? I wonder.

"You wished to see me," Mikiel says to his Brilliance. Appearing surprised to see me, he takes a step back.

I go to him and hug him and the baby he holds. Inhaling his sweet scent reinforces that he truly stands before me. Overjoyed that he's alive, I beam. But doubts steal my bliss. Taking my free hand, the other still holding Cila's, I pinch the skin of my arm to make sure I'm not dreaming. Then I pinch Mikiel.

"Meelah, what are you doing?"

He waits for an answer and remains pensive. This has everything to do with me. I recall his somber demeanor when I left him here with Leva. After all we have been through, we must move forward from our past. Here and now, none of that matters. He's alive and he's carrying what I believe to be his son. His sword is resting in its sheath. This brings further peace to my heart.

Breaking the silence, I hear him intone, "This is my son." He looks at me as if he fears that the news of his child will cause me pain.

"Congratulations, Mikiel, he appears healthy and he's beautiful."

"And he is without a mother."

"And I have faithfully pledged my heart to Kriyo." I hear him inhale the air around me. He breathes in deeply as if he can smell Kriyo's touch. If he can, there is a great deal to intake. His attention finds its way to the bundle within his arms. If he's hurt by my union with Kriyo, his son readily alleviates it. Still holding Cila's hand, I take a step closer to both of them and remark, "He looks like you, Mikiel."

"His name is Talus."

"You named him after that creature? What planet was he from?"

"Hetion," he answers. "Talus was a true friend. Only you would recall him."

"I do," I affirm with a chortle. "His scent was similar to rotten fruit. He was difficult to forget."

"He didn't smell that bad."

"Really?"

"Perhaps he had a slight scent, but I moved past it."

"Indeed. You with your fine-tuned sense of smell, did look past it. I don't know how."

"Are you happy?" he asks me. "You look as if you have been crying."

"Kriyo makes me very happy. Earlier, I was crying, but thankfully there is no need now."

"Will you explain the being that has her hand in yours?"

"You haven't met Cila!" I reflect on this. I introduce them, saying, "Mikiel, with honor, I would like you to meet Cila. She is a munad and a special part of my family."

"Thank you, Meelah," she says to me. "Mikiel, it is a pleasure to meet you and Talus. My kind speak of your son," she says, with a reflective pause. "They speak of his destiny and all the good he will do. Bringing him into this reality was the right choice."

"Thank you, Cila. But weren't the munads recently destroyed?"

"They shifted," she explains. "No essence can truly be destroyed." She directs her statement to me.

Her words come with profound understanding. Jael's essence is with her and when she leaves, I believe that he will become what she will. Energy merely shifts forms. She must have required more time or perhaps more fortitude for our plan to work. Jael needed resolve from the guilt that he was caring. Both needed the other.

She says, "I was diminishing far too quickly. This will afford me the time I need. Then he and I will brighten the sky."

"Why didn't you simply tell me your plan?"

"Kriyo saw these events within a drawing of Faro's. The Timeera told him to only share this information with me. Knowing Kriyo as I do, I propose that perhaps he also wished to test you."

"I told him that my heart belonged faithful to him. What if I failed? Why risk that?"

"I seem to be missing a huge piece of this conversation," Mikiel expresses.

"You don't need to understand any of it," I answer him. "But I wish for no more tests of my loyalty."

"Growth is comprised of tests. They are also referred to as acts of free will," the Light interjects. "Bastaine, the leader of the Timeera, explicitly advised Kriyo to withhold his father's vision from you. He also honors free will. Think about it, Meelah. Your free will has brought you here with a renewed perspective. It has polished your unwavering connection to Kriyo and your destiny. It has also empowered the munad by fusing her essence with a Churrian's soul. Free will creates remarkable realities. "

"It certainly does," I agree. But the matter of free will doesn't intrigue me as much as the name I keep hearing. "Bastaine," I announce, aloud. The sound or resonance of his name stirs something in me, an indiscernible memory perhaps. Hoping for clarity, I repeat the leader's name in my mind, *Bastaine... Bastaine*. I feel affected strangely by it, but I suppose the meaning of this association will be realized in due course.

Next to me, I hear Cila and Mikiel conversing. On my other side, I see the Light, His eyes are closed. Even though He appears connected to someone or something, I feel Him take my hand. He links me to a private conversation. My eyes close, bringing me to a new space. When I open them, I see a robed being enshrouded in golden rays. Facing me is Bastaine. I know this and I know him; however, I don't understand how. His radiance is similar in color to Natiya's. His face is blurred. I try to get a clearer view, but he chooses to keep it a mystery. Although I'm unable to make out his face, his energy is apparent and quite unique. The Light Force has left us alone, though He's still near. He's watching. He is also wondering why this leader is here.

I stand strong. I know who I am. I am not intimidated by his presence. Bastaine senses this, I can feel it. I seemed to have piqued his curiosity. He walks around me. I maintain my forward gaze. I have nothing to hide. Stopping before me, he looks into and through my chest.

"Concealing the amulet was wise," he states in a deep voice. I lower my head in acknowledgement. He's right. "You will soon require its force. But you haven't deciphered all the information from the last stone I gave you."

"You returned what already belonged to me and my amulet. Why did you remove what wasn't yours to take? And, why did you personally return it to me? Before you address my questions, I would like to answer yours. When I am ready for the information stored in my stone, I will be guided to it. I have faith in this process"

"Do you dislike me, Meelah?"

"How could I dislike someone I don't know. If I have given you this impression, I am sorry. I'm merely trying to make sense of matters. Could you please answer my questions?"

"I will," he replies in earnest. "You needed to declare your oath to the Light Force in your present physical form. This action reinstated your leadership of the Light Warriors and your connection to them. The last stone opened specific memories. You stored the source of your power and your bond to each Light Warrior in this particular gem. If your free will didn't bring you to this reinstatement, you wouldn't require this knowledge. We kept it safe. I myself protected it. There is another memory awaiting you. As to why I brought the stone to you, allow your faith to guide you to this answer. Since you have confidence in this process, you shouldn't mind waiting."

I appreciate his candor, also I am grateful. Expressing this, I continue. "I appreciate the clarification. I'm grateful for what you've done. You kept my memories safe and in good hands, thank you." He lowers his head to me. The intrigue continues to drive me. About to ask my next question, I realize that each time I met a Timeera, this leader appeared. Why? Surely the head of the Timeera has other pressing matters to tend to. Nonetheless, it was he who gave me the chest housing my amulet, then the correct stone. I even recall seeing his discernible image in Kriyo's eyes. Hungry for understanding, I use this time to inquire, "May I ask you another question?"

"You may."

"With all due respect, why are you here?"

"I heard you utter my name. Why have you summoned me?"

"Did I summon you by merely uttering your name?"

"No," he answers flatly. "Though I am curious as to why you whispered it, twice."

"It was not my intention to summon you though I appreciate you candidly answering my questions. I repeated your name because somewhere deep within me, I feel as though I know it."

"You do."

"Will you enlighten me as to how?" Again he encircles me.

"In time. Allow your faith to reveal our connection, though I have already given you a place to find the answer; your stone."

He will soon leave, I feel it. I have many questions, but there is something else I must convey. The one I love has blossomed in the mere presence of these beings. I must acknowledge this. "Kriyo is thriving under your influence. He truly resonates with the energy of your kind. I appreciate the care and the knowledge that you have bestowed on him."

Without delay, I hear, "We know who and what Kriyo is, but do you? Do you even know what you truly are, Meelah?"

"Kriyo doesn't need to be defined. I love him for who he is, not for what he is. As for me, perhaps you should ask my creators this question."

"You don't know! Aren't you curious as to your true identity?"

Wisps of light dance in his eyes. He seems to enjoy the fact that I don't know. Truthfully, I don't need to know. I have faith in the Creators. They answered this question. They only provided me with a basic overview yet it satisfied me. When I require more information I will learn it. But why does the being before me care to know? Intently, his eyes don't look at me, they see through me. He's utterly intriguing.

"Whatever I am, it doesn't need to be named. Why does this matter to you?"

"Meelah," the leader intones in a whisper.

Next to me the Light appears. I feel Him take my hand in His. It's time for us to leave. He is smiling at me. Once more I feel as though I have been tested. The leader before us, or his energy field, lowers his head. While dissolving into the background, Bastaine's focus shifts, centering directly on me.

"You matter to me," he announces.

His tone is powerful. Its force remains suspended around us. "I matter to him?" I mutter aloud. Looking at the Light Force I ask, "What was that meeting about?"

"I have theories. He asked my permission to meet with you. I assumed he did this because of where you are, in my domicile. Meelah, I need you to understand." He stands facing me. In this moment I witness His genuine nature. He wishes for us to have no secrets. He knows me well. I despise secrets. "Your last and only other lifetime, you were gifted to me, but now you belong to no one. That is why Bastaine held onto your stone, since he's neutral where I am not. My natural light could have influenced it. Honoring your free will, you chose to avow your oath and lead my warriors again. You don't belong to the light, the dark, or the indifferent, but you are all three. I hoped that your destiny and your free will would guide you back to me and the Light Warriors. You will always be their rightful leader. It is time that you understand your connection to the three components that complete reality. It's your choice whom you align with and what you do with this alignment."

"On some level I knew this. I feel the connection to both you and your brother. Also, I honor a new tie. Somehow I am connected to the indifferent ones and with Bastaine. With time this relationship will become clearer. I assure you; my alliance, or alignment as you've stated, is to you and my destiny."

"Perhaps Bastaine's visit was for us both. We needed to be reminded of who you are, whatever that is." He smiles and so do I. "Meelah, there is a wave affecting all in existence, even Bastaine. Regardless of what happens after the war, a fated change in leadership will occur. I initially thought his visit may involve this pending transformation. You and your destiny will influence more than you realize, Meelah."

"Will this change affect you?"

"No, but the outcome of the war will. The Timeera, my brother and I are immortals. Each of us represents a facet comprising reality as it is known to all. There is the light, the dark and the Timeera, who stand amid the perception of this duality as the impartial ones. Though none of us can cease to exist, the change that evolution brings will transform each of our realities permanently. This conversion will occur after the war."

Again, we stand in the presence of Cila and Mikiel. My hand is still connected with hers. Neither of them seem to realize that I left for a spell.

"Bastaine is indeed unique," Cila says to me. Apparently she didn't miss a thing. "Some of your memories have been removed. Not removed exactly, they have been concealed. Your essence knows him and he knows you."

"I would know if Bastaine and Meelah share memories," the Light tells her.

"Perhaps you do. Our Creators know what they are doing for it was they who hid this information from the both of you. What I know is this. The gap of time between Meelah's death and her rebirth was a span of one thousand years. You met Bastaine then," she explains.

"How do you know this, Cila?" I ask her.

"My father told me. He also told me that Bastaine witnessed the consummation of your union to Kriyo. My father wanted you to know this."

The Light Force is pensive, we both are. The mystery continues to deepen. Though I'm unsettled, I need to ease Cila's concerns. "Kriyo explained to me that our personal moment was recorded. Why Bastaine chose to see it is not a matter I choose to understand at this time. There is work to be done. I have faith in the process," I add, looking at the Light. His face registers a sense of peace, though moments ago, it did not. Perhaps our makers have revealed the memories in question.

"We have," I hear Feena's voice declare. "When you are ready, we will open these memories for you as well. We know you. We recognize what you can handle. You gave us consent to withhold them until you are ready. When we restore these remembrances you will remember this as well. Meelah," She includes in a serious tone of voice. "You must understand this! Sooner than you realize, you will require the information stored in the last stone given to you. There is a gift within this stone from Bastaine. It will protect something close to your heart. You are more than you know. You and he are connected. You will require this connection after the war. How you choose to wield your free will is still unwritten. The end of an era is upon us."

By my next breath, She's gone. The Light was also present to hear Her, so I turn to Him, hoping for understanding. Instead, He gives me a reassuring grin and a nod of His head. When I am meant to, I will comprehend my connection to Bastaine and the information he left me. I have faith in this. Here and now, I connect to my solemn oath. I am of service to the greater good, this is by my free will.

"And how will this free will further satisfy your destiny?" the Light Force asks me.

"I need your help. Take my hand and I will show you our plan."

Taking hold of my hand, the Brilliance sees how we wish to proceed. He also sees what I'll require of Him. As I open my eyes, I notice Mikiel has joined our vision. He is holding Cila's hand. I observe their exchange. Cila is one of a kind. Their hands continue to remain clasped. It mustn't have been easy for Mikiel to overhear the conversation about Kriyo and I consummating our union. I appreciate his son's presence. It has pleasantly redirected my dear friend.

Mikiel asks, "My liege, when do we leave?"

"I don't think it's wise for you to join us, not even to meet with Reetra."

"I know where to locate him. I was the one who initially contacted him for this purpose."

"You have a son and as you said, he doesn't have a mother. He needs his father. He needs you."

"I have spent my entire life fighting for this cause. I had to let you go! Don't ask me to surrender our mission as well! I must do this. I wish to battle by your side, not only for me, but also for my son. Allow me to show him what honor brings."

"Follow your heart, Mikiel. Let it be your guide. But I wish for your son to have his father. You need not risk your life. I will give you a few moments to decide."

Without a second thought, he replies, "I will fight by your side until the end of time, my liege."

Respecting his courage, I lower my head to him. He loves me and I love him, but it has changed; we as individuals have changed. Our love is what it should be. Though I give my consent, there is another I must ask. "Cila, are you strong enough to camouflage all of us?"

"It seems I don't have much of a choice," she answers, as Mikiel places his son in the arms of a female Light Warrior.

"Was Jael strong in spirit?"

"Yes!" both Mikiel and I answer.

"Good, I will draw from that strength."

"I can give you something else, my blood."

"No, Meelah. That will not be necessary. Jael will provide me with the strength that I require. I will only have days when we return to Churria."

"Doesn't it benefit you that Jael was Churrian?"

"Not in the aging process. His essence doesn't change my physical body. With what I must do, my body will age faster than it did before. I will have no more than two days once we return, but this is two days more than I had. If I didn't leave with you, I would have perished today."

"Kriyo will be heartbroken."

"And his heart will heal with your help. You will gain a chance at having a future, all of you will. Meelah," she says, "both of us will soon satisfy our destinies." To Mikiel, she adds, "Allowing other destinies to manifest."

"Do you feel as though you're always left in the dark?" I ask Mikiel.

"At times, yes," he answers with a grin. "Though Cila is correct. We will gain a future, everyone will, even Talus."

"We will return with warriors," I affirm to the Light.

"I will see you then. Be careful, Meelah. *He* seeks you and Cila." His words fade and so does He.

"Cila, are you positive that my blood will not benefit you?"

"I am quite certain and I am also at peace with what lies ahead for me. Soon, I will be with my father and you will witness your father's true light."

I have never considered Jael as my father, but the words feel true. I am proud of his recent selfless decisions. Uncertain of his fate, he surrendered the last of himself for the greater good. There's nothing more noble and reverent than that. I will make certain that all will know of his sacrifice. Cila takes hold of Mikiel's hand.

She warns, "Mikiel, keep hold of my hand and do not let it go! If you do, *he* will find you then locate us!"

"You have my word," he answers.

Together, with three strong hearts, we prepare to depart. Each one of us must succeed for the sake of love. I, for the love I possess for Kriyo and the Light; Mikiel, for the love he has for his son; and Cila, for the love of fulfilled destiny. One by one our eyes close. I hear our heartbeats as they begin to synch and our hearts beat as one. I command, "Bring us, Mikiel. It is time to meet Reetra's army."

Chapter Eighteen

We stand within a massive gorge. Still hand and hand, I take in the barren scene. Around us are mountains that appear to have seen the effects of war or a natural disaster. No life exists here. Inquisitively, I look at Mikiel, whose eyes remain fixed on something in the gloom ahead of us. I do not sense anything but his intent focus churns my curiosity. As time passes, and our stillness persists, I close my eyes and listen.

I hear voices, many of them. They are circling around us. I also detect their benign nature and I sense Mikiel does as well. Then something small lands on my shoulder. I feel its little feet navigate my collar bone as it nears my neck. There is kindness in this being, so I resist the urge to flick away whatever it is as it nears my ear. As this creature burrows through my hair, its little hand grabs the lobe of my ear. Opposing the desire to shrug my neck as this miniscule being tickles me, I release a little laugh.

"Keep your eyes closed," a wee voice says into my ear. "Reetra has been waiting for your arrival. He has been waiting for all of you. He is coming now."

Moving through my hair again, the tiny life form then leaps off my shoulder. The voices fall silent and I sense someone or something standing directly before me. Its moist and unusual breath swirls around my face and I raise the corners of my lips to a smile before lowering my head.

"You may all open your eyes," we hear Reetra state.

His eyes meet mine and he delves into them. Remaining resolute, I do not waver. Whatever he needs to find I will provide for him. His yellow eyes, similar to a reptile's, penetrate my soul. Leaning in, getting closer to me, he persists and I again smell his rancid breath. Pulling back, I watch as he lowers his head to all three of us. Calmly, he turns around and proceeds back into the surrounding murky and unsettled mist.

Mikiel takes a step forward. Not moving, I affirm, "Reetra wishes for us to remain here."

"That's correct," I hear another small voice spout.

A magnificent little being is hovering to our left. About three inches high, a winged, redheaded female bows to us. Wearing a white-and-orange embroidered gown, she flutters over to Mikiel.

"You look well, Mikiel," she says to him.

"Salfilia, you're looking healthy. I would like to introduce Meelah and Cila to you." He addresses us, "This is Salfilia, Reetra's assistant."

"This is Meelah?" Salfilia interrupts. "She is the one you fawned over…forever? She's not that special!" She scoffs, while fluttering her tangerine-colored wings in my face.

Remaining silent, I smirk. Why this little being despises me so, is her burden. I feel Cila give my hand a little squeeze; she too finds humor in this.

"Meelah is quite special, Salfilia. She is my leader, and she has chosen to be with another."

"Do you wish for me to injure her? I see that she has injured you!"

"No, that will not be necessary," he promptly answers her with a chuckle.

"How is Talus?" she asks, batting her long lashes. "If he possesses your physical features, I wish to be with him—eternally."

"Talus is fine. But he has been born with a destiny. He cannot be yours."

"Is it because of my size?"

"No," he answers with a gentle voice filled with amusement. "Talus must journey his destined path."

I feel sadness hearing Mikiel's words. Any and all destinies occur with limited options. I pray that Talus will find meaning and love on his path. Blending his destiny with his heart's desire, he will not harbor regret. Then again, I sense Reetra. Emerging from the swirling, fog-like atmosphere that hovers close to the ground, he comes into view. But he is not alone; another, wearily at his side, approaches us as well. Appearing female, and quite weak, she joins us. Her eyes are also yellow and the color of her skin is a dull red tone. Devoid of any body hair or a shred of clothing, extending her hand, she waits. I place my free hand in hers. She turns it over, revealing my wrist. I know what she wants, I feel what she needs.

"After she receives this exchange, we will depart with troops, at least two thousand strong," I affirm.

As Reetra lowers his head, I give my consent. Opening her mouth, I see her reveal her fangs. As if she's ravenous, she tears into the skin of my wrist. Squeezing Cila's hand, I resist the urge to reveal the pain. I feel Mikiel's distress as he watches in horror. The female fiercely intakes my blood. Her curved shoulders move in cadence with her gulping. When she swallows, I sense her ecstasy as my essence nourishes her. Moving her head back and forth, she opens wounds, drawing more blood. She's skilled, she's voracious and I begin to feel weak. I direct my gaze at Reetra. I wish not to hurt the female but I will, if I must. I send this message to him as well.

"Enough!" Mikiel yells.

After two more swigs, she removes her fangs from my vein. Licking my wrist, like a dog would a serious wound, she rises. My body begins to heal though I am left weakened by this healing. The female before us has been restored. Her physical form is now a vibrant red color and her yellow eyes are agleam. Her health and vigor have returned.

"She is Veta," Reetra states. "And she will rebuild the army. Your blood is like no other's. After the last dose, Veta was able to birth over one thousand Retza warriors. We have prepared them." Looking at Salfilia, who is suspended midair, he instructs, "Ready the strongest and most able warriors. Meelah requires an additional one thousand."

"I will have them ready."

Salfilia flutters off into the gloom. Now, standing before us is Veta. Bowing first to me, then to the others, she proceeds back from whence she came. Only Reetra remains. His gaunt reptilian form with a scrawny midsection above his two scaly legs makes him exceptional in appearance. Within his incomparable form is integrity. He embodies truth and exudes honesty. His facial expression softens as he senses my view of him. Pressing his staff onto the rocky terrain underfoot, he ambles closer to me.

"You will have one chance. Do not fail."

Turning around, he hobbles toward the ambiguous mass. Pausing, he strikes his staff onto the ground, one, two, three times. The vibration travels beneath our feet. It also separates the gloom, revealing a hidden passageway. Proceeding onward, he trudges ahead until he is lost from our sight. The cloud-like murk settles again, camouflaging the opening to his home. That he revealed it to us plainly illustrates his trust and his accord with our plan of defense. I allowed him to view our plans when he delved into my eyes. It brings me solace that he also believes we'll succeed. He, like many leaders, is an ageless being. After thousands upon thousands of years they've spent in hiding, the victory of this war will change theirs and everyone's reality. Freedom is upon the horizon. So is a life with hope.

Hand and hand, we wait, but not for long. They materialize from the mist. Retza warriors emerge two by two, blue-skinned and red-skinned. Their gear includes knives affixed to their belts and concealed in scabbards, a staff with a blade, and armor covering their chests. Young and strong, these warriors are ready for what lies ahead of them. They personally know of the Epoh's tough hide and toxic horn, this I saw within Reetra's eyes. I begin to taste my destiny, though it will come at a great cost. Many have already fallen and more will certainly join them.

Standing before us, the warriors have all come forth. I know how to bring them to their safe place, though I haven't shared this with Cila or Mikiel. The Timeera gave Cila permission to use the decahedron chamber, though I am uncertain if she knows this. I say, "Cila, you and Mikiel must return to Churria."

"And leave you unprotected?" Mikiel asks.

"Mikiel, you must trust me. I need you and Cila to obtain some things for me."

"What things?" he asks, intrigued. "The surface of Churria is consumed with Epoh."

"Yes, but you have Cila, and under the cover of night, they will not detect you. Cila knows what I require."

"This is dangerous."

"I wouldn't place you in danger, Mikiel," I assure him.

"I am not worried for me. This is dangerous for you. Once you release Cila's hands, the Darkness will locate you and this army."

"Reetra has that covered. Go! That is an order." To Cila, I instruct, "Be certain to stick to the plan. As soon as you get the vial of blood, and the rest of the warriors, return to the decahedron chamber. The Timeera have also granted you permission to use it. Mikiel and the others will protect you."

"I will wait until Reetra gives you the signal. Then I will release your hand, Meelah. Are you certain you are strong enough? Veta drained quite a lot of blood from you."

"I must do this, Cila. I will be fine. Mikiel, keep her safe. I am glad that you are by my side."

"Not exactly, Meelah. You are asking me to leave you."

"I know what I'm doing. Darkness has fallen on Churria. Give Mikiel the gudra root and prepare to leave."

"I know gudra root, it's revolting!"

"And it will conceal our scent," Cila counters, handing him a small piece.

I can't help but smile as he puts the root in his mouth. Immediately, he quivers as if to shake the repugnant flavor from his mouth. I also shudder, as my senses recall its vile taste. As the air encompassing us fills with the heinous odor, it is time. I feel it and Cila knows it. I follow her gaze to the skyline and we wait. Then we see it in the dark sky above us. A flickering light similar to that of a new star is the awaited sign. Reetra has veiled his kind and now I must remove these two thousand beings before the Dark Force locates me and destroys them.

"Are you certain you can move all of them?" Mikiel asks.

"Mikiel, go," I say, as Cila releases my hand.

"She knows what she must do, Mikiel! Bring us to Churria. There are Light Warriors in hiding who are awaiting us. Bring us to them, now!" Cila demands.

I sense their departure as I close my eyes. In my mind, I gather all of the warriors. Then I feel *him* as *he* locates me. The ubiquitous Darkness surges downward. Nearing me, approaching the warriors with vengeance, *he* swiftly descends. As *he* closes the gap between us, I am ready. Opening my eyes, I use my power and remove every warrior. Successfully, I bring them to the domicile of the Light Force. Once we're there, I release my hold on the mass and depart again. Appearing in space, I cut into my hand and lure the Darkness my way. I watch as a stream of my blood remains suspended around me. *He* will catch my scent. This distraction will lure *him* away from Reetra, Veta and all of his kind. I wait, but not for long. In the nearing distance, I sense Shadows as they also pick up my scent. I will enjoy destroying them as well. Coming my way, they are almost seamlessly blending into the natural dim light around me. But their malevolence makes them appear as clear as day. I sense their raw evil. Finally, *he* has located me. Disbursing *his* Shadows, *he's* behind me.

"Your blood," *he* says, drawing it into *his* mouth. "It's grand; moderately sweet with a spike of tartness. I could market this to all the bloodsuckers."

Facing *him*, I reply, "The munad lives."

"For now," *he* replies. "She is already waning."

"You fooled me before, I'll give you that."

"I have many talents, Meelah."

"Too bad you failed," I goad *him*.

"Did I? I wouldn't be so sure."

"I would." I sense the Light Force as He beams behind me.

"You have vacated your domicile! Isn't that against the rules, brother?" the Darkness shouts. "You have defied our creators for this? Have you come to save your little pet?"

"She doesn't belong to me, brother. Meelah has chosen to honor me and her destiny, again. Ironically, whether it's in this lifetime or her last, she detests you." Appearing before me, the Light Force states, "Go, Meelah."

"I'll see you soon, Meelah. The only thing that separates us is time and it's nearing an end."

"No, brother, your illicit behavior is nearing an end."

"Aren't you exhausted? Tending to all of these living beings' needs all…of…the…time! Join me and together we'll rule creation. Together, we would be stronger than the Creator. Collectively, we'd be unstoppable!"

"You still don't understand," the Light puts in plain words. "It isn't about the need for power over another. It isn't even about power."

"What's more relevant than supremacy?"

"Everything!" the Light responds. "The balance will soon be restored."

As anger wells in the Darkness, out comes the presence of another, the Creator. *He* asks, "Do we really require another family reunion?"

"You will abide by the universal laws or we will destroy you and make another in your place. All laws will be obeyed," the Creator declares.

"Then what will I get?"

"You will receive the gift of time," the Light Force answers. "The results of this war are final. No more of your antics."

"And if I win?" *he* asks mischievously, licking *his* lips.

"You will not be victorious," the Light quickly replies.

"But if you do prevail," the Almighty One affirms, "you may keep your army."

"That violates free will!" the Light cries.

"The Epoh will belong to your brother."

"And they can reproduce," the Darkness adds cunningly.

"There is an additional addendum," the Creator adds. "If Meelah wins this war, you will nullify her contract with you."

"So, if my brother wins, I get sent back to my domicile, forever, and I must void her contract! Why would I do that?"

"You already have Leva, all you will require is a mate for her. Honoring free will, you could raise an army of your own. But you will void Meelah's contract or we will destroy Leva."

"In short, if I win, I get an army. If I lose and cancel my contract with that little vixen, I get to hand-pick a sorry mate for Leva and raise an army. Either way, time, as you stated, brother, time will create my unstoppable force."

"Are you in agreement?" the All Powerful asks sternly.

"Yes," the Gloom answers. "Either way I get to continue my life's work of killing and pillaging. What more could I ask for?"

"When Meelah is victorious, you will remain in your domicile!" the Light proclaims.

"Yes," *he* answers flatly. "Either way, I'll make it work for me." Sniffing the air, the Darkness asks, "Have I been delayed here intentionally?"

"No one has coerced you to remain here, brother."

"You are all so clever," *he* states. "I'm quite proud of you," *he* announces to the Light. "I didn't think this was in you. It seems that there's hope for you after all. Remember, as a team, we'll be unstoppable," *he* sings. "Well, I must be going. Are we done here? Do you wish to add another addendum?"

"There is nothing more," the Creator states, fading into the surrounding obscurity.

Sensing that the Light will imminently depart as well, the Gloom inserts, "Too bad, brother." Seizing his attention, *he* asks, "Will you shed a tear?"

"Stop the riddles and speak your peace."

"I am going to slash Meelah limb from limb then watch her pathetic soul rise, only for me to destroy it as well. She will be gone, vanquished, no more. Her finite existence will permanently come to an end," *he* exclaims with enthusiasm.

"Then I will do the same to Leva, ending all chances of raising an army. An eye for an eye, brother. Meelah will be victorious."

Sneering, the Dark Force answers, "I would enjoy watching you shred Leva into tiny little bits. She hasn't fully committed to my level as darkness anyway."

"I have my faith, brother. What drives you?" the Light asks.

"Rage, mainly. I can hardly wait for the end. The anticipation is wickedly delightful!"

Chapter Nineteen

There is a storm brewing, I feel it, and all life in this universe and beyond senses it. With the Darkness briefly distracted, I meet with the Sirians. They are also concerned with the looming tempest. Every moment, it grows in intensity and force. I require the aid of these beings. Their intervention will give my warriors the advantage we require. I've asked the Sirians to block the light of day on Churria. I've also requested that they delay the arrival of dawn. It is now that I wait for their answer.

Circumventing the proper channels, they give their consent and I return to Churria. From above and through the swirling dim mist, I witness the enormity of the army below. I recall my nightmare and I hear Drana's haunting words in my mind, *earth will be next*. This army must be stopped. This will end here. There mustn't be a *next time* for them. I oppose the feeling of terror as it attempts to develop within me. We are greatly outnumbered. However, we will not be outmatched. I visualize my plan and run it through my mind over and over again. Soon it will be realized.

"It is no longer safe for you, Meelah," I hear the Light Force say in my inner being. "*He* will end you if you fail."

"Everything I know will end, if I fail," I send from my heart. "Failure is not an option."

I prepare to leave the scene below me. Soon I will be immersed in their darkness, but not today. With my intentions strong, I return to the decahedron chamber. As the luminescent room comes into view, I see Kriyo. Once I fully materialize, we fall into each other's arms. After I inhale his sweet scent from the nape of his neck, I pull back and state, "No more tests from you."

"The Timeera demanded that I allow your free will to create the right outcome."

"It was Bastaine," I tell him.

Pulling back, he asks me, "How do you know of Bastaine?"

"I met him. I even sense him at this moment. He's attuned to our conversation. Most relevantly, he's connected to me." At hearing these words, Kriyo closes his eyes. When he opens them, his expression validates what I already know. I continue. I want Bastaine to hear me as well. "I will say this now, not only to you, but also to him. I wish for no energy to stand between us, even if they're the Timeera. No more secrets." After I voice this, I rest my forehead against Kriyo's. "No secrets," I whisper. I show him my meeting with Bastaine, all of it. I include the Light Force's explanation of my three parts, even Cila's wisdom, including that it was Bastaine who witnessed our love. Kriyo remains in this space for a few moments. Reflected in his expression is something I can't clarify. "Time will bring the answers to both of us. Our love is true. No one will stand between us, not even secrets."

"Meelah, " he says softly, stroking the side of my face. "I know who and what you are. This truth has been etched on a special wall here in the Underground City. When you're ready, you will also know. You wanted it this way. That is why I haven't mentioned it. You documented that wish before you were born into this existence. I love you for who you are. I always have. And I am quite proud of what you are." I smile at him, remembering that I chose similar words, though admittedly, his sentiment is better phrased. My grin is contagious, as I see his face create one, lifting the heaviness around us. "My love, I didn't know about your connection to Bastaine; perhaps I'm not meant to interfere at this time. I also didn't know that he was the Timeera who witnessed our loving union." He adds, holding my hands, "I will do my best to honor your request, but the Timeera are not our enemies nor can I control what they ask of me."

"I don't wish for control, Kriyo. I hope for honesty. My love, time is fleeting. I must review your father's illustrations. He demanded it."

"You saw him?"

"I met with more than just your father, but you probably know that."

"No, tell me. I want to hear everything about your journey."

"Have Cila and Mikiel returned?"

"Yes, and my heart nearly sank when you weren't with them and the warriors."

"They found them! I knew the Light Warriors were alive. What about Grawl and Grutiri?"

"They buried themselves deep within the sand surrounding the back wall in Drista. They are unscathed and ready. Mikiel gave the vial of Grawl's blood to Trall."

"Kriyo, they're immune to toxins from the Epoh's horn. I hope to find an antidote."

"And the Retza army?" he asks, preparing to open the chamber door.

"They are ready and waiting in the Light Force's domicile."

"And Mikiel, does he know about our union?" he asks pointedly.

"Of course he does," I eagerly answer. "Mikiel has a son."

"I thought that the Light Warriors didn't reproduce?"

Pressing the door closed, I answer him. "Mikiel and I were given that ability, though neither of us knew at the time. I chose you in that lifetime, then again in this life. I've seemed to have fallen into the same pattern," I say, kissing his soft lips. "Leva and Mikiel are the parents of Talus and he is beautiful."

"Talus, that's a strong name."

"Talus was the name of a dear friend of Mikiel's a long time ago."

"So Leva can also procreate?"

"Leva has betrayed us. She was banished from my domicile."

"From your domicile?" he asks.

"Old habits," I answer him with a grin.

"I've missed you, Meelah," he whispers, pulling me again into his arms.

I wish to remain in the embrace of the being I love. He is my home. He is my life, my resilience. Taking a few breaths, I linger, but my thoughts prevent me from fully committing to the moment. I mustn't fail. Too much is on the line and there is still a great deal of preparation to do. I need not say a word, he feels the rising disquiet within me as if it was his own and it is. My burden affects everyone.

First his arms cinch even tighter around me. He reminds me that I am not alone. Next, he releases his grasp, looks into my eyes, and I wish I could freeze time and remain in this safe space. But transition is inevitable and time moves us onward. Lowering his eyes, severing our connection, he turns and opens the chamber door.

I readily take his extended hand as we step out of the room. Both Ruzi and Lador are faithfully waiting. I hear Ruzi say, "My liege!"

Lowering my head to my second in command, I get to the business at hand. "There is a great deal we must do. Please gather all of the Light Warriors and the trained Churrians. We all will return to our creator's kingdom. Only there will I reveal my plan."

"Consider it done. When will we leave?"

"I must confer with the Timeera and review some of Faro's drawings first. Prepare them to depart in two hours. We will meet here."

"I will see you then, my liege."

Bowing to us, Ruzi begins his mission. I feel Kriyo's attention on me, as it nearly warms my cheek. I realize that I should have shared this plan with him.

"Forgive me, Kriyo. My mind is so consumed that I failed to include you."

"You are a leader, Meelah, but please do include me."

"I will do my very best," I answer him as we proceed down the corridor.

Upon our journey I see a wondrous thing—Teese. Coming toward us, he wears a smile. I am relieved to see him alive though I knew he would be. New to battle, he has persevered against the odds, revealing there's greatness within him.

With good humor, I feel Kriyo squeeze my hand as the handsome Light Warrior continues directly my way. Light Warriors are easy on the eyes, that's for sure, but none of them are a match for Kriyo. A light smile graces Teese's face. His light brown wings, flecked with gold, are drawn tight behind him. His flaxen hair is short and tidy and his eyes are cinnamon brown. The armor covering his chest shimmers as if he's just polished it. The sheath of his sword is worn. He seems to have put this weapon to use. Muscular and lean, he now stands before us. When he is bowing before me, I politely remind the young warrior to honor the Head Elder as well. Showing authentic reverence to Kriyo as well, he rises.

"My liege, I knew you would come for us. We couldn't leave. We tried over and over again. The Dark One trapped us on the surface."

"I am sorry that it wasn't sooner. The Dark Force knows what he's doing. Trapping his prey is one of his tactics. I am glad to see you alive. I knew you would be."

"If it weren't for that time here, I wouldn't be able to learn their weaknesses."

"Please share this knowledge." I see him hesitate, so I add, "The Head Elder is also my partner. Anything that you would share with me, you may share also with him."

With respect, he lowers his head again before addressing both of us. "The Epoh have considerable weaknesses. We survived because we remained out of their reach. They're also significantly limited in the dark. This time, we observed them solely rely on their sense of smell, which is extremely acute. Their hide appears impenetrable, but an area below their shoulders is quite supple. I took down more than twenty by running my blade into this weak spot. This kills them within seconds, and when standing at their side, their toxic horn is no threat. They are not skilled at battle or tactical maneuvers. They appear to just charge their opposition. In a group, their horns are nearly impossible to avoid, but one on one, they are easy to take down."

"I am relieved that you survived. The Light Force will be quite proud of you. I am proud of you. Have you shared this information with Ruzi and Mikiel?"

"Yes."

"Good. Prepare for our departure. I have a few matters to handle before we leave."

He honors both Kriyo and I with another bow before proceeding onward. Something else I've forgotten to mention to Kriyo is my meeting with the Sirians. With Lador ambling behind us, we continue down the endless corridors. "I met with the Sirians. I have also witnessed a weakness with the Epoh. When darkness surrounds them, they are vulnerable. I asked the Sirians for their help."

"What did you ask of them?"

"They will blanket Churria in darkness. There will be no dawn until the battle is won."

"What happens if we fail?"

"We mustn't! If I fail, darkness will envelop all space. All that we know will fall. Kriyo," I say, softly, waiting for our eyes to meet. "I will not fail."

"We will not fail," he repeats.

Finally, we have arrived. Our chamber door, decorated with the glyphs depicting our union, is in my direct view. Running my hand over the etchings, I hear their meaning. This fuels me. It's this love, this passion that drives me. I cannot fail. Opening our chamber door, we proceed in. Faro's drawings come to mind and I ask Kriyo to show them to me.

Gathering the rolls of parchment, he hands them to me. "While you review my father's drawings, I'll confer with the Timeera. Do you wish to use the decahedron chamber to depart?"

"Is there another way?"

"The other way is from the ground. I'm certain that it's heavily guarded by Epoh."

"Thank you, Kriyo." Forgetting that I didn't share my meeting with his father, I take his hand and send him this information. I include his father's sense of well being. No words are needed. I release my telepathic link and he brings my hand to his lips. Lowering my arm, he connects with the Timeera.

I settle my focus on Faro's illustrations. Opening the rolls, the first few sheets are events that just occurred. It would have benefited me to have reviewed them before I left. Here I see Jael handing me a vial. Faro didn't include himself in this drawing. I wonder if he knew he would be there in spirit form. Seeing all of them was an incredible gift. Their warning saved Cila's life. Unrolling the next sheet, I am baffled; it's blank.

Returning my attention to Kriyo, I hear him on the other side of the room. He must have concluded the conference with the Timeera, freeing him for my question. "Did you review all of your father's work?"

"Yes," he answers, as he comes into view, wearing attire near and dear to my heart. "Ruzi lent this to me," he explains, seeing my expression.

My eyes singe him with pure ardor. He's combined two very special elements, himself and the uniform that I battled beside for centuries. He is utterly gorgeous. Every part of me wishes to be with him, every part, but the one that doesn't understand the meaning of this blank piece of paper.

"Meelah," he says with a smile.

I allow the blank parchment to rest. As I rise, I take in Kriyo's smile as it shifts into a beaming glow. He knows exactly what he's doing.

"You like the uniform?"

Already standing before him, I close my eyes and bring my lips to the soft skin of his neck. As I kiss him, he asks, "Do you wish that I could fly so we could be together as Light Warriors?"

"I am the light, the dark and the indifferent. I am no longer just a Light Warrior. I simply am, whatever that is." Whispering into his ear, I add, "My wish is to be with you; right here, right now."

Our lips meet and I melt into his presence. He sweeps me into his arms and with every step we take, his sweltering mouth covers mine. Lowering me to our bed, he sits me down. Slowly he undresses me until there is nothing else to remove. Rising to a stand, I begin to remove the uniform that fits to every contour of his perfect body. Each piece of his uniform is tossed to the side until he too has nothing else to shed. Our love brings us together. Our fervor each for the other brings with it an intense unity. Slowly and with control, we are able to linger in this place, just the two of us. No Timeera, no thoughts of what lies ahead. We commit ourselves fully to this brief moment, one that could be our last to share. Our heated moment of pure love comes to an end. He takes me in his arms and I rest my head upon his chest. I hear his heartbeat settle as does mine. This incredible exchange must end. Releasing his arms, I intone, "I must get ready."

I watch as he closes his eyes for a few breaths. Upon opening them, he says, "All right. But I will never forget."

"Forget what?" I ask.

"Your face," he answers.

"I hope not. Lador and Ruzi will be instructed to NEVER leave your side. I will return to you, I promise this."

"Meelah, I have decided to remain here when you and the others leave for the Light Force's domicile. I must ease the fears of the elders and the Churrians. They feel the unrest that haunts us. My place is here."

"It is," I say in agreement.

"There is more. The Timeera have also asked me to remain. They wish to meet with me before I join the battle."

"Do you know what it is they desire?"

"I have my suspicions," he answers. "But that is all I can share with you at this time. I'm honoring your request of no more secrets the best that I can."

"And I thank you." Sitting up, I remain on the side of our bed. Looking at him from over my shoulder, I include, "When I return, I will only bring a few Light Warriors with me. We will clear the entryway for you, Seli and Cila to exit. After you close the doors, we'll take to the skies. When the time is right, our army will arrive, but I must pave the way first." He sits up and rests his forehead against mine. In this space, I show him what is also fated to occur tomorrow. I sense his pain as he witnesses Cila's role as the amplifier. I also show him my destined task of returning the Darkness back to his domain.

"I know it's you who must return *him*. But how will you leave? That monster will trap you there."

"Did your father draw this reality?"

"No. It is merely my nightmare."

"I will leave that place. I have already been given a warning by the Light Force. I will have a small opening and I will use it. My heart is tethered to yours. It will bring me home."

Rising to a stand, he extends his hand to me. Ending the conversation is wise. Neither of us possesses control over the future. That being said, we can only have faith, anything else is futile. Walking past his father's most recent creations, I ask, "Have you seen this blank page? Is this a coincidence or is this a message of sorts, and are a few pages missing? The depictions are out of chronological order."

"I may have rearranged them in error. The blank piece was his last sheet."

"Did you remove any of the pages? Is there something that you are not telling me?"

"You confer with every force known. You know more than I do."

"We both know that's not entirely true."

As he washes up, I watch him. I know him, and he has chosen to hide a few of his father's drawings from me. Perhaps one of us will be harmed mortally? Consumed by questions and theories, I remain still.

"Meelah," he says, stopping my reeling thoughts. "I did remove a few of my father's drawings, but not because they revealed anything negative. They showed me something quite wonderful and I will share this development with you once your destiny is realized."

"Why didn't you simply say that?" I query him, relieved. "If you feel the knowledge from your father's creations has no relevance to what we face, then I will not insist. Instead, I will respect your decision."

"They are not significant in any way to the war. I would never put you in harm's way," he assures me, putting on his golden robe. "Look at you," he adds with a grin. "You can't leave as you are. I will share you with no other and no other will see what I do."

"I would have it no other way," I reply, dressing.

Finally, as prepared as I can be, I learn through Kriyo that the Timeera have granted all of the warriors the use of their sacred chamber. In my mind, I thank Bastaine, and with my eyes, I thank Kriyo. Together we are separate leaders and now our paths must veer apart.

"It is time," I state. "They are waiting for me."

Opening our door, we begin our approach to the decahedron room. With Kriyo's faithful friend in tow, we move quickly. Around the next corner, I see Cila. Again her hair is gray and the skin of her face, weathered. She hugs me and I whisper in her ear, "How much time?"

"I fear I'll have less time than I thought. Tomorrow," she adds feebly.

"Tomorrow it will be. I have shown Kriyo," I say, including him in the conversation.

"I have seen your death," he tells her poignantly. "I wish for another way."

"What you perceive as an ending, I see as a beginning. Tomorrow, I will go home and in that freedom something will rise—a future," Cila enlightens him.

"Tomorrow has not come. After Meelah departs, I wish to spend time with you."

"That sounds lovely," Cila answers, taking Kriyo's arm.

"Meelah!" I hear Trall spout. "Meelah!" he yells again, from behind us. "I have it!"

Leaving the group and striding toward Trall, I close the gap between us. I see a vial in his hand. He's created an antidote.

"I did it," he explains, breathless. "I only had time to create one and I'm not certain that it will work. I didn't get to field test it."

"Make as much as you can then give it to Kriyo. Thank you," I say, giving him a hug. "Truly, thank you."

Trall grasps my hand and presses the vial into it. I lower my head to him, then join Kriyo and Cila. I must ground myself. I almost left without the antidote. Now, I advise Kriyo of Trall's creation. I ask him to bring what Trall makes when they leave tomorrow. We both know that many will fall. If we can save even one, that's worth it all. Around the next corner of the maze, they appear, all of them. I behold the young Light Warriors' faces. The sight warms my heart. Next to them are about forty Churrians and Kriyo joins their group to address them.

Using this time allotted to me, I find Ruzi and grab Lador. Handing Ruzi the glass container, I say to them, "This is for Kriyo, it's an antidote."

"How?" Ruzi asks. "There is no known remedy."

"There is now," I state plainly. "More will come, but not nearly as much as we'll require. This one is for Kriyo, if he has need of it," I repeat. "I trust no others to protect him. Keep the Head Elder safe. Keep my Kriyo safe."

"Yes, my liege," Ruzi answers.

"I will remain by his side honorably," Lador assures me.

"Lador, leave with Kriyo tomorrow. I will clear the path so the doors can be safely opened. With my heart, I thank you both."

Bowing to them, I then continue on through the group. I prepare myself as I stand before the chamber door. With warriors ready and standing behind me, I realize that this moment is the beginning of the end. It's within sight, and soon it will be within grasp. Closing my eyes, I ask the doors before me to open.

Kriyo hears Meelah's request. He locates Mikiel amidst the warriors. Intently, he walks his way. "Mikiel, I would like to have a word with you." Lowering his head, Mikiel follows Kriyo away from the group. "At the cost of being blunt, we both love Meelah. My physical form limits me from doing what you can. Go where I cannot and keep watch over her."

"Always," Mikiel answers.

"There is more," Kriyo says quietly. "Meelah is with child. My father included this in his drawings."

"Does she know?"

"No," Kriyo answers.

"You should tell her."

"She cannot afford distractions, not even this. But if you know, perhaps you will keep a keen eye on her."

"I will," he states adamantly. "Be safe, Kriyo, and congratulations."

"It is I who should congratulate you. Talus is a powerful name. I feel as though I know it somehow."

Taking the Head Elder's hand, Mikiel presses it against Kriyo's chest. Mikiel then brings his hand to his chest and bows forward. This is the sacred gesture between Light Warriors.

"I will protect Meelah to my last breath," Mikiel proclaims.

"I know you will and I thank you. Be safe, Mikiel."

Rejoining the group, Kriyo sees Meelah enter the chamber. Behind her, a portion of the group proceeds in as well. His heart beats faster and faster as anxiety mounts within him. The door closes, leaving a fraction of warriors behind. Then once more it opens. As the final group, including Mikiel and Ruzi, enters, both Light Warriors honor Kriyo with a nod of their heads. He returns the kindness. At present, he is the only one left standing outside the door as it closes.

She has gone. He feels a gentle touch on his shoulder. Turning, he sees Cila's kind face, and Lador, who is also waiting for him. He joins them to begin their destiny. He notes how difficult the walk is for Cila. Before his very eyes, her back curves. Kriyo halts her steps, about to bend down and pick her up, but Lador sweeps Cila into his arms.

"Thank you," she says to him.

"No need to thank me," Lador answers. "You are bestowing on us all that you are. It is I who must show the gratitude. Thank you."

"We could continue this exchange for days, but I simply don't have the time," she jests. "You are welcome."

Releasing a chuckle, Lador proceeds onward. Kriyo shakes his head at Lador. "You always have to get the attention," Kriyo says to him.

"Not always," Lador answers.

Then from behind them they hear, "Kriyo!"

My voice halts their step. Taking to the air, I fly over to them. As my feet touch the ground, I bow to Lador and Cila. With kindness registered on their faces, they continue on their path, affording us a moment alone. Lador cradling Cila is quite the sight. Her thin frame is lost within his large arms. When Kriyo lowers his forehead to meet mine, we share a very brief moment to express our love. The next time we will see each other, this kind of exchange will not be possible. I feel his soft, warm breath as it caresses my lips and I resist the urge to close my eyes.

"I will always love you," I say to him. "We found each other again."

"We did," he answers solemnly. "I will see you tomorrow."

"I will be waiting for you right outside the doors."

Sliding his lips against mine, we briefly kiss. As our lips part, so do we, each walking in the opposing direction. I don't look back. I can't look back, but I feel him as he does. About to round the corner, I pause and look. Our eyes connect for a fleeting glance before I proceed to the chamber. Again, I open the double doors and step over their threshold. Standing in the very center of the room, I prepare myself to join the group already in the Light Force's domain.

I feel the storm as it surges around me. Even the air encircling me seems infused with strife. This distinctive feeling hangs in the atmosphere before a tornado touches down, changing everything one knows and understands. All I know will soon be put to the ultimate test.

Again, I sense Bastaine. A message from him, whispers around me. "We are connected. Soon you will require this bond."

I acknowledge him and our connection with my heart. I need all the help I can get. The space encompassing me falls dark and everything becomes still. This is the quiet before the violent unrest locates me. I will weather whatever arises, but I will not ride this storm alone. Focusing my thoughts, I return to the Light Force's domicile. It has begun.

I now stand before thousands, by the ones who will fight with me. They will battle for freedom. This moment, we are all dry and safe, but soon we will face the elements. We will thrash the storm. Then and only then will we witness another dawn. With our victory the light will shine again, bringing with it hope, bringing with it life.

Tomorrow hasn't yet arrived and this is beneficial, for now there is work to be done. Like the ever-present tempest, we'll intensify our fortitude and prepare. And, on this next day, we will battle for our very existence.

Chapter Twenty

"Meelah," I hear the Light Force voice softly. "I mustn't remain in my realm for too long with the mortal warriors here. As you know, my presence, my high vibration puts them at risk so I'll be brief. Our Creator has insisted that both my brother and I wait in their presence from this point on. Your infallible free will must guide you now. I believe in you, I always have," He says. "Defeat my brother's army then return *him* to *his* domicile. Our Creator will bring you to *him* after *his* army has been destroyed. My brother will be weak, but don't be fooled. Once *he* steps foot in *his* domicile, *his* powers will return in full."

"As soon as I get *him* there, I will depart. I have Kriyo waiting for my return. I made him that promise."

"I will not be able to intervene, it has been forbidden." Placing us before the warriors, He bellows, "The fate of all we know rests in all of you! My heart is with each of you." Deep within my soul, He privately includes, "This is why you were created, Meelah. Fulfill… your…destiny." Both He and His passionate words fade from me.

Again, I face the warriors. I observe the magnificent arches of the Light Warrior's wings as they rest nearly a foot above each of their heads. The Retza, donning protective, black armor and geared with heavy armament, remain in pairs, one with deep blue skin and the other with red. These pairs are scattered throughout the sea of warriors before me. I see Wazuli, a Churrian from Bursa. He is no longer wearing the customary robe; he is outfitted in attire similar to that of the Light Warriors, gilded body armor, a shield and a sword. He stands between Nala and a Retza pair. This acceptance and diversity will give us strength. Together we will fight with one pursuit.

"It is time for us to prepare!" I exclaim.

Closing my eyes, I go within. The soft din from the warriors swiftly ceases. Silence affords us the connection that we'll require. I tune into the thousands of heartbeats before me. Different rhythms, diverse patterns of beating, separate us. I home in on the Light Warriors and in time, the specific cadence of their life-pulse becomes one with mine. Steadily, we beat in harmony. I hear our unified heartbeat; I feel it as it moves through me. Again, I try to include the Retza and the Churrian but their signature doesn't fall in accord with our balance. This discord reveals the course that will best suit us. I see the strategy that we must utilize and I send it telepathically to every warrior before me. I illustrate my plan, then I ask all to bear witness to even a mere fraction of the light that will destroy the Shadows. Again, I focus on the synchronicity of the Light Warrior's driving force, the component that grants us life. My amulet, concealed in my chest cavity, begins to emanate extreme warmth. This heat rises, mounts, then explodes. Pure radiance bursts forth from me. One by one the resonance connecting us spreads the radiant light to the Light Warriors.

Together, we are one, and we all experience this powerful union as it builds in intensity. This purity coupled with Cila's ascribed inherent gifts, will further magnify our glory in extinguishing the darkness.

Gradually, I regain control of our radiance and diminish it. Opening my eyes, I see that all before me are bowing. I return the reverence, fully understanding that without each of them, victory would be out of reach. As they rise, telepathically, I continue streaming strategies and tactical maneuvers that we, the Light Warriors have used and perfected for ten thousand years.

Opening the forum, the leader of Retza warriors begins explaining his experience with the Epoh. He also shares the docile demeanor of these creatures before the Shadows consumed them. It is my intention to free them from the shackles of possession, but I will do what I must to end the tyranny of the Dark Force. As the Retza continues, I marvel at the passion emitted from this leader. His thick craggy skin is deep red in color. Yellow and intense, his eyes are commanding. The top of his bald head is festooned with a headdress decorated by black feathers. Covered in heavy, black armor, his chest and back are well protected. Physically lean and appearing quite strong, this being and all its shares, validates how grateful I am for their alliance.

Teese comes forward and shares his most recent encounters with the creatures and what he and the other Light Warriors have learned. Mikiel and Ruzi add accounts of their thousands of years of battle against the Darkness. In totality, they agree with the vision that was shown to them. A plan of attack has been solidified. There is one more tedious component to consider, the gudra root. In abundance it is passed out to them, even to me. Raising my hand, to first seize the attention of all, I bring the noxious camouflaging agent to my mouth and begin to chew. I watch as they do the same. The Retza appear to like its vile taste, but the Light Warriors and Churrians all seem to avoid the inevitable swallow. In time, they do that act and this is critical. This may save their lives, though many have already embraced whatever fate will hand them.

"Two elements have been shared," I avow. "We have eliminated their ability to catch our scent with the gudra root. The heart of this herb will sit in our digestive tracks. It will break down slowly and maintain our camouflage. Next, the Epoh rely not only on their keen sense of smell, but also on their sense of sight. This is greatly compromised at nightfall. With the assistance of the Sirians, there will be no dawn; no daylight. The moons and stars around Churria will also grow dim. We will battle in twilight. We will remain in this obscurity until our objective is realized. We do this for a future! We do this to right the balance! We will fight for our children, our progeny! This is our right. This is our destiny!" Pausing, I breathe in their alignment, their passion. This is no longer my destiny alone; it belongs to all of us. Failure is not a consideration. I needn't say it; I know they all realize what we risk.

In my mind, I cull out the twenty or so Light Warriors that will personally come with me, Ruzi being one of them. Mikiel will open the portal and leave with our remaining militia. I send this message to all and instantly Mikiel appears before me.

"I must remain with you, Meelah. I have always battled at your side," he states adamantly. "I wish to remain with you," he adds.

There is more to his plea, but now isn't the time to decipher it. Nodding my head, I agree. I team Teese and Nala together to lead the militia. Nala knows how to open the portal and her wisdom will be fruitful for the young, yet promising Light Warrior. But before I formally make the change, I confer with a dear friend. Stepping over to Ruzi, using the surface of my eyes, I share my plan. In his eyes, I see his response. This is no longer about them. If death arises, then it was for the greater good and whether they are together or apart, at that point, it will no longer be of consequence. His warm smile solidifies my new choice of leadership and I make it known to all.

One more time, I review the plan. They've got it, I see it. Providing them a few moments to tighten their gear and sharpen their blades, I also prepare. Nala stands before me with the balance of my equipment.

"I appreciate the honor," she says judiciously to me. "Teese and I will lead with fierce reverence," Nala confirms, handing me my apparatus. "It is time, my liege, right the balance once and for all."

"We will," I assure her, affixing my body armor. Taking hold of my helmet, I include, "As one, we will have our victory."

Standing before the mass again, but with Nala and Teese to my right and Mikiel and Ruzi to my left, I address everyone for a final sendoff. With the raising of my arm, the din settles and silence finds its place in all of us. I use no words, I express my message from my heart, which is my sheer gratitude. A surge of luminosity emits from me and radiates into all of them. This illumination binds us. Our essences, though they are each separate from their neighbor's, have now been tethered by light. This bond fortifies us all.

It is time, I feel it and all know it. Nala and Teese take my place as I step aside and join the small group to my left. All of the Light Warriors in this intimate group slide their helmets on and I do the same. Together we will liberate the munad. Cila, our key, along with Kriyo and Lador, will be solely under our protection. I appoint the two Light Warriors who are to take to the skies with Lador while the rest of us will protect Cila and Kriyo.

"Are you ready?" I ask them. Each Light Warrior nods in agreement. "It has begun."

Using my powers, I take the group and we leave the Light Force's domicile. I bring them to space, to the area above Churria. From this vantage point we all bear witness to the power of the Sirians. Cloaked in a solid veil of darkness, this star has been blocked from all illumination, all light except for what we will soon project from within us. In this space, all appears peaceful, though we sense the storm as it brews beneath us. We connect to the unrest, to the tempest as it prepares to strike once we're within reach. When our eyes acclimate to the darkness, we are ready to descend into the constant state of night below. The war has nearly commenced.

"Meelah!" I hear Mikiel shout.

I feel the Dark Force as *he* surges my way. "Go!" I yell to them. "Initiate our plan!"

"I will not leave you," Mikiel shouts back, drawing his sword.

"Yes, you will," I say, using a power that I hadn't recognized as available to me before.

Encasing Mikiel with a shield, I send him down with the others. For a brief moment, I watch as he fights my will. But his place is now with Kriyo and the others. I face the demon. I have no fear. Prepared to disappear from sight to elude *his* rage, I spot something incredible upon the distant horizon. Although *he* is ready to destroy me and everything that I embody, I point to what I see before I vanish from *his* sight. Reappearing out of *his* line of vision, I eagerly watch. The Creator, with incredible energy and presence, overtakes their son. Though *he* resists, *he* is no match for them. Obstinately, *he* tries to oppose them. I am concealed in the obscurity, but somehow *his* eyes find mine and I see within them, *his* wrath.

"It is up to you to right the balance," I hear from all around me. "No one can intervene from this point on. All eyes are on you, Meelah. This outcome will either raise the vibration within space, bringing forth evolution, or everything, everywhere, will fall. We are watching. Honor your destiny."

Again, I face Churria. Sensing the ethereal cord of light that binds me to my warriors below, I allow it to guide me to them. Descending, I hear a battle. Nearing the entry to the Underground City, I see remnants of Light Warriors. The mass of Epoh blocks the door.

"We must lure them away," I transmit telepathically.

"We have tried!" Ruzi exclaims. "Several Light Warriors landed on the surface and quickly they were ambushed."

"Sadly, I saw their remains. We must learn from their death. The Epoh expect us."

"Even though they cannot see clearly nor can they locate by their sense of smell, once we're in their territory they thrash about until they locate their target," Ruzi explains.

I sense Mikiel beside me. "Don't push me away again. I have sworn to protect you." He continues earnestly, "Allow me to honor this oath, Meelah."

"I appreciate your support. But right now, we must draw the Epoh away from the entry and I have an idea. I know what the Shadows can't resist."

"I don't like the sound of this."

"Mikiel, I will survive this, all of this," I state adamantly. "You must have faith in me, so must Kriyo. I know that both of you care for me, but neither of you can hinder me. If we fail, everything will fall. It must end today!"

"Yes, my liege."

"I will lure the Epoh to our battleground. That is where the rest of these beasts have gathered."

"That's too dangerous!" Ruzi exclaims.

"I know what I am doing. After they step through that door, make certain that Kriyo closes it. We cannot risk a breach to the Underground City. Do you still have the vial?"

"Yes," he answers.

"I hope that you will not need to use it, but something is unsettled within me that portends otherwise."

"Like your plan unsettles me," Mikiel states. "I wish to go with you."

"Ruzi, can you spare Mikiel?"

"Yes," he eagerly answers. "It is wise to have him by your side."

Amidst the obscurity, I command Ruzi, "Protect the Head Elder and Cila."

"I will, my liege."

"Wait until you are certain that all of the Epoh have vacated the area. It will take Seli a short run before he can take to the sky, especially since he'll be carrying two."

"I will, my liege."

"Thank you, Ruzi. I leave you in charge." Turning to my protector I say, "I will draw them to me. You will never touch the ground! You must give me your word."

I see his resistance as he grapples with it. Finally, he consents. "I give you my word."

"Good. I trust your word. I know what it means to you. Now, keep a keen eye on the path ahead of me."

As he nods his head, I see an opening below and descend. My feet touch ground and I am ready. I wait for them. I grind the soles of my boots into the soil. I want them to detect my movement and hear me as well. The ground beneath my feet swiftly begins to shudder.

"They're on their way to you!" Mikiel shouts from above. "Five approach steadily from behind you. More are coming," he adds. "About six...no, eight are to your left. Lift up, Meelah, they're surrounding you!"

I brace myself as they come into sight. I see them, I feel their thunderous weight as it pummels the ground. Their stench consumes the air. Raising my shield, I am fully encased by it. They come right at me! Charging with full force and from every direction, they continue to smash into me. My shield protects me from their horns, but my body takes some of the effect of their persistent bashing. The small scuffle gets the attention of the other Epoh. A message from Ruzi notifies me that the creatures perched outside the entryway have departed. Most likely, they too will join in the frenzy that I've caused. I lift from the ground and draw my sword. Out of their reach, I hover above them and cut into my wrist. Blood flows from my fresh wound. As I cough, more ejects from my mouth. I must have sustained some internal injuries. My body heals and I cut my wrist again. My blood tantalizes the Shadows within the Epoh. It creates an enticing agitation. Jumping and thrashing about, they desire to get to me, to kill me.

I lure them through Bursa. I sense Mikiel as he watches my path. More Epoh join the chaotic madness that swells below. I no longer can see the wooded area of the entryway. My heart hopes that Cila and Kriyo make it out safely.

An Epoh leaps into the air, atop another. As it ascends quickly, my leg narrowly avoids contact with its horn. For a third time, I slice into my arm. Again the fresh scent of my vital essence rouses the herd. Looking around, I do not see or sense Mikiel. Practically out of Bursa, I keep at a consistent pace, but worry begins to set in. I call to him in my mind.

"I am ahead of you," he readily answers.

Following the sound of his voice, I see him vaguely in the far distance. I also sense something and I feel Mikiel does as well. The Shadows are wise. Above me, Seli with Kriyo and Cila soar overhead. I also feel Ruzi and the others, but this is foreboding.

"Ruzi!" I state telepathically. "A few Shadows have left their host and have brought the battle to the air. They will pursue Cila!"

I feel him acknowledge me then I fly to where Mikiel has waited. I don't see him. Calming myself, I listen for his heartbeat—I feel it below, but it seems to be on the surface. In the nearing distance is a herd of Epoh. Raising my shield, I land and swiftly search for him. The land shakes and I near panic. They are coming! Finally, I see a portion of his wing beneath several branches of a humbra tree. Removing the debris, I see him and he's unconscious. Encasing him within my protective cover and shielding him with my body, I am attacked by the massive herd. Safeguarded from their horns, but not from their sheer mass, we are hit over and over again. Coughing again, I bring up blood. I drop it into Mikiel's mouth. My blood slips down his cheeks and paints his clothing red. As the herd moves onward, I shake Mikiel and shout for him to wake. Outside our encasement, I sense Shadows as they begin to encircle us. They sense my blood and they want it. Scoring my hand, I press the wound against Mikiel's lips. I cannot remain here nor can I leave him to die. His lips cover my gash and I feel him intake my blood.

"Mikiel!" I order. "You must get up!"

Slowly his eyes open and with my help, he sits up. "Shadows," he whispers.

"Yes, many have left the Epoh and have taken to our skies. We must go! Can you stand?"

"I have no choice," he answers, wearily rising. "Your blood, you didn't have to sacrifice for me."

"Oh yes, I did," I reply, looking beyond our safe space, and my heart nearly fails. "The Shadows are everywhere. Are you able to fly?"

"Yes, I'm regaining my strength with every breath."

"Close your eyes and hear my heartbeat," I say to him.

As we both close our eyes and allow the chaos to fade away, our hearts connect. This curative, brief moment restores the two of us. Using our innate ability, we disappear from the Shadow's grasp. I bring him to Grawl and Grutiri, where I expect to find Kriyo and Cila, but they are nowhere in sight.

"Where are they?" I ask, nearing panic. "Where are Cila and Kriyo?"

"They have not arrived," Grawl answers. "We have been waiting for them."

"Something has happened." I feel this truth and unease mounts within me. "Remain here, Mikiel, and continue to regain your strength. Warn Teese and Nala of the Shadows."

He acknowledges my instruction and I take to the sky. Soaring, I sense the looming Shadows. I also see Seli with no rider, below. He's running frantically. As he is averting a pack of Epoh, I tell him to fly. I'm unsure if he'll hear me through his panic or even if he'll grant this request since I'm not his rider. Thankfully, he does. He lifts from the ground. Continuing to scan beneath me,

I see Lador on foot with Cila in his arms. I descend, halting his swift gait.

I ask, "Where is Kriyo?"

"The Noori fell. Darkness overtook them. A Light Warrior caught Cila, but Kriyo fell into the herd. Ruzi attempted to locate him, but no one could have survived that."

I call to Mikiel and he appears by my side. He sees my anguish, even though I do my best to restrain it. "Mikiel, please bring Lador to the wall. It's too dangerous for him to travel on foot. I will keep Cila with me. Our army will be here momentarily. Lador, thank you for protecting Cila. Now go!" I demand, trying to maintain my focus.

Mikiel leaves with Lador. Holding Cila in my arms, I note how weak she is. Her heart beats slowly. Time is scarce. The Epohs have scattered, so have the Shadows. My plan to gather them has failed. My Kriyo, my heart, has fallen. I resist the urge to fall as well. This is larger than me. I must pull myself together.

"Believe," I hear Cila whisper. "It is not the ending."

"Indeed, it's not," I answer her.

I look into the gloom, to where I sense Kriyo, then, with deep pain, I turn in the opposite direction. Encasing Cila in my shield, I take us to the sky. Warm tears journey down the contours of my face as I increase the distance between us and Kriyo. I feel Cila give my hand a little squeeze. She also knows that the right path most often is more difficult to tread. Hovering above a gathering of Epoh, we wait. Swirling around us are Shadows, but more, many more, are spread throughout this star; we will need to draw them to us as well. Cila's eyes lovingly connect with me.

"Soon I will leave this physical form. Do what you must."

"How do you always know what I'm planning?"

"Those whose hearts are connected, share a unique bond," she whispers.

"Will I see him again, Cila?"

"Yes," she answers readily. "Sooner than you may realize. Don't lose faith."

Lifting her hand from mine, she pulls something from her pocket. The object she places upon her chest is a small knife. Again her eyes meet mine. "Right the balance, Meelah. Fulfill your destiny and free me. I am ready."

Midair and under the veil of darkness, I remove one of my hands supporting Cila. As she gives me the knife, I sense Teese, Nala and the army. I feel the thunder of their feet as they meet the ground in the near distance. I slice into my arm, then I press the blade of the knife into Cila. Feeling her body tense with the pain, I watch as her arm falls. It surrenders into the open space and hangs lifeless. The blood from the two of us rains down. Every Shadow, whether they are within the Epoh or flying in the atmosphere, catches the tantalizing infusion of the blood of a munad and the destined one. The frenzy intensifies. More and more Epoh join in the agitation. Farther than my eyes can perceive, the Epoh loom. Around us the Shadows bash into our encasement, determined to tear us apart. They taste the blood that seeps through our barrier. A small pool remains, and I use this to move the mass below. I relocate them to where my army is waiting. Though my blood ceases to flow, Cila's does not. Aware of what little life is within her, I command Teese and Nala to begin. The Shadows congregate in such great numbers that pure madness has now ceased my ability to see. No longer able to use my eyes, I close them. In this space, I hear Cila's heart as it beats indistinctly. She appears lifeless, though she has not given up. I feel Jael within her. His strong spirit helps to tether her to this moment. Together, they resist leaving the physical form, an act that will soon be the key to everyone's freedom.

I begin. Searching for my connection to the Light Warriors below takes a few moments. Upon the ground, they are an easy kill, but this is where we will obtain our victory. I feel their hearts beating. As the heat within me begins to rise, Cila and I arrive at the very epicenter of the Epoh, the crux of it all. Amidst my explosion of light, all around me becomes illuminated, bringing with it clarity. I hear the surrounding Shadows as they writhe in pain. The very outside perimeter is enclosed by Light Warriors and Retza. Still emitted from me, this luminance connects to every Light Warrior. As intense as this moment is, something unexpected occurs. Cila falls through my arms and through my shield. I watch her descend, as if in slow motion. Dropping into the light streaming from me, she unites with me on a profound level. Her heart beats for the very last time, and I experience it as if it were my own. The life within her magnifies the radiance. It consumes all space, every Shadow, and all darkness. Its raw vigor creates a force that surges with such power that it radiates beyond the limits of this star. Light devours the dark. It travels like a wave and steadily this luminescent undulating motion wanes. Weakened, I submit and I fall. Someone catches me, it's Mikiel. His warm arms cradle me. Opening my eyes, I see the most wonderful thing—Kriyo! Gently, I feel him take me into his arms. I witness within his beautiful eyes, our success. Softly, everything is again illuminated. The dawn of a new day has blessed us. Gleeful bouts of cheering fill the air. Sitting up, I lean forward and melt into Kriyo's embrace. Cila was right—she always was. Gazing up into the atmosphere, I look for a new star and finally

I see a twin begin to sparkle. Two new lights take their rightful place in space. With my heart, I thank both Cila and Jael. I feel Kriyo follow my lead as his heart does the same. Rising to a stand, with Kriyo's hand entwined with mine, I know with certainty there is more that I must do.

"Go," I hear Kriyo say. "Fulfill your destiny."

As our eyes meet, so do our lips. I feared that he was lost. Wrapping my arms around him, I hear the call summoning me from above.

"I love you," I say to him.

Fading from his sight, I appear in space. All is vibrant and alive. I follow my intuition, allowing it to guide me. As I soar, I feel my strength return. In the near distance, I see *him*. Cast away and appearing lifeless, the Dark Force floats amid the darkness. I grab *his* hand and bring *him* home. *He* is weak. *He* has been defeated. A piece of me feels sadness for *him*, but only for a brief moment. *He* has created *his* reality. Many good beings have lost their lives because of *his* evil acts.

Finally, I see it ahead. *His* domicile is a dark place. Perhaps *his* home is a mere reflection of *him*. Regardless, I am nearly there. On the perimeter of *his* nefarious nest, I avoid entering it. I push *him* into the outside wall, but it doesn't work. Begrudgingly, I step into *his* lair then proceed to pull *him* in. Why this worked, when I couldn't push *him* in, eludes me. Quickly, I proceed to leave.

Something strikes the back of my head. In shock, I turn around and discern the presence of Leva, then darkness overtakes me.

"Happy day, happy day," I hear the Dark Force chant as I awaken. "I get to tear you apart," *he* sings, sharpening a blade. "I will end your miserable existence, slowly."

Leva is standing by *his* side. Sitting up, I watch as *he* scans what looks like ancient tools. One by one the monster picks them up and inspects them. This is bad, very bad! I assess where I am and think of an escape, but... "There is no escape," I hear *him* whisper into my ear. *He* lingers and sniffs around the nape of my neck. Grabbing my arm, *he* makes a tiny cut into it. As I try to pull my arm from *his* grasp, but cannot, *he* licks my blood.

"Will you always be so difficult!" *he* shouts. "I just require one more little taste. I love your flavor," *he* adds cunningly. Cutting into my arm again, *he* looks at me and winks. *He* lowers his disgusting black lips onto my wound and draws my vital life force into his mouth. "Yes, yes, and yes!" *he* yells, *his* mouth dripping with blood. "Meelah, you are such a vixen! If things were different, we could have quite the future together," *he* states.

"What are you saying?"

"I would have made an honest woman out of you." Then getting into my face, *his* wickedness licks my cheek. I can't help but cringe. "You are as sweet as honey. You are also pregnant with two." *He* studies my face, and though I try not to reveal my astonishment, *he* sees it and laughs. "Leva, what is the incubation period of a Light Warrior?"

"She is not a Light Warrior!"

"Answer me!" the Dark Force demands. "I may have no use for you after all."

"I birthed my son in a month's time."

"Then you, Meelah, have a month. When your progeny are born, we'll reassess your worth to me. Leva, tend to our guest. She seems to be bleeding." Coming close to me, *he* chains both of my wrists and I spit at *his* face. "Keep your strength," *he* warns, wiping *his* cheek. Rising to a stand, *he* approaches Leva. "If you harm her in any way, I will use these tools on you! Don't cross me!" Sauntering out, *he* mumbles to *himself*, "Recruits. I have so much to do in such little time!"

Leva remains, though I wish to be alone. I fight the tears as they fill my eyes. Collapsing forward, I can no longer resist them and I release them. Wishing to wipe my face, I pull against the taut chain. My hand cannot reach my face or any other part of me. In the darkness, ironically the same essence I just defeated, I am trapped. I bring my mind to the light that resides within me, but here it has no power. Here, I have no power.

"Yes, you do," Leva says, hearing my thoughts. "There is a reason why you and I can enter and remain in his domicile. We are connected to it. Embrace that connection and your powers will return."

I hear her words, but I am not ready to believe nor utilize them. Instead, I allow my sadness to overtake me. With time, Leva leaves and I am alone. In the cold, in the darkness, I hear the two heartbeats growing within me. I haven't heard them before this moment. A bond between us is eternally forged. For them, and to hold Kriyo again, and to show my children the light, I realize what I must do. I unlock the message stored in the stone of my amulet. This is the gift from Bastaine. I feel him, though I know he's not here, but a part of him is, his light, even his love. I encase my progeny with it. I feel his smile as I do so. He knew this too was a part of my destiny. He tells me of something else, my key to survival in this domicile. Ready to utilize this knowledge, I allow some of the abundant darkness to enter me. As natural as breathing, it consumes me, but I cannot control its hold over me. Regaining my strength, my powers return. Rising, I rip through the chains.

The Dark Force now stands before me and when our eyes meet, *he* sees my black eyes and with deep satisfaction, *he* grins. Bringing a small cup gently to my mouth, the darkness within me opens my mouth and I intake the solution. I fight against the iniquity, but it has a stronghold. Wishing to rewind time, I realize that I'm losing control. My connection to the Light and all heart-centered reasoning begins to slip from my grasp. Valiantly, I attempt to keep hold of it. I retain the last bit of light within me and swiftly conceal it. With this minute amount of brilliance tucked behind my heart, I consent to play *his* game. Somehow, I will gain my freedom!

Before me, I see the Dark Force as *he* lowers to one knee. "You will be mine."

I have no fear. I will go home. But, here and now, the games have begun. I simply smile.

A soft whisper spreads to all the levels of consciousness. The gentle voice of the Creator simply proclaims, "*Destiny reborn.*" Though many have heard it, even Meelah, only a few understand its meaning. But with time, countless more will experience this truth. Though a war has been won and the balance restored, it has arrived at a cost. All things occur with a higher intrinsic divinity, even this. Soon, destiny will be reborn, and a wave of transformation will affect all that is.

Glossary

Ameira – Located on Churria, its glass-like reflective surface is the strongest teleporting station.

Amulet – A powerful talisman consisting of four stones. Each stone is from a quadrant of Churria. This charm was created by the Ultimate Force for Meelah. It holds unique powers as a result.

Ascend – Churrians at the age of roughly 750 to 950 years of age move on to a higher dimensional state of consciousness, taking their physical form with them.

Bastaine – He is the leader of the Timeera.

Biser– Hollow instrument used by the Viox that shoots dart saturated with sedating oils.

Blessing – A female Noori that is a winged-equine. This creature has bonded with Meelah.

Bursa – This is the greenest quadrant of Churria. Home to the majority of the Elders and to the Head Elder, this quadrant is known for its omnipresent flora.

Calla – A river on Churria. She is very much alive and a part of the eco-system on Churria.

Churria – A star located in the Pleiades. It is home to the Churrians and Ameira.

Churrians – Beings from Churria. Most beings are similar in appearance to humans. They stand at a minimum of six feet and a maximum of eight feet, although a height of fifteen feet is possible.

Cila – She is the half-sister of Rhana. Cila is both elf and fairy. Residing in the Realm of the Mystics, she flees to Churria to give birth to a daughter who is named Cila.

Cila II – Born on Churria, this special being is a munad. Her father is Hanu and her mother is Cila, Rhana's half-sister. She, being the last of the munad, is the key to restoring the balance.

Creators – This being or these beings are the creators of every soul and all emotion. They are referenced as: He, His, Him, She, Her, Hers, They. They are the Almighty.

Dark Force – This being personifies the darkness in all perceptions of reality. He is the Dark son of the Creators. Evil and monstrous, he is referenced as: *he, his, him.*

Dimension – A level of consciousness, existence or reality.

Drana – The current Queen of the Realm of the Mystics.

Drista – This is the arid and driest quadrant of Churria, with sandy terrain and clay-like homes encircled by the Dristan wall.

Dristans – Churrians who live in the quadrant of Drista.

Dryads – The spiritual beings eternally connected to one tree.

Elders – Churrians who have been appointed by the Head Elder to teach and/or oversee their quadrant. They make up the political bodies of Churria.

Faro – A humble yet prophetic Dristan. He is the father of Kriyo and the partner of Pasha.

Feena – The female polarity of the creators.

Grawl – A male invertebrate over twenty feet in length. He and Grutiri are the guardians of Drista. He is an eternal being who is rich with character.

Grutiri – A female invertebrate over twenty feet in length. She and Grawl are the guardians of Drista. She is an eternal being who is full of personality.

Gudra Roota – A foul tasting herb that is used to camouflage one from emitting a scent.

Hanu – He is the last of the munad.

Head Elder – This is the leader of Churria. This position is nominated solely by the Elders and it must be won by a majority vote. The Head Elder remains as the leader until ascending.

Jael – He is Meelah's biological father. From Bursa, this elder resists the idea of change.

Krall – An elder from Bursa.

Kriyo – A handsome young adult Dristan. He's the son of Pasha and Faro and the student of Trall. He is appointed to the position of Head Elder. He has close ties to the Timeera.

Kune – The current King of the Realm of the Mystics.

Light Force – This being personifies the Light in all perceptions of reality. He is the Light son of the Creators. Judicious and honorable, He is referenced as: He, His, Him. The Light Force is the creator of the Light Warriors.

Light Warriors – Winged warriors created by the Light Force. They protect the innocent throughout the universes. Their mission is to enforce the universal laws.

Luther Rutherford – A disheveled male being who shape-shifts into a Galidrome.

Meelah Neegry – Young adult female being that appears to be human. She has sleek dark hair, olive skin and a grand destiny.

Mikiel – A strapping blond Light Warrior selected to protect Meelah when she is on earth. He is second in command of the Light Warriors

Mikshe – A female Bursan who is the assistant to Head Elder Shria.

Munads – These evolved beings are masters of camouflage and reflecting light.

Nala – A female Light Warrior with speckled brown-and-white wings. Bold and precocious, she proves to be a great ally to Meelah.

Natiya – The mother of Churria. She is intricately connected to all life on this star. She keeps it harmonious and balanced. Natiya is powerful and her purpose is to maintain the thriving existence of all who make Churria their home.

Noori – A winged-equine residing in the Realm of the Mystics. A Noori waits until their essence bonds with a rider, making this rider the only one in its life.

Pasha – Middle-aged female who oversees Religards, AKA Ms. Lucy. She is the leader of the Northeast Team, mother to Kriyo and wife to Faro.

Plai – This quadrant of Churria is supported and surrounded by water. Plaian live in castle-like structures and are deeply connected to the energy within their encircling waters.

Plaians – Churrians that live in the quadrant of Plai.

Ralta – This quadrant of Churria is composed of enormous pieces of quartz, crystals and other minerals.

Raltans – Churrians that live in Ralta.

Raza – A female Churrian from Bursa, who gave birth to Meelah.

Rhana – A siren with golden hair and sensual charm.

Reetra – The leader of the Retza Warriors.

Retza Warriors – These warriors are born as twins; one is blue in color and the other is red in color. They are exceedingly skilled in combat.

Ruzi – A highly trained male Light Warrior with dark wings and a dark complexion. With a deep sense of integrity, this being is very judicious.

Samuel Neegry – He is the pure-hearted and kind Churrian who raised Meelah.

Seli – This creature is a male, pure-black Noori. He becomes bonded with Kriyo.

Shadows – These energies were members of the army of the Dark Force, but their physical forms were destroyed by the Light

Warriors and only their vigor remains. The Dark Force uses these energies to possess beings.

Silvera – Churrian herb that releases emotion from the heart chakra.

Sirians – The evolved life forms from Sirius A, Sirius B and Sirius C.

Ta – The male polarity of the creators.

Tagers root – A mild-favored herb used in tinctures. Grown in Bursa. Low growing pink flowered. The root is nutritious.

Teese – A young-male, Light Warrior who is a promising warrior.

Tella – Underwater creatures resembling whales. These beings protect the quadrant of Plai.

Thames grass – A palatable herb used to make tinctures. It grows in abundance in Drista. It looks like a purple-colored grass.

The Dark Force – His energy personifies malevolence. He is the son of the Ultimate Force and brother of the Light Force. He is referenced as: *He, His, Him.*

The Light Force – This being personifies the Light in all perceptions of reality. He is the Light son of the Creators. Judicious and honorable, He is referenced as: He, His, Him. The Light Force is the creator of the Light Warriors.

The Ultimate Force – This being or these beings are the creators of every soul and all emotion. They are referenced as: He, His, Him, She, Her, Hers, They. They are the Almighty.

Timeera – Impartial beings who reside in the Underground City beneath Churria. These beings are record keepers who simultaneously watch for imbalances between the Light Force and the Dark Force.

Tincture – A liquid herbal drink made by Churrians.

Trall – A wise Elder of Ralta and the Father of Samuel.

Universal Laws – Laws created by the Ultimate Force to maintain balance.

Viox – Special unit of Light Warriors that spare the innocent from a shadow

Yall – Churrian room similar to the kitchen.

Zaltan – Microscopic life forms that thrive on the energy emitted by the Plaians. They have created a foundation that the Plaians have built their quadrant on. Their relationship is truly symbiotic

About the Author

S.M. Huggins lives in a quiet town in Connecticut with her exuberant husband, six entertaining children, six crazy dogs, two elderly horses, and a crazy barn cat that has surpassed its ninth life. Amidst life's frenetic pace she has thoroughly enjoyed writing this page-turning series.

For S.M.'s full biography and upcoming projects, visit her website. www.SMHuggins.com

Acknowledgements

As always, I would like to thank my incredible husband for believing in me and in this dream. I love you! I would also like to mention my children for their unwavering patience and faith in their mother. With appreciation, I express my gratitude to: Heni, Bessie and Jenna, my sisters, Robert Plunkett, my grandfather and to all the fans of this series. Thank you for loving my dream.

Furthermore, a special and profound thank you goes out to Kathleen for editing my vision. Your polishing helped to make this book shine. I would also like to acknowledge Laura Gordon, the creative genius who designed the cover.

Finally, I would like to mention my muses, George Lucas, J.R.R. Tolkien, J.K. Rowling for opening the minds of millions of readers to unknown universes, worlds within worlds and magical realities. These highly regarded authors have forged the path to the unlimited joy we can find in reading their science fiction and fantasy works. Their belief in the imagination has given rise to the success of the subsequent writers who also reflect life outside the ordinary. I acknowledge the brilliance of these and the many other authors who keep dreams alive.

www.ingramcontent.com/pod-product-compliance
Lightning Source LLC
LaVergne TN
LVHW011758060526
838200LV00053B/3625